CW00506201

the life of blur

the life of blur

Martin Power

OMNIBUS PRESS
London / New York / Paris / Sydney / Copenhagen / Berlin / Madrid / Tokyo

Cover designed by Fresh Lemon
Picture research by Jacqui Black

ISBN: 978.1.780.38697.3
Order No: OP54912

Exclusive Distributors
Music Sales Limited,
14/15 Berners Street,
London, W1T 3LJ.

Music Sales Corporation
180 Madison Avenue, 24th Floor,
New York,
NY 10016,
USA.

Macmillan Distribution Services,
56 Parkwest Drive,
Derrimut, Vic 3030,
Australia.

Typeset by Phoenix Photosetting, Chatham, Kent
Printed in the EU

A catalogue record for this book is available from the British Library.

Visit Omnibus Press on the web at www.omnibuspress.com

Contents

Chapter One

The Road To Colchester

"We think we're very, very clever and we'd like everyone else to think that as well."

Damon Albarn

There are several possible beginnings to the story of Blur. One might invoke the rich history of Essex, with its ancient occupying forces, legendary warrior queens and bloody, embattled Britons. Another might focus on a beery, yet extremely productive rehearsal in a London studio that bound four musicians together as the eighties fell away to a new decade. Both points of entry have their merits. Both are reasonable starters for ten. But despite any arguments he might offer to the contrary, Blur's story and the band's two-plus decades of success will always be linked to the relentless ambitions of Damon Albarn. And so the story begins, and will probably end, with him.

Albarn was born on March 23, 1968 at Whitechapel Hospital in the heart of London's East End. Fifteen minutes' walk to the left was Aldgate. Ten minutes to the right, and Bethnal Green was yours for the taking. Throw a stone hard enough and there was real danger of hitting Mile End or London Fields. An area that announced itself in the bloodiest terms some 80 years before, when Jack The Ripper claimed the lives of five prostitutes among its slums and poorly lit backstreets, Whitechapel was still host to some faintly menacing place names in the spring of 1968. 'Raven Row', 'Artillery Lane' and the rather worrying 'Jack's Place'. All seemed steeped in magic and intrigue, all sounded terribly British. But if one wished to escape, the A11 at the top of Whitechapel High Street led all the way to Colchester, Essex, its progress snugly following a Roman road laid some two millennia before. Albarn would make that trip, albeit reluctantly, some ten years later.

For the first decade of his life, he would call Leytonstone home. Seven or so miles from Whitechapel along the Hackney Marshes, Leytonstone had no Jack the Ripper lurking in its historical record, but was none the worse for it. A vibrant, occasionally lively suburb of East London, the town was populated by a mix of English, Irish, Pakistani, Portuguese, Afro-Caribbean and Brazilian communities, all vying for space and reasonably priced rents. With Walthamstow Market nearby, Cathall Road swimming baths defining its centre and "The Flats" marking its borders with Epping Forest, Leytonstone was emblematic of a new type of multicultural London: one where first and second generation immigrants shyly forged alliances and lives alongside those whose ancestors had defined both the streets and culture. Though progress to harmony was sometimes slow (East Enders were well used to immigrants, but there still were pockets of racism within the community), it was still a good enough place to call home. Ethnically diverse, soaked in humour and birthing more than its fair share of icons – footballer David Beckham, cricketer Graham Gooch and photographer David Bailey among them – Leytonstone and its surroundings would leave a lasting impression both on Damon Albarn's future work and his view of a Britain once again struggling to be great.

Though Leytonstone was an essentially working class neighbourhood at the end of the sixties, Damon's parents did not quite fall into that demographic. Born in 1939, Keith Albarn could claim strong ancestral ties to Nottingham, his surname known, if not exactly common in that part of the North. Keith's own father Edward had actually settled in Lincolnshire, where he spent time working with various farming communities. A man of strong principles, political opinions and Quaker stock, Edward Albarn was a conscientious objector during World War Two, imbuing his own family with a free-thinking independent streak that manifested itself in his son's eventual choice of career. Having studied architecture and sculpture for three years, Keith became a Fellow of the Chartered Society of Designers, before beginning work in earnest as a stage designer for the theatre. By 1964, Albarn had his own company, juggling various theatre engagements with the building of modular furniture and learning toys for infants. But it was his forays into events design that opened doors to the world of music.

In 1966, Albarn helped conceptual artist Yoko Ono confound, then delight London's critics when he assisted in the staging of her first major exhibit at the Indica Gallery. "My dad was into psychedelia," Damon later remembered. "He was one of the prime movers in the psychedelic movement. He actually put on Yoko Ono's first exhibition." While Ono would become arguably more famous for marrying Beatle John Lennon than her own endeavours, the experience did Keith Albarn no harm at all, gifting him a pass key to the heart of a city then creating some of the most expressive, challenging and influential art of the modern era. By 1967 and the summer of love, he was running a modest, but profitable shop just off Carnaby Street, then the epicentre of London fashion. Specialising in alternative furniture with a mathematical bent, Keith's store also sold pieces of exotic ephemera heavily influenced by his interest in Islamic art.

Elsewhere, things looked equally bright as Albarn took on associate management duties for Canterbury progressive rock pioneers Soft Machine. A band heavily aligned with all things psychedelic, Soft Machine had already earned a reputation for putting on quite the show at underground clubs such as UFO and Middle Earth. But Keith's gift for creating "environmental happenings" took things to new heights when the group performed a series of gigs along France's Cote d'Azur in July 1967. Approaching his craft with considerable gusto, Albarn built an enclosed space named 'Discotheque Interplay' on a beach in Saint Aygulf, under which Soft Machine played their set as a beer festival raged outside. After five dates, the Mayor of St. Tropez declared Albarn's work an eyesore and ordered it closed. When told that all such art was protected by French law, the Mayor had it shut down for reasons of health and safety instead.

This exercise in tomfoolery seemed to spur Albarn on rather than put him off. As Soft Machine were embraced by the French art crowd for their daring, he secured a presenter's position on BBC One's *Late Night Line Up* – a prototype arts programme whose menu of live music, poetry performances and panel discussions provided a template for the likes of *The South Bank Show*, *After Dark* and *The Culture Show*. By the mid-seventies, Keith had added the title 'Author' to his CV, penning heady tomes such as *The Language Of Pattern* and *Diagram: Instrument Of Thought*, the latter co-written with Jenny Miall-Smith and given to exploring the strange worlds of symmetry and geometry. Stage and furniture designer, band manager, TV presenter and Islamic art expert. In short, Albarn had all the makings of a contemporary renaissance man.

Damon's mother Hazel was also a gifted individual. Like Keith, her family had their roots in farming, again in Lincolnshire, and also displayed strong liberal sensibilities. If reports are correct, they even offered a portion of their land for the placement of German and Italian prisoners during World War Two. Having already established an abiding interest in sculpture as a child, Hazel trained in stage design and following her arrival in London with Albarn in the mid-sixties, took a job with the prestigious Theatre Royal Stratford East. Led by renowned director Joan Littlewood – whose previous productions included the groundbreaking *A Taste Of Honey* and *Oh, What A Lovely War* – Stratford East was at the vanguard of a new type of theatre which Littlewood christened 'Sinn Féin'. Here, the onus was on dispensing with the traditional presentation of classics, in favour of fresh material given to "anti-form and anti-structure". While pregnant with Damon, Hazel provided stage designs for Littlewood's satire *Mrs. Wilson's Diary*, a slim tale drawing its central conceit from the imagined home life of Prime Minister Harold Wilson and his wife, Mary. Though motherhood temporarily became a full time role for Hazel, Keith Albarn briefly continued the family's association with Joan Littlewood, aiding her with design ideas for a 'Fun Palace'. Best described as "a mobile bubble theatre" that could be transported to parks, the seaside or even town centres, Littlewood hoped such an installation would break down the barrier between performer, stage and audience. Unfortunately, despite a dry run at the Tower Place festival in the summer of 1968, it all came to naught and Keith moved on to other projects.

Given the artistic pedigree of his parents, their choice of careers and the world which they inhabited, it would be perhaps fair to say that Damon Alban was not raised in the most conventional of environments. This was borne out by the aesthetic aspects of Albarn household, where the weird rubbed shoulders with the wonderful. Aside from silver-painted walls and six blue plastic chairs – a gift from the singer/songwriter Cat Stevens, who gave away all his worldly goods on converting to Islam – their Leytonstone home was festooned with various bits of art and craft, one more eye-catching than the next. More, the Albarns' door was always open to a plethora of musicians, sculptors, writers and artists, with spirited conversations taking place day and night at impeccably designed tables creaking under the weight of food, wine bottles and rapidly filling ashtrays. "I had a very open childhood. People were smoking dope and getting pissed," Damon once recalled to Q. "Taking drugs... never had that allure for me (because) pop culture was never something 'new' to me."

Taken at face value, such a statement might infer that Albarn was brought up in an anarchic, almost rootless atmosphere. Not so. In fact, his parents ensured that despite the collection of bohemians, intellectuals and other exotic creatures vying for attention in their living room, Damon enjoyed as normal a childhood as possible. An interest in football was actively encouraged, resulting in his life-long devotion to Chelsea FC. He was also fully supported in his school activities, with the Albarns' open door policy extending to both his classmates and other local children. All and all then, while the environment around him might have been a tad unconventional it was also completely angst-free, and by the sounds of it, extremely entertaining. "My parents were artists, quite eccentric. I liked the idea that when anyone came around to our house, they'd be (open-mouthed) because it was so different. The only time I'd get embarrassed was when my mum danced..."

By 1973, Damon was attending George Tomlinson Primary School on Leytonstone's Vernon Road, where he would soon be joined by his sister, Jessica. Three years his junior, Jessica shared the Albarn family trait for huge blue eyes, and perhaps unsurprisingly, exhibited a natural talent for fine art which she would cultivate successfully in later life. It was around this time that Damon experienced his first brush with the concert hall, attending an Osmonds gig with his parents at Hammersmith Odeon when the toothy Mormon brothers were at the height of their fame. Keen to extend their son's cultural perimeters beyond 'Crazy Horses' and 'Puppy Love', Keith and Hazel soon organised a visit to singer Harry Nilsson's new musical *The Point!* at London's Mermaid Theatre. Inspired by an LSD trip Nilsson had taken ("I looked at the trees and (houses), and realized that they all came to points," said Harry), *The Point!* starred former Monkees Davy Jones and Mickey Dolenz, and received rave reviews for its bizarre, but beautiful songs and innovative stage design.

With Cat Stevens and Soft Machine's Robert Wyatt regular visitors to his childhood home, and a growing list of widely disparate bands and shows informing his experience, one might have thought Damon's early musical tastes would veer a little off the beaten track. So it would prove. But it took a seemingly innocuous, country-tinged tune to really start the ball rolling. "One of my most vivid memories of primary school is the song 'Seasons In The Sun'," he told *Melody Maker* in 1993. "It had naughty lyrics, and while I can't remember quite what they were, they really got me going. It had a quality that's quite orgasmic for an eight year old, if that's possible." Albarn – even if he didn't quite understand why at the time – was essentially correct. Terry Jacks' 'Seasons In The Sun' was actually a sly cover of an old sixties tune written by Jacques Brel. A highly literate Belgian songwriter who specialised in the French 'chanson' style, Brel's original recording of 'Seasons...' was full of pathos and sarcasm, its lyric devoted to a man coming to terms with his wife's infidelities before death took him. If Jacks' version jettisoned much of the scorn and disdain, it still retained an ominous, uneasy tone – and one which Damon obviously responded to. This was a good spot for a young boy, and while his interest in Terry Jacks proved brief,

Albarn would later reap a decent harvest from further explorations of the chanson style.

If the sixties were about making their mark and starting a family for Keith and Hazel Albarn, then the seventies were given to consolidation and establishing firm roots outside the swirl of London life. Hence, when Keith was offered a lucrative position as Head of the North Essex School of Art in mid-1978, he accepted the post immediately. In practical terms, this meant upping sticks to a small village near Colchester, where the job was based. To facilitate the move, a 500-year old, four-bedroomed house backing onto a river and nearby wood was duly purchased for the not unreasonable sum of £9,000. At the time of the great upheaval, Damon was actually on a three-month holiday with a friend of his parents in Turkey – a decision that in principle was probably made for the best of reasons – but which ultimately led to some teething problems for the boy. "(Turkey) was great but when I came back, I found my sister Jessica had got herself settled and was very popular, whereas I struggled with all of that," he later told *The Sunday Times*. "Maybe being a bit older than her, I found the transition a lot harder and felt more aware of being the outsider."

As anyone transplanting a family from one area to another during childhood can confirm, such a move is often easiest on the youngest sibling. Certainly for Jessica Albarn, this proved the case. "We lived in a very old Tudor house in a close-knit village," she said, "and most of my childhood was spent running around the countryside, making dens in woods and playing down by the river with my friends. I also had lots of guinea pigs, a rabbit and a cat, (so) I was really happy and had a lot of freedom." While Jessica might have been over the moon with her new surroundings, Damon was not. "That move was the beginning of the end for me, really. The moment I was shoved into right-wing Essex, it all went wrong."

Unlike the town he had left behind, Colchester circa 1978 was somewhat lagging behind in the UK's slow but sure move towards multiculturalism, its origins and development taking a markedly different path to Albarn's beloved East End. Fifty odd miles from London, and housing some 75,000 inhabitants, Colchester was then best known as

'The Oldest Recorded Roman Town in Britain' (its existence is even mentioned in the records of Pliny the Elder). Originally settled by Celts who called it 'Camulodunon', Colchester had seen mass destruction before the first Gospels were thought written, with Queen Boudicca raising the place to the ground as part of her uprising against the Romans in 61AD. Rebuilt and rebooted – with a rather imposing set of walls and nifty chariot race track – Colchester subsequently fell to the Danes, Saxons and Normans before being given a royal charter by Richard the Lionheart in 1189. By 1648 it was in the wars again, this time acting as the site of a particularly ugly 11-week stand-off between Cavaliers and Roundheads which resulted in the execution of two prominent Royalists in the grounds of the town castle. Fast forward 237 years and it was an earthquake reaching 4.7 on the Richter scale that threw the town into chaos, destroying houses and roads across the length of its borders. Even if things had quietened down considerably by the late 1970s, only a fool would deny Colchester's sturdy character or ability to keep builders employed on a semi-permanent basis.

Of course, this was all small beer to Damon Albarn, whose first impressions of the town – and indeed, Essex in general – were largely unfavourable. "I was a complete fish out of water," he said. "It was almost an exclusively white community... pretty racist. They (would take) to Thatcher's dream and really go for it. The price (of that) was too much for me. The environment was fucked up, the vibrancy of the countryside was all gone. After Thatcher, the fields I was playing in one year (became) housing estates the next."

Albarn's observations had the ring of truth to them. By the time he was entering adolescence, Prime Minister Margaret Thatcher's dream of a New England was taking on full capitalistic shape. Across Essex, and in corresponding southern areas such as Milton Keynes, Northampton and Peterborough, new homes had sprung from old soil to accommodate waves of house buyers priced out of London's spiralling property market. The phrase 'Satellite Town' was now common parlance, its connotations of tired commuters making tired journeys back and forth from the smoke all too familiar to those lined up on station platforms across the south east. "We'd traded community for a disenfranchised life of Barratt homes and neuroses," Albarn later told *The Face*. "You see, we all need to fit in, to belong somewhere."

Back in 1979, Damon was still trying to find his own particular way forward. Luckily, there were several potential avenues to explore, most involving flora and fauna. Having temporarily lost his keys to the city, Albarn had at least gained access to a new world of woods, rivers, wildlife and the occasional witch. "It's not to say I didn't love the countryside. I'd often go fishing before school, (and) it was quite a magical place. In fact, there was a strong sense of witchcraft in the area, and we weren't averse to a bit of magic. We're not witches but we weren't scared of them either."

Away from such arcane distractions, Damon could keep himself busy by helping his mother out at the local arts and crafts shop she now managed. Failing that, there was always the prospect of riding lessons, again organised by Hazel for the benefit of local children. "For a while," he said, "I went from being a complete urban child to a country child. It was all fishes and birds." This paradigm shift from city slicker to country gent manifested itself through a rapidly expanding collection of fossils and several stuffed birds, all to be found on various shelves throughout his bedroom. Fishing too would have its place, with young Albarn even photographed for *The Angling Times* after catching a particularly weighty Chubb. "I had loads of fossils and stuffed animals. I even had a stuffed fox. I was a very keen fossil hunter, fisherman and bird watcher... very into nature."

Obviously, Damon was at least making a go of the country. But the true test of his assimilation into Essex life came when he joined Stanway Comprehensive School as a pupil in the autumn of 1979. Located just three miles outside of Colchester town centre, Stanway was to be home to the youngster for the next seven years. Once again, there were teething problems. "Well, I was as bohemian as you can get in an Essex comprehensive."

Raised by liberal-minded parents, well used to conversing with artistic types as a child and brought up in one of London's more cosmopolitan boroughs, the earring-wearing Albarn must have presented quite the puzzle to his fellow pupils. "They just thought I was a posh-gay weirdo.

I didn't fit in at all." Unlike many who might have folded under such pressure or sought to conform, Damon simply upped the ante by exhibiting a confidence and extroversion that must have confused and infuriated in equal measure. "I was quite an odd little fellow," he said. "When I should have been chasing girls... I started reading Karl Marx and playing the violin. Really, I just wanted to stand out, but you learn at that age that standing out doesn't really pay. It just makes you unpopular."

At first glance, such attention-seeking sounds like a rookie error, or as likely, a mild case of proto-adolescent belligerence. Yet, it also marks the first real example of a stubborn streak that became familiar in Albarn's later dealings with the world. Whenever presented with the opportunity to tow the line or follow the crowd, he was as likely to take a bus in the opposite direction or simply design his own method of transport. "I've inherited a desire to keep things simple from my mother and a desire to complicate things from my father," he once said.

Little by little, Damon eventually found his way at Stanway, even if it took time and tide to get there. One positive came from his skills with a football, a simple but effective method of gaining acceptance from those who might view him with suspicion. And if some classmates were still put off by his confidence, others seemed oddly drawn to it, with several of Stanway's braver souls forming tentative friendships with "the school weirdo". Just as well, as Albarn was never destined to become captain of the soccer team. "At the school I went to, you either played sport or played music. You didn't do both," he told *Planet Rock*. "So I gave up playing sport and started concentrating on music."

According to Jessica Albarn, the first signs of Damon's musical nature had manifested themselves well before his discovery of Terry Jacks. "Right from the start Damon was musical," she said. "Mum said he could play a mouth organ in the pram, and I can half-believe that because he just took to instruments straight away. He always had that natural ability. We both had piano lessons, but I knew Damon had something special. Whereas I'd come home and practise my sheet music, he'd already be banging out his own stuff. He was always free like that, you couldn't contain him." As evidenced, by the time he was 12, Albarn was already taking formal lessons in both violin and piano, this yearning towards music steadily creeping up on him over several years. Aside from the sly delights of 'Seasons In The Sun', he had taken to raiding his parents' record collection at will, pulling out a wide selection of LPs, singles and tapes: *Sgt. Pepper's Lonely Hearts Club Band*, Soft Machine's *Volume Two* and various other Pink Floyd releases were all plonked on the Dansette at one time or another. It didn't stop with progressive pop and rock. Indian ragas, Cuban dance, New Orleans jazz and even the gentle classical strains of Vaughan Williams' 'A Lark Ascending' all found their way into Albarn's curious ears.

Like many fledgling teenagers, he was also making musical discoveries outside of the family nest, though again, Jessica Albarn might have offered a little help on the way. "My sister made me a tape of Rod Stewart's 'First Cut Is The Deepest'. I played it over and over. I played it beyond the point of nausea and it still sounded great." If Damon was strongly taken by Stewart's way with a Scotch-soaked ballad, then he was simply transported by the Burundi drums, carbonised guitars and white face paint of Adam & The Ants. "Adam was the first and only pop star I ever wanted to be," he said. "Adam was the full stop after punk."

While Albarn was a tad too young to truly engage with the punk revolution of 1976/7, he found himself at a perfect age when the next wave of new wave struck. By 1980, the UK was in complete thrall to '2 Tone', a hugely addictive meld of Jamaican ska, rocksteady and reggae beats with a punk rock sensibility firmly at its heart. Driven by Coventry/Birmingham bands such as The Specials, The Selecter and The Beat, and further supported by their North London counterparts Madness and Bad Manners, 2 Tone promoted the idea of racial equality, sharp suits and even sharper social commentary. In Madness' case, that template was stretched to include a gift for true lunacy seldom found again in the British charts.

Suffice to say, Albarn was a zealous convert to the 2 Tone cause. Aside from the music and rude boy clothes, it greatly helped in forming a stronger connection with his classmates at Stanway. "When I was 12," he recalled, "I went to the Great Tey youth club in a little village outside of Colchester. I had my brogues, my little pork-pie hat and my little badge, and I used to get in a 'hokey-cokey' circle with all my mates and pretend to be Madness." To Damon, wearing the right threads and shoes – the self-same ones Suggs, Chas, Terry and Jerry all wore – was not only a point of principle, but also a badge of honour. Therefore, when he later met a younger Stanway pupil letting down the side, it could not go without comment. "I remember (Damon) in a black Mac," Graham Coxon told Q. "He was wearing a very white shirt, with a small 'Cary Grant' tie knot. Very nice rude boy brogues. He was messing with his hair (and) pouting in any reflective surface." Seconds later, Albarn made his play. "Damon came up to me and said 'They're crap shoes, look at these brogues, they're the proper sort.' You see, his soles were made of leather, and mine were made of rubber. Then he sort of put his hair right and walked off. I thought 'God, cheers', you know. I'd never met anyone with such a full-on attitude." That Coxon takes pleasure in telling this story some 30 years later continues to tickle Albarn. "Well, he obviously still holds it against me."

In fact, Graham Coxon was already well aware of Damon Albarn before their one-sided exchange outside the music room Portakabins at Stanway. "Damon was in the year above and I first noticed him singing 'Please Officer Krupke' from *West Side Story* in school assembly," he recalled. "I thought 'what a particularly extrovert chap.'" Though Coxon was amused by Albarn's nascent experiments with musical theatre (a subject to be covered in due course), he unknowingly shared several commonalities with the older boy, even if their individual journeys to Stanway were markedly different.

Born in a British military hospital near Reiten, Hanover on March 12, 1969, Graham was a true army baby, his father Bob then serving as a bandsman in the Worcestershire and Sherwood Foresters, one of the many regiments posted to Germany as part of post-WWII peace-keeping force. By the time he was four, the family – which included mother Pauline and older sister Hayley – found themselves living on an estate close to Montgomery Barracks in Berlin, their new city location affording Graham an opportunity to attend his first pop concert. The group concerned had a depressingly familiar ring. "It was The Osmonds. I got a plastic Osmonds hat."

A year later and Graham was on English soil, sharing a house with his grandfather alongside a motorway flyover in Spondon, Derby while his father served a tour of Northern Ireland during the height of the troubles. If it all sounded a tad grim, the memories were not. "I used to hear my dad playing stuff when he was home," Coxon said. "In fact, one of my first (musical) memories was my dad putting on Beethoven during an Easter egg hunt." An excellent saxophonist and clarinet player, it was perhaps inevitable that Bob Coxon would encourage his son towards a musical instrument, though the instrument concerned proved a surprising choice. "I played the Fife," laughed Graham. A staple of military marching bands, the fife was a high-pitched, small wooden flute comprised of six finger holes. Extraordinarily loud even in the right hands, one can only marvel at Coxon Sr.'s bravery in presenting Graham with such a prize. Thankfully, the child's experiments with the grim reaper of the flute family were brief, and he soon moved on to drum, clarinet and saxophone lessons, the latter of which he showed a natural aptitude for.

In typical army fashion, the family were soon on the move again and Bob Coxon's latest (and as it turned out, last) posting brought them to Colchester in 1977. By the end of the decade, Bob had handed in his military cards and taken a civilian job as leader of the East Constabulary Police band. To supplement his income, he also secured a post as covering music teacher at Stanway Comprehensive School, where Graham joined him as a pupil in the autumn of 1980. Given that he spent his earliest years in close proximity to assault courses, bunkers and bomb craters, one might have supposed young Coxon to be a tough army brat, keen to test his mettle against the best Stanway had to offer. The reality was somewhat different. By all accounts Graham was a quiet child – who like the rest of the new starters – lived in mortal fear of having his head flushed down a toilet by older kids. A keen *Blue Peter* fan (he was to appear on the legendary children's show twice), who harboured a mad crush on children's TV presenter Floella Benjamin and numbered the chocolate milk drink *Nesquik* among his major enthusiasms, Coxon was no trainee bully looking for fights in the playground. "I was pretty good at athletics though, 100 and 200 metres, high jump and discus," he said.

"If it wasn't for Dominic Pritchley, I'd have been fastest in my year, but he was pretty advanced as a human being, so there was no hope..."

Away from sport, there were two subjects that Graham really excelled at: music and art. In the latter case, Coxon had begun drawing as an infant, sending crayon pictures to his father whenever he was posted away from home. Teachers were quick to spot his efforts, and by the time Graham arrived at Stanway, his skills with a paint brush were being actively encouraged – a future career in design or advertising now a strong possibility. That said, both nature and nurture had dealt a fine hand in Coxon's favour, as he was also showing real promise as a musician. While the mini-drum kit in his bedroom remained more a hobby and less a vocation, he was beginning to make extremely promising noises with the saxophone his father gifted him with some years before. The only kid in his year – and indeed, school – with such an instrument, Graham again piqued the interest of his teachers who stepped in to offer formal lessons.

When free from the discipline of learning scales, correct embouchure and the relative merits of conical bores, Coxon also had the world of pop music to call his own. Like Damon, Graham's first brush with such things might have been The Osmonds, but his formative studies didn't end there. As with so many future musicians, it was The Beatles that took a firm hold of Coxon's ear and refused to let go. "I'm very fond of The Beatles' *Abbey Road*, probably because my dad used to play it to me in the womb," he said. "I had it floating around my head before I was born. With 'I Want You (She's So Heavy)', I can remember bouncing around on a Spacehopper to it, this cyclical riff just going round and round." And round. *Rubber Soul* too, was soon liberated for Graham's own ends. "I loved 'The Word' on that LP. I always thought it was incredibly groovy, with that great harmonica riff. I really wanted to be John Lennon. John Lennon in The Beatles he really wanted The Beatles to be." At nine years old, Coxon was parting with his own pocket money to soothe his ever-growing habit, purchasing a mint copy of The Police's 'Roxanne' at a local record store. "I'd loved The Beatles' backing vocals, and 'Roxanne' had great backing vocals." And if Graham didn't quite have the right Brogues for 2 Tone, it did little to curb his ardour towards the sound. "Bands like The Specials were so sharp and musical," he said. "They created a completely different world."

The real breakthrough came for Coxon at the age of 12 when he happened upon Paul Weller's Epping-based Mod revivalists, The Jam. Astounded by what could be achieved with just drums, bass, a growling vocal and treble-charged Rickenbacker, Coxon's world-view was forever changed. "I just had to have a guitar so I could play along with The Jam." Hoping that his son might gravitate towards jazz saxophone, Bob Coxon was a tad unsure when Graham asked for his first six-string, but the instrument was purchased nonetheless. "I used to buy all the Jam albums and songbooks and sit in my bedroom trying to pick up the different chords."

To Paul Weller's credit, he was never shy of name-checking The Jam's formative influences, and where the inspiration for songs such as 'In The City', 'Eton Rifles' or 'Going Underground' had come from. Hence, Coxon pursued Weller's recommendations with vigour, adding several albums by The Who to his ever-growing collection. "I absolutely loved The Who's Pete Townshend and was obsessed with *The Kids Are All Right* (documentary), though I was always scared of playing my Who records too loud in case my mum thought I was some nasty hooligan mod!" Pauline Coxon had good reason to worry. By 13, her son was a fully evolved mod revivalist. "I had the Parka, the boots, well, you know the drill. I'd wear the slimmest-cut school trousers I could find, and alter my blazer to three buttons instead of two. On 'civvies day', when you could wear what you wanted, there would be fights on the field between the mods, skinheads and casuals. As soon as it was break time, us mods had to run somewhere safe. There were only six of us, you see."

When The Jam ceased trading in 1982, it must have hurt Graham Coxon a little. Having never seen his heroes in the flesh, he had to make do with witnessing Weller's new and decidedly different band, The Style Council, at Ipswich Gaumont instead. But by then, the die was already cast: with a room festooned in posters, a small drum kit in one corner, a saxophone in another and his electric guitar taking pride of place on the bed, Coxon was now a confirmed musical junkie. "I dreamed of owning a real Rickenbacker," he said. "Two or three dreams, actually. Dreaming of guitars when other boys of my age were dreaming of something else altogether."

With the benefit of hindsight, it is tempting to formulate trite theories as to why Graham and Damon would strike up such a close friendship, despite the shakiest of starts. Perhaps it was the fact that both were new to Colchester, their backgrounds and experience marking them as different from the pack and more likely to bond as a result. Maybe the two instinctively sensed in each other a commonality of purpose, the skinny ties and 'Tuf' brogues early tribal signifiers of the road they would explore together. One might even argue that the younger Coxon was drawn to the older boy's innate self-confidence. Then again, perhaps not. "Damon wasn't liked much at school," Graham later said. "Even I thought he was a vain wanker." Or as most every teenage boy knows, an insult thrown on a playground is often a true precursor to friendship. Whatever the case or cause, Albarn and Coxon were soon to become the best of mates, an arrangement neither would break for the best part of two decades. "You know," Damon later said, "Graham and I went through the 'funny time' together. School, adolescence, all of that... even if he would disappear when I got into fights..." Given Albarn's ongoing habit of getting into a scrap when the occasion demanded it, and sometimes when it didn't, Coxon would turn that disappearing act into a work of art in years to come.

Chapter Two

Stirrings In The Portakabin

From the outside looking in, Damon Albarn and Graham Coxon must have made for an odd pairing at Stanway Comprehensive School. Albarn was all earrings and bleached hair, with a bead necklace his mother made for him years before hanging around his neck – a good luck charm never to be removed. Confident, gregarious and more than a little cocky, the adolescent Albarn was already half way to being a pop star, though that was not his intention at the time. "When I was young, I never had a real interest in 'pop music'," he later admitted. "I was just on this big 'This is going to happen' thing. I know from the age of 11, it's quite insane to say 'I'm going to be great', but that's what I did." Coxon, on the other hand, was a natural introvert. Reserved, even sweet (though he might hate that description) and just rid of the braces on his teeth, Graham's central focus were guitars and art, with an occasional charge up and down the running track the only real distraction from all the plectrums and paintbrushes. Yet, come their teenage years, the duo were to forge the closest of alliances. "I knew Graham before he even drank or smoked," Albarn once recalled. "He was the sweetest bloke alive."

As one might expect of soon-to-be best mates, their bonding routines followed a familiar pattern. As the Coxon family home backed onto Stanway's playing fields, Graham and Damon would invariably head there after school every day. Friday nights, however, were spent at the Albarn household where Coxon tried dodging free art lessons from Damon's mother. As the two grew slightly older, their attention turned to the illicit thrills of underage drinking, with cans of cheap cider and stolen bottles of Keith Albarn's homemade wine dunked in the river at the end of Damon's garden to make them cold enough for drinking. "Just teenage things, really" said Graham. "It was all quite... Enid Blyton."

Away from the booze and the odd cigarette, secrets were also exchanged. Coxon owned up to a mad crush on Kate 'Wuthering Heights' Bush, prompting Albarn to reveal one of his prize possessions – a suspiciously well-preserved photo of the raven-haired singer dressed in a figure-hugging leotard. "I used to fancy her terribly," he later admitted. And when boredom set in, there was always their shared hatred of Colchester to fall back on. "At school," said Graham, "we were asked to bring in photos of what people thought of Colchester, and some people brought in pictures of men digging holes. I took pictures of gravestones. It's death for young people, (that) place."

There was also some serious work going on. As Damon professed, while he was undoubtedly drawn to music – his studies in piano and violin confirming it – there was no mad rush to immerse himself in either the history or culture of pop. In fact, he seemed just as content to enjoy the Adam Ants and The Specials of this world for what they were: delightful entertainment. Graham, however, was far more serious when it came to such matters. Already besotted with 2 Tone and the mod revival, Coxon had set out to discover where it had all come from, tracing the roots of Madness to Prince Buster and The Jam to The Who and back again. It was knowledge he was eager to share with his friend. "Graham introduced me to a lot of music and attitudes when we were at school," Damon later told *The Face*. "We were both into 2 Tone, but he had a great collection of records I was totally unaware of. He really schooled me."

Aside from playing Albarn old Kinks and Jam LPs, Graham also commandeered the family video recorder, allowing his mate to enter the world of The Who with the full-length band documentary, The Kids Are

Alright, and *Quadrophenia*, the feature film based on Pete Townshend's 1973 Who album which follows the story of a young London mod and his adventures during the Mods v Rockers disturbances in Brighton in 1964. Like Coxon before him, these made a huge impact on Albarn – all those parka coats, bulls-eye T-shirts and draped Union Jacks not only visually confirming The Who's quintessentially British appeal, but also how insightful, impactful and important pop could be in the right hands. "I used to play Damon all these things that I thought were incredible and he'd absorb them," said Coxon. "In a way, I programmed him..."

Outside of the musical and filmic bubble they had constructed for themselves, there were other characters and events conspiring to shape Albarn and Coxon's future. At approximately the same time Damon arrived at Stanway, a new Head of Music Department was appointed. Having marked himself out as a teacher of promise at Hedingham School some thirty miles away, Nigel Hildreth came to the position with a clear mission in mind. "There had been a tradition of music making at Stanway but the department needed uplifting," he said. "This was a challenge, but there was a positive atmosphere in that the deputy head teacher, Yvonne Lawton, had been a previous head of music and therefore supported my activities." With the full backing of his Deputy Head, Hildreth's plan was bold and wide-ranging in its scope. "I wanted to raise standards by involving the youngsters in productions, then through ensembles and choirs (with that) also leading to individual achievement for the students. I started an orchestra and a large choir who became involved in larger scale performances, including 'The Messiah' and 'The Return of Odysseus' at the Royal Festival Hall... and 'Belshazzar's Feast' as part of an Essex-wide choir at the Royal Albert Hall."

Hildreth was also keen for such performances to be staged at Stanway School itself. To this end, he wrote an ambitious 'rock opera' retelling the legend of Faust with multiple harmonies, added percussion and a blast or two of orchestration. Entitled *The Damnation of Jonathan Fist!,* the production featured a 13-year-old Albarn making his theatrical debut as a millworker. "In his first performance, (Damon) was in the chorus," said Nigel. "But on stage your eyes were drawn to him. I clearly remember a former drama colleague from Hedingham called David Chapman commenting on that very fact when he saw the show."

Albarn's gift for drama was to become something of a dilemma, not only for him and his family, but also Nigel Hildreth. While Damon had already caught the music teacher's ear as a violinist of some potential, it was also becoming obvious that the youngster was also drawn to acting as a possible career – an ambition fully supported by his parents. "Keith and Hazel Albarn encouraged their children to engage in a wide range of artistic and academic activities, and were both eminent artists in their own right" Hildreth confirmed. "(But) I believe they thought Damon's true talents might lie with acting." As enamoured by Phil Daniels' nervy portrayal of 'super mod' Jimmy Cooper in the film *Quadrophenia* as he was with Madness or The Specials, Albarn would wrestle with the choice of drama over music well beyond his years at Stanway.

For the time being, however, there was plenty of opportunity to combine both interests as he worked his way out of the chorus and into the role of leading man. Damon's first shot as a principal actor came in Hildreth's production of Sandy Wilson's sunny musical *The Boy Friend* in 1983, when Albarn played the equally sunny 'Bobby'. Taught to dance the Charleston by Nigel's wife Wendy, Damon not only seemed to enjoy his proverbial moment in the sun, but also the female interest it brought him. "He had a good voice and (by then had) learnt aspects of stage craft," Hildreth recalled. "He clearly relished the attention and had a certain confidence which meant he could now partner older female leads." Albarn consolidated his new position as Stanway's go to lead in *Guys And Dolls*, where he took on the part of Nathan Detroit, a role once played with considerable humour (but no great singing voice) by the 'Method Acting King' himself, Marlon Brando.

Though a year younger than Albarn, Graham Coxon also got in on the musical act at Stanway, even going as far as to tread the boards with his friend on two occasions. When Hildreth delighted Damon's parents by staging a production of their old friend Joan Littlewood's *Oh, What A Lovely War!*, Albarn and Coxon were both key ensemble players, appearing together throughout the show. "Graham always had a pleasant voice, some great comic timing and soon had his own cachet from being in school productions," said Nigel.

The music department's next project – *Orpheus In The Underworld* – took things even further by giving Coxon and Albarn clearly defined roles, with Graham cast as 'Styx, god of the underworld' and Damon as 'Zeus, king of the gods'. "Damon was Zeus, which just about says it all," Hildreth laughed. "He was in a toga and chucking thunderbolts around." Albarn's part as Zeus was his last appearance before exams beckoned, but he did find time to help out backstage for *The Bartered Bride*, a Czech comic opera Stanway put on in collaboration with The Royal Opera House. On this occasion, Damon's younger sister Jessica was also a member of the chorus, while Graham's role required him to sing with his trousers firmly tucked into his socks. "I don't think I ever got over it," he later quipped to *Select.**

If Damon was seriously contemplating a life on the stage while at Stanway, he was also bright enough to continue his music lessons, though again, there was an issue or two to contend with along the way. At first, he was heavily drawn to the violin, playing with the school ensemble and much larger Colne Valley Youth Orchestra. But as time passed his attachment to bow and resin was superseded by a growing love of the piano, causing a loss of interest in his original choice of instrument that translated to both class and stage. "Damon could be absolutely infuriating," said Hildreth, "because he had lots of talent (but) he didn't always focus it."

For Albarn, there really was no dilemma. Having made the decision to concentrate on the keyboard, he augmented his studies at Stanway with private lessons from a local jazz pianist called Rich Webb. Inevitably, Damon also began to tentatively experiment with his own compositions. This time, Nigel Hildreth had no issues. "As a composer myself, I really wanted to encourage the students to write music," he said. "Both Damon and Graham, along with other musicians at Stanway

* BBC children's programme *Blue Peter* actually filmed one of these performances, earning Coxon another badge for his troubles. Sadly, the footage has been lost, depriving fans of an opportunity to see Graham in one of his more flamboyant guises.

such as Lucy Stimson and Jane Graham (were soon) participating in a town-wide competition with their own pieces."

The road to these competitions began for Damon and Graham when they stopped going back to the Coxon home at lunchtime and hung out instead at Stanway's music Portakabin – the very same place that the two had first met. "We used to hang around the music block, mainly because that was where 'the lads' never went," remembered Graham. "They'd be off on the field playing football and beating people up. I suppose we were the school freaks in a way." A safe haven from the killing fields outside, the Portakabin not only provided refuge but was also an ideal environment to tinker around with music. "Unlike many music departments (with a) number of practice rooms, Stanway only had a couple with the addition of a Portakabin just outside of the music area," said Nigel Hildreth. "But it did have a piano and music stands in it, and was available at break times and lunchtimes. It provided a bolt hole for some of the students who wanted to escape the weather or maybe develop some of their own music." In addition to a piano, a pile of sheet music and various songbooks, the Portakabin also housed a record player, several dozen LPs and a video recorder. On a good day, Albarn and Coxon could practice their instruments, work out the chords to 'Pinball Wizard', listen to The Beatles' *White Album* and still have time to watch a few minutes of *The Kids Are All Right*.

After a number of fledgling attempts at writing a tune, Damon Albarn finally came up with something he quite liked. Feeling that it "needed saxophone", Coxon was duly contacted and the pair met up at the house of a mutual friend/fellow musician Michael Morris for a jam. Though the moment, and indeed the tune itself have been lost in time, it remains the first time Graham properly contributed to one of Damon's musical ideas. It would not be the last.* For the moment, however, the notion of actually writing something together was not on the cards as both boys were expected to concentrate on individual compositions

* For the record, the song in question might have been called 'From A Basement Window'. If so, Damon and Graham eventually performed it together at a Stanway youth concert in 1985.

as part of their 'O' Level music course. To this end, Coxon wrote a short piece for piano and woodwind which he entitled 'Sonata'. "God, it sounds so pretentious now," he later joked. Nigel Hildreth was not laughing when he heard it. "Graham was obviously talented and he had a real musicality about him." 'Sonata' was subsequently performed by the Essex Youth Orchestra (EYO). Albarn's classical efforts were also highly commendable. Like Graham, his first submission was played by the EYO, while a later piece actually won a regional heat for *Young Musician Of the Year.*

While Damon and Graham were encouraged to pursue individual goals for the sake of their formal qualifications, they could not be stopped when it came to forming a band. Albarn had already dipped a cautious toe into this area when he joined up with classmate James Hibbins for Stanway's annual *Summer Extravaganza.* On the night in question, the duo played one of Damon's own songs, though he was content to stick with keyboards while Hibbins sang his tune. It wasn't long before two became six, with Michael Morris and Paul Stevens joining on guitar, and Kevin Ling on drums. Still not quite sure of his own skills with six strings, Graham filled in the remaining musical blanks with the odd sax line.

Content to use Stanway as the site of their furtive experiments, the sextet appeared at another school show some months after, performing two more of Albarn's compositions, "and a tune about Chess" by Hibbins. However, the line-up had been trimmed to a four-piece by the time they had a proper name. Calling themselves 'The Aftermath', Albarn, Coxon, Hibbins and Stevens' most notable appearance was at eight thirty in the morning before a school assembly of fourth and fifth formers. On this occasion, they played a raw, but spirited cover of Jimi Hendrix's version of 'Hey Joe' before shuffling off hurriedly behind the curtains.

Present throughout many of these performances was Nigel Hildreth, who had the unenviable task of balancing Albarn and Coxon's experiments with pop and rock alongside their official studies. As an interested – indeed, invested – observer, he witnessed both Damon's undoubted charisma and Graham's inherent gifts. Yet, there was no

'Eureka' moment that confirmed that either boy was bound for future glory. "Damon always had a stage presence and a confidence in his own abilities," Hildreth confirmed. "He could lead and engage with others. But no one could possibly know that he would go on to be such a multi-talented musician and artist. Likewise, Graham had sparks of real musicality that were obvious to all, but his quiet, sometimes nervous personality didn't give much of hint of things to come."

In fact, Stanway's Head of Department had his work cut out just getting Albarn to focus on one thing at a time. Increasingly working to his own personal agenda, Damon's growing interest in song writing, bands and the possibilities of film acting made for several potentially embarrassing moments onstage. During later school productions such as *Orpheus…*, Damon began to miss cues or fluff lines, his innate ability to improvise dialogue papering the cracks in his performance. While many in the audience failed to notice the slip ups, Hildreth was increasingly irritated by them. "There were times when he was just in a world of his own," said the teacher. Thankfully, if Graham showed similar signs of going off-piste, there was ex-military help at hand, both in-house and at home. "Bob Coxon was a peripatetic teacher who visited Stanway on a weekly basis," said Nigel, "And I'm absolutely sure he encouraged Graham in his musical development (at home) too..."

Despite Albarn's occasional theatrical lapses and his continuing internal debate regarding the worthiness of acting over music, his examination results were hardly a disaster. "I've got four or five 'O' Levels in the end," he later said. "I got a 'B' for English and the rest were 'C's." One of those 'C's was in music, thus allowing him to pursue the subject to 'A' Level at Stanway's sixth form college, alongside English and History. If reports are to be believed, he celebrated his good fortune by getting drunk with Graham. After smoking two huge cigars, the pair were violently sick. When Coxon passed his 'O' Levels (including music) a year later, the celebrations continued, with the pair joining Graham's parents on holiday in Romania. Sneaking off to drink the occasional beer or three at the local disco, the teenagers' mission to meet some real Romanian girls was also a success, though both returned home still hiding love bites underneath their shirt collars.

As one might expect at their age, Albarn and Coxon's socialising was now no longer confined to Portakabins, riverbanks or parentally assisted holidays. Instead, it was conducted in the pubs and clubs of Colchester. Alternating between the joys of Abbots Ale, Holsten Pils and Strongbow cider, Damon, Graham and several of their mates would often start the night off in 'The Cups' before heading off for a 'dance and a snog' at Brites nightclub. Now a huge Smiths fan – with a Morrissey-like quiff to prove it – it wasn't long before Damon drew the attention of several off-duty soldiers stationed at a nearby barracks. "When I was about 16, I'd get my head kicked in by local squaddies," Albarn later told *FHM*. "I was a Smiths lookalike and drinking in pubs filled with people who'd just got out of the army remand centre. I understand (why it happened) now. But I was clueless then, and deserved everything I got."

According to Graham, it wasn't just squaddies who took exception to Damon's hair "and rather big gob", as the local 'crustie' community joined the queue to make his acquaintance. "Damon was always getting duffed up in the toilets," he said. "We'd be on the town and he'd get beaten up by the New Model Army crew. We used to go to a pub and every time he'd go to the loo and he'd have his beating up. He'd go 'Graham, Graham, I've been beaten up', and I'd go 'Oh my God.' So he'd go 'I'm going'. And I'd say 'No, stay, have another drink'. And then he'd go and I'd stay behind and get drunk with the people who beat him up." (As stated, Albarn remembers things slightly differently. "Every time a fight started, Graham just disappeared...")

Colchester's New Model Army fans were presumably not in the audience to witness Albarn and Coxon's latest band Real Lives, who by now had begun playing gigs at local pubs and clubs such as The Affair, Oliver Twist and marginally less glamorous Woods Leisure Centre. With singer/guitarist James Hubbins having left the line-up to pursue a more 'prog rock' direction, new boy Alistair Havers had taken his place on vocals. The Jimi Hendrix cover versions had also been jettisoned, with Damon now having written enough original material for a half-hour set. As with The Aftermath, Real Lives proved a brief affair, but the group stuck around long enough to wobble the roof of Stanway's assembly hall when they appeared before an audience of first and second year students. "I remember going (along) as a member of staff to make sure there was nothing riotous going on," said Hildreth, "and although I cannot pretend to remember much about the music, I was struck by the way Damon was able to interact with the audience. The band were very successful on that night and that was when (Damon) started really being screamed at."

Sadly, no tapes or videos of The Aftermath or Real Lives have ever surfaced, though an amateur promo of the latter band was shot on the banks of the Colne River sometime in 1985/6. Similarly, if Damon Albarn has copies of any of his songs from this period, they also remain strictly under lock and key. Yet, it seems a fair bet that the material must have been extremely eclectic, given what he and Graham were listening to in the mid-eighties. Aside from their shared love of Madness, The Who, The Kinks and The Smiths, the pair had also discovered the joys of post punk and electro pop, with Albarn particularly drawn to XTC and The Human League. Coxon was also now heavily smitten with The Yardbirds, his continuing explorations of the guitar and its rich history inevitably leading him to the discovery of sixties gunslingers like Jimmy Page and Jeff Beck. "I loved 'Stroll On' from the film, *Blow Up*. It was from a time when volumes were going up and the existing amps couldn't handle it... the birth of feedback. You were getting these brilliant, anarchic aggressive sounds... the sounds of semi-acoustic guitars getting completely trashed."

This growing obsession with guitar thuggery would eventually draw Graham's ear to the racket and rapture of another cult sixties band, The Pink Fairies. "Their song 'The Snake' had this mean, devilish sort of riff," he said. "It absolutely screams in the middle section too. Just the best type of heavy rock, riffing with glee."

Though Albarn might have been left cold in the middle by some of his friend's more anarchic discoveries, there was one group Coxon threw his way that absolutely knocked him for six. "Syd Barrett-era Pink Floyd," said Damon. "It was just great English song writing, and I learned it inside out as you do with the greats... Ray Davies, The Beatles and Syd." On yet another mission to find some guitar music that "didn't rely on embarrassing, despicable mind-blowing solos that go on for hours", Graham came across Syd Barrett's peculiar genius while again visiting the record shop on Colchester High Street. "I'd been through The Beatles and The Who, and then at about the age of 16, 17, I discovered Pink Floyd's first album, *Piper At The Gates Of Dawn*. I was struck by the freedom, wit and confidence of it. Syd's guitar was like a sonic paint brush. He was so expressive, so experimental. That stuck." Entranced by the likes of 'Lucifer Sam' and 'Interstellar Overdrive', it wasn't long before Graham and Damon had accessed Syd's post-Floyd solo material, the two debating the worth of 'Baby Lemonade''s bluesy meander over the backwards-guitar waves of 'Dominoes'. "My parents had Floyd's *Atom Heart Mother*, and I loved that," said Albarn of the band's 1970 Syd-less album. "But Graham really got me into the Barrett era. I wasn't interested in it (before). I got interested in it because it was a way of hanging out with Graham, really."

In the end, all the passion in the world for the likes of Syd Barrett and early Pink Floyd could not keep Real Lives together, nor dissuade Coxon and Albarn from putting aside their musical studies in favour of Art and Drama respectively. With Graham, the decision – while surprising – was taken for the best of reasons. One of a number of talented pupils in his year, he had got to Grade Five in his saxophone exams and passed music 'O' Level easily enough (he also gained 'O' Levels in English, Biology and Art). But the demands of music 'A' Level proved a different matter, causing him to quit the subject after just six months to fully concentrate on his first real love: painting. "Graham found the demands of 'A' Level music pretty difficult," said Hildreth, "whereas his decision to follow art instead seemed more natural."

Damon, on the other hand, seemed capable of doing what was required of him, yet had simply lost interest. Having now set his heart on a place at drama school, studying the finer details of harmony and counterpoint no longer held much appeal. It all came to a head in the summer of 1986 when he arrived at his final exams with no musical scores to hand. "Damon had completed his studies for music 'A' Level, (but) in those days, students studied a number of set works and needed to bring these into the exam hall," said Nigel. "As I was told afterwards, he did not remember these scores, and thus was not able to answer the questions in the detail required. Unlike today when other factors would have balanced that out, in those days the emphasis upon the final exam was absolute." In short, Albarn had just failed his 'A' Level. "Damon's compositions and performance were very good," concluded Hildreth, "but most of the exam concentrated on musical analysis and it really didn't help that he (forgot) to bring his scores with him..."

Damon's 'A' Level results were so disappointing he couldn't even bring himself to tell his parents. In addition to failing music, he only managed a 'D' in English and an 'E' in History. Finding a good university place would be difficult. As luck would have it he didn't need to, having already secured his place at East 15, an "on the up" drama college but a short bus ride away from where he had grown up in Leytonstone. Graham too, had no issues with academic placement following his days at Stanway, taking up a two-year foundation course in Art and Design at the North Essex School Of Art, where Keith Albarn had recently been promoted to Director. "No nepotism, though," he later joked. With 50-odd miles now between them, and two very different choices of potential career, the Albarn/Coxon double act looked like it might finally be breaking up. At the time, neither of them would have looked at that way. Too melodramatic by half. Nonetheless, after all the Portakabins, Who videos, odd little bands and countless pub fights, things were about to change. For the better, as it turned out.

Chapter Three

A Very Middle Class Contract

At the tender age of eleven, Damon Albarn set off on a personal crusade "to be great". On paper, that ambition might appear overtly optimistic, a tad grasping, and given his youth, precocious in the extreme. Yet, when weighing up the evidence gathered over the years at Stanway, he might well have been onto something. Guided by family, teachers and friends, Albarn had shown much promise, first as an instrumentalist, then a fledgling composer and potential band leader. More, his forays into musical theatre seemed to confirm him as an actor of real talent – showy, occasionally unfocused, and again veering towards conceit – but talented nonetheless. "He had a rare magnetism on stage," said Nigel Hildreth, "and many teachers thought he could make it as an actor."

For a while, Damon fought quite the battle when it came to the matter of his future career. That battle was surely made worse by the fact music and drama seemed to come naturally to him, thereby muddying which road to take. But by the end of his school days, drama had won out and Albarn was on his way to East 15. Unfortunately, it was not his wisest decision.

When Albarn arrived at E15, hopes must have been high. A drama school whose former alumni included the respected actors Anne Mitchell and Alison Steadman, as well as upcoming writers/directors such as April

De Angelis and Stephen Daldry, East 15 also had a good reputation for placing its pupils in work. In a world where a reported 95% of Britain's acting community were 'resting' (i.e. claiming unemployment benefit), this was some boast. Another plus for Damon was East 15's location. Situated in the leafy grounds of an old Victorian manor, the school was only a five minute walk from Debden underground station, which in turn was only six stops away from his beloved Leytonstone. "In Damon's mind," said a former Stanway pupil, "he was going home."

Indeed, he was. On arriving in London, Albarn headed straight to his former stomping ground, taking up a flat share not far away from his family's old home. With a place to finally call his own, and a small grant with which to support himself, the 18-year-old was ready for his close-up.

At first, things went well enough. A new student in a new environment, Albarn's initial days were spent locating his classrooms, soaking up the curriculum and scoping out the competition. One immediate surprise was how young he was in comparison to everyone else, with the average East 15 student at least three years older than him. For a youth brought up among artists, designers and professional bohemians, this raised no great concern, other than to underline the fact he was once again a new boy rather than the wizened sixth former of Stanway. East 15's approach to drama, however, did give him severe pause. Like many such institutions at the time, the school took its cue from Konstantin Stanislavsky's 'Method' system, where an actor fleshes out their role through a combination of emotional cues and personal memories. When the Method worked – as with Robert De Niro's portrayal of the unravelling vigilante Travis Bickle in the film *Taxi Driver* – the results were astounding. When it didn't or was taken too far, the actor concerned could appear little more than a bizarre composite of facial tics, verbal pauses and bulging eyes. An instinctive performer who drew much of his energy from the audience, this 'Method' business was all a bit much for Albarn. "It was up its own arse." Still, if it had worked for Marlon Brando in *Guys And Dolls* and *On The Waterfront*, then Damon was at least willing to give it the old college try. Over the next few months, he would find himself inhabiting the roles of a mediaeval troubadour, pre-Regency landlord, singing cowboy, jobbing prostitute, prissy secretary, and perhaps most improbably, the Iranian leader Ayatollah Khomeini. All in all, it was a long way from 'Bobby' in *The Boy Friend*.

Seeking some comfort from days spent dressed as a gypsy tramp or 17th century malcontent in *The Duchess Of Malfi*, Albarn once again turned to piano. Thankfully, East 15 could assist his endeavours in this area, with many of their in-house productions requiring musical accompaniment. One story from this time has Damon writing a cod-country & western song for a comedy skit named 'A Night In The Longhorn Saloon', while another has him penning an Irish air for use by a friend in a short play. But in the main, his instrumental efforts were serious and surprisingly heartfelt. This was nowhere more apparent than when he performed as part of the college orchestra for Bertolt Brecht and Kurt Weill's collaboration *The Threepenny Opera* during the spring of 1987. In the audience was an old friend. "I went to see *The Threepenny Opera* at East 15 as I knew Damon and Catriona Martin of the student cast," said Nigel Hildreth. "I was surprised to see that he wasn't acting, but was actually playing (piano). After the show, my wife and I took the two of them for a curry, and learned that Damon was leaning again towards music. In fact, he was going to take up some other musical opportunities, including working with the Berliner Ensemble." Albarn got his chance to work with the esteemed German theatre company some three weeks later, when they appeared at a Brecht/Weill festival in nearby Ilford. Describing it as a "fantastic all round experience," Damon's growing appreciation of ...*Threepenny* and its creators pointed clearly at things to come. "It's overwhelmingly articulate music," he later said, "and it gave me a real taste for performing good music well."

It is perhaps worth taking a moment to understand Albarn's interest in the work of poet/theatre director Bertolt Brecht, and in particular, the composer Kurt Weill. If reports are correct, Damon first came across *The Threepenny Opera* in his parents' record collection. Suffice to say, he was immediately fascinated. Debuting in Berlin during the summer of 1928, just as Germany's Weimar Republic began to crumble away to the Nazis, *Threepenny...* was both a well-aimed critique at the perils of capitalism and a revolutionary pot-shot at the then stuffy values of traditional opera. Full of quirk and satire, Brecht's sweet/sour lyrics were magnificently supported by the melodies of Weill: simple yet angular, jazzy yet populist, compositions such as 'Mack The Knife' and 'Pirate Jenny' enraptured Damon as much as 'Baggy Trousers' or 'Ghost Town' ever did. Further, unlike the mass appeal of 2 Tone or the musical discoveries unearthed by Graham Coxon's detective work, *The Threepenny Opera* felt like it was all his. "Kurt Weill was a marvellous find for me," he later said, "It was more important than any pop record." Of course, Albarn wasn't the first to discover Brecht and Weill's wares: both The Doors and David Bowie had covered 'Alabama Song', while Nina Simone and Steeleye Span provided their respective audiences with extremely different takes on 'Pirate Jenny'. But Brecht's gift for lampooning the pretensions of high art and Weill's ability to remould classical themes into easily accessible tunes struck a profound chord with Damon, and would again exert a strong influence on his future work.

The next opportunity for Albarn to reactivate his interests as a pianist and songwriter did not come via East 15's music department, but from a fellow pupil called Eddie Deedigan. A quick-witted drama student who spent the early eighties whittling away his time in pop-folk group Random Gender, Deedigan shared Damon's gift of the gab and love of a song. Having struck up a sturdy friendship through their mutual distaste for East 15's teaching methods, the two subsequently become flatmates in Leytonstone. However, while Albarn had stopped working with bands after the dissolution of Real Lives, Eddie's last group – the curiously named 'The Alternative Car Park' – were still committed to a gig at Gold Diggers in Chippenham, despite the fact that they had broken up some weeks before. One reason Deedigan remained keen to honour his commitment was The Car Park were supporting legendary German chanteuse and former Velvet Underground singer Nico. A huge fan of the Velvets – and Nico in particular – Eddie was not going to miss a chance to meet his hero, even if it meant pulling together a collection of misfits, trainee actors and non-musicians to do it.

Hastily assembling a huge-lunged backing vocalist, promising, but largely untested sax player and a drummer whose talents ran to playing a snare drum but little more, Deedigan reached out to the one person who might actually be able to carry a tune. In keeping with his general disinterest in the history of pop (New York 'Avant Garde' branch included), Damon Albarn was clueless as to Nico, and more worryingly, had never heard of Velvet Underground. But after a quick whizz through 'I'm Waiting For The Man' and 'Venus In Furs', he was in. By all accounts, Albarn's one and only appearance with The Car Park went very well indeed. Cheered on by a few dozen East 15 types bussed in especially for the occasion, he was even granted a brief solo spot at the end of the set, performing a ballad called 'Rain'. According to Eddie – who incidentally met Nico for a beer afterwards – Albarn all but stole the show.

Despite such temporary distractions, by mid-1987 Damon had grown disenchanted with East 15 and was ready to quit. Disillusioned by the school's ethos, bored with having to fight for a seat due to high class numbers and thoroughly convinced an actor's life wasn't for him, the thought of returning for another year was simply "draining". Looking back, there were occasional highlights. For instance, he narrowly missed getting a part in the film adaptation of Martin Amis' coming of age novel *The Rachel Papers*. "When I got down to the last four, I thought 'I'd better read the book,'" he later said. A small role in a theatrical update of Terrence Rattigan's *The Browning Version* went the same way. But all in all, the lows outweighed the highs by a considerable margin. "I felt hopeless, unhappy and really dissatisfied with what I was doing," he told writer Stuart Maconie in 1998. "I just didn't feel any connection with the school at all." Uncertain how best to proceed, he returned home to Colchester to weigh up his options.

Back in Essex, Albarn saw that his old mate Graham Coxon was having the time of his life. Finding things at the North Essex School Of Art much to his liking, Graham had come on in leaps and bounds since Damon headed to London 12 months before. Not only were his grades exceptional, but he also about to embark on his first serious relationship with 'a rather pretty girl'. In keeping with this general upswing in his fortunes, Graham was exhibiting a distinctly rosy outlook, despite the fact that the mock spectacles that he once wore in honour of Smiths frontman Morrissey "were now a medical requirement".

There was progress on the musical front, too. Enjoying a generous amount of down time between classes, Coxon had taken the view 'Have sax, will travel' and chucked in with a variety of local groups, including The Curious Band and the cunningly titled Hazel Dean And The Carp Eaters From Hell. With Jessica Albarn in the year below him, and serious talk among his tutors of a possible placement at one of London's best art schools, being Graham Coxon circa 1987 was really rather good indeed. "I was having a lovely time," he might have said.

With Damon back on the Colchester scene, Coxon was eager to find out how his friend's song writing had progressed. The results were surprising. "I used to go around and see him," said Coxon, "and he'd play me this weird stuff that was just endless piano with no singing on it at all. It was just nuts." Knee deep in the music of Kurt Weill – Albarn was by now deconstructing the composer's most complex opera, *The Rise and Fall of the City of Mahagonny* – and still coming to terms with his negative experiences at acting school, Damon appeared in no mood for pop, rock or any other type of frippery. "I really was in the doldrums most of the time."

Ultimately, it took an inheritance of £3,000 from his grandfather to snap him back into shape, and again focus his attentions on what he wanted to do with his life. With his acting ambitions rapidly evaporating, the onus was now on creating music of enduring value. But he was realistic enough to know that while indulging his love of cult German composers might lead to fine reviews, it was also likely to guarantee artistic obscurity. This was not an acceptable option. "I think I was one of those people who had to become quite successful in order to feel normal."

The first stage of Albarn's new masterplan saw him move back to London, where he secured a number of part-time jobs in order to pay the rent. One such stint found him serving drinks at the swanky Portobello Hotel in the heart of Notting Hill. According to Damon, U2 singer and general demi-god Bono was rude to him at the bar, though fellow bandmate The Edge remained a perfect gentleman. Albarn's time at the Portobello proved short, but his next stint as a sales clerk at *Le Croissant* in Euston Station was a much better fit, if only for its central London location and closer proximity to the music business. With some of his £3,000 inheritance already spent on new equipment and fledgling recordings, Albarn was determined to use the remaining funds to make a professional demo of his three best songs. As the legend goes, he purloined a copy of *Yellow Pages* and scanned it for likely studios in the area. At the top of the alphabetical list was *The Beat Factory*. Keen to get things moving, he made an appointment to visit.

By the time Damon Albarn came calling, The Beat Factory had been a going concern for some four years. A short walk from Euston station, it was owned and managed by Graeme Holdaway and Marijke Bergkamp, who worked as engineer/producer and studio manager respectively. A former student at the Central School of Speech and Drama, Holdaway's fascination with bands and brief tenure as a semi-professional guitarist eventually led to a love of the recording process, his first real jobs of note running tapes for reggae acts such as Black Uhuru and Black Slate. "I actually became pretty good at dub techniques," he said.

In Bergkamp's case, the road to music was a little more circuitous. Born in Holland, she had lived out part of her childhood in Australia before coming to England to study Drama and History at the University of London. Having been introduced through mutual friends Graeme and Marijke soon became an item, and later married. Already a personal partnership, it wasn't long before they decided to make it a professional one as well. "We were young and ambitious, and to us," said Bergkamp, "It was all an adventure."

Long taken with the idea of owning a studio of his own, and with a partner now in full support of that ambition, Holdaway and Bergkamp purchased the Beat Factory site in 1983. They then spent the next year getting it ready for action. Tunnels were built to bring air into the premises "because we couldn't afford air conditioning at that time" with Hessian, Velcro patches and huge cushions stuck to the walls to aid soundproofing and create the right atmosphere. Bright lights were also hung around the studio, making the best of the building's available space. "It was an intimate place," said Graeme, "quite cosy really, but a good place for bands to come."

And come they did. Within a year of opening, The Beat Factory had mustered a strong reputation with both unsigned bands and major record labels. "We weren't specialising in one type of music," Holdaway confirmed. "We had soft metal bands, dance acts, there was a whole range of stuff, actually. I loved the variety of that, because I didn't want us to be typecast." Some of those walking through the studio door at the time included veteran prog rockers Wishbone Ash, Welsh songstress Bonnie Tyler and up and comers like Belouis Some and Fundamental. On one occasion, they even had rock royalty come visit. "Yes, The Who's Roger Daltrey did a session," said Graeme. "He was the loudest voice I've ever recorded, with the biggest lungs. I had to put him about 12 feet away from the microphone!"

An established concern, with various artists coming and going at all hours of the day and night, Damon Albarn was yet another potential client when he came to visit Marijke Bergkamp at The Beat Factory in October 1987. It didn't stay that way for long. "What first struck me about Damon was his intensity and commitment," she said. "He had about £1,000 (left) as an inheritance from his grandfather and wanted to record three songs. This was a huge amount of money for him, and he was very concentrated, very intense. He really wanted to get those tracks finished. And that's what attracted me to taking the project forward – not so much the music – but the level of commitment he showed." Impressed by the teenager's attitude, Bergkamp introduced him to Holdaway, who in turn listened to the songs Albarn wanted to record. "I wasn't that keen at first," he admitted. "Maybe I was a little tired, or overworked at the time, but I remember the first session as being a bit awkward." After working with Albarn for a while, his mood began to improve. "There was never any doubt that Damon had talent. But his approach was disparate. He could play, he could sing, but really it was the intensity that drew you in. He had the demeanour of an artist."

Unfortunately, there were no records taken of the three songs Albarn brought with him to The Beat Factory, but Holdaway and Bergkamp remain reasonably sure that 'Burden Of These Dreams' and 'Can't Live Without You' constituted two of them. In the case of 'Burden...' at least, it is easy to confirm the producer's contention that Damon undoubtedly had talent. A slow-building, two chord vamp redolent of Simple Minds or Peter Gabriel's 'Biko', 'Burden...' exhibited little indication of what was to eventually come from Albarn, but the signs of a promising songwriter were nonetheless there: working from a premise of 'tension and release', the tune was full of subtle keyboard flourishes and stray substitutions, with Damon's vocal pulling the central melody line to an emotive climax.

Suffice to say, the meeting between both parties went well enough for Albarn to return as a paying client a week or so later. On one session, he had Graham Coxon in tow. "Yes, Graham was on the first recordings," recalled Marijke. "He got lost on the way to the studio and Damon had to go and find him. At that point, he was technically anaemic, and white as a sheet... really in a bad state. He could barely lift the sax, but he could really carry a tune." The cause behind Coxon's sorry condition was a combination of working late shifts at his local Sainsbury's and a newfound interest in "protest vegetarianism". Taking Morrissey's edict that 'Meat Is Murder' to heart, Graham had changed his diet so radically he ended up in hospital with anaemia – his days reportedly spent cagging cigarettes from fellow patients, drawing old men urinating into jars and listening to The Smiths and Fleetwood Mac on a spare C90 cassette. However weak he was at the time, it did not stop him making the session. "Damon was like a big brother to Graham," said Bergkamp, "and Graham was very important to Damon. Damon was also very protective about Graham. They were almost bound together."

Following the pattern of their first encounter, Graeme Holdaway remained unsure about the overall quality of Albarn's material. "The early sessions were like building a Meccano train, adding bits together that worked. We even sequenced a keyboard drone from Eric Clapton's soundtrack to the thriller *Edge Of Darkness*. But there was an emotional quality to his voice even then. I do remember it as being hard work, though. In fact, it drained me."

There were other concerns for Holdaway. Damon's energy levels were commendable, but he could change his mind on a whim, shooting from one musical style to another in the time it took to make a coffee. Equally, while Coxon had come along to lend a hand, Albarn was approaching the overall project as a solo artist, which meant supporting musicians would have to be found, charts written and sequencers programmed. In short, a lot of hard work. Then there were Damon's myriad influences to contend with. "The musical influences were not just regular 'pop' influences," said Graeme. "There was Kurt Weill, Brecht, Avro Part, some really wide-ranging, left field stuff." But the tapes they made together kept drawing him back. "He was a musical chameleon, but there really was something there." Like Holdaway, Bergkamp also had issues with Albarn's songs, finding them to be more ordinary than extraordinary at the time. But she was also convinced he had the right stuff. "After the session, (we had) a difference of opinion about him," said Graeme. "She agreed with me that (the songs) weren't that great, (but) she felt very strongly that Damon had a quality about him... the air of a promising artist whose songs would get better if he were (pointed) the right way."

Following a somewhat lively discussion between the two, Holdaway and Bergkamp decided to offer Albarn a production/management deal. To sweeten the pill, he would gain access to the studio when it was unused. To sour it a little, making the tea would also be part of the package. To ensure everything was above board, Marijke visited Damon's parents to talk through the offer. "Damon was still at East 15 at the time," she said. "I think he trusted me and understood there was a relationship that could develop between The Beat Factory and him. We could see talent there, but (becoming a professional musician) was potentially life-changing. He had a very strong family background, so I went to see his parents to discuss how things might be taken forward. They were genuinely nice people, genuinely interesting people from a middle-class background who wanted the best for their son. They were a hugely important part of his life, and weren't going to let Damon prance about with no direction. So I wanted to show that from our point of view, we were showing a commitment to his progress. Really, for him, it boiled down to East 15 or a career in music, and he wanted to get it right."

With his parents' blessing, and principles agreed between all parties, Albarn signed a contract with The Beat Factory. Given he would be with them for the next two odd years, it is perhaps worth exploring that time in a little detail...*

At the top of everyone's agenda was getting a record deal as fast as possible. Twenty odd years on, Graeme Holdaway now feels that if a little more attention was paid to musical direction and overall strategy from the start, things might have progressed better. "Getting a deal was the central focus, and for good or ill, we started to craft the songs in that direction, without really having a template in place." Holdaway was also having the devil's own job in slowing Albarn down.

Working from home with a keyboard, Damon would turn up most days at The Beat Factory after his shift at Le Croissant, often with several new ideas on tape. From the winter of 1987 through to the spring of 1988, the best of these were developed, with rough piano and guide vocals being fed into the studio sequencer to see what came out. Of the material from that time, 'Bitter Sweet', 'The Red Club', 'China Doll' and 'Free The World' found Damon again flitting between various musical forms, with faux-soul, electro-pop and even world music all providing an influence here and there. But the sheer breath of styles only served to confuse the record labels who heard them. "After the original demos, we went to the record companies and solicited some interest with 'China Doll', 'Bitter Sweet' and several other tracks," said Bergkamp. "But they were still quite disparate, and the companies – as they do – wanted to categorise him. At that point, Damon was like a

* In some accounts of the Blur story, Damon had already left East 15 before signing up with The Beat Factory. That his first visit to the studio was probably in October, 1987 (some weeks after term time had started) certainly gives credence to this version of events. However, Marijke Bergkamp seems sure the decision to leave East 15 was taken only after he signed with the studio.

sponge soaking up various sounds and influences, but they wanted a nice, neatly packaged thing."

In truth, Albarn, Holdaway and Bergkamp were all learning their trade at the same time, with each party making their best efforts to secure that elusive record contract. It wasn't easy for any of them. "I didn't really know how to rate record company responses at that time," admitted Marijke. "Clearly though, there was more involved in getting a deal than just turning up at the office! In fact, Damon would be waiting for me when I came back. He'd ask 'How did it go? How did it go?'" Graeme felt much the same way, admiring Albarn's decision to stick with them when the labels clearly weren't biting. "I actually felt sorry for Damon, because he hung so much importance on our ability to get that record company interest," he said. "We were ingénues on the business side of things. There's no doubt in my mind that that was the case. But he stuck with us. The Beat Factory gave him a base to create, to mess about with sound canvasses, to experiment, to develop. And the better Damon got, the more I could do with it."

Though Albarn showed great loyalty with The Beat Factory after his initial efforts were rejected by record companies, he was nonetheless impatient for progress to be made. Having cut ties with acting, thrown in his lot with music, spent his grandfather's inheritance on demos and tested the support of his parents, he still found himself serving fancy breads to rush hour commuters in a busy train station just to earn his keep. This might explain why Damon briefly abandoned his efforts as a solo artist in favour of teaming up with fellow songwriter Sam Vamplew in the duo Two's A Crowd. "We weren't getting (anywhere) with the disparate stuff," said Bergkamp, "so maybe Damon thought 'This could be that neat little package the companies were looking for'."

A huge 'northern soul' fan, Vamplew was a regular visitor to the studio, cutting various tracks during early 1988. With Damon also recording songs and making the occasional tea, it was not long before the two met. However, no-one – least of all Graeme Holdaway – was expecting them to join forces. "Sam had a potent voice but to be honest, only about 10% of the talent Damon had. We were tearing our hair out at the idea, but Sam was incredibly persuasive. I think there was a feeling that the sum of the parts might make for a greater whole. And they came to us with a fait accompli, really. I think Damon was drawn to it in an almost perverse way. You know, 'Let's try this on for size'. And we enabled it, gave them studio time to explore the possibility, but..."

During their brief life span Two's A Crowd recorded at least five tunes, mostly Vamplew's, but with a couple of Albarn's thrown in to make things more interesting. Among their better efforts were a soft-soul shuffle with electronic overtones christened 'Waiting', a funky little number called 'Bad Religion', and two fair-to-middling pop tracks entitled 'Running' and 'Let's Get Together'. Lost somewhere between Colin Vearncombe's Black, early Pet Shop Boys and the tail end of Go West, Two's A Crowd were interesting, but no more so than 100 similar acts doing exactly the same thing during the same period. By the time publicity shots of the duo were taken at The North Essex School Of Art (presumably at the behest of Keith Albarn) and demos shopped around to the labels, Two's A Crowd were also finished. "It all went horribly wrong," said Graeme. "Sam wanted to carry on without Damon, and we had to remove Damon's parts from the demos. You know, I absolutely hated that period. I'd come to understand Damon's range, but Sam, well Sam was completely off the wall. Let's just call it an interesting experiment." (Sam Vamplew later contributed to the soundtrack of *The Lion King*, before reportedly pursuing other interests outside music).

In a classic case of 'Back to the drawing board', Albarn returned to his former status of solo artist, writing several more songs in the early summer of 1988. The results were promising. In 'Black Rain Town', he began to explore the darker side of his musical nature – the melody slow and unsettling, the atmosphere decidedly grim. "There were lyrical images of trucks loaded with plutonium being shipped at night across a rain-drenched city," said Holdaway. "Very evocative, very dark. At that point, I think we all knew he was getting somewhere. He was starting to get properly into the driving seat." Another new composition 'Hippy Children' (actually co-written with Graeme Holdaway) even solicited mild record company interest. "I came up with the riff, and played guitar on it. Damon added keys, we got a great session sax player in, and added some strong backing vocalists too. It was bouncy, it really had something, so we threw some money at it." Yet, still no one bit. "It was an uphill struggle," Holdaway continued. "None of the record companies were really signing anyone at that time, so we had to work on the songs, build the appeal, keep going."

Sick of bringing demo tapes to the record companies, Bergkamp now decided to bring Damon instead. In a bold move, a morning slot with EMI's chief A&R man Dave Ambrose was booked. Then overseeing the interests of acts such as Queen, Pink Floyd, Duran Duran and the Pet Shop Boys, Ambrose had also personally signed Kate Bush, Dexy's Midnight Runners and Sex Pistols (albeit very briefly) to the label. A veteran of the music wars, "Dave Ambrose knew his apples." However, as much as he liked Albarn, he heard nothing particularly riveting at the time. "We went to Dave's offices in London and did live versions of the songs with a guitar (and backing tapes)," said Bergkamp. "Damon just sat there, singing. We tried it this way and that way, but still nothing." With almost a year of such rejections behind him, Albarn had had enough. "Damon had just reached that point," Holdaway remembered. "He said 'I need a band...'"

Chapter Four

Convergences

Since the autumn of 1987, Damon Albarn had been trying to get a record deal. Though his agreement with The Beat Factory allowed him access to high quality studio equipment, production assistance, managerial representation and an opportunity to progress on his own terms in "an organic way", none of it had worked. Bored by failure and desperate for success, he made the decision in the summer of 1988 to end his career as a solo artist and instead form a band. Having briefly toyed with the idea of marketing himself as 'Circus', he simply transferred the name to that of his new group.

The first recruit to Albarn's cause was an old friend from college days named Tom Aitkenhead (though he would actually leave fairly soon after). A chisel-featured sort with a knack for technology, Aitkenhead had backed Damon when he performed a thinly attended solo concert at the Colchester Arts Centre some months before, making sure all the sequencers, drum machines and tape loops ran to order while Albarn sang from the front. The next to join up was Eddie Deedigan. Like Damon, Eddie had jacked in East 15 at the end of his first year and had been looking to put a band together ever since. With Deedigan came Dave Brolan. Likable, waggish and then sporting a quiff Morrissey would have been proud of, Brolan was a fine bassist and a spirited guitarist to boot. Next through the door came "The blue eyed boy," Darren Filkins. Like Brolan, Filkins was another of Deedigan's connections, having served time in The Alternative Car Park before it all went south. Last, but certainly not least, was Dave Rowntree.

Born at Colchester Maternity Hospital on 8 May, 1964, Rowntree's background was not dissimilar to that of Damon Albarn or Graham Coxon, albeit with its own set of twists and turns. The youngest of two children (his sister Sara was born five years before him), Dave's father John was one of those lab-coated sound effects engineers that made the BBC such an interesting place to visit during the sixties. A keen amateur musician, John Rowntree also worked on many of The Beatles' radio broadcasts at the corporation from 1963–65, his behind the scenes efforts ensuring that John, Paul, George and Ringo could be clearly heard above all the static. Dave's mother Susan was more front of house, playing viola with several classical orchestras until she became tired of the lifestyle and settled with her husband in Colchester. With music such a huge part of the Rowntree household, Dave was expected to learn an instrument from an early age. "I was forced into it," he once quipped. His first task was to conquer a mini set of bagpipes called a 'Chanter' before he got to experiment with the real thing. "It was like playing a bloody hot water bottle." When all the drones and bellows failed to interest the young boy, Rowntree's parents relented and gave him a chance to learn a military drum instead. Taught by a burly Scotsman who taped a sixpence to the skin – the coin signifying where Dave should strike for maximum efficiency – things went well enough until he missed the spot, at which point he risked being struck by his ex-army teacher instead.

Such punitive measures didn't put Rowntree off. Quite the opposite, in fact. By the time he was 12, Dave was regularly drumming with a young American pianist named Buddy Hassler, whose family originally came to Colchester as part of the US Airforce. With Rowntree's sister Sara offering occasional support on tambourine, this curious trio made their live debut at a street party thrown in honour of the Queen's Silver Jubilee. By all accounts quite the performance, Sara sang The Beatles' 'Yellow Submarine' while Dave and Buddy bashed away in the background. "At least Buddy could open the piano lid." There were more formal lessons ahead. Alongside his father, Rowntree was a regular attendee at Landermere Music School in Thorpe-Le-Soken. Here, he learned percussion and music theory, playing with string quartets, woodwind sections and even traditional brass bands, for which he developed a particular affection. "The drum parts were pants, but it was a great feeling to be in the middle of it all."

It wasn't all jazz and brass, of course. Even if his parents were schooled musicians, the Rowntree family record collection fully reflected popular music of the time, and Dave was scouring each and every LP they owned for drummers to latch onto. "My parents were sixties kids, so I was constantly listening to Cream, the Stones and Hendrix," he later confirmed. "That's the stuff I was listening to when I was growing up. I was obsessed with Cream's Ginger Baker and 'Strange Brew'. I just played that song until I'd worn out the groove. I wasn't really into Ringo back then, to my eternal shame, though *A Hard Day's Night* was my favourite Beatles album."

Eager to get his new drum kit out of the bedroom and into a concert hall, it wasn't long before Rowntree began mucking around with local bands, the first of which was a trio jokingly named The Strategic Arms Quartet. "Hilarious, eh?" When the joke fell flat, Dave threw in his cards with Idle Vice, another Colchester act whose repertoire mostly extended to jazz-punk songs of the instrumental variety.

It was during this period that Idle Vice guitarist Robin Anderson introduced Rowntree to Graham Coxon, then alternating his musical efforts between The Curious Band and Hazel Dean And The Carp Eaters From Hell. During conversation over a couple of pints, it transpired that Dave had actually been taught by Graham's father Bob at Landermere School on Saturday mornings. "We became mates soon after that," said the drummer. Mates and soon-to-be bandmates, as it transpired. With the Colchester alternative scene an exceedingly small affair, it wasn't unusual for groups to share or swop personnel with each other, their line-ups as fluid and interchangeable as the music they played. Hence, Idle Vice's Anderson had already lent a hand in ...The Carp Enders when the occasion warranted it. Keen to get a brass section attached to his own band, the guitarist asked Coxon to consider playing saxophone with the Vice. Within the space of a month, Graham was doing the odd gig with Rowntree at The Hole In the Wall, Oliver Twist and several other pubs in the area.

The arrangement didn't last long, however, as Rowntree left Colchester to pursue higher education. By his own admission a relaxed sort of pupil during his time at Gilberd Grammar School, he still did enough to gain a place on a HND Computer Science course at Thames Polytechnic, then based in South East London. Given later achievements, it was the first clear manifestation of Rowntree's ability to smoothly move between the demands of music and the more material world. Fascinated by all things mega-byte related, he had spent many an after-hours session at Gilberd working his way through programmes and sub-routines, having picked up the bug at an electronics show his father took him to as a child. By 20, that fascination was a potential career, as he became one of a new generation of IT kids able to turn raw data into something rather wonderful. Far ahead of the game due to his own studies, Rowntree spent his two years at Thames Poly on easy street, with lessons an idle distraction from regular pub crawls around his home in Woolwich and the odd jam with fellow students. He even found time to set up a music society.

Once qualified, one might have thought Dave would have parked his musical ambitions in favour of making a killing on the London job market. After all, by 1986, Thatcher's Britain was well out of recession and truly back in the black, with demand for those who understood anything at all about computers beginning to spiral. Rowntree, however, was not one of Thatcher's children. Politically far left of centre, the drummer was more Marxist Agit-prop/hippie than yuppie at the time, even going as far as model patched trousers and a woolly Kaftan when the mood took him.

Temporarily turning his back on the analogue world, he re-established contact with Idle Vice's Robin Anderson, added a chap called Jim on bass and set about forming a punk/rock/power pop trio. With no regular income to speak of, the band took advantage of London's vast, but edgy squat scene, first moving into a shabby flat in North London's

Kings Cross, before upping stakes three miles down the road to Crouch End. Commandeering a disused, five floor community centre with his and hers toilet facilities, the group (which now included the regally named Charles Windsor on vocals) couldn't believe their luck. "We actually got a floor each," laughed Rowntree. But a run in with the local police and a summary eviction notice soon changed their minds. On the dole, scoring only the occasional gig (often as not in other squats) and soon to be homeless, the quartet decided to buy a van, vacate North London and try their luck in France for a year.

What followed can best be described as a brush with feast and famine, albeit of the Gallic variety. Living "hand to mouth, really", the band subsisted on a diet of baguettes, cheap local plonk and if the budget ran to it, the odd splurge on some good quality cheese. With paying gigs sporadic at first, they often as not busked in town squares across the country, saving money by sleeping in tents, or when the weather deemed it necessary, their rapidly unravelling van. If things went well – as they did in the coastal region of Pas-de-Calais – Rowntree and his colleagues amassed a healthy local following and enough money to move into a hotel. When they didn't, as in Paris and Tours, then it was straight back to Pas-de-Calais. "They really loved us there," he said. As their profile in northern France grew, there was serious talk among the musicians of making the move permanent. But faced with another year of uncertain fortunes and a never ending cycle of tent/van/hotel, Rowntree made the decision to come home.

Arriving back in a Colchester dole queue at the end of 1987, Dave finally gave in to the other side of his nature and took a job as a computer programmer with the local council. There were benefits to it. The role itself wasn't particularly taxing, but soundly remunerated. Further, unlike the private sector where appearance was sometimes as important as performance, Rowntree's publically funded position meant he could dress more or less as he pleased, as long as a jacket and trousers were in there somewhere. Given the fact he had recently taken to sporting a luscious Mohawk, this was something of an advantage. "It was a Mohawk, not a Mohican," he later emphasised. "A very 'Colchestrian' difference. The Mohican was thin, the Mohawk was thick." Best of all, by returning to the town of his birth, he could once again look up a few old friends in the hope of finding a new group.

One of these was Graham Coxon, who was still making occasional noises with The Curious Band at the time. When talk turned to music between the two, Coxon invited Rowntree to see an old friend from his Stanway days play a short set at The Colchester Arts Centre. Taking up the offer, Dave joined a dozen or so other punters in the audience to see Damon Albarn's first 'solo' gig. "I'd already heard tapes of Damon from Graham, and thought the stuff was great." Impressed by Albarn's performance, Rowntree handed over his telephone number at the end of the night with the words "If you ever need a drummer, just give me a ring." In October 1988, the call finally came. "I had an executive, sitting behind the desk, high powered job, and I gave it up to be a drummer..."

The band Rowntree found himself joining was a real hotchpotch of musical influences, with a shared love of The Smiths the only real constant among them. As a solo artist, Albarn had drawn variously on David Bowie, Kurt Weill, The Pet Shop Boys, plastic soul and even Peter Gabriel for inspiration. Now, with several other members keen to throw in their tuppence worth, the palette was widened even further to include Talking Heads, a bit of folk and even Elvis Presley (bassist Dave Brolan was a huge fan of 'Blue Moon' at the time). Still overseeing production duties as well as providing a base of operations, The Beat Factory's Graeme Holdaway was unsure of Circus as a long-term prospect right from the start. "For Damon, Circus was about getting the experience of being in a band. I think he knew it wouldn't last, but it was all part of the learning curve." That said, early signs were encouraging. The group quickly established a strong work ethic with Albarn and Deedigan providing the lion's share of song ideas between them, including the likes of 'Happy House', 'She Said' and 'Salvation'.

By the early winter of 1988, they were ready to cut their first demos. Unfortunately, guitarist Darren Filkins had other ideas. A keen amateur photographer, Filkins had recently scored his first professional commission and chose to leave Circus just two days before recording was to begin. "Wow, that was a long time ago," said Filkins in 2013, "and a really interesting time. But I decided to leave while on a photo shoot in St. Lucia in November 1988. I loved music, but I have no regrets. I've had a lot of fun..." For Albarn and Rowntree, there was never any doubt as to who would replace the errant guitarist. "We just called Graham."

Happily, Graham Coxon was no longer living in Colchester when Circus came calling. Having done extremely well in his final exams at North Essex, he accepted an offer to study Fine Art at Goldsmiths College, subsequently moving to South London in the autumn of 1988. Now a student at England's most prestigious art school, Graham was sharing paint and conversation with some of the brighter minds in the country. "You were mixing with people who had really different ideas," he later said. "Fine artists mixing with sculptors mixing with graphic artists. Quite heady." Though there were occasional doubts about some of his colleagues – "(The place) was full of cunts and posers who thought they were intellectual" – Coxon still loved Goldsmiths' atmosphere and ethos. After all, this was a college with a reputation for encouraging its charges "to risk falling on their arse" in order to produce their best work. "A fine artist," said Graham, "might find themselves incompetently doing some graphics which actually turned out (to be) quite exciting and less precious than a traditional graphic artist (might achieve)."

Outside the classroom, he was also having a ball. Living in Goldsmiths' halls of residency deep in the heart of New Cross (then as now, a lively part of the world), Coxon had access to cheap pubs, even cheaper student bars and with The Venue, an intimate, if scruffy concert hall populated by a variety of then up-and-coming bands. "When I was in New Cross, I was just going to see these little groups, you know, who then went on and got big," he said. "The Stone Roses, Inspiral Carpets… they were all just starting out."

Unsurprisingly, Damon Albarn had been a regular visitor to Coxon's digs since his friend had arrived in London some months before. Impressed by Goldsmiths and Graham's positivity towards it, he even enrolled on "a part-time, two classes a week spurious music course just to get myself on campus, really." But with the clock ticking and Circus ready to record, Damon was now visiting New Cross on business. Though Coxon had both his guitar and sax with him, he had thus far been reluctant to take out his toys at college. "I always felt slightly ashamed of the musical side of myself at Goldsmiths, really. It was a very serious art school at the time." This was different, of course. Having worked on and off with Albarn for years, and already contributed to several of his demos at The Beat Factory, there was no way Graham was going to miss out on the party. "I'd just sneak off to rehearse at night, then paint in the morning. Or eat a pizza," he laughed.

Graham Coxon's first rehearsal with Circus was something of a shock for all concerned. Seen primarily as a sax player, no-one but Albarn and Rowntree knew how far the quiet chap with the glasses had come on six strings. "In the build up to Circus, Graham was still really playing sax," said Graeme Holdaway. "But he picked up my Mansun guitar, and I was completely gobsmacked. I just said to him 'Why are you playing sax?' I just couldn't believe how good he was. He would do these incredibly over-the-top things, dropped tunings, feedback... just brilliant, even then."

In an interview with writer Martin Roach, Eddie Deedigan confirmed a similar sense of awe. "He fucking licked it, mental playing, unbelievable. We just couldn't believe what we were hearing. It was so easy for him." Self-raised on Weller and Townshend, Coxon hadn't just stopped with the mods. By 1989, he had not only incorporated the work of classicists Jeff Beck and Jimmy Page into his sonic armoury, but also added a new batch of greasy noise merchants then doing the musical rounds. In Dinosaur Jr.'s J Mascis, Sonic Youth's Thurston Moore and My Bloody Valentine's Kevin Shields, Coxon had found a school of guitar playing that spoke to him directly – its use of atonality, alternative tunings, waves of distortion and droning feedback opening up the instrument for him all over again. "It was like a new vocabulary in a way," he later told *Guitar*.

With Graham now on board, the band set about recording demos of Albarn and Deedigan's songs in the winter of 1988 for a 'mini-album' to be touted around the record companies. As before, interest in the finished product was slight, with only EMI faintly complimentary of their efforts. Never convinced of the fact that Circus would work, Graeme Holdaway continued to watch from the wings as the storm clouds gathered. "Circus was like two bands coming together," he said. "Eddie Deedigan and Dave Brolan were like an Irish folk-rock outfit, very much their own band. And on the other side were Damon, Graham and Dave, who were very much of themselves too. There were really two leaders, then. I knew that wasn't going to work. Marijke knew it wasn't going to work and I suspect Damon knew it wasn't going to work. But they were damned if they were going to admit to us it wasn't going to work. So they went for it." The next stage was getting out of the studio and onto the stage. To facilitate Circus' live debut, Eddie's wife booked the band a gig at the Victoria Hall in Southborough, Kent on January 26, 1989 with local chancers Whale Oil in support. "It was all a bit shambolic," said Bergkamp of the concert, "with Eddie and Damon ribbing on stage, but also quite a lot of fun."

It was Circus' first and last gig. Though Deedigan and Albarn were close friends, they were also becoming diametrically opposed when it came to matters of musical direction. With Graham Coxon, Circus had acquired a hugely talented guitarist, but one that brought with him a love of power chords, raw experimentation and a mad crush on Big Black and My Bloody Valentine. While Albarn and Rowntree were more than happy to incorporate such influences into the group's sound, the more melodically inclined Eddie and his corner man Dave Brolan were less sure. When the end came, it was mercifully quick. "Circus actually broke up in the middle of a recording session at The Beat Factory," said Holdaway. "There was a big argument and Eddie and Dave Brolan walked out. The others stayed." Two decades later, there is still some confusion as to what exactly actually happened on the day. According to Deedigan, he and Brolan simply left the band citing musical differences. Others have it that Dave Rowntree actually sacked Eddie and Brolan walked out in solidarity at his friend's dismissal. Whatever the truth of it, Deedigan and Brolan were soon back on the gigging circuit with a promising, Celtic-tinged folk-pop outfit called The Shanakies. Circus, on the other hand, were missing a bassist.

Enter Alex James.

Unlike Damon Albarn, Graham Coxon and Dave Rowntree, Alex James had no real connection with Colchester. Nor did he enjoy any prolonged musical training. That said, whatever he lacked in either area was more than made up for in swank, swagger and bags of self-possession. "I think I always wanted to be a pop star," he later said, "or an astronaut..." Born on November 21, 1968, Stephen Alexander James spent his bucket and spade years growing up in the sleepy seaside town of Bournemouth. Then perhaps unfairly known as "one giant retirement home by the sea", Bournemouth had little of the cosmopolitan allure of Brighton. Frankly, it would not even trouble Torquay or the Isle of Wight in the glamour stakes. But according to James, it was nonetheless a fine place to idle away his summers as a child. "It was nice growing up by the seaside. There was lots of opportunity for vandalism." Alex's father John was a navy man in his youth, eventually leaving the service to work as sales manager for a firm specialising in waste compactors and baling machines. Alex's mother did local voluntary work in Bournemouth and its surroundings, helping old and infirm residents with a 'Books On Wheels' service. "My grandparents were really working class, and my dad earned money and would be classified as middle class," Alex said. "But I don't really think any of it matters."

If James' background sounded fairly anodyne, he could still claim some exotic types lurking elsewhere in the family records. "My uncle was a jazz pianist and my granny's sisters were on the stage," he said. "In fact, my grandma was actually part of a glamorous dance troupe called 'The Dolly Sisters'." Alex's grandfather Emrys was equally off-beat. The owner of a 13-room guest house in the centre of Bournemouth, he was also a working chef, his abilities in the kitchen making a striking impression upon his young grandson. "My granddad was a cordon bleu chef in a five-star hotel in Bournemouth, where I grew up," James later told *The Sun*. "From the age of seven, I'd help him make the breakfasts. I was in complete awe of his skills." When Emrys passed, the James clan moved into his old home, with the 11-year-old Alex, his younger sister Deborah, one or two guinea pigs and their favourite pet "Sparky the Wonderdog" now spoilt for choice when it came to potential play areas. "Deborah was two years younger than me, and we were always very close but very different," he said. "She was really good at painting and drawing. She's got strong visual acuity."

Alex James' thirteenth year was marked by his first real dalliance with a musical instrument. Having objected to the smell of recorders as an infant and tested the patience of his teacher on violin aged eight, he suddenly expressed a mild interest in electronic keyboards. Being something of an amateur player himself, John James purchased his son a £100 upright piano for a birthday present. Unfortunately, while Alex enjoyed watching his dad bang out the odd rock 'n' roll lick, he felt little drive to learn the piano himself. "My dad showed me how to play blues. But really, I just wanted to be a footballer like all the other boys. Besides," he concluded, "only wankers were into music." All that changed when Alex turned 16. "I heard 'Blue Monday' by New Order," he said. "Everything about that record was unconventional. It's an odd length, the bass was doing one melody and the guitar's doing another, and you've got these great, very honest lyrics (on top). It was sophisticated in a very primitive way... a bunch of Herberts claiming high art as their own."

With New Order bassist Peter Hook his new hero, and Duran Duran's John Taylor providing a look to aspire to ("He had a really good haircut"), James harangued his parents for a bass guitar of his very own. They caved in soon enough. "I got my first guitar as a fashion accessory," he later said. "It was a Fender Precision bought from Southbourne *Exchange & Mart* for £50. Quite nifty, too."

James' first band was unusual, principally for the fact that he was the only member. Calling himself The Age Of Consent, the 'group' consisted of Alex shouting "1,2,3,4, take it away" into a tape recorder before dropping the needle of his stereo on Fleetwood Mac's 'The Chain'. This combination of live shouting and recorded music was then presented to friends as evidence of The Age Of Consents' uncanny skills and James' personal dexterity on bass. It didn't wash. That said, he eventually did learn to play 'The Chain', Led Zeppelin's 'Whole Lotta Love' and even New Order's 'Blue Monday' as part of an unnamed "bedroom band" consisting of several schoolmates and the wonderfully named Rut The Nut. But again, it proved "more of a laugh" than anything worth taking seriously. "When you're 11, you and all your mates want to be footballers, but then when you're 16 you all want to be in a band," he said. "Everybody in my class was learning one instrument or another, so it was quite easy to join in."

While James' efforts on bass guitar might have lacked necessary rigour at the time, his academic prowess could not be faulted. At the same age he was plucking away at 'The Chain', Alex passed no fewer than 13 'O' Levels, marking him out as one of the smarter boys not only in Bournemouth Grammar School, but also the entire south west coast of England. Sadly, the wheels came off soon after, as the once model pupil set about expanding his studies to include underage drinking, wobbly dancing in even wobblier nightclubs and the pursuit of several dozen local girls. By 18, James' nocturnal activities had conspired against him, resulting in the death of countless brain cells and some quite shocking 'A' Level results in Physics, Chemistry and French. Now unsure of finding a university place, he chose to gather his thoughts by taking a gap year. What followed was 12 months of social and career inertia, as he spent his nights drowning his sorrows and his days recovering in a variety of temporary jobs. During this wilderness period, he worked variously as a labourer on the grounds of Winfrith Nuclear Power Station, a navvy on building sites and a shelf stacker at Safeway's. Away from the beer bottles, pick axes and detergents, there were also a few garage bands to distract him, as James threw in his lot with The Rising, The Victorians and the improbably titled Mr. Pangs' Bang Bangs, the latter named in honour of his then landlord – a footballer with Southampton FC. As with The Age of Consent, none of these acts were to ever trouble the charts.

It all came to a merciful end when one of Alex's former teachers provided a strong enough reference for him to gain admission to Goldsmiths College studying French. Having by now experienced life up a ladder, down a hole and at the wrong end of a bullying supermarket manager, he grasped the opportunity with both arms and legs. Arriving at Goldsmiths during the autumn of 1988, James took to university life like a proverbial duck to water, his timetable marked by occasional lectures, heady after hours discussions concerning the merits of French

Romanticism and weekend trips into the West End. With the possible exception of the lectures, most of these activities seemed to involve copious amounts of alcohol, for which Alex had obviously developed quite the taste. In fact, when his own personal stash of wine and beer ran out, he simply solved the problem by liberating another student's supply from the shared fridge in his halls of residence. He was never caught. "All in all, I was at the best art school in the world and having a wonderful time," James later said, "I mean, how could you not?"

Things got even better when Alex became acquainted with Graham Coxon, whom he had first seen unloading belongings from his parents' car on the opening day of college. Though Coxon was covered in paint and appeared oblivious to all and sundry, James took to him immediately. "Graham was pulling a guitar out of the back of the car and dressed in a stripy sweater and glasses," said Alex. "I just liked him on sight." Proving synchronicity to be a wonderful thing, it transpired Graham roomed directly above Alex in the student halls at Laurie Grove near New Cross. When finally introduced by mutual friends, the pair's conversation immediately turned to music, with James owning up to the ownership of a bass guitar. "It went from there, really," he said.

What followed was a short, but crucial period of 'Getting to know you'. Coxon became a sceptical member of James' new art movement 'Nichtkunst', which seemed to consist of both making charcoal pictures of various objects until one or the other fell asleep. Several drunken debates were also had about the merits of rock vs. pop, with Graham loudly extolling the virtues of The Pixies and The Pastels while Alex listened to *Sgt. Pepper's Lonely Hearts' Club Band* in the background. On one occasion (possibly during an argument), an extractor fiound its way out Coxon's third floor window. As the two were again drunk at the time, they simply forgot about retrieving it, only to learn the next day that the thing had become irretrievably stuck in the wheel of the Bursar's VW Camper Van. Such was the road to friendship. "Graham really was quite cool," James later said, "He even knew the third years..."

Having happily fallen in with Coxon and the Goldsmiths art crowd, it was only a matter of time before Alex James was introduced to Damon Albarn. That invitation came in December 1988 when Circus were throwing a party at The Beat Factory to mark the end of recording for their mini album. Keen to see what Coxon was getting up to outside college, and extremely eager to meet the mysterious Albarn – "Graham talked about Damon a lot" – it was an offer James could not refuse. It turned out to be an interesting night. Expecting to find someone rather similar in style, mood and temperament to Graham, James was instead confronted by a rather arrogant young man with "old fashioned" spiky hair and sandals on his feet. Worse still, Albarn found the fact that Alex had never been in a recording studio before the sign of a lesser mortal. Irritated by the slight, James answered honestly when asked what he thought of Circus' songs. "Damon had completely pissed me off," Alex recalled. "(So) I told him they sounded like Brother Beyond."

If James' words were designed to offend, they seemed to have the opposite effect. Following the departure/removal/sacking of Eddie Deedigan and Dave Brolan several weeks later, Alex was hastily summoned to The Beat Factory where he was handed a can of lager by Coxon and a bass guitar by Albarn. "An audition of sorts," he later quipped. What happened next sealed his fate. Idly strumming out a chord sequence he had been playing around with in his Goldsmiths digs, Graham began embellishing James' melody and adding the odd lyric. Not to be left out, Damon provided a rough drum pattern and some more words, including the chorus' key line. "She is so high, she is so high..." When Dave Rowntree later added a few beats of his own, the quartet had their first song and rather a good one at that. "'She's So High' was fully formed right from the beginning," said Graeme Holdaway. "They didn't change the structure, the instrumentation, anything. It was just there, and didn't change from demo to record." (Astoundingly, 'She's So High' also marked the last time the group would write together in such a fashion).

What followed this beery session was six months of hard graft, with all four members of the new enterprise fully committing their time and effort to a mutually shared cause. "Graham was already in the band with Damon and Dave, and Damon already had got this management deal with keys to the studio," said James. "So we just locked ourselves in for six months and worked and worked on making ourselves brilliant."

Unlike Circus, there were few fights over musical direction, no matter how odd or left-field the influence involved. Having recently fallen in love with the odd meters and climbing chromatics of English art-rockers The Cardiacs, Albarn was now writing songs with a quirkier, almost atonal approach to melody. When combined with Coxon's efforts to emulate My Bloody Valentine's "sheet of sound" guitars, the results could be overwhelming. "I think Damon was almost cynical about it all at the start of the new group," said a watchful Marijke Bergkamp. "By then, he'd tried solo projects, duos and now it was bands. (But) there was still a feeling he just wasn't getting anywhere. So I genuinely think he started writing 'Anti-music'."

Early recordings from this period bear out Bergkamp's contention. 'Fried' for instance, was a mad four-man charge in search of a tune, with Albarn yelling over the top until his lungs gave out. 'Shimmer', too, was another experiment with the music of extremity. Combining waves of discordant guitar with a jabbering vocal from Damon, it also featured a super-speed middle section The Cardiacs would have been proud of. Taken together, these were less traditional songs and more experiments in sound. "The band's early sessions were all about energy," said producer Graeme Holdaway. "'Fried', 'Shimmer', all that stuff. There were a lot of emotions flying around at those sessions." When these demos were taken to the record companies, the reaction was bleak.

"Oh, we really had to learn to temper our (original) sound," said Graham. "The first recordings we made as demos, well, people like Creation Records told us to get out. It was fairly unlistenable. But most of the recordings were influenced by those (Creation) bands, plus some psychedelic and out-there stuff. We were an amalgam of early Pink Floyd and My Bloody Valentine, but we were proud of it. That was our heritage. The Rolling Stones had the blues. We had My Bloody Valentine."

When the band were not rehearsing or recording, they were drinking. "Dave was a really nice bloke," said Holdaway. "A quiet, polite guy, though he was wearing pyjama bottoms that were stitched around the middle. But boy, could he drink. Ten pints, easy. But they were all drinking. We'd break from recording and they'd go to the pub. Damon and Dave really were as strong as an ox." Unfortunately, Graham Coxon didn't share their intestinal fortitude. "At that point, Graham didn't really have the constitution for really heavy drinking," said Holdaway. "Three pints would have the same effect on him as ten pints on someone else. He was still weakened (by anaemia) at the time." By all accounts, Alex James was almost as bad as Coxon. "To be honest, I thought Alex was a complete oaf," said Graeme. "He was drinking even more than Dave, so it was difficult to get anything out of him. He couldn't really play a note then, either. But you know, there was no doubt he looked the part..."

After several months of writing songs, recording demos and abusing their livers, Albarn, Coxon, Rowntree and James were ready to take to the stage. Intent on not trading under the name Circus, they were nonetheless having trouble coming up with a suitable alternative. In the end, the group opted for Seymour, reportedly taking their cue from the titular character of J.D. Salinger's 1959 novella, *Seymour: An Introduction.* Given the fact that Salinger's most famous work, *The Catcher In The Rye,* all but defined teenage angst, and *Seymour...* itself was written in a style not dissimilar to the rambling missives of Syd Barrett, it really wasn't a bad choice of moniker for an upcoming art-pop band. However, Seymour's somewhat arch connotations still managed to confuse many on first hearing. "Well, it did raise an eyebrow or two at the record labels," laughed Holdaway.

Confusion also reigns over the date and venue of Seymour's first gig. Some would have it that their debut appearance was an impromptu slot at Goldsmiths in front of the student union during the autumn of 1988. Unlikely, as Circus were still a going concern at that time. Another possible lead has them playing at a squat in Clapham during the same period. Given Dave Rowntree's links with that scene were long over, this again seems unfeasible. Therefore, it remains a more likely bet that Seymour opened their live account at The East Anglian Railway Museum, near Colchester in the late spring of 1989. "It had a fantastic landscape, a Victorian viaduct," Damon later remembered, "and it's where Graham and I did a lot of our early mucking about as teenagers." Though details of their performance remain sketchy, Alex

James once offered a memory or two about the show. "We had just enough songs to play for about half an hour," he said. "I remember Damon's granny saying it was great. Surprising really, as we were very drunk and horrible."

As legend has it, Seymour remained "drunk and horrible" for many of their earliest appearances, with Albarn a ball of energy from start to finish. "Our early shows were just chaos," Graham later remembered. "Damon would bomb Alex, chase me around, then get sick behind the amps. The set would only last 15 minutes. He just had so much energy. I hated it, though. I wanted to play all the songs." According to Marijke Bergkamp, Albarn's occasional vomiting was less about the amount he drank before the show, and more about the level of ambition swirling inside him. "Damon wanted it so much," she said, "He was even being sick at the microphone."

This combustible attitude to gigging also brought its downsides. Following a support slot at Camden's grungy Dingwalls to alternative rockers New Fast Automatic Daffodils in November, 1989, Seymour's high spirits transferred themselves from the stage and into the audience. When a friend of the band exposed himself as a joke, the club bouncer took immediate exception, first spraying mace into the offender's eyes, before doing the same to Albarn and Co when they tried to protect him. All five ended up in the local casualty department where they received treatment for their injuries. Bizarrely, *Music Review*'s write-up of the gig failed to mention the incident, though journalist Leo Finlay was extremely complimentary about a group called Feymour. "This unsigned Colchester band played a blinder," said Finlay. "There may well be a gap in the market, and Feymour have the charm to fill it." Even if he got their name wrong, his heart was at least in the right place.

Despite such occasional hiccups, Seymour were beginning to build a steady following by the autumn of 1989, as the group continued to concentrate its efforts on gigging in London and the south east. Away from the madness of Dingwalls, they also performed support slots and the occasional headliner in tried and tested music industry pubs such as Finsbury Park's Sir George Robey, Kennington's Cricketers and The Camden Falcon. While attendances might have often been below 100 at these concerts, word was still spreading. "We did a couple of gigs and people were already talking about us," Alex remembered. "We were arrogant, but you need arrogance, self-confidence. And don't forget, we were brilliant." A definitive set list was also taking shape. With 'Fried' and 'Shimmer' now consigned to the musical dustbin, funkier newer material such as 'I Know', 'Close' and the excellent 'Explain' all illustrated that Seymour were at least paying some attention to the pop scene around them.

It was just as well. At the same time the quartet were making a small, but substantial splash in London, a growing nationwide movement called 'baggy' was taking lessons learned from the recent wave of 'Madchester' bands and giving them an even more pie-eyed makeover. Following in the footsteps of The Stone Roses and Happy Mondays, acts like The Soup Dragons, The Charlatans and The Farm were all upping the neo-psychedelic guitars, 'funky drummer' beats and loved-up lyricism to new heights and appreciative crowds. Crucially, the record companies were also starting to circle, with cheque books at the ready to sign anyone with a bowl haircut, loose cut jeans and an ecstasy habit. If Seymour were to stand any chance of being picked up by a label, then at least one or two of their tunes would have to reflect – or at least be manipulated to reflect – this growing sea change in Britain's musical and fashion tastes. It was a thought to be parked, but also returned to.

The first real sign that Seymour's time was nigh came in late November 1989, when Food Records' Andy Ross came to see the band at the Powerhaus in Islington, north London. Though Food were no industry giant, they did have form, push and a certain clout. Set up by former Teardrop Explodes producer/manager/keyboardist Dave Balfe in 1984, the independent label had started out by signing cult fare such as Voice Of The Beehive, Zodiac Mindwarp and Crazyhead. But the acquisition of electronic indie-rockers Jesus Jones in 1989 changed both Food's profile and fortunes, eventually netting band and record company a number one album in the UK and a number one single in the States. A growing enterprise whose product was funded and distributed worldwide by "super label" EMI, Dave Balfe was nevertheless keen to retain Food's creative independence despite such resounding success. To aid him in this ambition, help ease his workload, and scout other potential signings, Balfe brought former *Sounds* journalist Andy Ross on board as his partner.

Unlike several before him, Ross was immediately taken with Seymour when he heard their demos in late 1989. "I went to see Andy Ross and played him the tapes," said Marijke Bergkamp. "I remember he had these three trays on his desk. One of them said 'Do now', another said 'Do later' and the last one said 'Do me a favour'. But he liked Seymour, so he turned up to see them. Again. And again. Then Dave Balfe turned up too." As stated above, Ross' first experience of the band came at Islington's Powerhaus in November 1989, but he was to become a repeat attendee at several more shows before the year was out. "I saw these four lunatics jumping all over the place," he later confirmed, "and I don't know why, but I thought 'This is good'. So I got my partner Dave Balfe along to see them too..."

At the same time that Food Records were ramping up their interest in the band, Damon Albarn and Seymour's relationship with Graeme Holdaway and Marijke Bergkamp at The Beat Factory was coming to an end. "Damon and Seymour had become more and more independent," said Bergkamp. "They had been spending a lot of time together, writing, rehearsing... still fighting for recognition, still fighting for the record deal." There were other problems to contend with from The Beat Factory's point of view. As this sense of independence flourished, the band – and Damon in particular – had started to distance themselves from both the studio and the production/management duo, resulting in uneven communications, simmering tensions and the occasional argument (by all accounts, Damon had even wrested control of some recording sessions from Holdaway, much to the latter's irritation).

While Bergkamp continued to book gigs and produce flyers, she also sensed the end might be in sight. "The contract with us was up for renewal (at the end of 1989) and I made a conscious decision to wait (before trying to renew)," she confirmed. "I could have said, 'If you want me to book these gigs, well...' But I waited. You know, if it works, it works. Then Damon went AWOL for a few days. By this point, he'd had meetings with (record companies) on his own, and they'd had some press write-ups too. We were all excited because it looked like it was really going somewhere. Then he turns up and goes into this big spiel about the fact that no one could understand what they were doing with us, and particularly me. He also had issues about the fact that Graeme and I were splitting up at the time." Suffice to say, Albarn did not renew the contract, and Seymour, Holdaway and Bergkamp parted company soon after.

When asked about his days at The Beat Factory, Damon Albarn has always been dismissive, variously describing that period in his artistic development as "utterly vacuous" and "totally unfocused". He has even ended enquiries about the likes of Two's A Crowd with a simple, but emphatic "I don't want to talk about that." Of course, these negative views may have been consolidated by the fact that Graeme Holdaway sold some of the demos at auction during a particularly cash-strapped period in the mid-nineties. It is also fair to say that until the formation of Seymour at least, nothing of great or lasting musical value was achieved in that time. However, Damon's experiences at the studio remain a clear and compelling record of an artist trying on various hats and styles until he finally came across one that suited him. "I genuinely think Damon might not have got there if he didn't have someone to help develop him as an artist at that time," said Graeme Holdaway. "If not us, then perhaps someone else. I really think he would have been a different artist. But we can look ourselves in the eye and feel proud of what we did. But I have to be honest here. (The experience) did change how I viewed other artists in terms of trust for at least another year. In fact, I actually became a bassist afterwards, but that's a whole other story..."*

With The Beat Factory contract having lapsed, Seymour were now untethered from any management obligations and free to negotiate on their own terms with Food Records. By the end of February, 1990,

* The Beat Factory was finally sold in the mid-Nineties. After a spell as a jobbing musician, Graeme Holdaway became a successful media services manager, while Marijke Bergkamp pursued a career as a video editor (working on *Rob Roy* and *Mission Impossible*), before becoming a consultant for hire. They remain friends.

they had signed to the label. "Quite cheaply, it has to be said," laughed Andy Ross, "but it all worked out in the end." As part of the deal, the group would receive Dave Balfe and Ross' full attention, worldwide distribution rights through EMI and an up-front advance of £3,000 to cover essentials, clothes and other sundries. "Not quite millionaires, then," quipped Alex James. There were caveats. In a jokey aside, Food's contract stipulated that Dave Rowntree was no longer allowed to wear his beloved pyjama bottoms while on stage. More seriously, Balfe and Ross asked the band to discard the name Seymour in favour of something more commercially viable. Both group and label went to lunch to bash the matter out. Having recently played alongside indie-darlings The Keatons at a gig in Highbury, Graham Coxon favoured something equally arch and suggested The Becketts. It was dismissed. The Shining Path was also nixed due to the Communist Party of Peru sharing the same appellation. Sensitise, Whirlpool and The Sunflowers were all discussed as possibilities, only to be thrown out as too 'baggy'. But there was one name did not offend anyone. Though nebulous and unspecific, it also carried connotations of lightning speed, shifting shapes and constant motion. By the time lunch ended, all were agreed. Seymour were no more. From now on, they were to be called Blur.

Now officially part of the Food records roster, there were other business matters for the newly christened Blur to attend to. First on the list for Graham Coxon and Alex James was parting company with Goldsmiths on good terms. "The director said to me, 'I know what's going on, I've seen it all before'," Coxon confirmed. "(He said) 'Why don't you take a year out and see how it goes? And if it all falls to bits, like it so often does, well, you can come back.'" Perhaps more importantly, the band needed to secure a publishing deal for their songs. Again, this proved relatively easy with MCA's head scout Mike Smith eager to offer them terms. "I'd seen a show by Seymour at Islington's Lady Owen Arms, and then a bunch of shows by Blur at the Bull and Gate in Kentish Town (in early 1990)," Smith later told *The Guardian*. "Watching Damon back then was like watching Iggy Pop. He would climb along the pipes on the ceiling and then slap down on to the crowd below him. The combination of the front three was incredible.

It was obvious that Graham was a great musician, Alex looked like he'd walked off the set of *Brideshead Revisited* and Damon, with this big shock of blond hair, looked like one of the children from *The Village Of The Damned*. There was something intense, spooky and unreal about him. There were a couple of bands I'd been excited about, but nothing that had hit me between the eyes like that." A deal for £80,000 was agreed soon after.

There was one more thing to take care of. While Blur had now acquired a record label and publishing deal, neither Food nor MCA had the time (or inclination) to deal with press enquiries, studio bookings and potential tour itineraries. This was the job of a manager. Having dispensed with The Beat Factory's services, the search was on for a suitable candidate. Balfe and Ross favoured the safe hands of Chris Morrison, a wise old stager who had previously handled the affairs of Thin Lizzy and Ultravox, among others. But Blur were less given to the Irishman's strongly corporate approach to the music business, at least at that time. Instead, they elected to sign with Mike Collins, a benevolent raconteur who had once overseen the careers of chilly art-punk quartet Wire and post-new romantic electro dabblers Propaganda. As the story goes, Collins was a fine teller of tales and bought Blur an excellent lunch. In the band's mind, he also carried 'the cachet of cool', his links to Wire far more credible and cutting edge than Chris Morrison's championing of older, more industry-friendly acts. Regrettably, Blur's relationship with Collins would end unpleasantly down the road.

With their house apparently in order, and a spray of gigs around the London area keeping them busy into late spring of 1990, Blur were now well placed for what was about to follow. "We had a ridiculous self-belief, even before we got a deal," Alex later recalled. "We really felt that we'd had a vision of the future and what we were doing was genuinely groundbreaking." It was also accurate to say that the key driver behind the band's success thus far, and indeed, the likely focus of much future attention was their frontman and chief songwriter, Damon Albarn. "Damon's got an enormous amount of energy," continued James. "He's probably got three balls. Graham, (Dave) and I would probably still be sitting around drinking and picking our noses if there wasn't somebody around with that much energy and drive."

Albarn could feel well pleased with himself. Following an uncertain 12 months at East 15 drama school, he had taken a chance and committed body and soul to a career in music. And if the road was hard, frustrating or even embarrassing at times, he never once took his eye off the prize. "I was very driven and was prepared to do almost anything to succeed," he later told Q. "And I did go through some alarming manifestations..." With the advent of Seymour/Blur, things had changed for the better. By surrendering some of his own artistic ambitions to a larger (and extremely talented) whole, there was a real chance the success he had craved since adolescence was now within grasp. Yet, according to Damon, it was going to be a journey without maps. "At the start of it all, Blur wanted to confuse, to be as complicated as possible. If we had a 'manifesto'," he concluded, "that really was it..."

Chapter Five

Escape Velocity

For many a band, the acquisition of a record and publishing deal marks the end of several years' hard work, a just and fitting reward for time served in dingy rehearsal rooms, box-like demo studios and playing sweaty, cramped clubs to sweaty, indifferent audiences. Air becomes fresher, outlooks rosier, and best of all, one can boast to all and sundry that your group, your gang, are now professional musicians. In Blur's case, the journey from indie-minded hopefuls to promising recording artists had actually taken months rather than years, but there was still a sense of a job well done. "It's great being in a band at that age," Alex later said. "Thinking about what you want to be, doing manifestos, thinking about your image. And then it happens."

Of course, the reality of Blur's new position was less romantic. They were a young group carrying real debt and real expectations, and as such no different from any other marketable commodity. An investment had been made in their talents, and a return was due. From now on, success would be measured by high chart placings, well-reviewed tours to sold-out crowds and T-shirts, programmes and other forms of merchandising flying off the concessions stand. Blur had entered a numbers game, and signing a deal was very much the beginning rather than an end.

Of prime importance in that equation was the choice of the band's first single. For Graham Coxon and MCA's Mike Smith, 'Won't Do It' and 'Repetition' seemed likely contenders, their choppy, atonal qualities indicative of Blur's more experimental, independent-minded side. But neither song had a traditional hook and, frankly, were as likely to alienate mainstream audiences as attract them. For Dave Balfe and Andy Ross, it was a toss-up between 'I Know' (Blur's most obviously 'baggy' tune) and the sedate, yet pleasantly hypnotic 'She's So High', both of which displayed strong melodies, and had a chance of cracking the charts. "'She's So High' showed that they had a clear grasp of the facets of simple song writing," Andy Ross later told *Record Collector*. "Everything was in the right place and in the right proportion." Suffice to say, sanity – and sound business acumen – prevailed, with Blur entering Willesden's Battery Studios in North West London during the summer of 1990 carrying two songs that might yet make them stars.

The production team accorded the responsibility of turning 'She's So High' and 'I Know' from edgy demos into potential hits were Steve Power and Steve Lovell. Liverpool born and bred, Power and Lovell had come to prominence via that city's rich music scene of the late seventies/early eighties, when they provided keyboards and guitar respectively for cult art-pop act Hambi And The Dance. "I was part of the Liverpool scene, and even shared a flat with Wayne Hussey – later of The Mission – in the early days," said Power. "There was always talk between us of putting together a band, but it didn't come to anything, though Wayne did join an early incarnation of Hambi And The Dance." When Hambi... eventually signed to Virgin, Power took his share of the advance and built Pink Recording Studios so that the band had easy and cheap access to studio time. Inevitably, other fledgling Liverpool acts came to use Pink for their own demo recordings. "Yeah, we had The Lotus Eaters and Frankie Goes To Hollywood as early clients," continued Power, "and Steve Lovell and I were in a band with (Frankie... singer) Holly Johnson for a while. Actually, I say a band. It was more a group of people talking about being in a band. We didn't play a great deal!"

Following Hambi...'s demise, Power and Lovell turned their hands to engineering and production work, establishing a solid reputation through sessions with The Jazz Babies and astoundingly coiffured pop stars A Flock Of Seagulls. "I mixed a live gig at Eric's in Liverpool for the payment of having my hair cut by Flock's singer Mike Score, who was a professional barber before he became a star," said Power. "Still, it really was like 'Would you let this man cut your hair?' Plainly, I'd been on drugs that day..." By the mid-eighties Lovell and Power had moved to London, the former producing ex-Teardrop Explodes frontman Julian Cope's debut album *World Shut Your Mouth*, while Power (who also contributed to *World...*) secured a house engineer's job at Battery Studios. Here, he worked alongside renowned producer Mutt Lange on Billy Ocean's 'When The Going Gets Tough' and 'They'll Be Sad Songs'. Stints with Level 42 and indie sweethearts/festival darlings James soon followed. But the allure of striking up the old partnership became hard to resist. "I always liked the 'team' thing about production," Steve said. "So if I got a job, more often than not, I'd say 'Why don't you come and do it with me, Mr Lovell?' It was more like a gang. I liked his views and approach on things and vice versa. So we ended up doing the likes of A House and The Railway Children together, good, indie guitary bands..."

Given the fact that the production duo had a strong track record, Dave Balfe was a former member of The Teardrop Explodes and Damon Albarn was an evangelical Julian Cope fan, it seemed obvious that Blur and Power/Lovell were going to be a snug fit. "My first memory of Blur was going to see them play and they were incredible," said Steve. "I thought they looked fantastic and sounded fantastic. It was one of those 'The sum are greater than the parts' things. The band was electric and the atmosphere, too. 'She's So High' was the stand out, so it was agreed we'd do that with 'I Know'. Then, it was just a case of rehearsing the band before recording started in earnest." With Jesus Jones' success still ringing in his ears and at cash tills on both sides of the Atlantic, Dave Balfe was keen success be achieved, and quickly. "I knew there was pressure on them from Food... from Balfe, really," said Power. "If there wasn't immediate success, there was the chance that they'd be dropped."

If Damon Albarn was feeling a certain tightness around the collar concerning Food's hopes for Blur, he hid it well in interviews at the time. "We'd like a lot of people to buy our records and they will," he bullishly told *Sounds* in June, 1990. "We'd be really disappointed if (the single) didn't chart." Albarn carried this attitude into Battery Studios, where Power observed Blur's frontman at close quarters. "They were kids really, but there was a great group dynamic, even if Dave Rowntree got a bit sat on at the start. Damon was good-naturedly ribbing him a lot, I seem to remember. But then, Damon was the natural leader. He spoke for all of them, really."

Over the course of five days at Battery, Blur and their producers worked hard on capturing the group's live energy on tape. Sessions typically ran from 10 in the morning to 11 at night, with breaks taken for lunch, dinner and the odd game of football. "The World Cup was on at the time," Steve said, "So, we'd work, eat, then watch a second half here and there. Brazil versus whoever, you know. Because the studio space was quite big, we'd even end up playing the odd game inside. As Graham didn't really follow football, he'd be the keeper. I remember him walking back and forth on the goal line like a space invader." By all accounts, it was one of the few times Coxon let down his guard during the sessions. "Graham was unique, a fully formed musician, but he was incredibly quiet. A bit taciturn, actually," Power continued. "I felt that we really had to gain his trust, though that did come towards the end. At the start of recording, he was a bit suspicious of it all. Like many young bands, he might have been worried that what (we'd record) wouldn't be at all what the band actually sounded like. Perhaps he'd had that experience before. It was like he was thinking 'How's this one going to go wrong?'"

Whether Coxon's reserve was due to suspicion, previous disappointments at The Beat Factory or pure fear, his overall contributions to the recording of 'She's So High' and 'I Know' cannot be understated. "Oh, Damon respected Graham, all right," said Power. "He knew how important he was to the sound and the scheme of things." This fact was underlined when it became clear James was having difficulty nailing his bass parts during the sessions. "Alex was still finding his feet at that point," Power continued. "It was his first time in such an environment, so Graham and I sat with him for a few hours trying to get him into the groove." Despite their best efforts, Alex's best efforts still fell short of the mark. As a result, Coxon heavily fortified the bassist's melody lines on both tracks. However, it didn't stop James inviting his parents along to Battery to see him at work. "He came to Lovell and me and quietly asked whether his mum and dad could come to the studio," said Power. "Such a polite boy, Alex. So they came in and had a look. Genuinely lovely people, they were. It was a shame to see them go." After two further days of mixing, the tapes – as they say – were in the can. "The general feeling was 'This is a completely unknown band. Will the public get it?'"

The results of Blur's endeavours at Battery still retain a curious, beguiling quality some two decades on, their colour and shape indicative of a band finding its own feet while also acknowledging what was going on around them at the time. In the case of 'I Know', the influence of The Stone Roses was evident for all to hear, Graham's clipped guitar figure, Dave's bouncing snare and Damon's heavily reverbed vocal all recalling the Mancunian quartet's signature sound. "Yeah, we did defer to the baggy thing a little on 'I Know', mainly to keep the sound current," said Power. "So we looped Dave's drums and added a few other little bits, you know. By osmosis, Blur were linked with the baggy thing that was happening. But at the same time, they weren't keen to be associated with that and I agreed with them. If you step onto the baggy bandwagon, you'll go under with the baggy bandwagon when it crashes. Damon was really strong on that. So, the idea was to go a little baggy on 'I Know' so we didn't have to do that on 'She's So High'".

Unlike 'I Know', which made great, if reluctant play of clutching at the coattails of a movement then sweeping Britain, 'She's So High' was a different beast altogether, and all the better for it. Based around Graham's simple, circular guitar riff, the song had a lazy, almost anaesthetised feel, with Blur's rhythm section pulling gently but insistently against Damon's vocal. "She is so high," sang a woozy-sounding Albarn, "I want to crawl all over her..." This sense of cool serenity was again emphasised in the tune's middle section where Coxon let loose with some distinctly psychedelic backward-sounding Les Pauls. "The backwards guitar came out of a real Beatles influence," Power confirmed. "They wanted a far-out, almost trippy feel that was also true to the band, so Graham recorded those sounds and did a very good job of it, I must say." The end result obviously appealed to Coxon, who placed a call to Power and Lovell three days after recording concluded. "He rang up after the session and thanked us for how great it sounded. I genuinely think he thought it was going to go wrong. I was like 'Wow', because he hadn't said anything like that at the time."*

The general consensus was that Blur had delivered on both tracks and the decision was made to release them as a double A-side (with the My Bloody Valentine-referencing 'Down' making up numbers on the CD single). In addition to a hastily arranged 21-date British tour to illicit maximum publicity, Dave Balfe put his weight behind making a suitably esoteric video for 'She's So High', which he chose to direct himself. The end result was eye-catching if a tad confusing, as a somnambulant Blur mimed to camera while encased in what appeared to be a giant electrical cable. "Balfe had a vision for 'She's So High' which included making a neon jellyfish," said Rowntree. "He called it his 'ring of rings'. It consisted of rings and ropes strung together with three guys pulling on the ropes to make it wobble. I remember him shouting 'I haven't seen the definitive wobble yet...'" For added surrealism, the sleeve chosen to house the single featured Blur's new, distinctive logo amidst multiple portraits of a naked woman astride a smiling hippopotamus. The work of figurative American painter Mel Ramos (who reportedly disliked the songs), this striking image was created by design firm Stylorouge, who would forge an extremely profitable association with Blur in years to come. At the time, however, the cover provoked some controversy,

* For Steve Power, 'She's So High'/'I Know' marked the end of his association with Blur, though he did record (unused) versions of 'Bad Day' and 'Close' with the band in late 1990: "We were asked to do more, and Steve Lovell did return to the Blur camp a few months later to cut some tracks." Power was to become one of the nineties' most in-demand producers, cutting a string of multi-platinum albums and singles for Robbie Williams, including *Life Through A Lens* and the monster hit 'Angels'.

with several student organisations deeming it sexist rubbish. In fact, reaction to Blur's "sexy hippo" was so negative at Warwick University, the band's merchandising stand was attacked when they appeared there.

With a whiff of mild hullaballoo surrounding its sleeve – never a bad thing in pop – and Food Records' A&R staff more than happy to take advantage of the fuss, 'She's So High'/'I Know' was released on October 15, 1990. Eager to align themselves to a band for which great things might be expected, both *NME* and *Sounds* awarded Blur 'Single of the Week'. "This debut sees the guys doffing their cap to the indie/dance scene, while flouncing way beyond it," said the latter music paper. "How can you resist a love song opening with the lines 'I see her face every day, it doesn't help me'? This stands comparison with anything in the last five years, (and) Blur are the first great band of the 90s."

Elsewhere, the reception was frostier. On BBC1's newly-revived *Juke Box Jury*, hosted by a pre-*Later...* Jools Holland, talk show host Jonathan Ross gave 'She's So High' a resolute thumbs-down. Playing it for laughs, the Leytonstone-born Ross (who incidentally went to the same primary school as Albarn) ended his critique by pointing to the size of Damon's eyeballs – a sly nod to the drug ecstasy. After a brisk shuffling of papers from Holland, the show proceeded apace.

Despite their obvious qualities, the one-two punch of 'She's So High'/'I Know' had to make do with a moderate number 48 placing in the UK charts. For Dave Balfe and Andy Ross, this was a respectable enough start for any new band. But for the impatient Blur, the single's failure to clip the Top 30 was a crushing disappointment. "I was really pissed off," Alex later said. "I genuinely thought it would go higher than that. Actually, I thought it was the best single ever."

There was little time to dwell on any such notions of failure. Throughout October and November of 1990, the group found themselves traipsing up and down various motorways around the UK, with gigs ranging from Brighton to Newcastle and back again. Until then labelled as an "indie-friendly band" with an audience to match, the tour brought Blur their first taste of an entirely new type of fan. "We've now got these Japanese girls that follow us around everywhere," said Albarn at the time. "They're so polite and have these incredibly expensive video cameras. They love waving too. When you get on the tour bus, they all wave. I think their idea of sex is waving and bowing."

According to the singer, there was also a much darker group of individuals drawn to Blur shows – the type that were looking for more than just a smile or a wave. "Recently, people have been coming along to gigs just in case I really kill myself." he said. "When we first started, I was like a human whirlwind, just everywhere, not singing properly, just being really crap. I jumped off everything, careered into anything and everybody and just didn't care. I thought it was great to have a bloody nose and feel sick. Then, people started shouting 'Hurt yourself! Jump off the PA! Be sick!' It became a cliché quickly and made me think about what I was doing more."

Alex James was undergoing no such existential crisis. "(Being on tour's) a dream," he said. "You don't have to pay for anything. You go to different places every day. Everywhere you go, you get beer and drugs free, and girls scream at you. You feel... well, you feel like shit most of the time, but it's all good."

With a record deal, Top 50 single, sold out show at London's ULU and a critically lauded end of year support slot to the baggy-approved Soup Dragons at Brixton Academy, 1990 had been kind to Blur thus far. But the group, and Albarn in particular, wanted more. "The Beatles are the role model, the band everyone should aspire to," he said. "One style an album. All those episodes I'd like to try. I'm really looking forward to our Maharishi period." Big words, well said. Yet, there was still the nagging matter of following up 'She's So High' with another single – one that might even prize them into the Top 30.

Somewhat uncharacteristically, the band appeared in no particular hurry. "We've already noticed that when people love us, or expect certain things we shy away from it," said Damon. "We don't want that kind of pressure. The more you do, the more popular you become, the more you have to force it." Again, these were strong sentiments, even if they masked the actuality of Blur's situation. During the early months of 1991 there was much forcing to be done as the group locked themselves into the studio to work on their debut album. Avoiding pressure, no matter how artistic the reasoning behind it, was never an option.

Predictably, on those occasions that Blur did escape from their responsibilities, drink provided both steer and succour. Having already established a formidable reputation as semi-professional soaks, the band could often be found perfecting their skills in various pubs and clubs across Central and West London. Preferred tipples during this period included Guinness, beer, wine and a semi-lethal combination of Pernod and cider, sometimes with added blackcurrant to give it the "authenticity of a cocktail". Still, for one member of Blur at least, the road to excess didn't always lead to the palace of wisdom. "I can get pretty offensive, (because) I get helpless," Coxon admitted to *Melody Maker*. "I'm perfectly charming, and then at that point where I start forgetting what's happened, I get drunk and turn into a horrible bastard." The admission also came with a strong caveat. "That doesn't make me an offensive person," he said. "People need space and respect, and shouldn't be judged on everything they do." Not yet, at least.

By April 15, 1991, Blur were back in the singles wars, though with much greater success this time around. That said, any grand plans to introduce the Great British public to the more extreme elements of their sound were once again stymied by a far more important goal. "Our record company wanted to get their money back," remembered Alex. "So they said, 'No backwards drums, use these drums and you'll have a massive hit.'" Like 'I Know' before it, Blur's second single 'There's No Other Way' was in thrall to baggy, both in terms of production and sound. Thankfully, it was also rather good. A chunky tune – heavily reliant on looped beats, another slippery riff from Coxon and an insistent, sixties-sounding chorus that made best use of Albarn's breathy vocals – 'There's No Other Way' provided listeners with a honeyed, accessible take on The Stone Roses and Happy Mondays, with an echo – both lyrically and melodically – of Pink Floyd's second single 'See Emily Play' which was written by Syd Barrett. And if Blur had little or nothing in common with either band or the scene that surrounded them, so be it. Commandeering the odd drum loop or cycling bass pattern was a small price to pay in the general scheme of things. "It was a kind of exercise," Coxon later admitted. "We just ripped off a few dance beats. It wasn't something we greatly cared about or felt we needed to do. It was just a scam, really. We weren't baggy at all, just frustrated young punks. Baggy was all about the North, and we were a London band."

One wouldn't have known it from the press releases that accompanied advance white label copies of the single. "Those baggy buggers Blur (are making) a welcome return (with) a top notch slither of guitar dance," ran Food's alliterative copy. "One play is all you need to get those bowl haircuts on the floor to this corker of a track." And bowl haircuts were certainly the order of the day when it came to the accompanying video, with both Damon and Graham looking as if they had escaped from an old episode of *The Monkees*. "I had such a long fringe at the time that they couldn't see my eyes," Albarn later complained. "So they cut a huge chunk out of it. It ended up looking like a fucking window."

Filmed in a mock-Georgian mansion outside Isleworth and again directed by Dave Balfe, Blur's latest promo was a knowing homage to the kitchen-sink realism of film director Mike Leigh – its shots of crammed dinner tables and runny gravy mocking the inanities of British family life. "The family (who lived there) were really thrilled we borrowed their house," Damon said. "(But) they didn't realise we were going there and burying them in their own lives. When the video gets shown on *Top Of The Pops*, there'll be millions of people watching it and it's going to be like a mirror into their own homes, into their own lives. It'll be like we've got a camera looking at them. That amuses me."

Albarn's confidence that 'There's No Other Way' would get them on *Top Of The Pops* was well placed. The single debuted on the charts at number 20, thus allowing Blur a spot on the UK's most popular and enduring music show. "Being on *TOTP* for the first time is a massive responsibility," Damon confirmed at the time. "I mean, you're representing youth in front of this incredible audience of 10 million people and it's your duty to... put the knife in. That's the point when you should become incredibly great. There can be no modesty. I don't believe in modesty when you're playing in front of 10 million people. I believe in blossoming into something great, something legendary."

After Coxon jeopardised Albarn's plans for greatness by arriving late for the recording, getting into a fight with the studio doorman and almost being turned away, Blur eventually took their place in front of the cameras. Far from appearing to be pop's true saviours, however, the band more resembled whirling dervishes, with Damon and Alex spinning perilously around on some self-imagined axis while Graham stared with something resembling amazement. "They looked," said one critic, "as high as fucking kites."

Blur's odd, if curiously touching debut on *TOTP* ultimately provided the group with the escape velocity they were seeking. 'There's No Other Way' shot up to number eight, and went on to sell over 150,000 copies during its eight week run on the charts. Always eyeing the next stage in Blur's development, Albarn played coy at the time – "I think we'd like to be a band judged on its albums rather than singles. After all, singles are such a liquid thing" – but that frightening self-belief was never far from the surface. "I've always known I'm incredibly special," he told *Select*'s Dave Cavanagh. "All my life, you know? It's not a big deal. It's just confidence, unbelievable confidence." His colleague stage right was somewhat less ebullient. "'There's No Other Way' was histrionic, if thoughtful," said Coxon. "But I do quite like the guitar tone..."

Somewhat ironically, Blur marked their accession to the Top 10 with a homecoming gig at the University of Essex in Colchester. "What am I expecting?" Albarn mused to *Select* on his way to the venue. "A pretty negative audience, I suppose. Places like Colchester celebrate the mediocre, you know? In Colchester, there's an unwritten rule," he continued. "'You can talk about it, but never achieve it.'" As if to spite him, Blur's return to Colchester was a near sell-out, with nearly 700 fans turning up to the show. Evidently, while Damon was in no mood to forgive being lambasted for his ambitions as a teenager, the town's inhabitants were now willing to pay good money to see him on stage.

Blur did not spend another six months considering a follow-up to 'There's No Other Way'. Instead, they were back promoting a brand new single by late July 1991. Entitled 'Bang', it was the band's first real mistake. Written in response to Food's (rather loud) demand for another hit, 'Bang' took Blur only 15 minutes to complete, the song bashed out during a rehearsal at jazz studio The Premises on Hackney Road several months earlier. Again heavily beholden to baggy values (though there was a little Smiths influence in there too), its main point of interest was

Alex's snaky bass line, its lively twists and turns showing just how much he had improved from the days of Battery Studios just a year before. Regrettably, the rest of the tune lacked any real snap, crackle or pop, its verse as bland as vanilla, its chorus dry as toast: "'Bang'," Albarn later observed, "was just shit."

This time, professional video maker Willy Smax was charged with making a silk purse out of a sow's ear, his time-lapse promo capturing a moody Blur amid the streaking car lights of London's West End. "(The promo's) a fine advertisement for the city, really," said Albarn. "I just remember two nights of wandering around being lit well." Indeed he was. Now sporting a mod haircut that made the best of his face, Damon looked less like an extra escaping from the set of *The Monkees* and more the perfect pop star. "Well, it's inevitable when you're in our position that you're going to be seen as teeny idols," he told *NME*, "and it's not something we're really keen to cultivate. But then again, what can you do?" In 'Bang''s case, hope that those self-same teenies were not exercising any form of quality control when it came to their pocket money...

Supported by the band-produced B-sides 'Luminous', 'Berserk' and 'Uncle Love', 'Bang' was greeted with little enthusiasm by the music press and no great affection by the public, the single nudging the charts at number 24 before falling into oblivion. Though it was a little too early to call the career ambulance, the failure of 'Bang' to consolidate or improve on the success of 'There's No Other Way' again highlighted the perils of Blur's position. As their latest release confirmed, they were a London-based group predominantly trading on the sound of another city, their links to baggy culture more a flag of convenience than a banding together of like-minded brothers. Worse still, it irritated the hell out of them. "Those (Manchester) bands were looking to LA for inspiration, buying guns and playing at being John Wayne," Coxon later confirmed. "We had nothing to do with the Americans at all. We were quite content to deal with life in England."

There was also the problem of future marketing to contend with. Blur had originally been sold in to the press as an "indie-loving, baggy-friendly" proposition, albeit one with strong commercial ambitions.

However, when 'There's No Other Way' was picked up by a wider audience who did not take their immediate cues from *NME*, *Melody Maker* or *Sounds*, it placed the band uncomfortably between two stools. If 'Bang' had again gone Top 10, the issue might have been solved. Freed from any irksome labels or shackling connotations, Blur would be able to trade on the strength of their own name and brand. But the single's rapid descent into the bargain bins proved the tricky journey from the music weeklies into the traditional mainstream was far from over. This was a group still reliant on the critics to plead their cause and help them build a stable, sustaining fan base. "I think I'm probably overconfident all the time," Albarn conceded. "I don't know my limitations yet and that's probably quite a dangerous thing."

The dangers of this indie/pop duality was underlined by Blur's almost religious attendance of Syndrome, a tiny nightclub located just metres away from Tottenham Court Road station in the heart of London's West End. In truth, Syndrome's decor was undistinguished (wonky tables, wonky bar), its dance floor minute (60 legs at a push) and its entrance perilous (turn right quickly, or all was lost). But most every Thursday night, the subterranean hotspot played host to some of the brightest sparks then on the independent scene, the likes of Lush, Moose, Chapterhouse and See See Rider all drinking behind its creaky doors. As time would tell, some of these bands came to brief prominence, their reputation for moody sets, out-of-focus guitars and introspective lyricism being rewarded with a Top 30 album here or Top 20 single there. But in the summer of 1991, no one knew what was around the corner and music journalists made a point of sharing beers and stories with the acts they hoped might provide next year's front covers. *MM* scribe and future *NME* editor Steve Sutherland even went as far as to christen those attending Syndrome 'The Scene That Celebrates Itself', his barbed description referencing the fact that many of these bands not only drank together, but were also regular visitors at each other's gigs.

For Blur, Syndrome was probably just a place to escape accusations they were "Baggy from the back of a van", their attendance at the club more about meeting fellow My Bloody Valentine fans than aligning themselves with another burgeoning movement. But for Food's Andy

Ross, there were pitfalls between all the pint glasses. "[Syndrome] was about 'Shoegazers'," he said. "Blur were not shoegazers." In Ross' mind, this was a crucial distinction. Unlike Lush, Chapterhouse or Thousand Yard Stare – who were gaining a reputation for staring at the effects pedals beneath their feet rather than the audience in front of them – Blur had already broken into the Top Ten and Food were expecting more of the same. The game now was to pull the group away from such lazy tag-lines or career-limiting associations and put them back at the top of the charts. "I didn't want Blur to be just an '*NME*' band," Dave Balfe later said, "I wanted them to be stars..."

As Blur's debut album *Leisure* confirmed, there was a little more work to be done before Balfe's plans for total domination were fully realised. Released on August 26, 1991, *Leisure* was to have been called 'Irony In The UK', but both band and label had dumped the Sex Pistols-referencing title by the time it arrived in shops. At first sight, the augurs were reasonably good, with the album's cover shot of a fifties model smiling innocently from beneath a bathing hat both cheeky and eye-catching. Even the back-sleeve image of the group sitting moodily in a field of cows had its own Syd Barrett-like charm. But the music contained within was more of a puzzle. On one hand, *Leisure* displayed moments of genuine brilliance, the occasional song confirming the group as potential world-beaters. Sadly, such moments were few and far between, as the listener was often left wanting more if not really knowing why. Some 21 years later, that combined sense of longing and confusion still holds true.

As is often the way with debut albums, two previous singles – 'She's So High' and 'Bang' – were chosen to kick things off, allowing one's ear a sense of familiarity before the onslaught of any new material. Unfortunately, when it did arrive, there was immediate disappointment. Drowning in a torrent of Sonic Youth-like guitars and rattling cymbals, 'Slow Down' had no great sense of atmosphere or any real tune to speak of. Fighting to be heard over all the power chords and crashing percussion, Damon was left with little choice but to croon a few 'Ahhs' and 'Ooohs' in lieu of a proper chorus. Thankfully, the old Seymour stalwart 'Repetition' was far more impressive and indeed original sounding, with Graham's guitar droning away like a drunken computer game behind Albarn's heavily compressed vocal. A bit of a gimmick perhaps, but one that still made for a satisfying, if queasy listening experience. Coxon's beloved Les Paul was again at the front, centre and end of 'Bad Day', his continued interest in creating backwards soundscapes helping deflect attention away from the song's rather pedestrian structure.

Thankfully, things took an upward turn immediately after, with the forlorn psychedelia of 'Sing'. Again harking back to the days when Blur traded under the name Seymour, the song had been lifted wholesale from a demo cut by the band at Chalk Farm's Roundhouse Studios. Full of wistful vocals, insistently struck pianos and reverberating guitars, 'Sing''s all pervading sense of melancholia at last pointed to the band Blur could be rather than were. "Even people who hated us would come rushing up and say, 'What was that song?'" said a proud Coxon. Following 'There's No Other Way''s not unwelcome reappearance, the Smiths-lite musings of 'Fool', stunted aggression of 'Come Together' (a live favourite perhaps, but not well served here) and baggy-leaning 'High Cool' all conspired to ruin the party before Blur returned to their formative roots to save *Leisure* from itself. Best described as the bastard son of early Pink Floyd and Sonic Youth, 'Birthday' was another Seymour-era gem, the song's gentle, orchestral opening soon crumbling away beneath the strength of Coxon's heavily fortified guitars. A natural end to the album, Blur inexplicably chose to finish instead with 'Wear Me Down'. Given its strong central melody and successful blend of pop and indie flavours, 'Wear Me Down' was no doubt a steady pointer to all future endeavours, but surely better placed ahead of the weary, but wise 'Birthday' than behind it.

Full of clever guitars, funky drums, popping basses and pleasant, if detached-sounding vocals, *Leisure* wasn't a bad album. But by leaping between myriad styles at a moment's notice, it also lacked cohesion and focus, with Blur's efforts to be all things to all men giving the record a choppy, almost schizophrenic quality. More, its lack of truly memorable tunes and "wilfully banal lyricism" (to which we will return in due course) meant that one had to fight for any real pleasure gained, as song after song melted into the next. That said, not all blame for *Leisure*'s shortcomings could be placed at Blur's feet, as the album had seen several producers come and go before its release. In fact, when Lovell/Power originally left the project – or were pushed for getting Graham to shadow Alex's bass parts on 'Bad Day' and 'Close' – Food had real trouble finding able replacements. Former EMI A&R scout turned studio whiz Mike Thorne came in to oversee three songs, his previous credits on Soft Cell's 'Tainted Love', The Communards' 'Don't Leave Me This Way' and many a dance-orientated 12″ giving him strong credentials to plug the gap. But for one reason or another, it wasn't to be. "Lovely bloke, Mike," Graham later said. "He'd jog home from the sessions every night and get lost." As evidenced, Blur had also tried their hand at the production game, though the sterling job they made of 'Sing' was more likely a case of beginner's luck than much else. In the end, it was another type of happy accident that finally gifted the band a man best suited to maximise their talents, even if he temporarily disappeared again upon completing the project.

Like so many other successful recording types, Stephen Street had begun his pop career as a musician, playing bass in various groups throughout the late seventies before settling into the line-up of Ska-popsters BIM. When that act folded, Street swopped four strings for studio life, taking a job as an assistant engineer at Island Records' Fallout Shelter in Hammersmith, West London. Fortune smiled when the 24-year-old found himself engineering The Smiths' fourth single 'Heaven Knows I'm Miserable Now' in 1984, its blend of jangling guitars and sardonic lyricism a refreshing alternative to all those synthetic bleeps and beeps then bothering the charts. "I'd seen The Smiths on *TOTP* doing 'This Charming Man'," Stephen said, "and like most other people, was really excited by them." The Smiths obviously liked Street too, as he was asked to engineer their next two LPs *Meat Is Murder* and *The Queen Is Dead*, before receiving a full production credit on the band's 1987 swansong, *Strangeways Here We Come*. His continuing association with Smiths singer Morrissey brought more accolades as the Street-produced *Viva Hate* stole the UK number one spot and a Gold disc to boot.

Despite further production credits with the likes of Psychedelic Furs and The Triffids, Street was at something of a loose end in 1991 following the dissolution of Foundation Records, an independent label he set up with writer Jerry Smith two or so years before. This temporary break in schedules allowed him to be in front of his TV set when 'She's So High' fell foul of Jonathan Ross on *Juke Box Jury*. Unlike Ross, however, Street immediately connected with Blur's sound and image, a connection that sufficiently inspired him to arrange a meeting with Dave Balfe. When that went well, Street was subsequently invited for a beer with Blur near Food's offices at London's Piccadilly Circus. "Well, they were Smiths fans and were keen to meet me too," said Street. "We agreed to do a test session of two songs, one of which was 'There's No Other Way'. I went off somewhere for a couple of months and when I got back to England it was in the charts, and everyone was getting quite excited."

Recorded in early January, 1991, 'There's No Other Way' allowed Stephen Street his first taste of "the Blur experience". At the session – recorded in Fulham's Maison Rouge Studios – the producer earned his crust immediately by speeding up Damon's original tempo for the song and introducing the distinctive loop that made '... Other Way' so baggy-friendly. He was also sympathetic to Alex's role within the band, bolstering the young bassist's confidence by allowing him to work steadily on the track without threat of Graham replacing his parts. Strangely, it was actually Coxon who proved hardest for Street to read at first, the guitar player's initial shyness being misconstrued as truculence or worse. But the two soon formed a mutual appreciation society, with Graham enjoying a chance to again indulge his passion for backwards taping and the producer coming to the conclusion that "He was the best British guitarist since The Smiths' Johnny Marr." Following 'There's No Other Way''s chart success, Street cut five more tracks for *Leisure* across the spring and summer of 1991, including the good ('Repetition'), the bad ('High Cool') and the downright ugly ('Bang') before again going on his way. "I didn't know it then," he later said, "but it was the start of a long and fruitful relationship..."

Back in the late summer of 1991, of course, the riches reaped by Blur and Stephen Street's future collaborations were still some two years away. Of far more compelling importance at the time was what press and public made of *Leisure*. In the case of the music papers, response was divided, and then some. "There is no mystique to Blur," reasoned *NME*'s Andrew Collins. "They are standing next to you at the Moose gig. They spend less money on clothes than you do. They make Ride look like Duran Duran (and) they have taken 'Ordinary Ladness' to new and frankly depressing extremes. *Leisure* is quite an engaging debut album with at least five songs that justify the tenner. But it ain't the future. Blur are merely the present of rock."

Melody Maker, on the other hand, was rolling out the red carpet. "Blur's ambition is so naked, there's a disarming purity about it, a naive exuberance," said Steve Sutherland. "They may be riding around in cabs right now, but *Leisure* suggests that they will be the first of the new breed to be chauffeured around in day-glo Rolls Royces. Others may choose to stare at their shoes, but Blur look full into mirrors and there, they see stars." Such divisions were understandable. For some, Blur represented "British pop's uncomfortable present," a time where decades of glamour and artfulness had been usurped by bands who looked exactly like their fans, and in the majority of cases, acted a lot worse. "Baggy songs, baggy clothes, baggy attitudes," observed one critic. But in the other corner, Blur's ambitions were meritorious, their starry (if largely unearned) arrogance a welcome antidote to those groups whose gaze lingered on their trainers rather than the skies above.

One area that all critics seemed to agree upon, however, was the undistinguished nature of Damon Albarn's lyrics. While Blur's music obviously showed pockets of real promise, Albarn's wordplay was ordinary at best, vacillating between half-developed observations on English culture and whimsical commentaries on love and loneliness. On occasion, such as the opening line of 'There's No Other Way', Damon's relaxed approach to the disciplines of penmanship had a certain curt charm – "You've taken the fun out of everything" – raising a knowing smile or two. But when confronted with the likes of 'Bang''s chorus – "Bang goes another day, where it went I could not say..." – the urge to grind one's teeth in despair became overwhelming. Of course, Albarn could plead the influence of Syd Barrett as a mitigating factor, the former Floyd man's whimsical, almost childlike rhymes a profound influence on his own approach to lyric-writing. But as he was to later admit, inherent laziness played a far greater part in the overall picture. "I often wrote the lyrics five minutes before singing them," said Damon. "Back then, I was an appalling lyricist. Lazy, conceited and rather woolly." As was so often the case with Blur's frontman, he would correct the fault over time.

If Albarn's sluggish approach to wordplay had capsized *Leisure* on occasion, he showed no such indolence when meeting the press to promote *Leisure*. In fact, it was as if he had been saving all his best work for interviews. "If I felt I could do more for the world by giving this up and travelling around England with a guitar and just singing, I'd do it... but we live in such a complex society that my role as someone who entertains and lifts spirits only works on a level by me becoming incredibly famous and successful." For those who doubted the veracity of his self-proclaimed gifts – or those of his band – there was also an answer. "I don't claim that we're stunningly original. I just firmly believe in writing brilliant songs with an incisive message," he said. "This band is about basic things, and just playing with those basic things. There's nothing else to us. I hate for people to listen to us and think 'God, what a mastery of words, what incredible musicians'. It's all just crap."

While *Leisure* was no monument for new British music, nor Blur as yet the band Albarn claimed them to be, both LP and group were accorded a winning response from the general public. Debuting on the UK charts at number seven, *Leisure* soon fought its way to Gold status, its 100,000 sales easily recouping the £250,000 it had cost to record. For Damon, this was validation at its most pure and simple. "There's nothing more up to date and relevant than Blur," the singer proudly told *Q*. "We're like The Jam, The Smiths and The Stone Roses were in place and time."

He even took the opportunity to bite the hand that had originally fed him, using the album's success to distance his band from any further accusations of bandwagon jumping. "When we came out with 'There's No Other Way', everyone lumped us in with the whole baggy movement," he said. "But if you play *Leisure*, it's a lot tougher and less dancey than all the Baggy bands. *Leisure* (will) kill off that whole baggy thing."

For once, Albarn was wrong. *Leisure* didn't kill baggy. Grunge did. And for a while at least, it looked like it might kill Blur too.

Chapter Six

Diver Down

Two days before *Leisure* was released on August 26, 1991, Blur put in a strong, if occasionally sluggish shift at the annual Reading Festival. Sandwiched between Zen-like rappers De La Soul and the grimy Northern genius of The Fall, the band performed a mix of the old, middling and new, opening with the up-tempo, bluesy strains of 'Explain' before rolling through well-executed takes of 'Bad Day', 'Wear Me Down' and 'There's No Other Way'. Of the fresh songs on show, 'Turn It Up' snapped nicely at the heels, even if it had little musically new to say. 'Oily Water', on the other hand, found Graham teasing ears with a jerky tremolo effect as Albarn sang of suspicion and decline through a recently acquired megaphone. The overall effect may have sounded like the aural equivalent of a hangover, but 'Oily Water' was nonetheless an impressive addition to the band's rapidly growing canon of songs.

Uncharacteristically, Damon was a more subdued presence than usual at Reading, his trademark energy somewhat lacking as he clung to the microphone stand for long periods of the set. Perhaps such behaviour was designed to present the band in a different, more mature light. Perhaps he was simply the worse for drink. Whatever the truth of it, *NME* picked up on the change in their review of the gig, conferring Albarn with the title "Anti-frontman". Thanks to the antics and behaviour of another performer at Reading, that phrase would soon be worn as a badge of honour on both sides of the Atlantic Ocean.

One day before at Reading, a little known trio called Nirvana had delivered a truly psychotic performance that peaked when their singer/guitarist launched himself off the stage to convene with fans some 15 feet below. For many in attendance it was their first experience of Kurt Cobain, though as the cliché goes, it would not be their last. At the time, Cobain and Nirvana were only three weeks away from releasing their major label debut, *Nevermind*, recorded on a budget of $65,000 dollars and from which an equally modest return was expected. However, due to the astounding success of its lead-off single 'Smells Like Teen Spirit', frontman and group soon found themselves reluctantly spearheading a new American movement called 'Grunge' that would make stars not only of them, but Pearl Jam, Alice In Chains and Soundgarden too.

Grounded in the classicism of seventies hard rock, but also keen to claim punk credentials, grunge was the very antithesis of the baggy ideal then sweeping Britain. Unlike the drugged-out bliss and whimsy offered by Madchester, the Seattle-based scene was trading on the harder lyrical themes of social dislocation, fractured psyches and strong feminism, all spun together in a brisk musical package of slow-building verses, raging choruses and the odd guitar solo or two. As with any youth cult worth its salt, grunge also came with a ready-made look and feel, its leading lights dressed in cheap flannel shirts, battered trainers and jeans in need of several patches to make them decent. Truthfully, neither the music nor attitude of grunge were particularly novel: Sting and The Police were using the formula of 'loud, quiet, loud' as far back as 1978, while The Pixies all but mastered the form with their seminal LP *Surfer Rosa* in 1987. More, the Sex Pistols, Joy Division, The Slits and The Raincoats had torn up the rulebook when it came to social complaint, inner turmoil and the championing of women's rights during punk/post-punk's heyday. But that was then, grunge was now, and despite the fact its influences were clear as glass, the music carried real pathos and power, two strengths long absent in both pop and rock. Never ones to let a good trend pass them by – and knowing baggy would soon be past its sell-by date – the press set about turning the UK's high streets into a sea of plaid over the next 12 months.

As autumn gave way to winter in 1991, the machinery that would point Britain's musical head in the direction of America's north west coast was still very much at the testing stage, with only Nirvana thus far breaking the transatlantic ice. Therefore, Blur were free to consolidate their latest victories both home and abroad. With *Leisure*'s strong first week showing on the charts, and the critics still more or less on their side, the group set about their task with a 16-date tour of the UK, culminating at Kilburn's National Ballroom on October 24. Unlike Reading, Blur were in far more energetic form at the packed National, their new, flowery, neo-psychedelic backdrop – all dancing fractals and spinning colours – a suitable foil for those oily megaphone blasts and trippy guitars. October also marked the group's first tour of the USA, even if it only amounted to a handful of dates at key locations such as New York's Marquee club, Chicago's Metro Cabaret and LA's Roxy Theatre.

Represented by SBK records in the States, Blur had received a modicum of interest from radio stations on the back of 'There's No Other Way', the song actually breaking into *Billboard*'s Top 100, where it stayed for six weeks. And with the grunge explosion at least six months off in the distance, the road still appeared clear for a new, on-the-up English group to present their wares across the pond. Playing to audiences of hundreds rather the thousands that greeted them on the festival circuit at home, Blur actually seemed to relish a return to the small, tightly packed venues that defined their station only 18 months before. "The US crowds seemed absolutely ecstatic," said Alex at the time. Marking their days with lunchtime gigs at various radio stations and their nights performing in small, but important sweat boxes on both coasts, Blur's inaugural Stateside visit may have lacked for glamour, but boded reasonably well for the future. "It's different here," said Albarn, "but a good gauge of quality. Mind you, if we spent too much time (in the USA), we might start getting away with being pretty shitty." As time would tell, the reverse proved true.

After further dates in Japan and Europe, the band's year ended at Brixton Academy on December 21 where they were honorary guests at Food Records' 'Christmas Party'. A charity-themed bash put together by Dave Balfe and Andy Ross in aid of Great Ormond Street Hospital, the group were appearing alongside label-mates Sensitive, Diesel Park West and a headlining Jesus Jones. Steeled by several months of consistent touring, Blur nearly stole the show from under the Joneses' noses, even debuting two new songs along the way. In the case of 'Never Clever', the emphasis was firmly on danceable pop-punk, albeit of the Hazel O'Connor 'Breaking Glass' variety. That said, the other debutant of the evening was an absolute corker. Like 'Oily Water' before it, 'Pressure On Julian' presented Blur as an "interesting work in progress", the quartet retaining their gift for swirling psychedelic passages, but now adding a murky, almost hallucinogenic quality to their sound.

For the first two thousand punters through the doors at Brixton there was yet another gift, this one in the form of a free cassette featuring two tracks from each band on Food's roster. Blur's contribution was a re-mixed (and frankly far better) version of 'High Cool' plus a dreamy new tune called 'Resigned'. "It was nearly Christmas," recalled Andy Ross, "and we didn't want to put out another (Blur) single just for the sake of it. So we did something that wasn't commercially available and didn't take the piss out of fans."

If Blur were taking stock at the beginning of 1992, they could feel reasonably content. Despite the minor problem of 'Bang' the quartet's return to the Top Ten with *Leisure*, a financially lucrative UK tour and a proper introduction to the joys of Europe, America and Japan had all helped salve the wounds of one misfiring single. The material debuted both at Reading and Brixton also pointed to bold new horizons, placing a little rock-friendly grit at the band's alt-pop centre. It must have all seemed a long way from their debut TV appearance on children's show *Eggs And Baker* only eight months before. "God," remembered Albarn, "there were four and five-year-olds sitting in front of us, wondering why we were there." Yet, for all the attendant positives, there was some real enmity concerning Blur's recent and rapid ascent. Those lingering accusations of the band using baggy for their own ends still hung like a bad odour over the desks of several music journalists, while Damon's ever more extreme pronouncements on Blur's worth did little to diffuse such opinion. "We're a band that could completely and utterly change everything," he told *NME,* with no obvious modesty. Of course, arrogance from a pop star was nothing new. T-Rex's Marc Bolan had relied on it to make headlines in the early seventies, while John Lydon worked it like a sharp knife into the heart of the press at the height of punk. But Blur were still at a sensitive stage in their public development, and one sour article, dissenting review or misjudged alliance might still cause them some problems. That fact was harshly underlined by the group's involvement with the 'Rollercoaster' tour of April, 1992.

Sponsored by *Melody Maker*, Rollercoaster was a very British answer to the wildly successful 'Lollapalooza' festival, which had travelled the US and Canada throughout 1991. Pulling together a richly varied musical cast that included Nine Inch Nails, Ice-T and headliners Jane's Addiction, Lollapalooza had changed the traditional notion of what a touring circus could be, offering rock, punk, hip hop and fire-eaters all on the same bill. In Rollercoaster's case, the bands involved were slightly less divergent, but still capable of providing a wide spread of sounds for several potential audiences. Leading the charge were headliners and feedback kings The Jesus And Mary Chain with support offered by the ever-fragrant My Bloody Valentine and American indie darlings Dinosaur Jr. "Our manager had the (original) idea for doing this tour, but we thought it would be far too much hassle to get it done," said Mary Chain singer Jim Reid at the time. "Then, we more or less decided if we could get the right bands, we'd do it. I thought we'd ask people and they'd tell us to fuck off, but everybody agreed to do it right away – the first three bands on our wish list. It's like a sixties pop package (with) Hendrix and Pink Floyd on the road together, or a punk packet with The Pistols, The Slits and The Clash. We want to get back to those days. It's not a new idea, but we can't understand why more bands aren't doing it."

To Graham Coxon, the idea of sharing the same stage as his teenage hero Kevin Shields while also getting to watch Dinosaur Jr.'s J Mascis mangle his Fender Jazzmaster from the wings must have seemed like manna from heaven. Even Damon couldn't curb his enthusiasm for the forthcoming gigs. "Without sounding really crap, I think it's the most exciting thing we've ever done," he said. "Actually, it's a bit difficult for me to talk about these bands because I'm honestly starstruck by it all." Starstruck, but ultimately disappointed. If Blur's involvement with Rollercoaster was meant to consolidate their appeal with an alternative audience, or at least confirm their credentials outside a world of *TOTP* appearances, it backfired badly. That Graham could hold his own – even far surpass the instrumental musings of Shields and J Mascis – was never in doubt. Nor was the fact that Blur were showing signs of becoming a fine live band. But as those who saw the Rollercoaster tour will attest, the quartet's wilful blend of scowling guitars and artful pop was an uneasy fit amongst all the "sturm und drang" going on around them. Worse, the gentlemen's agreement to rotate the order of bands each night under the Mary Chain seemed to put Blur at a permanent disadvantage. If they opened proceedings, the group appeared not unlike a light starter before a particularly heavy main course. Yet, if their spot on the bill placed them amongst My Bloody Valentine and Dinosaur Jr., there was the risk of being crushed between two very large chunks of alternative rock. In practical terms, it was a no-win situation.

Despite the drawbacks, there was no doubt Rollercoaster was a well-attended tour, giving Blur the chance to play their brand new single 'Popscene' to an audience of thousands each night in Birmingham, Manchester and London during April 1992. First unveiled at the Kilburn's National Ballroom some six months before, 'Popscene' was by a considerable margin the best – and somewhat ironically – loudest thing the band had involved themselves with yet. Produced by Steve Lovell (now temporarily back in favour with Dave Balfe) at Holborn's Matrix Studios, the song was a relentless ball of energy from start to finish: opening with the screams of Coxon's heavily-flanged guitar and pushed along nicely by Dave Rowntree's novel take on the drumbeat to Can's 'Mother Sky', 'Popscene' found Albarn protesting loudly about the inanities of a business he was now up to his neck in. "I never really stopped to think how... everyone is a clever clone, so in the absence of a way of life... popscene, all right?" By the time Alex

James had fused a nicely propulsive bass line on top of a stabbing brass part courtesy of veteran sessioneers The Kick Horns, a hit was all but assured. Or so Blur thought. "Yeah, I'd love 'Popscene' to be a big hit," Damon said. "It'd be great. But then again, there's a noisy indie group on *TOTP* every week now. All looking very satisfied with their Number 18..."

In the end, Blur would probably have killed for a number 18 slot, as 'Popscene' stiffed at an extremely disappointing 32 on its release. "'Popscene' is an Inspiral Teardrop of a song," sniffed *Melody Maker*, "just a directionless organ-fest in search of a good chorus." Given the music paper was currently sponsoring the band's spot on Rollercoaster, this was criticism at its harshest. That said, guest reviewers The Beastie Boys over at *NME* were in no mood to play nice either. "They should have a special note on there to play it at 33rpm (rather than 45rpm)." For Andy Ross at Food, this was all too much. "We were totally devastated... in a state of shock for months," he later told *Record Collector*. "We thought it was a brilliant single." With the benefit of hindsight, it is all too easy to see how the fates – and indeed, the critics – conspired to temporarily end Blur's winning run. Obviously, some in the musical intelligentsia had long been suspicious of their worth, with Damon's continued insistence that the band's songs would be sung around camp fires 100 years hence grating like cheese. But as also evidenced, the overriding factor that derailed Blur at the time of 'Popscene''s release was the growing shift by British journalists and music fans alike from home-grown bands of any persuasion to the thundering pleasures offered by Seattle's grunge movement.

"It was Nirvana that really fucked 'Popscene' up," said a rightly irked Coxon.

During an interview some two years later, Albarn confirmed much of the above, his sense of betrayal at the hands of the music press coming across in slow, insistent waves. "'Popscene' was a huge departure for us," he told journalist John Harris. "It was a very, very English record. But that annoyed a lot of people... and because fashion was becoming completely myopic about America at the time, we felt we were being mistreated. We knew it was good, we knew it was better than we'd done before, but certain reviewers hated us for it. We put ourselves out on a limb to pursue this English ideal and no-one was interested."

Though equally angry at 'Popscene''s failure and the reasons behind it, Dave Rowntree chose to view things in a slightly different manner, seeing Blur's lone stand against grunge as the first sign of an entrenched dogmatism that would pay big dividends in years to come. "It was completely ignored by the press, but it was at a point when we realised we weren't going to listen to what anyone else was saying. We knew we could work well in the studio and that we were capable of making great records. And to be honest, it didn't really matter whether journalists didn't seem to agree." This might well have been true. But in April 1992, 'Popscene''s non-performance on the UK charts halted Blur's future plans in their tracks, the band's next choice of single – 'Never Clever' – indefinitely postponed while Dave Balfe at Food gave their career options a serious re-think. Unfortunately, things were about to get much worse.

At the same time that 'Popscene' stiffed on the charts, Blur found out that their financial affairs were in complete tatters. Despite the fact that *Leisure* had done brisk business, and their recent tours were well attended, there still seemed to be a large hole in the group's profits. "We discovered that all the money we'd made from *Leisure* – which wasn't millions, but quite a reasonable amount nonetheless – had disappeared," said Albarn. (Reportedly, Blur had earned in excess of £400,000 since signing with Food in 1990, but were now in debt to the sum of £60,000, with a further £40k unaccounted for). While the band were quick to part company with those they deemed responsible for the mess (manager Mike Collins parted company with the band at around this time – possibly one casualty of their decision), clawing their way back into the black was another matter altogether. "Most people think that when you've had a hit single, you've got a million pounds," said Rowntree. "Whereas all it really means is you've spent a million pounds. So the more hits you have the more money you can (potentially) lose." Blur were not the first band to fall foul of sloppy managerial decisions or irresponsible accounting. Nor would they be the last. But the harsh reality of their situation meant that they had to all but start again. "We'd worked as hard as people like Ride or The Charlatans," Albarn told *NME*, "but we hadn't seen anything. We literally had no money and we couldn't even pay our rent. It got to the stage where it was touch and go whether we actually went bankrupt."

Though they originally rejected him as a potential manager only two years before, Blur now returned to Chris Morrison in an effort to steady the ship. Known in the business as a "straight shooter", Morrison's activities had not just been confined to vintage acts such as Thin Lizzy or Ultravox. A founding trustee of Band Aid, the genial Irishman had also worked alongside Bob Geldof, Midge Ure and Harvey Goldsmith in their efforts to raise funds for victims of the 1984 Ethiopian famine. By the late eighties, his managerial roster had expanded yet again, with Dead Or Alive, The Beloved and The Jesus And Mary Chain all signing up to his company, CMO. Having kept Phil Lynott out of jail for more than a decade, harangued the UK's biggest pop stars out of their beds on a cold Sunday morning to record a multi-million selling charity single and commandeered thousands of amplifiers for the Mary Chain to smash, Chris Morrison could surely sort out Blur's woes. Indeed he could. But that help would come at a high price. To ease the band's financial woes, Morrison quickly struck up a deal with a music merchandising company specialising in T-shirts. They would put up money in advance – thus nullifying Blur's current debt situation – while in return the group would undertake a comprehensive tour of the USA to pay off the loan. On paper, the arrangement pulled Blur out of their hole, put them back on solid ground and if T-shirt sales at gigs went nicely, might even return the group to moderate profit. In reality, they were about to enter hell.

Much has been written about Blur's American tour of 1992. For the most part, it makes for grim reading. This will be no exception. Landing in Boston on April 13, 1992 in preparation for a free radio station gig the next day at WCBN, the band's first night on US soil went reasonably well. Spirits were high, due in part to a well-received live session with BBC DJ Mark Goodier back in London. Sadly, this sense of ebullience was short-lived. Though Blur had no new product to sell, and were essentially touring an album that was nearly a year old, their US record company SBK was intent on getting its money's worth out of the band. Hence, in a schedule that might have broken a Navy Seal, Albarn and co. were allotted just two days off during the 44-date run. Worse, they were travelling "state-by-state, sixties-style" in a small tour bus, with the distance between gigs often clocking up hundreds of miles. After three nights of dwelling on such horrors, Blur had transformed into a four-headed beer monster and they hadn't even left Massachusetts yet. While on stage at the Venus de Milo, Damon's decision to repeatedly dowse the audience with water led to the concert being pulled by promoters after just four songs. Deprived of something to watch, the crowd focused their attentions on dismantling the venue. Blaming the band for the damage, the club's bouncers then set upon Blur, who in turn were forced to escape through a nearby window. This was only the start. On the way to Washington's 9.30 club several days later, a drunken Coxon became so enraged with his touring prison that he broke every window on the bus. A similarly drunk Rowntree somehow managed to sleep through it all. "The whole thing was fucking... awful," Dave later remembered.

To compound their misery, America had now fully woken up to the wonders of grunge, thus rendering Blur's latest British invasion completely obsolete. Whereas only six months before they could at least stir up some interest via tenuous associations with successful UK exports such as Jesus Jones and EMF, their music and image were now viewed as old hat and out of date. "Suddenly American youth culture had found a voice and a look and a hero (in Kurt Cobain)," Alex remembered. "We, as a young British band, were (now) totally superfluous to it all."

To rub more salt into the wounds, Blur were still expected to press the flesh of every DJ and record shop owner SBK could find on route. "We were being greeted by a record company rep who'd then put us in the back of a big black car and drive us to a shopping mall (for a) 'meet and greet'," said Albarn. "Then it was eating shit in a fast food store (before driving) to another radio station who thought we were from Manchester." Pickled in alcohol, homesick and sodden, and in their own words "feeling like complete outsiders", Blur turned on each other for amusement. "At one point, each of us had black eyes," said Alex, "and I had two."

Beneath the skin, things were far worse. The band's non-stop smoking meant that common colds soon became chest infections while Coxon's newfound allegiance to vodka brought on several bleeding ulcers. "We were all on the verge of being hospitalised." With little else to do but torment each other and watch old Benny Hill videos between shows, the group's sole consolation became playing live. "It was the only release we got from all the irritation," said Albarn. Yet oftentimes, the crowds who turned up to see them play had only a cursory knowledge of the band and their songs. "No-one knew who we fucking were," Graham later admitted. "Most of America probably doesn't even listen to music, anyway. They just go racoon hunting."

On May 29, 1992 it was finally over. After a 44-day zigzag ride through the likes of Ithaca, Providence, Trenton and Baltimore, Palo Alto, San Diego and Dallas, Blur made their final stand at Orlando's Edge Club before the now corpse-like band were dropped at the airport. According to Albarn, the only thing of real value he took home from the whole, sorry experience was a notebook stuffed with new song ideas. "During that whole period of alcoholically-induced homesickness, I started writing songs which created an English atmosphere."

Unfortunately, Blur could not outrun America or its influence by hopping on a plane. In fact, the whole grunge phenomenon that haunted their days and nights in the USA seemed to have caught an earlier flight, even finding time to prepare a thoughtful homecoming for the band. Before Blur left for the States, the only Seattle group to trouble the UK charts in any meaningful way was Nirvana. But by the summer of 1992, their down-tuned cousins had arrived too. After breaking into the Top 20 with their debut album *Ten* in March, Pearl Jam were well on the way to hit single number three with 'Jeremy'. Soundgarden had also taken advantage of Britain's interest in all things Seattle by scoring a mid-table position of number 39 for their third LP *Badmotorfinger*, while lead-off single 'Jesus Christ Pose' nudged its way into the Top 30. Within six months, Alice In Chains would join in with their own masterpiece *Dirt*, its dark, druggy contents for many still grunge's true defining moment.

Whichever way one cut it, American rock had settled in Blighty and showed no intention of going home for the foreseeable future. "You couldn't escape it on a fast bicycle," laughed Coxon.

Just a year before, Blur might have been tipped as *the* British band to see such intruders off, but again, much had changed since the release of *Leisure*. The honour of fighting grunge on the beaches now fell to newcomers Suede, though according to Alex James, "The Best New Band in Britain" was in fact living on, "Borrowed money. Borrowed talent. Borrowed quotes. Borrowed time." Like Blur before them, Suede had wasted little time in grabbing the attention of the music press or clipping the UK Top 50 with their debut single. Additionally, much of their immediate appeal was centred on the louche stage presence of singer Brett Anderson and twisting guitar theatrics of Bernard Butler. A record deal with an 'indie' subsidiary backed by major label muscle also ran some familiar bells. So far, so Blur. But that was where the obvious similarities between the two ended.

Unlike their Colchester counterparts, Suede seemed intent on bringing back an old-school, floppy-haired glamour to rock'n'roll, the group taking their musical cues not just from The Beatles and The Smiths, but also the outlandish genius of David Bowie. In fact, it was this precise sense of otherness that caught the attention of *NME*'s John Mulvey when he saw the band play London's ULU in October, 1991. "They had charm, aggression, and... if not exactly eroticism, then something a little bit new, dangerous and exciting." By April 1992, Suede had snagged the cover of *Melody Maker* and a month later, entered the British charts at number 49 with their first single 'The Drowners'. The follow up, 'Metal Mickey', consolidated the band's position, taking them into the Top 20 at a respectable 17. In fact, walk past any newsstand in the summer/autumn of 1992, and chances were that Suede's frontman Brett Anderson would be staring winsomely out from some music magazine or other. Damon Albarn remained unimpressed. "A friend of mine wondered how anyone could think of Brett as a sex symbol when he's got such a big arse."

The reasons for Blur and Damon's antipathy towards Suede – and indeed, vice versa – were many and varied, though previous romantic entanglements, displaced emotions, way too much drink and 'boys being boys' were enough to start the party. In mid-1991 (or thereabouts), Albarn had begun dating Justine Frischmann, a 21-year-old architecture student then studying at London University. The daughter of Hungarian-born engineering consultant Wilem Frischmann, whose designs were key in the building of London's imposing *Natwest Tower*, Justine had something of the debutante to her: striking, self-assured and "of impeccable background", she was also a huge music fan, whittling away her spare time as rhythm guitarist in Suede, a group she had helped found with singer and former lover Brett Anderson – and with whom she still lived at the time.

Just as Suede began their assault on London's club scene, however, Justine left the band. "I got sick of the 'pomp rock' thing and Bernard Butler and his ten minute guitar solos," she said. Bernard Butler remembers things a tad differently. "She'd turn up late for rehearsals and say the worst thing in the world: 'I've been on a Blur video shoot.' That was when it ended, really. I think it was the day after she said that that Brett phoned me up and said, 'I've kicked her out.'"

Whatever the case, Frischmann's departure from Suede and the flat she shared with Anderson seemed to act as something of an enabler for both singer and group. "If Justine hadn't left the band," said Brett, "I don't think Suede would have got anywhere. It was a combination of being personally motivated, and the chemistry being right once she'd left." In the end, all parties actually seemed to benefit from going their separate ways. Suede were soon picked up by Nude records and began having hits while Frischmann turned her attentions to forming a new band she called Elastica. More, Damon Albarn had got exactly what he wanted: To wit, Justine Frischmann. If things were left there, all might have cooled without major incident. Sadly, there were to be no dignified silences between Blur and Suede, as both camps set about waging a particularly ugly war of words, more often than not played out in the pages of the music press.

As one might expect, Albarn threw the majority of insults from the Blur camp, though his team mates were not slow on the uptake either. According to Damon, Anderson's band would still be languishing in obscurity if he had not stolen Frischmann away, the friction caused by the spilt giving Suede's singer the necessary impetus to write conflicted, lovelorn material such as 'Animal Lover' and 'Metal Mickey'. Several jibes concerning the similarity of Brett's 'Mockney' singing voice to Albarn's own vocal style were also thrown into the public domain. When Bernard Butler hit back on Anderson's behalf by pointing out that the lyrics to 'Bang' were the poorest he had ever encountered, Graham Coxon immediately sought to protect his friend. "Mr. Butler was Blur's guitar roadie for two years. He spent hours crying on my doorstep for us to take him out on tour." (It might also be worth noting that Coxon was dating Justine Frischmann's best friend Jane Olliver at this point.) From cheap shots at Brett's sexual orientation to sour allegations that he was a heroin user, it seemed that every time a member of Blur got drunk – and there were many – a journalist was there to capture it on paper.

In reality, Damon's various flare-ups were really those of a young man seeking to protect his position while also coming to terms with the fact his girlfriend's ex-band/lover were trouncing Blur in the charts. "It got to the stage that every time I got drunk, I got very nasty about Suede," he told *NME*. "It's not easy when you see your girlfriend's ex-band do well. I was a bit of a prat about it, but (I felt) I had to be at the time." Damon's thoughts on Blur's slide down the pop ladder at the perceived expense of Suede were echoed by Graham Coxon. "It was weird. We came back from America and suddenly Suede were everywhere and we were crap. I went down the Camden Underworld and no-one would talk to me. I was yesterday's guitar man." The whole sorry affair was later summed up by Albarn in nine telling words. "Suede had a really good year. We did not."

Blur's season in hell came to a sad, ignominious end when the group headlined 'Gimme Shelter', a charity gig for the homeless at London's Town and Country Club on July 23, 1992. Unofficially billed "as a sort of homecoming" following their excursions abroad, it was as good a time as any for the band to reassert their credentials after a period of uncertain sales and unpleasant press coverage. There was also the opportunity to see off potential rivals Suede too, as Brett Anderson's troupe had been improbably booked to open the show. "It was supposed to be our comeback," said an aggrieved Damon. Suffice to say, the night did not go well for Blur. As if following some awful pre-ordained script, Suede turned in a superb performance, their emotive set closer 'To The Birds' reportedly inspired by Anderson's break-up with Frischmann. Following a spirited 30 odd minutes from indie pop-punksters Mega City Four, it was Blur's turn to shine. The first words Albarn uttered set the tone for the rest of the show. "We're so fucking shit, you may as well go home now." After several numbers watching the group drunkenly reel into each other, while Damon set about the task of head-butting a speaker to death, a few dozen audience members took his advice and headed for the doors. For others, the sight of four individuals having a collective breakdown was too good an opportunity to miss. By the time they got to their final number of the evening – 'Coping' – the spectacle was akin to chaos. "We were," said Graham, "fucking disgusting. It was like being in a coma."

Blur's behaviour was prompted by a four-hour drinking binge before the show at their new home-away-from-home, Camden Town's Good Mixer, a pub located but yards from Food Records' latest offices. When Damon spilt wine all over his shirt, Dave Rowntree – who lived nearby – offered to return to his flat and wash the item. Temporarily absent for an hour or so, he became a semi-sober witness to what was to follow. As the alcohol consumption continued at the venue, with Albarn ranting about the sins of America to anyone within earshot, it became clear to Blur's drummer his band mates were in no shape to pick up their instruments, let alone play or sing. "I was thinking, 'Please stop this, please stop this...'". No-one did, leaving manager Chris Morrison and Food boss Dave Balfe to watch the spectacle unfold from front of house. "A complete fucking mess," being one short review of the gig. "Actually," said Coxon, "I think we'd done worse. It was just difficult to remember when."

Albarn and Co.'s antics at the Town and Country Club did not go without comment either from their manager or label. While Morrison expressed profound disappointment at their behaviour, Balfe took things several stages further. The day after the gig, he met with a hungover Damon and clarified Food's position. In his opinion, the band were "pissing" away their talent and a line needed to be drawn in the sand. If Blur could not take themselves seriously, then neither would he. The message was clear: 'Clean up your act or be dropped'. For Albarn, the moment of clarity had arrived: "That was rock bottom, really," he said. "All we had left was ourselves." Ultimately, it was Justine Frischmann who provided an answer of sorts for both Damon and the band. Having witnessed Blur's bumpy descent from promising newcomers to potential also-rans, and an increasingly pointless press war between her old and new boyfriend that did neither any favours, she offered some simple, but sage advice. "Justine told me to make more of an effort," said Albarn. "Because I'm quite a forceful character, nobody was really saying that to me. She made me feel there was more to being in a band than just writing vacuous songs."

Bruised, battered, and with their career in jeopardy, Blur were now in danger of becoming yesterday's men before they even had a chance to record their second album. Suffice to say, they came out fighting, this time with a bulldog in tow.

Chapter Seven

Selling Britain By The Pound

For those seeking evidence of just how far Blur had swerved off the beaten track by the summer of 1992, then the band's tour documentary *Starshaped* reveals all. In fact, even its title gives much of the game away. "'Starshaped' refers to the shape you find yourself in when you wake up on your face fully clothed, after passing out drunk," said Albarn. As anyone who has seen the film will attest, Damon was speaking from personal experience here. A cripplingly honest account of Blur's progress from 1991's Reading Festival to their first appearance at Glastonbury on June 28, 1992, *Starshaped* makes a strong claim as rock's first genuine video nasty. Brimful of beer-sodden tour buses, sweaty roadies, grinning drivers and four musicians fluctuating from drunken elation to hungover despair, *Starshaped* captures Blur in "all their gory glory", as the band test their livers, lungs, bones and brains to breaking point.

If one has a strong constitution, there are rich highlights to savour: Damon vomits backstage, then attacks a speaker cabinet with all too predictable results. An ill-advised climb up a lighting rig ends in even more injury. Graham sets off on a drinking binge, goes missing for an hour or so and is then found in a field. Alex turns smoking into an Olympic level event, his burnt tonsils making him sound like an indie-pop version of Keith Richards, leaving a pleasantly soused Dave Rowntree to stare into the distance at some object only he can see. Despite all the chipped bones and misplaced guitarists, *Starshaped* is also genuinely funny at times, with Coxon in particular a hoot throughout. More, there are some fine live performances from the band, including an astounding version of 'Popscene'. But for all its relative merits, *Starshaped* remains a strangely joyless experience, the sheer exhaustion of those involved seeping from TV set to viewer like some pixel-born infection. "We'd done two American tours promoting *Leisure*, and became incredibly depressed people," said Albarn. "We then had to come back to England again and take ourselves more seriously."

As evidenced, there was little seriousness shown by Blur during their set at the Town & Country Club in July 1992. A new low for the band, it even led Dave Balfe to issue a clear ultimatum, his threat to drop them from Food Records unless their behaviour improved not of the idle kind. No longer protected by the bullet-proof status chart success brought, Blur were now a group under considerable scrutiny, their behaviours closely monitored, their output meticulously checked. Following a familiar pattern, the band stumbled badly before again finding their feet. The first pratfall occurred when Balfe and Andy Ross set up a series of recording sessions for Blur with XTC's Andy Partridge, then working as a producer for hire while his own group renegotiated terms with their label, Virgin. True doyens of the new wave, Partridge and XTC had enjoyed a distinguished run of hits from the late seventies onwards, the likes of 'Towers Of London', 'Sgt. Rock...' and 'Senses Working Overtime' all displaying a fractured, eccentric, yet extremely melodic approach to the rigours of songcraft. It was hoped that Andy Partridge might now turn some of Blur's own set of oddities into multi-platinum sales.

Unfortunately, the meeting of minds did not go well. For his opening gambit, Albarn complimented Partridge on 'Making Plans For Nigel', arguably XTC's best known and best loved song. Sadly, Andy had not written it, that honour going to his band mate Colin Moulding instead. More frost descended as the producer's self-confessed "dictatorial" style clashed with Blur's own relaxed approach to recording. Worse, the sessions were being held at Church studios in North London's Crouch End, an area known to local residents as "one giant pub". With the Haringey Arms next door, The King's Head across the road and The Railway Tavern and The Queens left and right respectively, distractions surrounded Blur like sodden sharks. That said, work was done, albeit of the quirkiest variety. Sounding not unlike a conjoining of XTC and Wire with grumpier guitars and chirpier vocals, Blur's early versions of 'Coping', 'Sunday Sunday' (then called 'Sunday Sleep') and 'Seven Days' certainly presented the band in a different pose, but one they did not wish to share with the world just yet. A parting of the ways was inevitable. "It just didn't work for us," Albarn said sharply. Partridge was equally happy to terminate their brief association. "Dave Balfe really wasn't happy when he heard the final mixes," he told *The Independent*. "The band were also having a lot of internal problems... they were kind of confused at the time."*

After several further attempts at recording (which we will return to) it was Graham Coxon's improbable attendance of a Cranberries gig at London's Marquee club during the late summer of 1992 that finally set Blur to rights. While casually watching the Irish pop-rockers from the safety of the bar, Coxon ran into Stephen Street, who had co-incidentally just finished overseeing The Cranberries' debut album in Dublin. Pleasantries were exchanged, ideas traded and Graham was soon canvassing both his own group and Food records for Stephen's return as producer. Weeks later, Blur and Street were back in Fulham's Maison Rouge Studios furiously working on the remaining songs for their second album. Finishing just before Christmas, the quartet celebrated several months' hard graft by playing a 'fan club only' gig at Fulham's Hibernian Club on December 16.

A boozy night by all accounts, Blur were supported by a combination of the surreal and religious (the local Salvation Army Band) and the new and noisy (up and coming riot grrrl band Huggy Bear). To add to this overall air of oddness, they also gave away 400 specially printed copies

* The fruits of Blur and Partridge's collaboration would subsequently languish in the vaults until released on the *21* box set in July 2012.

of their own twisted variant on the traditional carol 'Here We Come A-Wassailing'. Now re-titled 'The Wassailing Song', the tune bounced along like a drunken Morris dancer, with Albarn and Coxon trading vocals over a droning accordion and thumping bass drum. Unfortunately, Dave Balfe was not in the mood for high jinks or wayward carols. When presented with the results of Blur's latest endeavours at Maison Rouge, Food's boss said he didn't hear a single. Hence, Albarn was sent packing to write one over the Christmas break. In the end, he managed two.

Almost twelve months after 'Popscene' fell away to bad reviews and general commercial apathy, Blur again felt ready to re-assert their wares in the marketplace on April 21, 1993. "*Leisure* was our 'indie detox' album," said Coxon at the time. "(It was) an album that allowed us to get all that Dinosaur, Valentines and C86 bile out of our system. Now, things are different." As lead-off single 'For Tomorrow' proved, Coxon wasn't exaggerating. An unashamed pop classic, full of strange key changes, stirring strings – courtesy of the Duke String Quartet – and a mesmerising 'La la la' chorus sung by Damon and several female backing singers, 'For Tomorrow' was the sound of a confident and re-invigorated Blur. Written by Albarn at his parents' piano on Christmas Day, the song completely eschewed any notion of grunge, instead taking its sonic inspiration from Ziggy-period David Bowie and mid-sixties Kinks tunes. In short, this was a terribly British record, giving absolutely nothing of itself to America; "We're a British pop band and pop culture is what excites us," said Graham at the time. "We're not a traditionalist 'rock' band in that way."

Further, Albarn had taken giant steps forward as a lyricist on 'For Tomorrow', his words this time neither vacuous nor banal, but engaging and on occasion, terribly sad. "She's a 20th century girl, hanging on for dear life..." With its images of a modern day 'Terry and Julie' lost somewhere on London's Westway as the metaphorical ice cracks around them, it was all a hell of a long way from "Bang goes another day...'. "You know, I wasn't confident enough back then to be a songwriter," Damon admitted in April 1993. "There were one or two little things, but I hadn't found the confidence to really... write." As is often the case when the general public is confronted with something novel or genuinely interesting, 'For Tomorrow' was given a quizzical thumbs-up from record buyers, but no more. Instead of a deserved place in the UK Top Ten, Blur had to make do with a desultory number 28, only four places higher than 'Popscene' had managed 12 months before. Not even a nicely evocative, black and white video from film director Julien Temple – which took the band on a bus ride from London's Trafalgar Square to the kite-flying playing fields of Primrose Hill – could prise it any higher. "Yes, we were disappointed," reasoned Alex, "but we also knew we were really onto something."

Like most everyone else, the music press were also slow on the uptake concerning what exactly that something might be. "First, they tried to kill baggy," said *NME*, "now they're after grunge. Our very own slacker boys are telling us to smarten up our ideas and go exercise the bulldog..." *Melody Maker* went even further, as journalist Cathi Unsworth decided it was time not to bury grunge, but Blur instead. "I suppose it was too much to hope we'd seen the back of them," she said before comparing their latest single to "the sound [of] Cockney Rebel doing a David Bowie karaoke night with extra prizes for T-Rex motifs". Not to be outdone, at precisely the same time Blur were trying to claw their way back into the public's affections, *Select* launched a 12-page 'Union Jack' issue, hailing cover stars Suede and Luke Haines' Auteurs (among others) as the saviours of British pop. With Blur not even mentioned in dispatches, it was 1992 all over again. "I really don't want to get into this," said an aggrieved-sounding Albarn, "but [of those frontmen] one's not good looking enough and the other's too obsessed with his own sexuality – or lack of it – to be able to articulate anything about Britain."

The extent of Damon Albarn and Blur's ambitions for British pop became clear on the release of their second album on May 10, 1993. Like *Leisure* before it, the record had laboured under a humorous working title – 'England vs. America' – but given the band's links to their US label SBK, such bear-baiting rhetoric was never a realistic proposition. "Shame though," Alex later quipped, "It probably would have sold twice as many in the States if it had 'America' in the title." Instead, Blur christened their sophomore effort in honour of a slogan they had seen stencilled on a wall along London's Bayswater Road. "(It said) 'Modern Life Is Rubbish'," remembered Damon. "It was the most significant comment on popular culture (I'd seen) since 'Anarchy In The UK'."

To compliment *Modern Life...*'s retrograde sentiments, design consultants Stylorouge again found a suitably eccentric cover shot, this time using an oil painting of a speeding train to evoke maximum visual impact. "(The painting 'Full Steam Ahead') was meant to evoke the feel of *Just William*'s... pre-war Britain," they said at the time. The disc's inner packaging was also striking. In a beautifully judged illustration by Paul Stephen, the four members of Blur were presented sitting on a tube carriage, their hands and knees folded, their very English Doc Marten boots jutting towards the artist. Of course, this sepia-tinged portrait provided a deliberately ironic counterpoint to the album's title and cover. Elsewhere, lyrics and actual music were neatly printed in the disc's accompanying booklet, Graham kindly outlining each chord to "demystify" the art of guitar playing. All in all, this was clever stuff.

The music wasn't half bad, either. Though Blur had drawn on a host of British influences from Madness, Bowie and The Buzzcocks to The Smiths, Lionel Bart and The Who to inform the record's sound and style, *Modern Life Is Rubbish* was also very much about the band expanding their own creative perimeters. Aside from the usual swirl of vocals, guitar, bass and drums, *Modern Life...* was awash with squeaky organs, bleating synths, orchestral horn lines and lilting string arrangements. For added satire and general contrariness, found sounds and FX gimmickry also snuck their way into the grooves, the tinkling of typewriters sitting nicely alongside samples from TV and radio advertisements. If nothing else, one could wallow for days with the right pair of headphones. Yet, it was the songs of *Modern Life...* that would make or break Blur's attempt at putting themselves back at the front of the pack. "You always have to remember that pop music is just a fashion," said Damon, "and you have to be one step ahead if you're going to last..."

From the seventies-tinged opening strains of 'For Tomorrow' to the neo-psychedelic coda of 'Resigned', Blur seldom put a foot wrong throughout *Modern Life...* though, as ever, there was the odd misfire: 'Villa Rosie' was a bit too knowing for its own good, while 'Turn It

Up' wandered around like a stray from the *Leisure* sessions, its buoyant chorus and winning guitar work the only reasons to merit inclusion. But these were only small beefs on an otherwise immaculately laid table. 'Advert' for instance, found the band harnessing the energy of their live shows for the first time on record, the tune's punk-friendly snarl a jutting addition to Blur's future set list. 'Blues Jeans' on the other hand, caught them in a distinctly Morrissey and Marr mood, its lilting chords and swaying melody recalling The Smiths at the most drowsy and relaxed. For lovers of quirky power-pop, 'Starshaped' also delivered much, leading one to wonder what XTC's Andy Partridge might have done with it had things gone better in Crouch End.

If old fans were somewhat confused by Blur's multi-faceted new direction, 'Oily Water' provided partial recompense. A staple of concert shows since mid-1991, the track was as unctuous as its name suggested. Contrasting grimy, but mellow passages against blasts of shrieking discordance, 'Oily Water' was a curiously erotic interlude, the sound of beer being poured down the sink after a dirty night out on the tiles. "It's gratuitously nasty and My Bloody Valentine all over," said Alex. 'Miss America' also had a sense of post-bedsit fumble about it, its shimmering guitar, dripping tap percussion and lazy, almost distracted vocals channelling the likes of Syd Barrett's 'Late Night', 'Terrapin' or at a push, 'Wined And Dined'. Completing the trio of hung over sounding tunes was 'Pressure On Julian', though unlike 'Oily Water' and 'Miss America' before it, '...Julian''s green about the gills guitar intro soon found itself hastily woken up by a catchy chorus and "sprint to the finish" ending. 'Coping' also showed signs of major resuscitation, the entertaining but slim tune recorded some months before at Crouch End's Church Studios filling out nicely in the bass, drums and keyboard departments.

Of the remaining songs on *Modern Life Is Rubbish*, future singles 'Sunday Sunday' and 'Chemical World' showed how far Albarn had come as "a writer of potential hits", how finely Blur enhanced his tunes and how thoroughly British the album actually was. Coming out of the traps like some long-lost Madness track, 'Sunday Sunday' was all tub-thumping drums, driving brass stabs (again courtesy of The Kick

Horns) and infuriatingly catchy chorus. It also had the temerity to speed up during the mid-section, a tactic Dave Balfe felt would see the song ousted from potential radio playlists (He needn't have worried. It didn't). With its multi-tracked "Ooh, ooh, oohs" and Beatles-approved descending chord pattern, 'Chemical World' was another radio friendly anthem – and just as well, because it had been designed specifically for that purpose. Not hearing an American hit on any of the demos for *Modern Life...*, Blur's US label had asked that Damon return to the drawing board and whip one up. 'Sunday Sunday' was the result. In reality, save for Coxon's beefed up guitar signal and a more sturdy drum track, there was little or nothing American about the song at all, with Albarn taking his cues from The Fab Four and The Kinks rather than Nirvana or Soundgarden. But for whatever reason, the ruse worked. SBK declared 'Sunday Sunday' delightful and the band got back to the business of finishing their album in relative peace.

If there was a highlight to be had on *Modern Life Is Rubbish* it was probably 'Colin Zeal', which ironically enough was written by Damon in the States while Blur were having their collective breakdown in 1992. Featuring James' rolling bass line, Rowntree's neatly tuned tom-toms and several seismic blasts of guitar from Coxon, 'Colin Zeal' was a curious beast in that it was difficult at first to ascribe a direct musical influence to it. Whereas elsewhere, one could easily join dots to Bowie or The Beatles, 2 tone or My Bloody Valentine, 'Colin Zeal''s mix of punk rock theatrics and art-house spin seemed to present Blur as a band of themselves, for themselves. However, one quick jaunt through The Teardrop Explodes' back catalogue and all was revealed. Not only did '...Zeal''s spinning guitar heavily recall Teardrop's 'Sleeping Gas', but Albarn's melody line also ran perilously close to Julian Cope's original vocal. As ever, Damon had an answer ready. "Really, there's no necessity for originality anymore. There are so many old things to splice together in infinite permutations, there's no need to create anything new."

With both sides of *Modern Life...* bookended by the frankly mad instrumentals 'Intermission' and 'Commercial Break' – two music hall-themed "roustabouts" the band used to enliven audiences when all else failed – Blur's second album was quite the achievement. Full of strong ideas, it admirably honoured Britain's musical past and present, while at the same time re-casting the band as a viable alternative to all those baritone grunts and growls from across the Atlantic. The record also made a star of Graham Coxon. While no one could deny that Alex James and Dave Rowntree both put in winning shifts throughout, it really was Coxon's gift with six strings, a sturdy amplifier and a nest of effects pedals that propelled the sound and spirit of *Modern Life Is Rubbish*. "I was getting a bit bored of this distorted sound everywhere," he said, "so I thought I'd try something new." Using an army of Les Pauls, Telecasters, various acoustics, flangers, vibratos and tremolo boxes, Graham provided a master class in punk, indie, rock and even folk guitar stylings. "You know, creativity can often come out of incompetence," said the ever modest guitarist. "I've always believed that incompetent musicians can sometimes make the best musicians. Accidents can happen when you're not the best guitarist and sometimes those accidents sound like the work of a genius when you hear them on record."

Of course, Damon Albarn could also take a bow for his efforts on *Modern Life Is Rubbish*. After all, it was his keen – some might say avaricious – mind behind much of the music, and indeed, the lyrics that accompanied them. And what a breath of fresh air those lyrics were. Rightly accused in the past of pure laziness when it came to putting words to song, Albarn was a changed man. No longer content with delivering 'sound poems' as a lyrical prop, Blur's frontman was now the keenest of observers, his critical eye probing most every facet of modern British life. From 'Chemical World''s rosy-cheeked check-out girl eating chocolate as she faces eviction to 'Sunday Sunday''s old soldier bemoaning the loss of an England only he can remember, each character (or caricature) rang a familiar bell. This was nowhere more apparent than on 'Colin Zeal'. An empty-headed vessel programmed to dream of impending wealth and foreign holidays while stuck in a traffic jam, '... Zeal' was emblematic of a certain type of new Englander Albarn knew only too well. "Colin Zeal lives in a new town in Essex," Damon told *NME*'s John Harris. "He's a modern retard and... represents the huge wave of sanitisation that's undoubtedly linked to America."

Damon's obsession with the 'Coca-colonisation' of Britain was also at the heart of 'Advertisement', the tune's aggressive structure augmenting his attack on maximum comfort for minimum effort. "Advertisements are here for rapid persuasion," he sang, "...you need fast relief from aches and stomach pains."

This theme of general malaise was all over *Modern Life Is Rubbish* like a rash. On the Dave Balfe-baiting 'Pressure On Julian' and 'Coping' – so titled to remind Food's boss of his unsatisfactory stint with The Teardrops' mercurial singer – images of yellow tongues, tired eyes and "pissy water" all jostled for attention. 'For Tomorrow''s golden couple also had their problems, both fighting the urge not "to get sick again" as they traversed the Westway. Even the voyeuristic protagonist of 'Chemical World' seemed unwell, prescribing himself "some sugary tea" to combat light-headedness. As some have observed, Albarn might well have been experimenting with darker hues here, his references to swimming heads and sweet-flavoured restoratives common parlance among heroin users. For the time being at least, such speculation went unanswered as Damon's cast of peeping Thomases, grateful exhibitionists, nervous, coughing men and knowing, naughty girls diverted attention away from the subject of hard drugs and onto mystical London bus trips from Primrose Hill to Empress Gate.

It was precisely this aspect of Blur's latest work that the critics honed in on, with the band's endless championing of British music and culture – in both its mundane and miraculous forms – at the heart of their reviews. "Blur have reinvented themselves in the image of their youth, sullen and suburban, as ghosts from a time when you could still be beaten up before assembly for wearing the wrong badge," said *NME*'s Paul Moody. "It's the Village Green Preservation Society come home to find a car park in its place. Unlike Ride or The Charlatans whose second albums barely limped into the breach, Blur have thrown on their old clothes and stormed into No Man's Land with all guns blazing." Sensing a band that might well be again on the up, the previously unkind *Melody Maker* now shifted their position from assassination to one of cautious support. "'*Modern Life...*' is admirably ambitious, (even if it) occasionally starts to creak under the weight of its own intent," said Paul Mathur.

"But it is (also) the kind of pop record that too few British groups are currently even considering throwing into the public consciousness. For that, Blur should be accorded some sort of wide-eyed respect."

Indeed, the fact that Blur had avoided the perils of "Beautiful South-style dreariness or Weller-style retro-ism" while making the thoroughly British *Modern Life Is Rubbish* was wholly commendable. More, their careful traipsing between the "radical and reactionary" without getting caught in either camp also pleased. Yet, whenever a whiff of pro-British sentiment was used to promote an idea or concept, there was always a risk that nasty word 'Nationalism' – or something very like it – was lurking in the shadows. Predictably, Blur were not immune to such charges, with their first set of press photos to promote *Modern Life...* threatening to derail their return to favour before it had even begun. Entitled 'British Image No.1', Paul Stephens' image of the band dressed in bovver boots, Fred Perry tops and waving a huge bull mastiff at the camera set off alarm bells with the media and public alike. Visually too close for some to the 'Oi!' skinhead movement of the late seventies – which unwittingly acted as a flytrap for a number of extreme right-wing types – Blur now found themselves battling accusations of racial insensitivity. If not handled well, this was Morrissey at 'Madstock' all over again. Quick to act, the group issued a second set of photos, cunningly titled 'British Image No.2', which re-positioned them as a camp foursome attending "a pre-war aristocratic tea party". Burnt by the criticism and keen not to have it repeated, Albarn met the press head on. "The notion of being lumped in with that kind of mindless ignorance is horrible. I really just wanted to make music that is more universal," he empathically stated. "There's no suggestion whatsoever in anything we've ever done that we glorify a white Britain. In fact, we're celebrating Britain today, which is not white."

Point well made. But away from defending lazy accusations of nationalism, racism or any other 'ism', there was a distinct feeling that Blur had more in mind than just celebrating Britishness. In fact, the more Albarn talked, the clearer his secondary agenda became. "If punk was about getting rid of hippies, then I'm getting rid of grunge," he told

NME. "People should smarten up, be a bit more energetic. They're walking around like hippies, stooped, greasy hair... It irritates me." Tired of newly plaid-clad DJs swapping old news items about Kurt and Courtney's latest faux pas, Damon was intent on bringing down grunge before it brought down Britain. "Everyone has become focused on America, and we're just trying to redress the balance," he said. "We have such a rich musical heritage that doesn't just start with rock 'n' roll. It actually goes back to the post-war period of Joan Littlewood and Lionel Bart, and before that, music hall. I'm not saying that everyone should put on a fake Cockney accent, and start singing about the Old Bull And Bush, but I do feel our culture is under siege and we're in danger of losing it. And because we're so mild-mannered and liberal, we just say 'Oh, it doesn't matter really'. Well, it does matter."

Truthfully, there was something very familiar about Damon's arguments and how he chose to express them. For starters, the ironic use of advertising snippets on *Modern Life*... and his lyrical obsessions with mundane objects and everyday situations surely had their origins in Britain's pop art movement of the early fifties. Like sculptor Eduardo Paolozzi and critic John McHale before him, Blur's singer was challenging accepted notions of what constituted high art by celebrating the ordinary and commonplace instead. Even the song title 'For Tomorrow' was indebted to Richard Hamilton's groundbreaking 1956 work 'This Is Tomorrow' – its images of musclemen and burlesque girls juxtaposed against Hoovers and coffee tables confirming the artist's view that beauty and glamour could also be found in simple, mass-produced items.

Further, Albarn's newfound habit of spray-painting the slogan 'Modern Life Is Rubbish' wherever he went – "I graffiti it everywhere. I think it expresses everything" – could be traced back to the French Situationists of the late sixties. The brainchild of Marxist theorist Guy Debord, Situationists (or SI) believed that if avant-garde images or confrontational slogans were placed in everyday environments, they would jar the observer's imagination and snap them "from casual spectacle into the living moment". Revived by The Clash in the seventies and taken to its logical extreme by Manic Street Preachers at the start of the nineties, the art of the slogan in commandeering cultural interest was again nothing particularly groundbreaking.

Even Damon's greatest fear and potentially strongest argument – that Britain was losing its musical and cultural identity to American influence – had the ring of old news to it. As far back as the forties, when US servicemen landed on English shores and Frank Sinatra sold a smooth new music into London's dancehalls, there were concerns that Uncle Sam was coming to "steal our daughters away". These worries escalated into rampant hysteria during the fifties as Elvis Presley and James Dean introduced Britain to the teenager, the old empire now under siege by a mutinous, home-grown army dressed in Teddy Boy jackets and crepe shoes. Yet, said Empire (or at least a bit of it) survived and five or so years later, the battle was even going the other way. Led by The Beatles, reinforced by The Rolling Stones, and with The Animals, The Yardbirds and Herman's Hermits all offering able support, the "British Invasion of America" in the mid-sixties turned England's crumpled old capital into the most fashionable city in the world – the term 'Swinging London' still carrying joyful connotations of stick-thin supermodels, bold experimentation and fabulous, fabulous bands. One might even argue Britain's musical/cultural invasion of the USA had never really stopped: from Led Zeppelin, Black Sabbath and Fleetwood Mac to Duran Duran, Depeche Mode and Jesus Jones, one band or another always seemed to be taking a bite at the US cherry. Perhaps the likes of Nirvana, Pearl Jam and Soundgarden – who lest anyone forget, all namechecked British bands among their primary influences – were simply redressing some odd cosmic balance.

That said, where Albarn and Blur could claim an empathic victory was how they had gone about the business of stripping away even a smidgeon of traditional Americana from the musical contents of *Modern Life Is Rubbish*. That grunge would never get a look in was all too obvious. But the album also managed to avoid delving into blues, jazz, R&B or even British-influenced US heavy rock for its inspiration. No overt homages to Muddy Waters, Duke Ellington, James Brown, Prince or even Van Halen here. Instead, like The Kinks, Madness and XTC before them, Blur presented listeners with a peculiarly homespun take on the twelve-note scale, with sounds and styles more likely drawn from Victorian music hall than the work of Black Flag or The Band. "When we released 'Popscene' in 1992," said Coxon by way of explanation, "the only bands people cared about were Nirvana and Pearl Jam. Now, people are beginning to talk about this new 'English' fashion in music. For us, it's nothing new. We've always made English pop records."

Whether *Modern Life Is Rubbish* was a reactionary solution to the problem of grunge, a radicalised commentary on the marvels and maladies of British life or simply dying embers stoked up to build new fires mattered not. Despite the fact that its influences were clear and standpoint somewhat familiar, *Modern Life...* remained a fine album, and one that ironically re-positioned Blur at the forefront of British pop – a band to lead and not to follow. Like *Leisure* before it, however, there was a real danger the record could have fallen prey to 'Too many cooks...' syndrome. Following their failed attempts to gel with Andy Partridge, Blur had used three further producers in an effort to complete the disc. Called back to active service after his efforts on 'Popscene', Steve Lovell lent a helping hand on 'Villa Rosie' and 'Sunday Sunday', while esteemed engineer John Smith received a co-production credit alongside the band for his work on five more tracks, including the wonderful 'Oily Water'.

But again, it was left to Stephen Street to help Blur over the finish line, even if Dave Balfe remained unconvinced by the results. "I remember finishing the record... and Balfe coming in and basically washing his hands of it... saying, 'It's crap, it's only going to sell to a few thousand *NME* readers and that's it. There's no hits on there'," said Street. "His vision, which had been distorted by the success of Jesus Jones in America, was to try and have another band that he could crack America with and obviously this album was not going to do that. But to be fair to Dave Balfe, it did spur Damon on to think, 'Well fuck you I'm going to write a couple of hits now...'"

Of course, in pop terms, sales and not philosophies dictated an act's commercial success and *Modern Life Is Rubbish* did respectable, if not astounding business for both Blur and Balfe. Released on May 10, 1993, the album peaked at number 15 in the British charts, selling some

40,000 units in its initial run. These sales were no doubt helped by a 14-date UK tour that found the band performing amidst a stage set covered in giant sofas, lampshades, duck ornaments and toasters. "It was like *Eastenders* had been dragged to Birmingham," one critic wryly observed. In a cod-homage to U2's *Zoo TV* spectacle of a year before, Blur also placed an out-sized television set onstage, blasting images of adverts and regional news at the audience. Though the British pop art influences were being pushed to extremes here, reviews for the group's live shows were uniformly positive, buoyed along by a re-invigorated four piece intent on reclaiming Britain's musical supremacy over Seattle. "People make the most absurd claims for Nirvana," said an irritated Rowntree, "But what have they actually done? Basically turned soft American rock into slightly harder American rock. Big deal. It might mean something to record companies that have to change their marketing strategies, but does it mean they're dangerous? Of course not. It doesn't mean shit."

To back up the tough rhetoric, Blur released a new single – 'Chemical World' – on June 28. Though it might have been written at the behest of their American record label to help the quartet's cause overseas, 'Chemical World' remained as British as pie and mash. "These townies never speak to you, just stick together so they never get lonely," sang Albarn as he stood under a tree surrounded by rabbits in the single's 'Country Life'-baiting video. Backed by a variety of CD and vinyl formats – which included a quite awful cover of Rod Stewart's 'Maggie May' on which Alex rightly refused to play – 'Chemical World' may only have nudged number 28 in the charts, but Blur's intent was still clear. "A modicum of success has allowed us to be what we always wanted to be," said Damon, "a very weird British pop group."

If Blur were having problems getting back into the Top Ten again, then at least momentum was slowly gathering elsewhere. Having toured the UK and played selected dates throughout Europe in May/June, the group returned to the outdoor circuit in early July, first appearing at Nottingham's 'Heineken Music Festival' before making their way to Reading a month or so later. Only a year before, Blur were in trouble – a band whose focus was lost in a sea of beer, petty rivalries and faltering record company support. At Reading 1993, however, both purpose and definition had been re-discovered, with a 15-song set played in failing light at Little John's Farm capturing the attention of thousands. "Blur were playing the second stage on a cold Saturday night," said journalist Steve Sutherland. "Gradually, as if by some pre-arranged signal, people started heading for the tent where Blur found themselves the focal point of festivities. By common consent," he concluded, "they became the hit of the whole weekend."

The fact that said crowd may well have been seeking shelter from inclement weather or solace from a reportedly dull night's entertainment on the main stage was irrelevant. Those at Reading voted with their feet, the music papers noticed, and for Blur, a corner had been turned. "The atmosphere at Reading was incredible," Stephen Street later confirmed. "All the fans knew all the lyrics to the songs (from *Modern Life*...), so we knew the record had reached those people and there was the beginning of something here. It really was the step up the ladder that they needed at the time."

Despite their triumphant set at Reading on August 28, there was no magical parting of the waves for Blur just yet. Yet another round of UK dates, this time sponsored by *Melody Maker* and christened the 'Sugary Tea' tour, took the band from Manchester to Brighton over the course of 20-odd nights during October 1993. To coincide with the trek, Blur released 'Sunday Sunday', the third and final single lifted from *Modern Life Is Rubbish*. Arguably the most sing-along moment on the album, even if Dave Balfe detested the triple-speed middle-section (itself another tribute to Albarn's beloved Cardiacs), 'Sunday Sunday' had all the makings of a Top Ten hit: big of chorus, jaunty of brass section and backed by a barking mad video Madness would have been proud of, it should have taken Blur over the top. However, the group were again denied victory as the tune stalled at number 26.

While some scratched their heads at this latest failure, others pointed to the dark lyrical undercurrent of 'Sunday Sunday' as one possible reason it had drawn a semi-blank. Written by Albarn as he watched shoppers tramp in and out of a Minneapolis mall during Blur's ill-fated 1992 US tour, the song was another thinly-disguised attack on consumer gluttony; its images of a family anesthetising themselves on bread, eggs and beef all for "that Sunday sleep" as glutinous and opaque as day-old gravy. However, blaming Damon's sour wordplay wasn't much of an excuse. From The Kinks' own 'Sunny Afternoon' to Monty Python's 'Always Look On The Bright Side Of Life', the Great British public had always been partial to a bit of satire as long as the accompanying tune could be sung in the bath. Like 'Popscene' before, it was much more likely that record buyers were still too busy spending their pennies on grunge to really invest in a new and improved Blur. Not that the band were bitter about it, though. "With Nirvana, it's really difficult to believe anything because every time they open their mouths, they sound really patrician," said Coxon. "Kurt and Courtney sound like your really embarrassing auntie and uncle."

Of perhaps more interest to long-serving fans were the B-sides chosen by Blur to accompany 'Sunday Sunday''s release. Plundering their own vaults, the group issued a raft of old Seymour material on various CD, 7″ and 12″ formats, including original Beat Factory demos of 'Mixed Up', 'Tell Me, Tell Me', 'Fried' and 'Long Legged'. "I think we realized that Seymour was still there in us and it was a shame to keep him locked up," said Coxon. To no-one's great surprise, these songs sounded raw, unfocused and occasionally unlistenable. Yet, even in such a primal state, they also strongly hinted at Blur's eventual future: the shrieking feedback that announced 'Shimmer', the mad charge of 'Tell Me' and 'Fried', even Graham's falsetto vocals on 'Dizzy'. Each track subtly reinforced Graeme Holdaway's contention that Seymour and Blur were always one and the same. "Oh, they say there were two different groups," he said, "but Seymour are Blur and Blur are Seymour. All they really did was change their name."

To further confound, Blur released two more surprises as part of 'Sunday Sunday''s multiple-format sales drive. Under the guise of 'The Popular Community CD', cover versions of the old music hall stalwarts 'Daisy Bell' and 'Let's All Go Down The Strand' found their way into the public domain. Given their quality, they really should have been redacted. Possibly the nadir of the band's recorded career, these punkified takes on post-Edwardian sing-song might have been philosophically congruent with Damon's equations on modern life and rubbish. But hearing him warble "Daisy Daisy, give me your answer do" like an ailing Lionel Bart did the band no favours and only reinforced journalistic accusations that Blur's latest gambit was all Mockney, no Cockney.

These monstrosities aside, Blur finished 1993 with dignity more or less intact. The band's grim, but riveting documentary *Starshaped* drew strong reviews when released in late September 1993, while a short tour of Japan in November reinforced their growing appeal in the Far East. There was even time for a quick return visit to the States just before Christmas, neatly coinciding with SBK's delayed release of *Modern Life Is Rubbish*. Unfortunately, there was to be no happy ending to Blur's experiences with their American record label. Even though the band played several well-received gigs on both sides of the country – drawing four encores from a rabid crowd at LA's legendary Whiskey A Go Go – their Stateside profile remained spectral at best. Unlike *Leisure*, which had at least sold nearly 90,000 copies in the USA, *Modern Life...* struggled to shift a quarter of that figure – a pitiful performance by anyone's standards. According to Blur's manager Chris Morrison, repeated attempts at persuading SBK to market the disc via college radio had all fallen on deaf ears, with the company preferring to target more traditional, but ultimately less sympathetic Top 40 programmers instead. To make matters worse, Morrison discovered the real reason behind *Modern Life...*'s tardy US release date was because the label had shut down their Alternative Music department the previous summer. "When I asked why (it had closed)," he confirmed, "They said it was because the girl had left." Of course, one should have felt some degree of sympathy for Blur here. But after all the anti-American rhetoric of the past six months, it was hard not to study the mess without the phrase 'Instant Karma' coming to mind: 'Britain vs. America', indeed.

In practical terms, Blur's real battle of 1993 had not been fought overseas, but resolutely on home soil. It was also one they were winning. By year end, this fact was reflected in the annual music paper polls where Blur not only took *Melody Maker's* 'Best Live Act', but also third spot for 'Best Album'. Thanks to his stonking performance in talking up the record, Damon also came sixth in the 'Lip of the Year'. To compound the singer's personal pleasure, Justine Frischmann's new group Elastica – who had only been gigging a matter of months – even won 'Brightest Hope'. But there was one fly in the ointment: Blur could claim only second spot in the 'Best Band' stakes as arch-rivals Suede clipped them to that coveted title. Come early 1994, Brett Anderson's troupe would also add an *NME* Brat, Brit award nomination and a much-coveted Mercury Prize to their tally. Typically, Damon had moved on from petty feuds to much bigger prizes by then. "*Modern Life Is Rubbish* saved us," he said. "It's given us an identity. We'd been told repeatedly that we were committing commercial suicide. But we had a really strong feeling among the four of us that we were doing something good. And you know what? We were."

Now all they had to do was to top it.

Chapter Eight

The Golden Year

While not quite a resurrection, *Modern Life Is Rubbish* had enabled Blur to salvage their reputation and re-position their brand, while also putting the negative events of 1992 far behind them. "Even though *Modern Life...* didn't sell an enormous amount," said Dave Rowntree, "it was extremely well received, especially by people whose opinions mattered at the time. And that in turn gave us a confidence in ourselves that we'd previously lacked." Some might argue that Blur, or at least Damon Albarn, had never lacked for confidence. But the threat of becoming yesterday's men so early in their career seemed to galvanise the band into action, their subsequent tirades against grunge and American consumerist influence resulting in a fine album and series of focused, occasionally brilliant live shows. "*Modern Life...* was our last chance really, before Food might have dropped us," continued Rowntree. "But in actual fact, it led us somewhere else entirely."

Of central importance to that "somewhere" was Blur's occasionally unsubtle, yet still touching adherence to British culture and music in the face of all things Seattle. By taking such a contrary – some might even say reactionary – stance, there had been a danger the band would appear out of step and out of time, an anachronism trading on the ashes of old empires. Instead, their rigid standpoint had entirely the opposite effect, laying the foundations for a still percolating, as yet unnamed movement that would not only do for grunge, but also reactivate interest in all things British at an international level.

Aware such a time might be near, Blur spent the winter of 1993 ensconced with producer Stephen Street at Fulham's Maison Rouge studios recording their next album. Over the course of three extremely cold months, the band stuck to a work schedule remarkably similar to the one followed when making their debut single 'She's So High' two years before. "We like working with Stephen because it's a very civilised process," Alex said at the time. "We take tea when we work, and we're out by midnight. No rock 'n' roll myth-building with us." Minimising distractions, Street arranged for food and drink to be delivered to Maison Rouge, with a short break for "leg movements" during mid-afternoon. As before, Albarn had brought an impressive number of completed songs with him, though there was still time for further experimentation and tweaking of arrangements. By late January, at least 20 tracks were down on tape, allowing Blur and Street to separate the wheat from the chaff. So confident were they in the material, 16 of those tracks made the final cut. Banging a now familiar drum, Food's Dave Balfe was sceptical about the record's chances, feeling that Blur's decision to amplify their essential Britishness would hurt their overseas sales. "This might be a mistake," he said. It wasn't.

Based on previous endeavours, it might be expected that Blur would choose something bold or brassy for the first single from their third album: a stirring, glam rock-inflected anthem perhaps, or a big-boned number full of jaunty asides. Instead, the group released a peculiar, almost robotic little tune that puzzled as much as pleased. Yet, after one or two listens, one realised Blur had a masterpiece on their hands. Unlike the Ziggy-like strains of 'For Tomorrow' or the 'Rat tat tat' of 'Sunday Sunday', 'Girls And Boys' was a true child of the eighties, its mechanised drum beats, jerky synth patterns and heavily flanged guitars recalling a time when Gary Numan, Duran Duran and Human League ruled the UK's airwaves. "Ah, girls and boys," Alex later said. "Disco drums, nasty guitars and Duran Duran bass. Damon's singing about shagging, too." Indeed he was. Twisting his vocals around a genius turn from bassist James, 'Girls And Boys' had Albarn slyly pontificating on the dubious pleasures of Club 18-30 holiday culture, the singer perfectly capturing all the desire and despair of young Brits "following the herd down to Greece..."

Sexually ambivalent (listen well to the chorus), but keen not to judge those under scrutiny, 'Girls And Boys''s wily lyric came to Albarn during a brief visit to Magaluf with girlfriend Justine Frischmann in the summer of 1993. "Yeah, it's about those sorts of holidays," he told *The Guardian* a year later. "The place was equally divided between cafés serving up full English breakfasts and really tacky Essex nightclubs. There was a very strong sexuality about it. I just love the whole idea of it, to be honest. I love herds. All these blokes and all these girls meeting at the watering hole and then... copulating. There's no morality involved, and I'm not saying it should or shouldn't happen. I suppose my mind's just getting more dirty. I can't help it." Fast forward a decade, and Damon had slightly modified his position, casting an even more honest light on the motives behind the song. "(I was watching) with a combination of desire and disgust," he said, "though half of me... just wanted to get right in there, in the middle of it." Another quantum leap forward for Albarn as a lyricist and Blur as a potential hit machine, producer Stephen Street recognised 'Girls And Boys' worth the second he heard it. "When Alex started playing that ridiculously funky, sexy bass line, you just knew it was something we had to run with," he said. "Great chords, great chorus, and everyone could relate to it."

As ever, Food were keen to maximise the single's chances with a strong promotional campaign. Hence, former 10cc songwriter turned video maker Kevin Godley was charged with filming Blur against a bluescreen backdrop as images of suntanned teenagers boozing themselves into oblivion were projected behind them. A perfect visual accompaniment to Albarn's tale of rutting Brits abroad, Godley was aghast at the finished product, disowning it as "Page 3 rubbish." Blur, on the other hand, absolutely loved it. "Oh, it suited the song perfectly," said Rowntree. To cap it all, designers Stylorouge provided a wonderful cover for the single, featuring a young couple caught in silhouette against a golden sunset. The photograph in question had been lifted directly from the front of a condom packet. Wave-drenched beaches, beer-drenched lovers and a safe sex message to boot, this was marketing at its very best.

A cunning distillation of all that was right and wrong with Britain's youth culture at the time, 'Girls And Boys' provided Blur with their biggest-selling single yet. Released on March 7, 1994, the song immediately climbed to number five on the UK charts, a pattern subsequently repeated throughout Europe. Though expectations for 'Girls And Boys' were high behind the scenes, the level of its success still took some in the band by surprise. "'Girls And Boys' going Top five was a bit of a shocker," said Graham Coxon. "Mind you, it is a horribly catchy bugger, isn't it?" Having waited patiently since his 16th birthday to become a "proper pop star", Alex James turned philosopher king when his time finally came. "In a way, pop songs have to be brutal to be successful. There's seldom room for ambiguity," he said. "So to have a 'brutal' pop hit with a seam of ambiguity also running through it... well, you're doing quite well, aren't you?" Dave Rowntree, who by his own admission had done little more than programme the song's electro drum beat, was also in a curiously detached mood. "I'm (not) really in it," the drummer observed. "(But) it's cool not being in your own song."

For Damon Albarn, emotions were mixed. Having spent nearly half a decade telling journalists Blur were the band to "change things at a fundamental level", he was now potentially able to make good on his astounding promise. Suffice to say, the first wave of sound bites from Blur's singer were a joy to behold. "'Girls And Boys'?" he said. "Four notes. And the chorus is 'Boys, girls, love'. That's quite a universal message, isn't it? I just can't believe I didn't think of it earlier. Easy." Privately, it was a different matter. Albarn had long exhibited the type of staggering confidence usually associated with coked-up city brokers, free-wheeling stunt cyclists or just plain madmen. Now, through a combination of steel-capped will, acute self-visualisation and more than a little talent, the dream was within his grasp. He reacted by getting the worst kind of shakes. "Actually, I had my first panic attack about two weeks after 'Girls And Boys' entered the charts," he later confessed. "Everything had changed." Unfortunately, these panic attacks would worsen in the coming months, their level of severity concurrent with each new stage of Blur's blossoming fortunes.

That Albarn had to suffer such attacks for the sin of dreaming himself to stardom seemed a somewhat unjust reward for time and trouble served. Yet, across the Atlantic, Kurt Cobain had reacted far worse to the demands of fame. Long troubled by drug problems, uncertain health and various psychic wounds that simply refused to heal, Nirvana's frontman took his own life with a shotgun on April 5, 1994. A terrible waste, Cobain was just 27 years old. Having spearheaded the rise of grunge and become its most vocal, if reluctant spokesman, the fall out surrounding Kurt's suicide was immense. Candlelight vigils were held in various cities around the world, while Seattle briefly became a mausoleum to the songwriter's memory. Elsewhere, various commentators took to theorising about a 'Culture of despair' enveloping the young, with grunge's self-loathing lyrical content and links to hard drug use poured over in microscopic detail.

Blur were in a difficult position here. On the one hand, they were on the verge of a major breakthrough at home and abroad, 'Girls And Boys' opening a door to a potential level of fame it would hard to tolerate losing. But as anyone who had read a music paper in the last 18 months knew, they had also fought a one-band British war against grunge in general and America in particular. Worse, their pronouncements regarding Nirvana's worth were particularly sour. In callous terms, should Cobain's death bolster a new, sympathetic wave of interest in all things American, then Blur's previous growls of dissent might cast them as villains rather than heroes, thus ending any momentum thus far achieved. An acquaintance of Kurt and his wife Courtney Love since the two had visited Syndrome in 1991, Albarn chose to address such issues in an open and refreshingly honest manner. "It was very strange, actually," he said of Cobain's passing. "I'd just got through a month of working ridiculously hard, during which I went through 12 countries in ten days and was suffering from nervous exhaustion. It was horrible because, at the same time that I was on these covers looking like this ironic, chirpy Englishman, there were all these other covers with these harrowing pictures of this quite beautiful man who was the same age as me who killed himself. Just... horrible."

Truthfully, Kurt Cobain's death – while both tragic and wasteful – was to serve as a natural 'beginning of the end' to grunge's dominance of the international music scene. Like many before it, the movement may have been wide-ranging in its appeal, limitless in its potential selling power, but it was also ephemeral in its timescales. At some point, whether distant or near, grunge would inevitably have lost its youthful audience as they moved towards the impending responsibilities of adulthood – nappies and season tickets replacing CDs and posters. That such a fate was unfair or unjust was not at issue. It was simply the way things worked. After a respectful period of mourning for Cobain and what he represented, the search for new stars and sensations, scenes and cults would start all over again. Somewhat paradoxically, Blur were now well placed to lead that search back towards British soil. "I never said I hated America," Albarn made clear. "I simply think we've undervalued our own culture and overvalued theirs."

Though it didn't have an official name yet, Britain's newest pop movement held its first proper party at East London's Walthamstow Stadium on April 26, 1994 to mark the release of Blur's third album, *Parklife*. An auspicious gathering that included the likes of Food label mates Jesus Jones, shoegazing buddies Lush, The Cranberries, Pop Will Eat Itself and even veteran punk Eddie 'Tenpole' Tudor, Blur proved themselves genial, if very drunken hosts. For every old friend in attendance, there was also a new one keen to get in on the fun. Having just provided Blur with a fresh dance re-mix of 'Girls And Boys', The Pet Shop Boys came out of the studio and onto the dog track, as did surrealist comedian Eddie Izzard and nascent indie-rockers Sleeper. Elastica were also there to offer their support, Justine Frischmann's band having released their second single 'Line Up' only two months before. When questioned about the similarities between 'Line Up''s quirky, asymmetrical structure and Blur's own 'Girls And Boys', Frischmann was on top form. "We don't talk about that," she hissed. "Those sort of things cause divorce."

The night went exceedingly well until the Blur-sponsored 'Parklife Stakes' set things on an anarchic spin. First, one of the greyhounds got stuck in its trap, causing severe delays. When the race finally got underway, the track's electronic hare soon became derailed, causing chaos among the chasing hounds that were unsure whether to savage it or each other. As several attendants fought to calm the unfortunate animals down, the race was declared void. "All the people at the track were saying it was unprecedented," said Rowntree. "No one had ever seen anything like it in the history of dog racing." Strangely enough, the abandoned race proved a good omen for the band. "I didn't get my Trifecta, though," quipped Coxon.

As *Parklife*'s cover photograph illustrated, there was both rhyme and reason to Blur's choice of Walthamstow Stadium for the launch of their new record: with its two snarling greyhounds on the turn towards the finish line, Bob Thomas' lively image was a clever nod to one of the British working class' favourite pastimes. "That image came to a head when Damon actually bought shares in a greyhound," said Stylorouge's creative director Rob O'Connor. "The photographer couldn't believe we wanted it for a record cover. I'm sure if he'd thought about it, he'd have asked for a bit more money!" A perfect blend of high and low art, Thomas' shot resonated strongly with the band. "The greyhounds had an aggressiveness we liked," said Coxon. "We chose the ones with the most teeth. They look deranged, just longing to kill, (with these) bizarre looks on their faces. You don't get that look with a footballer... well, maybe a little bit." *Parklife*'s accompanying booklet continued the sporting theme. Designed to look like a racing chit, it also featured several shots of Blur taking in the action at the East End's most famous dog track. "In a way," Graham confirmed, "the *Parklife* sleeve is all intellect and no soul, but it's also sensational, graphic and perfect."*

With *Modern Life Is Rubbish*, Blur had raised a sturdy platform from which to promote their music and philosophy. With *Parklife*, they

* Destined to become one of the more enduring images of nineties UK pop, Bob Thomas' *Parklife* photo was subsequently honoured by the Royal Mail, who turned his work into a stamp as part of their 2010 'Classic Album Covers' series.

now added a set of "fuck off speakers" to shout that message from the rooftops. A crystal clear distillation of their influences, values and attitudes, the album's working title – 'British Pop 1965–82' – said it all, really. Dipped in mod and seasoned with 2 Tone, punk, glam, new wave and new romanticism were also present in each and every groove. It didn't end there: sixties beat groups, flashes of psychedelia and even the whiff of prog rock were never far from the surface either, making *Parklife* a compendium of classic old sounds presented in clever new ways. "By the time we did *Parklife*," said Alex, "we were coming off a good record, had been around for a few years, felt confident as musicians and had a great relationship with our producer, Stephen Street. In short, the stars had aligned and we were primed to explode."

As with many a classic album, *Parklife* began with a hit, this time provided by 'Girls And Boys'. Not particularly indicative of the record as a whole, 'Girls..." buoyant chorus nonetheless created an immediate sense of optimism in the listener, alerting them to pleasures yet to come. "'Girls And Boys'," concluded one critic, "is the sound of Duran Duran drowning in a beer barrel." Opening with a splash chord of which Pete Townshend would have been proud, Graham Coxon's rude guitar next announced the arrival of 'Tracy Jacks', immediately pulling Blur out of the materially-minded eighties and back to the swinging sixties. Its jaunty tones recalling both The Who and The Small Faces, there was also an unabashed element of XTC and Wire to 'Tracy Jacks', all those post-punk twitches providing spiky contrast in a tune honouring "Those great sixties 'name' songs like The Kinks' 'David Watts'." Away from the gentle pop tones of 'End Of The Century', 'Clover Over Dover' and the marvellously syrupy 'Badhead', *Parklife* also offered several sound musical thrashings. 'Bank Holiday' fused a Cardiacs-like love of speed-riffing with the blunt post-punk thrills of 'Hersham Boys'-era Sham 69, while 'Jubilee' borrowed David Bowie's platform boots (and the chorus from Toni Basil's immortal 'Mickey') to make its point. Bowie was again a reference on 'London Loves', though this time it was 'Fashion' rather than 'Suffragette City' to which Blur were doffing their musical cap. "Yes," admitted Coxon, "it does have a funky sort of Fripp/Bowie thing going on."

Though it was easy enough to accuse Blur of liberating the occasional chord sequence or even downright pastiche at times, the band could also turn their influences into something both clever and wonderful. 'Trouble At The Message Centre' was one such moment. An astringent, emotionally detached tune that owed a debt of gratitude to the shivery thrills of Tubeway Army and Magazine, 'Trouble...' was still very much Blur's own beast. Beginning with Albarn's echoing, mildly dissonant keyboard line, 'Trouble...' soon developed into a strange brew of off-kilter guitars and creeping rhythmic shunts, its structure climbing ever upwards before finally collapsing under its own weight. 'This Is A Low' was even better. Described by Graham as "a kind of musical psychedelic dream about a shipping forecast," the tune was dreamy and sombre all at once, Coxon's Flamenco-style flourishes steadily driving '...Low''s lilting verse towards one of the strongest, most poignant choruses Damon Albarn would ever write. "We wanted each song to be in its own little world on *Parklife*," said Coxon. By that definition, 'This Is A Low' was its very own island paradise, albeit with a British rain shower gathering overhead...

As with any great record, there were always a lame duck or downright oddity to help define how marvellous the other songs were. *Parklife* proved no exception. 'Magic America' was one step too far even by Blur's eccentric standards, its hokey chorus and squelching keyboard part a little too close to the theme tune of cult TV cartoon *Roobarb And Custard* for comfort. 'Far Out' also lived up to its title, with "guest lyricist/singer" Alex James crooning the names of various suns, moons and stars over a wobbling, sci-fi-sounding background. As a delightful homage to the bassist's growing interest in astronomy, 'Far Out' worked well enough. Whether it was worthy of inclusion on *Parklife* was perhaps another matter, even if James' casual vocal delivery did confer a certain charm. In keeping with their love of odd instrumentals, 'The Debt Collector' added Austrian 'Oom-pah' music to Blur's catalogue. Full of comedic brass parts and swirling saxophones (courtesy of Coxon), 'The Debt Collector' once again emphasised Damon's love affair with Kurt Weill and vintage music hall. This fact was driven home by *Parklife*'s closing track 'Lot 105'. Starting out like the credits sequence to some long-lost seventies sitcom, 'Lot 105' quickly transformed into a lunatic waltz, Coxon's 2 Tone guitar chops mutating into full blown tremolo madness within the space of one hot minute. "Arrangement-wise, we were gaining confidence by *Parklife*," Coxon later said. "We could read music to the extent that we could give a brass section a score to work from. We were starting to get some real control."

Parklife's wide breadth of musical influences, odd meters and kinetic arrangements was also mirrored in the instrumentation and sound effects used to realise them. From the gentle harpsichords and squealing seagulls on 'Clover Over Dover' to the *Space Invaders* keyboards and nudging brass parts of 'Jubilee', the album was one giant sonic experiment. Central to realising this approach was Damon Albarn, who had pulled out machine strings, melodicas, recorders, vibraphones, Moog synths and even radio traffic alerts to add texture and sinew to the songs. Coxon's performance was also superlative, the bespectacled one's multi-tracked lead on 'This Is A Low', skittering Fripp-isms on 'London Loves' and ringing, Smiths-like chord work on 'Badhead' all consolidating his position as 'England's pre-eminent alternative lead guitarist'. "Oh, do go away," he quipped to *Guitar* at the time. Not far behind were Dave Rowntree and Alex James, who had often been overshadowed in the race to shower Albarn and Coxon in critical garlands. In fact, Rowntree and James were now a fine, inventive rhythm section, using economy and occasionally silence to mark out their own space within the band. "It's not where you play," said Dave, "It's where you don't." This "now-you-see-us-now-you-don't" approach was nowhere more evident than on 'Tracy Jacks' where the duo completely disappeared at times, allowing just strings and vocals to inform the central melody. "The Smiths were one of those bands that could do any kind of song and be instantly recognisable," said Stephen Street. "Blur are the same. They work as a unit for the benefit of song."

Immaculately performed, impeccably produced and ringing with memorable tunes, *Parklife* was thus far a pleasure on the ear. Yet, to truly qualify as the perfect album Damon Albarn wanted it to be, the stories that sat atop the songs would have to equally flawless. In the end, he turned to the work of British author Martin Amis for necessary inspiration. "I read *London Fields* when Blur were on their second tour of America," he said. "It saved me." A pitch-black novel with murder at its heart, Amis' *London Fields* was full of comedy, introspection and foreboding, its plotline sinister and twisting, its characters feckless and unreliable. Set against a backdrop of social and moral decay, with nuclear war an omnipresent threat, Amis' bleak creations cheated and manipulated their way out of trouble until the author finally brought their lives to a close in a maze of uncertain endings. One of the nineties' finer literary achievements, *London Fields* was not only memorable for its unsavoury cast list (the petty criminal Keith Talent being particularly repellent), but also where Martin Amis chose to place them. While nominally set in the western part of the city, Amis' London was an almost imaginary terrain, its topography shifting to suit wherever the writer's fancy took him.

For Albarn, *London Fields*' mix of gritty reality and curious artifice provided the perfect solution in how to frame his own characters and locations throughout the lyrics of *Parklife*. "Until then, I'd been quite traditional in my reading – Bukowski, Bellow, Hesse – but *London Fields* gave me so many options. Martin Amis gave me a key to a language I was interested in... A sort of dirty, speedy London dialect which he uses, and (which) I wanted to use in my songs. I also liked the way he can flip between high and low culture." In fact, Damon was so taken with Amis' most intensely realised character, the fickle, capricious Keith Talent, he actually upped sticks with Justine Frischmann to live in West London. "(It's the line) Talent 'moved to the good area to the east of Ladbroke Grove'," he said. "Keith was so English and I just wanted to be him."

Armed with a new palette of dirty colours to draw from, Albarn's list of hapless misfits, ne'er-do-wells and aging matriarchs covered *Parklife* like a tragi-comic sore. In 'Jubilee', an exasperated banker watches his slovenly son fade into the family sofa, the boy gone "all divvy" from watching "too much telly". 'Bank Holiday' was equally observant, as a grandmother orders a new set of dentures to better eat her pizza crusts at a looming family party. 'Trouble At The Message Centre''s all-powerful switchboard operator was another choice creation, advising her irritated customers that, "There's no calls today, dear, you'll just have to wait, dear." And with 'Magic America''s Bill Barrett, Damon gave us a protagonist so deliberately gormless one actually felt sorry for him. "La la la la la, he wants to live in magic America, with all the magic people." The latest in Albarn's series of thinly veiled warnings about Britain falling prey to the charms of Uncle Sam, 'Magic America' was so vitriolic in its anti-US sentiments that Blur's frontman felt he had to offer an explanation. "I just feel physically unwell when I'm in America," he said. "I can't help that I have this America-phobia. I don't want us to come across as these venomous, anti-American Brits, but I find it hard to adapt to the scale of America. America eats us up. So I had to write that one seething little song and get it out of my system. It's more subtle than you think." Only if one were applying subtlety with a large sledge hammer.

Amid all the copulating teens ('Girls And Boys'), chain-smoking speed freaks ('London Loves') and *Quadrophenia*-referencing suicides ('Clover Over Dover'), there was also a genuinely touching soul in 'Tracy Jacks'. Career civil servant, possible cross dresser, failing in health and unsound of mind, '... Jacks' was 'Colin Zeal''s older, sicker cousin, a man for whom life pleasures have all but disappeared. "He's getting past forty, and all the seams are splitting." Cautioned by the police while "running round naked" on a trip to the seaside, *Parklife*'s saddest creation is swiftly returned from whence he came, only to knock down his own home with a bulldozer. Part Arnold Layne, part Reginald Perrin but always terribly British, 'Tracy Jacks' was a BBC mini-series in just four verses and a rotating stanza.

"With the characters of *Modern Life Is Rubbish*, they weren't so nocturnal," said Albarn. "They lived in the day and didn't get up to anything naughty. On this album, they start out in the daylight, (but) quickly descend into the darker regions of themselves." However, Damon was also at pains to point out that these characters were no idle imaginings. Instead, they came from wilful observation and close scrutiny of the culture surrounding him. "I do not adopt a 'persona' to write," he said. "It's just voyeurism. Madness or Ray Davies never wrote a story about themselves. They just told great stories."

Several years later, that sense of voyeurism had been stretched to include Albarn himself as part of the equation. "You just write about yourself and put yourself into somebody else's shoes," he told *Mojo* in 2000. "The darker the part of your personality you want to talk about, the more complicated the character becomes... and the more disguised, I suppose."

An album so successful in celebrating the ups and downs of life in a capital city that Dave Balfe had wanted to call it 'London' and put a fruit and vegetable cart on the cover, *Parklife* was a record of which Blur could be justly proud. Luckily for the band, most everyone thought so too. "Clever without being smug, stylish without being facile, and accessible without a trace of triteness or banality," wrote *Q*'s Stuart Maconie. "It's hard to see a pop guitar album coming anywhere near *Parklife* this year in terms of inventiveness, wit and intelligence." *NME*'s Johnny Dee was also running out of thumbs to raise. "Where Ray Davies saw the beauty of the skies over Waterloo Station, Damon Albarn sees it in the mirrorball above a Mykonos dance floor. So often cast aside as a joke, a band who would turn up at the opening of a door if the invite included a free can of Heineken, Blur have made what will undoubtedly be seen as the greatest pop album of 1994. It is easy to forget that albums can be this fabulous."

A lone, if not quite dissenting voice in the wilderness, *Melody Maker*'s Simon Price was less sure, pointing heads toward the reality behind Blur's dog-loving, beer-swilling, London-centric image. "Like Morrissey, Blur are bourgeois indie softies who like a bit of rough," he said. "Maybe The Rolling Stones are a better analogy – nice middle class boys kidding the world they were East End yobs. Blur would actually have us believe that they are Essex lager louts. Nice try, bless 'em, but they'll always be more 'Itchycoo Park' than Upton Park. I like Blur, but I can't quite love them. Maybe it's because I'm not a Londoner..." Technically, neither were three members of Blur. But Albarn had brought a skewed romance to *Parklife* that only someone transplanted from the city at such an impressionable age could muster.

While several points raised by Simon Price would come back to haunt Blur soon enough, *Parklife*'s momentum could not be stopped by one cautious review. With 'Girls And Boys' alerting the general public something marvellous might be on the horizon and a distinct crackle of change in the air following the sad death of Kurt Cobain, the band were in Alex James' words "primed to explode". And so they did. A week after its release on April 25, 1994, *Parklife* debuted on the UK album charts at number one. The wait was over. Blur were officially stars. "Britain was waiting for a band who could walk it like they talked it, if you will," said James. "Suede had set things up – certainly in a press sense – but they still hadn't sold that many records. So when 'Girls And Boys' came out, that was it. We were off and running."

With a Top Five single and number one album in their hands, Blur were now ready to meet their adoring public face-to-face. Beginning an 18-date tour at Nottingham's Rock City on May 10, 1994, the band travelled across the UK, providing audiences in Wolverhampton, Bristol, Glasgow and several other cities a chance to see what all the fuss was about. With Sleeper providing attractive support, Blur's set list incorporated several new tracks from *Parklife*, including 'Tracy Jacks' and an anarchic 'Jubilee'. To give those new to the group something to focus on during the older material, Blur kindly provided a huge mirrorball above the stage while three giant lampshades towered over the amps. By the time the band got to London for two sold-out shows at Shepherds Bush Empire on May 26 and 27, they were on fire. "The Blur show is all high art, arch campness and lo-fi pantomime," observed *NME*, "with a little punk rock thrown in as well." Sadly, as Alex James stalked the boards in Shepherds Bush, his new flat in the heart of London's West End was being burgled. "There was a keyboard missing and some other stuff, but I hadn't really noticed," said the bassist. "Actually, I couldn't really bring myself to care. I don't give money to beggars in the street, so fair's fair, I suppose."

As Blur marked the end of their first round of UK gigs at Leeds' Town & Country Club on May 31 (the show was filmed by *MTV*), another single was released from their best-selling album. A winsome ballad in the French chanson style, 'To The End' was the only track on *Parklife* not to have been recorded at Maison Rouge studio or produced by Stephen Street. Full of lush orchestration, swooping strings and a choric refrain "sung entirely Francais" by Stereolab's Lætitia Sadier, 'To The End' was actually cut at London's RAK Studios under the guidance of Stephen Hague and long-time Blur associate John Smith. A quiet, methodical American whose first production credit was Malcolm McClaren's hugely influential 1984 hit 'Madame Butterfly', Hague's subsequent clients had included Pet Shop Boys, OMD, PiL and New Order. At demo stage, 'To The End''s French vocal interpositions had been provided by Justine Frischmann, and a very good job she did too. But feeling that an appearance alongside her boyfriend might be a tad vulgar – and possibly undermine Elastica's carefully constructed indie cred – Justine stepped aside, allowing native Parisian Sadier to take up the reins.

The result was another feather in Albarn's ever-growing musical cap. Having successfully tackled post-Edwardian-style instrumentals, Austrian-themed brass ostinato and even faux-Ronnie Hazlehurst TV tunes, 'To The End' now added French torch songs to his tally. Having loved Terry Jacks' take on Jacques Brel's caustic 'Seasons In The Sun' as a child, there was also something of a circle being completed here, as Damon handed in his own sweet/sour take on the perils of love. Written from the perspective of a couple trading insults and intimate asides from the bottom of their wine glasses, 'To The End' was pitched metaphorically higher than the more earthbound concerns of 'Girls And Boys' but was none the worse for it. "Been drinking far too much," sang Damon's young lover, "... neither of us can think straight anymore." To strengthen the single's chances, Blur flew to Prague with director David Mould where they filmed scenes for 'To The End''s moody, atmospheric video. Shot entirely in black and white, and based on the cult 1961 French New Wave movie *Last Year At Marienbad,* the promo cast Damon and Graham as penguin-suited rivals warring for the affections of a mystery brunette. Suffice to say, it did not end well for her or them. All a tad pretentious perhaps, but 'To The End' again found Blur admirably stretching their boundaries, and without a whiff of Britishness to boot. Regrettably, after the fun and frolics of 'Girls And Boys', it was a stretch too far for the British public, who awarded the tune with a number 16 placing in the charts.*

Unlike previous singles, Blur could easily absorb their disappointment with 'To The End''s relatively stunted performance. Still riding high in the charts after several months, *Parklife* was well on its way to 300,000 sales by the time the band returned to the UK following a 16-date European tour in late June. Its unit tally rose even further by the end of the month, as thousands of punters crammed into Michael Eavis' muddy fields to witness Blur's return to Glastonbury. Performing on the *NME* (or second) stage, the quartet were in excellent, if extremely theatrical form for the festival crowds. In honour of nearby Stonehenge, Albarn took to the boards in druid's robes, while Coxon paid inadvertent tribute to Salisbury army base 40 odd miles away by dressing head to toe in combat gear. Opening with the mad strains of 'Lot 105', Blur turned in a fine set that included no less than ten of *Parklife*'s 16 tracks, thus ensuring that even those living under a rock for several months (and there were surely several hundred at Glastonbury) could not escape their latest wares. Somewhat surprisingly, Blur only appeared second on the bill, with headlining status given to space rockers Spiritualized. It was an understandable oversight. Having booked their slot months before *Parklife* began its attack on the British charts, no one in their right mind could have imagined how far the group would come in such a short time.

While Blur returned to Europe to take advantage of the financially lucrative summer festival circuit, Food geared up promotional activities on the home front for the band's next single. To no one's great surprise, it turned out to be the album's title track 'Parklife'. First demoed in May 1993 at Putney's Ritz Rehearsal Studios, Stephen Street had leapt

* Always sure of its worth, Blur re-recorded 'To The End' with French singer/actress Francoise Hardy in early 1995. Given the slightly extended title 'To The End (La Comedie)', Albarn sang his verses in French this time around. "I loved doing that and Francoise is the perfect singer for the song," he said. 'To The End (La Comedie)' was released as a single in France and later found its way onto various Blur UK box sets and B-sides.

on the song when he heard it. "It was going to be a huge hit," he said. "There was no doubt about that." But there were problems. Albarn wanted 'Parklife' to have a narrative feel, the verses spoken rather than sung. Yet, when he attempted to voice the character he had written, it all fell a bit flat. "I didn't think I was Cockney enough," he said. "So I thought 'Fuck it. Phil Daniels can do it'."

Since Damon and Graham were old enough to buy their own videos, they had been in love with Phil Daniels. North London born and bred, the actor was a graduate of Islington's Anna Scher Theatre School, making his debut at the age of 17 in Alan Parker's 1976 kiddie gangster pic, *Bugsy Malone*. From there he had picked up roles in various TV series and plays – including the cult ITV drama *Raven* – before landing the job that for people of a certain age would forever define him: ultra-Mod Jimmy Cooper in 1979's *Quadrophenia*. Nominally based on The Who's ground-breaking rock opera, *Quadrophenia* took some of Pete Townshend's finest songs and turned them into an often funny, but ultimately grim movie detailing Jimmy's journey from pill-popping optimist to jaded cynic. Set amid London's shabbiest night clubs and the untidy splendour of Brighton beach, *Quadrophenia* was really a hymn to sixties mod life, its images of Parka-clad clans scootering up and down the A23 often more important than the actual dialogue. That said, Daniels' depiction of the rapidly unravelling Jimmy was sharp as a tack, channelling all the nervous energy, earthy romanticism and cod-philosophising of Townshend's original protagonist.

By the time Blur were cutting *Parklife* in the autumn/winter of 1993, Phil Daniels had long moved on from being Jimmy Cooper. In fact, he was then treading the boards of London's Shaftesbury Theatre as roustabout Jigger Craigin in Rodgers & Hammerstein's fairground musical, *Carousel*. But Albarn was still convinced he could put the actor's sparkling Cockney accent to good use. Phone calls were made. "I played football with Steve Sutherland, the editor of *NME*," Phil remembered, "and he mentioned that some young band wanted to do something with me. I said 'That sounds like a bit of fun', so I went off to some studio near Chelsea and met the boys."

If Blur were expecting a sharp-suited mod to stride confidently into Maison Rouge, they were in for a big surprise. In keeping with Jigger Craigin's vagabond image, a loose-jean wearing Daniels arrived at the studio replete with full beard and scruffy hair. Despite the radical change of appearance, he was still Jimmy Cooper to Blur. "They were massive fans," Phil said. "Graham was mad about *Quadrophenia* and kept on quoting me bits of dialogue." At first, Damon actually wanted Daniels to voice the character of 'The Debt Collector', but when lyrical inspiration failed to strike, the tune remained instrumental and the actor's talents were placed elsewhere. "Yeah, I had him in mind for that," the singer said. "But then I thought 'He could do 'Parklife' instead. It really was that random." Directed by Albarn and Street – "(They said) 'a bit faster, a bit slower', those are the only things I respond to" – Phil's contribution to the song took only three takes and 30 minutes. "It was over in a jiffy!"

Happy accident or not, Phil Daniels' involvement with 'Parklife' turned out to be a stroke of genius on Blur's part. Over a clattering background of low-velocity brass stabs and fiercely struck guitars, the actor took Albarn's words and turned them into a verbal assault on the senses. Cast as a cynical Cockney "giving it large" to passers-by as he strolls through his local park, Daniels' surreal chatter about well-fed sparrows, erectile dysfunction, rotating joggers and early-to-rise dustmen was funny, infectious and if truth be told, all a bit mad. "In *Quadrophenia*, Phil Daniels' character reflected all the things I love and hate in British culture," Damon later confirmed, "I've now met a lot of people I once idolised and he's one of the few who's even better in real life."

Riddled with memorable catchphrases and featuring a chorus most bands would happily kill for, 'Parklife' was another potential monster in the making. To make sure of it, Food hired film maker Pedro Romhanyi to direct a suitably eye-catching video. Daft as brush from start to finish, the final product had Daniels and Albarn playing a pair of oily double glazing salesmen, while Rowntree and James hammed it up as happy couple 'Ken And Cindy', the bassist dressed in drag especially for the occasion. All the good roles now gone, Coxon was forced to put on a fat suit to play 'Parklife''s least endearing character, the gym-shy 'Gut Lord Marching'.

With its barking dogs, laughing children and smashing glass (the dogs and children were both sound effects, while Rowntree really broke the glass), 'Parklife' had all the makings of the perfect summer hit, perhaps even taking Blur back to the top of the charts. Yet, when released on August 22, 1994, the single stalled at a number ten. Not bad, but not quite what the band, their producer or record company were expecting. "We thought it would be bloody huge," said Ross. Of course, there were several possible reasons for 'Parklife''s confusing fate. By the time the single hit stores, its parent album had already been awarded a Gold disc (500,000 sales), with talk of the record going Platinum (one million sales) in a matter of weeks. Obviously, it was now only the hardcore that would buy 'Parklife' for the B-side materials it offered. More, despite the song's undoubted worth, it also had a whiff of novelty record about it that might have put off the more discerning or serious music fan. Perhaps everyone went on holiday the week it was released. We will never know. Whatever the case, in subsequent years, 'Parklife' was to take on a life all of its own, serving as football anthem, pub singalong and background music in a hundred TV comedy, documentary and sports shows. When used as backing accompaniment for adverts, it was also hugely successful, with *Coca-Cola*, *Chanel* and *Nike* all aligning their brand to Blur's little tune at one time or another. "I guess when people think of us, they do think of 'Parklife'... especially in England," Albarn later said. "But whether it's our best song, well, that's another thing entirely..."

While 'Parklife' patiently waited to assume its iconic status, Blur got with the business of promoting their third album. Chancing their arm once again across the Atlantic, the band played nine shows in various US cities during September, including New York, Atlanta and LA. However, audience numbers seldom strayed above 1,000, a figure Blur could now reasonably expect to see them off at an airport back home. "The Blur audience in America is the most dysfunctional of all the dysfunctional tribes," Albarn sighed.

Given the immensely British contents of *Parklife* and Damon's continued rubbishing of grunge/slacker culture, it was perhaps a miracle anyone turned up at all. "Slacker culture says nothing to us about our lives. I believe we've sold ourselves as a nation, and we're so far down that road it's gone beyond anger," he told *The Face* in 1994. "American imperialism is endemic now – it's as much a part of (our) culture as all things British. But I believe America will reject slacker culture. They'll see it as useless and unproductive. They'll need bands that smile... take the piss and have a bit of cavort. (They'll need) something that isn't all aggression and neurosis." For the moment at least, America was content to decide what it needed, and it wasn't Blur.

Still, Albarn's intense sentiments continued to reap a fine harvest at home, and for the most part, anywhere that didn't fly a Stars and Stripes flag to identify its borders. In a blaze of activity towards the end of 1994, Blur were a ubiquitous presence across the UK, Europe and the Far East. October found the band performing a slew of concerts in Germany, Italy, Holland, France and Spain, while the following month they journeyed to Japan for a nine-date tour. Three years before, Blur could count their Japanese fan base as two giggling girls with a video camera. But a combination of hummable songs and cheeky smiles had changed all that. Continuing a rich tradition that began with The Beatles and reached a crescendo with Duran Duran, Blur were the latest British pop group to be drawn to the collective bosom of Japan's pop-mad teens. "It was absolute madness," said an impressed James. From the minute they stepped off the airplane, the band were followed everywhere by fans wanting them to sign album sleeves, teddy bears, and on the odd occasion, items of clothing that did little to prevent colds and flu. Seizing an opportunity to make capital from Blur's new status as "Pop gods", EMI Japan released a hastily assembled collection of flip sides, rarities and live tracks under the title: *Blur Present 'The Special Collectors Edition'*.

Though the financial motives behind the album's release were woefully transparent, *...Special Collectors Edition* served to test the theory that a band's true worth could be judged by the quality of its B-sides. Overall, Blur did better than most. Of the 18 tracks on show, 'Peach' was a real stand-out, its simple, evocative structure recalling a woozy Sunday afternoon spent at London's UFO club, circa 1967. A particular favourite of Albarn's, 'Peach' made good use of the battered Harmonium the singer had picked up for £20 in a Clapham music store. "He spent about £1,000 doing it up, though," laughed James. Married to Coxon's pulsing guitar, the old Victorian pump organ provided a lush undercurrent over which Damon sang of loaded guns and birds' nests. 'Badgeman Brown' was another sixties-themed affair, again confirming the depth of Blur's affections for the wayward Syd Barrett. Written for the soundtrack of a proposed arthouse film the band were supposed to make with Pink Floyd album cover artist Storm 'Hipgnosis' Thorgeson ("It all came to nothing"), '...Brown' remained a cunning update of Syd's immortal 'Vegetable Man'. "Dave Balfe and Andy Ross fucking hated it," said Graham.

'Es Schmecht', on the other hand, was choppy, angular and thoroughly modern. A misspelling of the German phrase 'Es schmeckt', meaning 'It tastes good', the song was heavily influenced by Krautrockers Can, right down to Alex's whirling, high octave bass line. But it was an old *Modern Life Is Rubbish* outtake called 'When The Cows Come Home' that really illustrated the tortures Blur had to go through when deciding which tracks made an album's final running order. Full of melodic surprises, its melding of *Magical Mystery Tour*-period Beatles and music hall brass was probably as good as anything on *Modern Life...*, yet it still failed to make the cut. "Songs are like your babies," continued Coxon. "It's horrible letting them go..."

One tune that might have been better served staying put on *Parklife* rather than making its own way in the world was 'End Of A Century'. Instead it became the fourth and final single to be released from the album. Much loved by Damon, Stephen Street and Andy Ross, even if Graham was less sure of its charms, '...Century' did have much to commend it: Cut from the same melodic cloth as 'Tracy Jacks', though much more doleful and resolute, the song's blend of sighing harmonies and keening trombone made for easy listening. Equally, Albarn's vocal – a masterclass of elongated vowels – was undeniably pleasant on the ear. But the singer's tale of a boy and girl more content to nestle together by the light of the TV than paint the town red was at times as musically lethargic as its subject matter. Making its way into stores on

November 7, 1994, 'End Of A Century' ground to a halt at number 18 before beginning its resigned descent back down the charts.

If 'End Of A Century' didn't quite capture the hearts and minds of the public, its accompanying video rubberstamped the growing eminence of Blur as a live act. Filmed at the band's appearance at north London's Alexandra Palace on October 7, 1994, the '...Century' promo was a perfect snapshot of one of the year's better gigs. Mirroring Glastonbury before it, when the band booked Ally Pally for their only London show of the autumn, there were serious doubts they could fill the venue. A huge aircraft-hanger of a place, it easily housed an audience of 8,000 with further room to swing a few dozen cats. Yet, such worries proved unfounded. Tickets for the event sold out in under a week, with buses even arranged to ferry punters to the gig and back from a pick-up point in Trafalgar Square. With benefit of hindsight, 'Parklife at the Palace' proved itself a pre-cursor for was about to come in British music. Opening the show were Supergrass. Alternative pop-rockers from Oxford who were still three weeks away from releasing their first single 'Caught By The Fuzz', Supergrass were full of tunes and cheek, their mutton-chopped frontman Gaz Coombes charming early arrivals away from the bar and into the main hall.

Further up the bill were Pulp, who had recently supported Blur on their fifth US tour. Unlike Supergrass, Jarvis Cocker's men (and woman) had been around in one form or another since the halcyon days of 1978. But the band's latest album *His 'N' Hers* had just nudged its way into the UK Top Ten and great things were now expected. Like Albarn, Cocker had always been obsessed with the minutiae of British life, all those furiously twitching curtains and hair-blocked sinks providing able subject matter for his pithy, sardonic lyrics. But unlike the eighties, when such lyrical concerns were often overshadowed by multi-platinum tales of avarice and materialism, British audiences were now demanding clever tunes about more down-to-earth concerns. Again, like Albarn, Jarvis Cocker could easily answer their call.

'Parklife at the Palace' proved a triumphant night for Blur. On stage for the best part of two hours, the band played 21 songs in all, with 'She's So High', 'There's No Other Way' and the great lost single

'Popscene' all recalled to their set. Away from this re-introduction of old friends, there were many other highlights. Freed from its studio constraints, 'Trouble At The Message Centre' took on a more frantic feel and delivery, causing Dave to almost tear a hole in his snare drum during the track's nervy mid-section. Always so coy on record, 'Magic America' also benefitted from its transfer from tape to hall, those wide-open chords allowing Graham to get in touch with his inner anarchist. Parklife's spry B-side 'Supa Shoppa' even gave Blur a chance to indulge their instrumental prowess, Albarn whizzing across the keys as Alex boogied along on bass. From the bingo caller who introduced the band to the disco lights that accompanied 'Girls And Boys', the onus at Ally Pally was always going to be on fun. As if to prove the point, Phil Daniels emerged just past the hour to join Blur for a chaotic rendition of 'Parklife', the actor as adept at pogo-ing as Damon himself. Yet, it was the show's closing track that lingered most in the memory.

'This Is A Low' had all but killed Damon Albarn during the recording of *Parklife*. Constantly struggling with the melody, the singer even took the song on holiday to Cornwall with him and his parents over the Christmas of 1993 in an effort to complete it. By early February 1994, it still lacked a definitive lyric and time was running out. Albarn was due in hospital for an imminent hernia operation and the band's block booking at Maison Rouge studios was nearly at an end. With his back to the wall, Damon turned to a small present Alex James had given him over the festive season. Bought from a travel shop in London's Covent Garden, the handkerchief in question had a map of Great Britain printed on it, replete with its shipping regions. Starting in one corner (The Bay of Biscay), Albarn kept turning the hankie until he had a sad-eyed traveller's tale of a journey around the British Isles. Replete with images of stalled traffic at Dogger Bank, Thameside taxi ranks and mad monarchs jumping off Cornish cliffs, the words fair popped off the page. There was a new title too. Originally called 'We Are A Low' (possibly a reference to heroin use), the song's central phrase now reflected both a character and a country living under rainy skies, waiting for the sun to break through. "It was just bloody marvellous," said Stephen Street.

Almost perfect on record, 'This Is A Low''s combination of keening verse and troubled, yet up-lifting chorus was just as good live, marking a natural end to Blur's Alexandra Palace experience, and indeed, many a show thereafter.*

There was one more gig for Blur to attend to before they could call it quits for 1994. However, it was played in neither a giant shed nor muddy field. Instead, the band ventured back to Colchester Sixth Form College just before Christmas to perform at a charity event organised by their former music teacher Nigel Hildreth. Keen to find new ways to raise funds for an Indian orphanage, Hildreth had contacted Keith Albarn with the idea of Damon and Graham returning to their old stomping ground to sign autographs for the cause. "Damon immediately dismissed that idea and put forward the suggestion that he bring the whole band, to do what he at first described as an acoustic set with the college orchestra," said Hildreth. Albarn's proposal didn't end there. "He also suggested that I could get the students to arrange Blur's music and that the orchestra could even play on stage with the band. Suffice to say, the tickets for the show were sold out in a matter of minutes. Some students didn't even believe it was happening."

On December 16, 1994, Blur arrived at Colchester railway station with several distinguished guests in tow. "Q magazine were there to cover the event and we therefore had a press embargo," confirmed Hildreth. "The BBC also came along to make *a Kaleidoscope* production for radio with Miranda Sawyer hosting."

Security was tight around the event. Five years before, the band could have walked the length and breadth of the town without an eyebrow being raised, but now things were different. Blur's appearance was kept under close wraps amid genuine fears the small gym in which the concert was to be played would be invaded by hundreds of uninvited fans. Thankfully, while a few strays turned up to knock at the windows, it all went off without a glitch. "The concert was a great success," said Nigel. "My orchestra rehearsed, amended and cut some bits of

* Blur's Alexandra Palace gig was released on video as *Showtime* in February, 1995. Sadly, the concert has never been updated to a DVD format.

the arrangements. Then we added some other elements so that we performed pretty comfortably."

Kicking off at five in the afternoon, Blur played a 15 song, hour long set, during which time they were joined onstage by Hildreth's orchestra for six tunes including 'End Of A Century', 'Tracy Jacks', 'To The End' and of course, 'Parklife'. For Albarn, an old debt was finally being repaid. "Nigel Hildreth gave me and Graham a real confidence about doing a lot of things," he told the BBC on the night. "Neither of us was incredibly proficient, so he gave us the confidence to busk it, really." With band, crew and engineers all giving up their time for free, Blur's return to Colchester raised £3,000 for Hildreth's chosen charity and a few quid more for the local landlord. "The performance was a real buzz and we all had a great time," said the teacher. "Afterwards we all went into the nearby town for a drink, going first to the Hole In The Wall pub and then later – after I had had something to eat with Mr and Mrs Coxon – to Colchester Arts Centre."

Blur's Colchester adventure marked a fitting end to a golden year for the band. Having begun 1994 under a pile of broken guitar strings and unfinished lyrics, they had ended it with their old music teacher conducting a 17-piece orchestra to several of their hits. All in all, it wasn't a bad return for 12 months' hard work. "'Girls And Boys' was a proper pop single, 'To The End' was a big-boned ballad, 'Parklife' was 'football' and then we had 'End Of A Century' which was again another pretty pop song," reasoned Damon. "We were sending out all the right signals to people who weren't necessarily drawn to alternative music, and it worked."

For once, Damon was actually understating the case. By the end of 1994, *Parklife* was well past the one million sales mark and chasing after a second platinum disc. By anyone's estimations, this was impressive stuff. "That level of success?" said Food's dazed, but exuberant Andy Ross. "Of course I didn't bloody expect it! To be honest, we'd have been happy to have shifted 200,000."

When assessing extreme levels of commercial success, it is sometimes difficult to understand why a particular band or album gains such affection with the public. Thankfully, this was the not the case with

Blur or *Parklife*. A wonderfully judged record full of wonderfully played tunes, *Parklife* was vital, entertaining, and crucially, arrived at a time when pop's tectonic plates were again shifting back from America to Britain.

"*Parklife* perfectly captured the moment," Dave Rowntree told *The O-Zone*. "That's the qualification for a truly great album, the ability to capture the moment. We went from being a struggling 'Music Press' band to being household names in a few months. That took some doing." There was one more thing the drummer wished to add. "Somewhere along the way, we also inadvertently invented Britpop..."

Things moved quickly now.

Chapter Nine

A Brief Word About Britpop

By early 1995, Britpop had swept across the UK like some benevolent airborne virus, bestowing upon its sufferers a combined sense of euphoria, a swelling in national pride and a soundtrack to get very drunk to. Described as a movement, it really was more a media invention, drawing together for a short time several mildly similar bands under one mutually beneficial umbrella. Yet, even the most hardened cynic would concede that Britpop was possibly the best thing to have happened to the British music industry in nearly three decades. Easy on the eye, exciting to the ear, and for record companies a source of extraordinary profit, Britpop shattered the notion that the UK's days as a quality exporter of international tunes had ended when The Beatles split up. At the forefront of Britpop, of course, were Blur. To understand how that came to pass one had to backtrack a little, first exploring recent events in the music press, then panning the search a little wider.

Unsurprisingly, the phrase 'Britpop' wasn't even new. Musician/ journalist John Robb had used it in *Sounds* during the late Eighties to describe a cluster of indie/alternative bands then making tentative waves on the music scene: The La's, The Stone Roses, Inspiral Carpets, The Bridewell Taxis. All were from the North of England. Most with similar haircuts. Some destined to succeed, others less so. But apart from a shared love of circular guitar riffs and rotating arpeggios, the similarities between these bands were often outweighed by their differences. More, the groups wished to be judged on their own merits, and not as some imagined whole. With nothing to be gained from it, *Sounds* dropped the term and all concerned moved on to varying degrees of notoriety.

In the meantime, the music press continued their search for home-grown talent that could be hastily assembled under a new flag of convenience. The benefits, after all, were measurable and lasting. Heavy metal. Punk. The new romantics. Each movement had begun with one or two bands leading the charge, only to be followed by a hundred, sometimes a thousand others. If played correctly, everyone would benefit. The groups got coverage, the record companies got product and the press got something to write about. Of course, the music weeklies' timing had to be perfect to make it all work. Hang onto a movement too long, and one risked going under with it. Let go too soon, or worse, run with the wrong alternative and circulation dropped. *NME* were often brilliant at the game. *Sounds*, which ceased publication in 1991, were sadly not.

As stated, in the years leading up to 1994, there had been several worthy attempts to find a cohesive movement to champion at home. For reasons of geography, analogous drum patterns and like-minded drug habits, 'Madchester' had worked a treat. It even allowed a few of John Robb's original 'Britpop' bands to be recycled under a new catchphrase. Madchester's scruffier offshoot 'baggy' was not quite as successful, however, its momentum lost somewhere in the long grass despite a strong start. With 'shoegazing' and 'the scene that celebrates itself', there was also some sense of early promise, but finding an apt band to push from the clubs into the stadiums from either camp was always going to be hard work. Then, seemingly from nowhere came 'The New Wave Of New Wave' or 'NWONW', and the typewriters were ringing again. Arriving at the gate at the precise time grunge was beginning to wobble, NWONW at least had a sense of energy and purpose to commend it. Of equal importance was that the groups being rallied under its flag sounded vaguely alike. From S★M★A★S★H and These Animal Men to Done Lying Down and Compulsion, the onus was on fast, frenetic songs played with real abandon: the lyrics acerbic, pointed and sharp, the image snarly, spiky and trim. Taking its lead from seventies punk icons such as The Clash, The Stranglers and Wire, NWONW certainly read well on the pages of *NME*. Sadly, what it didn't have was a preponderance of good tunes. Unlike 'London Calling', 'No More Heroes' or even 'I Am The Fly', one could not easily hum the chorus to S*M*A*S*H's '(I Want To) Kill Everybody' or Done Lying Down's 'Septic'. Attitude in abundance, they had. Crossover appeal, they had not.

Elsewhere, some progress had been made in finding that "Next big thing." In Suede, British pop at last had a genuine prospect on its hands. Armed with tunes and attitude to spare, the band were also in possession of a bombastic theatricality seldom witnessed since David Bowie threw a camp arm around Mick Ronson's shoulders on *TOTP* in 1972. Quick to rise, Suede's self-titled debut album was for a short period the UK's fastest selling record by a new band, an achievement rubberstamped by the committee for the Mercury Music Prize who honoured it with 'Best Album' of 1993. But shoehorning the group into an opportune movement was not without its difficulties for music journalists. When singer Brett Anderson appeared on the cover of *Select*'s 'Union Jack' issue of April 1993 under the banner 'Yanks Go Home', the best the magazine could find in the way of possible allies was Pulp, The Auteurs and Denim. Fine bands all, but comparing Brett Anderson to Jarvis Cocker or Luke Haines was akin to comparing distressed leather with herringbone.

There was another issue to contend with. If a blanket scene was to take off on the shoulders of one group, that group had to be truly reflective of its culture and time. Again, in this respect, Suede were a difficult sell. All clever angles and well-lit cheekbones, the band visually recalled the chilly drama of Bauhaus as much as the outlandish allure of Roxy Music. As such, Suede were always destined to be more cult act than true mainstream attraction – a cult that could number its followers in the hundreds of thousands perhaps – but a cult nonetheless. In reality, that was just the way Brett Anderson seemed to want it. Raised on a diet of Bowie and a little bit of The Smiths on the side, the Suede frontman's obsessions with sex, gender bending and the seedier side of human experience marked him as a man apart, with little or no interest in the celebrations about to start outside the walls of his bedroom. "I'd always been fascinated by suburbia and I liked to throw these twisted references to small-town British life into songs," he later said, "but we were never (going) to the party with the new lads..."

While Anderson might have held them in some disdain, the "new lads" were about to become mightily important as enthusiastic backers of the approaching Britpop phenomenon. In May 1994, a magazine was launched bearing the proud motto 'For men who should know better'. The brainchild of Mick Bunnage, Tim Southwell and former *NME* editor James Brown, *Loaded* was a celebration of all things male, its manifesto clearly detailed in Brown's first editorial. "*Loaded...* is dedicated to life, liberty and the pursuit of sex, drink (and) football. *Loaded* is music, film, relationships, humour, hard news and popular culture. *Loaded*," concluded the Editor, "is for the man who believes he can do *anything*, if only he wasn't so hung over. As Phil Lynott so wisely said, 'The boys are back in town'."

With its cover photo of Brit actor Gary Oldman puffing busily on a cigarette, its accompanying headline "Super lads... play to win," and scantily clad "Brit babe" Elizabeth Hurley contained within its pages, *Loaded* wasn't going to win any prizes for political correctness. What it did do, however, was capture a mood and mentality that had been brewing nicely in pubs and clubs for the last couple of years: in short, British males celebrating British values in exceedingly British ways. Within six months, *Loaded*'s circulation had hit the 350,000 mark, impressive for an established periodical, astounding for one just launched.

Only a fool would deny Blur were ahead of the game here, both in terms of opportunity and influence. Since 1992 and 'Popscene', the band had been banging a drum for home grown music, their stand against grunge singular at the time, now eerily prescient. *Modern Life...* had developed the conceit to new heights – the songs and attitude discernibly British, the band's image a natural accompaniment. And without doubt, Blur's image was always a key factor in the band's fortunes. Even in their baggiest days, they had reflected the fashion around them, the bowl haircuts, loose jeans and striped T-shirts putting little, if no distance between them and their fans. For a brief period, of course, they almost lost it. Damon's newfound affection for sharp suits and Graham's love of a good boating jacket confused the crowds at Glastonbury in 1992, a case of too much, too soon. The bull mastiffs and bovver boots of 1993 were no great improvement, causing the band to be labelled Xenophobic, or worse. But by 1994, Blur had got their Mojo working again, the casual trainers, sportswear, Harringtons and tweeds all acting as reflective surfaces to both their core audience and newer fans.

And then there was the message itself. A "one-man quote machine", Damon Albarn's mouth had been running in fifth gear for the best part of three years when it came to restoring matters of national pride. Anti-American imperialism, anti-grunge, antithetical in fact, to all but the notion that British music and culture had to reclaim its place at the top of the proverbial heap. This in itself would not have mattered greatly if *Parklife* had not backed up the rhetoric, but with one million sales and counting, any such problem had been alleviated. Blur equalled British, and suddenly, British equalled all things good. To bookend the idea, there was also the matter of how the band had chosen to comport themselves on the way to the top. Though it nearly did for them at the Town and Country Club in July 1992, Blur had – with one exception we will return to shortly – continued to count drink among their greatest pleasures. From Pernod with everything at Syndrome to the pint pot featured on the cover of the *Parklife* single, Blur and alcohol were synonymous. "We're just boozers," said Alex at the time. "Really, that's what we are. It's as bad as anything else, but you get spared the claptrap. It's a good pop drug."

No great thing for their livers, obviously, but entirely complimentary with where Britain found itself in 1994. As *Loaded*'s meteoric ascent confirmed, men were in the mood to celebrate being men again, and that deserved a drink. Or several drinks. However, getting in touch with one's inner beer monster wasn't strictly confined to the male of the species. In fact, since the early eighties, binge drinking had been steadily on the rise among Britain's female population, creating a party culture where young men and women went toe to toe and glass for glass with each other. This behaviour often reached its zenith in the clubs of cheap holiday destinations like Ibiza, Faliraki and Aya Napa, where British youths drank themselves to near oblivion before taking the party back to their bedrooms, or as likely, the nearest beach. To his credit, Albarn had captured it all brilliantly with 'Girls And Boys', his talk of herds, beer-addled brain cells and sexual opportunism ironically providing a soundtrack to all the "drinking and shagging".

Of course, Blur ran no obvious risk of being aligned with 'New lad' culture until 1994. As a band – and a young one at that – their behaviour was more likely judged against a rich history of off-the-hook pop stars than some emergent social phenomenon. If charged with boorishness, incivility or just plain bad manners, they could always play the artistic card. And frequently did. "We think of ourselves as sensitive lager louts," Albarn once said, while Alex James went one better. "We're hooligans with vision, if you will, more chaps than lads." But the fact remained they were the only group ever to confirm their drummer was in the pub rather than the studio in the liner notes of an album. "Dave Rowntree," ran the credits of *Modern Life...*'s 'Miss America', "The Plough, Bloomsbury." In the end, Blur's own gift for laddishness again dovetailed perfectly with where Britain was heading in the mid-nineties. From Damon's beery obsession with football, Alex and Dave's occasional punch-ups with other musicians and Graham once listing his home address as 'The Good Mixer, Camden Town', Blur didn't so much tick all the boxes as drown them in lager.

That Blur had engineered their own rise to the forefront of British music in 1994 was also incontestable. Confident in their position, sure of the goods they had to sell, and armed with steely, occasionally scorching rhetoric that set them apart from their peers, there was good reason for Dave Rowntree to cheekily claim the invention of Britpop as Blur's own. That other factors – from the demise of grunge to the emergence of 'new lad' – had helped that invention along was also beyond measurable doubt. But as with many a brand new device, keeping hold of how others used it was nigh-on impossible. And so was the case with Britpop. By the time *Parklife* picked up 'Best Album' at the Q awards at the end of 1994, Britain's record companies and music papers were eagerly searching for other acts that could be brought under Blur's newly opened umbrella. With the recent success of *His 'N' Hers* and a clear association with Albarn and co. via Alexandra Palace and elsewhere, Pulp were immediate and obvious candidates. Supergrass too, also began to receive increased coverage and favourable reviews. Another band to benefit from their link to the *Parklife* boys was Sleeper, their frontwoman Louise Wener's way with a sly quip drawing journalists like bees to honey.

It did not end with Pulp, Sleeper and Supergrass. As 1994 gave way to 1995, the list of acts potentially labelled with the Britpop tag had grown exponentially: Ash, The Bluetones, Cast, Dodgy, Echobelly, Gene, Heavy Stereo, Marion, Menswear, Powder, Salad and Shed Seven were all either releasing records, signing record deals or being talked up by the press as worthy of record deals. Pre-Britpop hopefuls and old stagers were in the act too. Both The Boo Radleys and The Lightning Seeds gained renewed interest from UK audiences as a result of all the fuss, while Paul Weller also benefitted from his past mod associations via an upsurge in sales for his latest album, *Wild Wood*.

As to be expected, there were also several bands that ran screaming from any notion of a new 'movement'. For reasons already outlined, Suede had built a large fence between them and the whole idea of Britpop, preferring to go it alone than risk any more Blur-associated headlines. In truth, they had enough problems of their own to contend with. By the time *Parklife* began its attack on the charts, Anderson's group was in disarray, their guitarist Bernard Butler ousted from the ranks during recording sessions for their second album. Though the band recovered well enough – their sophomore disc *Dog Man Star* debuted at number three on the UK charts in October 1994 – there was still much to be done before the ship was once again steady. Thankfully, *Parklife*'s success seemed to at last bring an end to the ugly feud between Anderson and Albarn. Given the circumstances, there was no longer much point in fighting. "You know, I've exorcised all my little hang ups now," Damon confirmed at the time. "I imposed them on myself in the first place, and (that) was probably unnecessary, but it helped them in the first place and it sure helped us. But now I think it's quits."

One or two other acts were busy creating their own space from the Britpop tidal wave. Always a band apart, Welsh contrarians Manic Street Preachers spent much time in 1994 rubbishing the whole idea before the sad disappearance of their spokesman Richey Edwards gave them more pressing matters to attend to. Radiohead were also less than enamoured with being linked to any phenomenon outside their own self-created universe. Like Blur circa 1993, they had clear plans of their own and that did not include being labelled 'Brit', 'pop' or anything else for that matter. Of the newer breed drawn into the Britpop orbit, Gene were perhaps keenest to gain a little distance for themselves, though there was the odd flirtation with the scene here and there before they truly struck out on their own.

Other bands simply boxed clever. Fellow newcomers Marion for instance, chose to emphasise their new wave credentials rather than risk being tarred with a somewhat fluffier brush, the band citing The Buzzcocks and Joy Division rather than The Kinks or The Small Faces as primary influences. Elastica, on the other hand, had to play it straight down the middle. Publically supportive of her boyfriend and subtly flattering to the general idea of it all, Justine Frischmann still managed to keep her group from falling too far into Britpop's slipstream. With their debut album destined to top the UK charts in March 1995, Elastica were also picking up real interest in the States where they were being pushed as an alternative rock band by their new manager, the ubiquitous Chris Morrison. Having seen Blur's US campaigns flounder in part because their music was targeted at the wrong audience by unsuitable DJs, Morrison was hell bent on Elastica avoiding a similar fate. Therefore, while the band could afford an inevitable association with Britpop and Blur at home, Elastica's American image was cultivated via college radio and alt-rock festival appearances. For Frischmann, being 50% of a high-profile relationship was always going to bring about such challenges. "I went into this with my eyes open," she told *Q* in 1995. "I thought if they can handle it, so can I. There's also the idea that if you have a (famous) boyfriend, then you want to be equal to him. You want to be as good as they are."*

In the main, however, there were no great complaints from anyone about the rise of Britpop. For the music press, it was as if all their Christmases had come at once. Only four years before, journalists had been tearing their hair out, moving groups like chess pieces from one potential movement to another in an effort to create something of lasting worth (lest we forget, Blur started 'baggy' before being lumped in with the 'shoegazers' and 'the scene that celebrates itself'). But by 1995, the hard work was being done for them as band after band emerged from the clubs and into the charts. Pick the right artist at the right time and a music weekly's circulation could rise by up to 15%. Golden days, as they say.

For the record industry, it was even better. Having seen sales disappear across the Atlantic for the last three years, Britpop was now redressing the balance: first Suede, then Blur, with Elastica, Pulp, Supergrass and Cast all following suit, labels such as EMI/Parlophone, Polydor, Polygram and Deceptive were all breaking out the champagne bottles to toast the new regime, and indeed, themselves. Smack bang in the middle of it all, of course, were Blur. Slayers of baggy, vanquishers of grunge, and now the undisputed kings of the British music scene. The fact hadn't gone unnoticed by Alex James. "Being in a band is fucking brilliant," he said. "People who say being in a band is boring are in rubbish bands."

Being in Blur was certainly brilliant in the early months of 1995, as the group began collecting a procession of honours for simply being themselves. Somewhat improbably, the band failed to duplicate Suede's achievement of 1993 by losing out to the anodyne funk grooves of M People in the race for 'Best Album' at the Mercury Music Prize Awards. But they fared considerably better at *NME*'s inaugural 'Brats', capturing 'Best Album' and 'Best Band' among other gongs. In record industry

* Despite such concerns, Elastica still turned up to perform on 'Britpop Now', a BBC 2 music special aired on August 16, 1995 and hosted by Damon Albarn. Aside from Elastica, Blur, Pulp, Supergrass, Gene, Sleeper, Echobelly, Menswear and Marion also contributed songs to the show.

terms, however, there was only one awards ceremony worthy of serious attention: the Brits. While it didn't have the creditability of the Brats (which were launched specifically to lampoon it) or the seriousness of the Mercury's, the Brits represented the British Phonographic Industry's yearly chance to honour those who had brought it wads of cash in suitably ornate style.

Broadcast on ITV in mid-February to an audience of millions, Blur stole the show, winning 'Best Album' and 'Best Video' for *Parklife*, Best Single for 'Girls And Boys' and just for the hell of it, 'Best British Group' as well. At the time, this was an unheard of sweep. "1994 was the year British music started to re-establish itself as a force," said Albarn, "It really is as simple as that."

Mildly soused on a combination of beer, red wine and champagne, Blur played up the cheeky chappies angle to maximum effect at the Brits, their raw live rendition of 'Girls And Boys' a breath of fresh air when compared to the stagey turns of Madonna and Elton John. Rowntree was in especially rude mood, scrawling 'Dave' on his cheek in mock honour of fellow Brit nominee Prince, who arrived at the show with the word 'Slave' written on his own face – a clear reference to the contract war he was fighting with record label Warner Brothers at the time. Yet, Blur's high spirits reached a crescendo when they were awarded 'Best British Group' by Vic Reeves and Bob Mortimer. Smothering the comedy duo in kisses, Alex proceeded to tell every teenager watching at home his life story before Albarn finally grabbed the mic. "Thanks to everyone who's had blind faith in us, past and present," said Blur's frontman, before adding "I think this (award) should have been shared with Oasis. Oh, and wake up America..."

Alex being a little squiffy on champagne was no great surprise. In fact, it was all rather endearing. And again, the casual rubbishing of America was nothing new. One had almost come to expect it from Damon. But Blur's attempt to share their success with another band was a little more unexpected. "It's not us on our own, you know," Albarn said after the ceremony. "We might have been the first to start shouting about British music from the rooftops, but look at Oasis. I really think this (award) should have been a joint thing that we shared with them."

From the look on his face, he meant every word. Who knows, he might have even prepared the speech beforehand. Nonetheless, it remained a magnanimous gesture, the architect of Britpop doffing his cap to a new and exciting group that he felt merited serious, lasting attention. Leap a decade forward, however, and it was all change. "Oh God, what did I say that for?"

Hindsight, they say, is a wonderful thing. It gives perspective to one's actions while also ensuring mistakes made are seldom repeated. Perhaps it was hindsight that changed Damon's mind regarding his view of Oasis. Maybe. Then again, maybe not. One thing remains clear. Until 1995 Blur – and Damon Albarn in particular – had been in full control of the narrative of Britpop, bending word and deed to need and want. With the arrival of Oasis, some of that control was lost.

Chapter Ten

Win The Battle

By the spring of 1995, Blur owned the British music scene. After their success at the Brits, sales for *Parklife* saw yet another rush, pushing the album towards double platinum status not even a year after its release. That the band had attained such notoriety by sticking to their pop guns rather than courting the more traditional rock market made that achievement all the more remarkable. "Rock would have been the easy option," Albarn said at the time. "You can write mediocre songs, mumble words, put a lot of attitude into it and (still) be successful. But pop is so much more of an exposé. If (*Parklife*) hadn't had something to say and the sounds that we used hadn't been thought through deeply, it would have just been embarrassing."

It was a sound point. Even in their leanest times, Blur had never seriously entertained the notion of beefing up their sound or turning up the volume to attract a rock audience. First and foremost, they were a pop group. Artful, clever and experimental, but a pop group nonetheless, and a very British one at that. "Pop (was) devalued by the slacker movement, but we stuck to that essential belief even when it wasn't fashionable," said Alex. "Blur are a band for the Hoovering classes, the Nanette Newman of pop, we're really a bit of a lift..."

They were also starting to get quite rich. Having shifted close to two million copies of their latest album at home, 'Girls And Boys', 'To The End' and 'Parklife' had also done well as singles in the European market. More, the group's success had re-activated interest in their back catalogue, with punters now catching up with *Modern Life Is Rubbish* and to a lesser extent, *Leisure*. Soon enough, Blur's high commercial profile in Japan would lead to the release of *Live At The Budokan 1995*, a two-disc concert set recorded specifically for Eastern territories. "It's not bad," said Damon of the album, "but I don't think we'll be inflicting it on the fans at home." (They eventually changed their minds in 2000).

More money was raised for the cause when in April 1995 the band signed a new publishing deal with EMI worth a reported £2 million. For Mike Smith, who originally brought Blur to MCA Publishing before progressing to EMI as Head of A&R, the decision to now reunite with them was comically easy. "Even when *Modern Life Is Rubbish* came out and wasn't hugely successful, you got the sense of a band who were revitalised," he later told *The Guardian*. "I was actually at Alex's place when the 12-inch of 'Girls And Boys' arrived. He put the speakers up at the windows and turned it up to the maximum volume so that everyone in Covent Garden could hear it. We were all dancing round his flat going 'This is it. This is blast-off time!'"

Each member of Blur reacted to their new circumstances in different ways. For James, this meant taking up semi-permanent residence at The Groucho Club, a members only bar in the heart of London's Soho that did "champagne on tap" and allowed him to smoke as much as he damn well pleased. (When the five minute walk from Covent Garden to Soho proved simply too much, then Freud's – a cocktail lounge just below his flat on Endell Street – or the nearby Mars Bar provided convenient substitutes). A born bon vivant, Alex took to the role of wealthy pop star with astounding alacrity, his public persona combining the charm of actor Leslie Phillips with the buccaneering ways of Rolling Stone Keith Richards. Whether linked in the press to an exotic supermodel or captured for posterity stumbling out of a bar – ciggie in mouth, champers in hand – James brought a lightness of touch to it all. "Oh, Alex is a natural," scoffed Graham at the time. "He was born to be a pin up."

James could also be genuinely funny. Disinclined to play the intellectual (despite all those qualifications), he could still pontificate with the best of them when the mood struck. "People say we're a British band, that we talk about mainly British things, and that's true to a point," said the bassist in late 1994. "But in the last (few months), I've only spent two weeks in Britain, and half of that was at Heathrow Airport. I think we're gradually becoming international creatures." With quotes like these, it was no wonder journalists loved him.

Graham, on the other hand, continued to downplay the fame game, his only real concession to changing circumstances being the purchase of a vintage 1966 Karmann Ghia. "It's a bit decrepit, and of all the vintage cars he could have bought, not a flash one," said Damon. "But he looks quite sweet in it with his little glasses." There was no great change in Coxon's choice of bar, either. When not at the wheel of his Karmann, he could more often than not be found at the back of Camden Town's Good Mixer pub, happily talking with local tradesmen. It was precisely this reluctance to engage with the responsibilities of stardom that was slowly turning him into Blur's greatest curiosity. Naturally shy, the guitarist also exuded a kind of befuddled charm, his detached pronouncements and occasional giggles during interviews marking him out as a cult figure for both fans and press. Seizing an opportunity to run with the image, music weeklies began printing little vignettes about British pop's "resident oddball." Though he took it all with good humour, Coxon really didn't understand why anyone was really that interested in the first place. "I really do try to be normal, and I think I am," he said. "But personally, I find this 'Unofficial Strangest Man in Pop' title a bit weird. Anyway, I don't feel famous. I suppose (I've made) an effort to be 'unfamous'. I picture myself as someone who's still getting pints of milk on the corner every morning."

Dave Rowntree had dealt with Blur's growing notoriety by getting his house in order, both personally and professionally. By 1995, Rowntree had not only married his Canadian girlfriend Paula and moved to leafy Hampstead, but was also now completely teetotal. Having established a reputation as a boozer of some distinction, the drummer was shocked into sobriety after a particularly heavy session with Siouxsie & The Banshees while on tour in Europe during 1993. "If I had to pin (stopping) down to one moment, I'd say it was after a heavy blow out with The Banshees," he said. "Around then, I was getting pretty close to the edge." While the decision to get clean took several tries before it truly stuck, Rowntree was sure it was the right move for both his mind and liver. "Do I miss the oblivion? Well, I can't say I do because I could never remember anything. The reason I stopped was because I'd woken up with a hangover every day for three years." One could only marvel at the discipline shown here. One quarter of one of the booziest bands in Britain, Dave spent his days surrounded by well-wishers and industry types hell bent on buying him a drink. "At the time, we were like kids being given the keys to the sweet shop," he said. "The trouble was, none of us knew that if we ate too many sweets we would be sick. You just had to find your own way."

For Damon Albarn, Blur's hedonistic ways had also brought genuine fear to the door. First struck down with panic attacks, the singer's woes escalated to include chronic insomnia, persistent shoulder pains and, more worryingly, bouts of occasional depression that left him exhausted and nervous. Convinced that he was seriously ill, Damon sought advice from a variety of sources including a faith healer and acupuncturist before taking the more traditional route to a Harley Street specialist. When faced with Albarn's admissions of heavy drinking, occasional drug use and a workload that would slay a horse, the doctor prescribed medication and a radical change in lifestyle. Fearful of becoming dependant on any form of medicinal prop, Albarn stopped taking his prescription almost immediately and joined a local gym instead. Though the drinking and use of soft drugs were not quite halted, anything heavier than the occasional spliff was strictly verboten.

"Ecstasy embarrassed me because I was far too nice to everyone, and I don't believe in being so for no reason," he told *FHM* in 1995. "I do smoke dope occasionally, but I tend to really enjoy it or become ridiculously paranoid, so there's not much point doing it all the time. I did cocaine for about a year and a half, (and it) seriously damaged my nervous system, so I thought 'Well, that's a bit stupid'. Basically, you've either got the constitution or you haven't, and I was very lucky that very quickly my body told me there was no point in taking drugs."

Albarn's accession to millionaire's row, however, seemed to leave him somewhat more confused. "He's never really had big money before," said Justine Frischmann. "He's been talking about (getting) a car. But he can barely ride a scooter, let alone drive." For all his banging confidence, Damon appeared as lost as anyone might when given the keys to the proverbial kingdom at such a tender age. "I did my growing up in public," he later said. "And I was really still a teenager at the age of 26..."

Still, being in touch with his inner 16-year-old did at least provide some compensation. When offered the opportunity to appear alongside his teenage hero Ray Davies on *Channel Four*'s late night music programme *The White Room* in March 1995, Albarn leapt at the chance. A self-confessed addict when it came to Davies' work with The Kinks ("What he did is in my blood"), he was reportedly in bits backstage before the show. But as the duo's acoustic performance of the immortal 'Waterloo Sunset' proved, he had recovered well by the time the cameras rolled.

"'...Sunset' is the most perfect song (anyone) could ever hope to write," he said. Having just duetted with Damon on one of his own songs, Ray Davies returned the compliment by breaking into an impromptu version of 'Parklife', his laconic North London voice a natural fit with Albarn's own posh/Cockney tones. "You know, I was actually in love with Ray for that hour."

Albarn was also temporarily smitten with Davies' former partner, Chrissie Hynde, joining her and The Pretenders onstage in London soon after *The White Room* appearance for another acoustic rendition of another Kinks song. "We did 'I Go To Sleep' from 1965's *Kinda Kinks*," he said. "The Pretenders' version is pretty good as well, though." Determined to make it a year to remember, Damon's next appointment was with former Special Terry Hall, the two meeting up in the studio as potential contributors to trip-hop guru Tricky's new album. "I thought it was bizarre that nobody from (the pop world) had worked with Tricky before," said Blur's frontman at the time. "It was really liberating, working with him." As with Ray Davies, Albarn's feelings for Terry Hall were something akin to love. "The Specials *were* my adolescence." Regrettably, the track Damon contributed to – 'I'll Pass Right Through You' – remains unreleased, the singer so disappointed with his performance he asked for it to be excised from Tricky's 1996 disc, *Nearly God*.*

Realistically, however, these sessions and appearances were little more than pleasant distractions from the next stage of Blur's masterplan, the details of which were announced to the press in April 1995. With a new single and album set for summer release, the band were to start the ball rolling with the biggest headlining concert of their careers at Mile End Stadium on Saturday, June 17. Given that the East End venue could accommodate an audience of 27,000, this was yet another confirmation that Blur were now officially the biggest pop group in Britain. "Well, Wembley Stadium was just a bit too big and Finsbury Park was a bit too... grown up, so Mile End was the one," said Albarn at the time. "Also, I was born just over the road from the stadium, so there you are."

To set the stage for their big day – and get themselves back into fighting shape after a paucity of gigs since Alexandra Palace in November 1994 – the group performed several overseas shows before a surprise visit to Camden Town's tiny Dublin Castle on May 18. In front of a crowd of just 250 people (including Justine and Donna Matthews from Elastica and Pulp's Jarvis Cocker), Blur handed in a somewhat shambolic set, in large part due to the pub's minuscule PA system. But for those gathered, many of whom were old school fan club members, it was one of the few chances left to witness the group without the need of binoculars or a telescope.

In typically obstinate fashion, the morning of Blur's Mile End show was marred by a combination of persistent rain and chilly breezes, turning

* It is worth noting that while 'I'll Pass Right Through You' didn't make the cut, Damon Albarn and Terry Hall had actually worked together before, co-writing the slight, but pleasing 'Chasing A Rainbow' in 1994. It was eventually released as a single by Hall a year later, and can still be found on the CD reissue of the former Special's first solo album, *Home*.

the site into a rain-drenched wind tunnel before a band had even set foot on stage. That said, opening act The Shanakies did their level best to bring levity and humour to proceedings. More used to venues akin to The Camden Falcon than Mile End, the group nonetheless showed considerable mettle, their particular brand of Celtic-tinged tunefulness going over well with the early arrivals. For Shanakies frontmen Eddie Deedigan and Dave Brolan, it must have been something of a bittersweet experience. Personally asked to do the gig by their old mate Albarn, the former Circus members were still without a record deal despite some strong tunes and a novel cover version of Orange Juice's 'Rip It Up' – which given the right backing – screamed 'hit single'. Sadly, the band broke up soon after, ironically the victims of A&R men more interested in signing Britpop hopefuls than a refreshing folk-pop alternative.

There were several more support groups to see before Blur took to the stage. Again appearing at the behest of Damon Albarn, The Cardiacs remained the acquired taste they always had been, their jerky rhythms and curious atonalities lost on many in attendance. Yet, if anyone really wanted to learn where some of the inspiration for Blur tunes such as 'Intermission' or 'Lot 105' had come from, it was staring them right in the face. Dodgy were an entirely different matter, their bottle-blonde brand of sunny Britpop shaming the downpours that continued to plague Mile End throughout the day. Unfortunately, veteran duo Sparks gained a reception mildly similar to The Cardiacs. Legends to a man, Ron and Russell Mael had been responsible for some of the finest music of the seventies and eighties, with hits such as 'This Town Ain't Big Enough For Both Of Us' and 'Beat The Clock' spanning glam to electro pop and back again. Sadly, for a young crowd growing progressively more impatient to see their heroes, Sparks were another oddity they could do without. The Boo Radleys fared better. Coming to the East End on the back of a recent number one album (*Wake Up!*) and Top Ten single ('Wake Up Boo!'), the former shoegazers were in decent form, providing a set of few surprises but several quality tunes.

And then it was Blur's turn. Arriving on stage at dusk, the band teased the audience with a few notes from 'The Debt Collector' before kicking off the gig with a rip-roaring version of 'Tracy Jacks'. For some,

Damon's decision to dress as an old man – replete with grey wig and pot belly – during the first number was bizarre as a bag of socks. For others, including *Melody Maker*, it was simply business as usual. "You can take the boy out of drama school," quipped the paper, "but you can't take the drama school out of the boy..." Once shed of his disguise (he was actually meant to be 'The Debt Collector' in human form), there was no real stopping either Albarn or Blur. Part greatest hits collection, part back-catalogue heaven, the group banged out no fewer than nine Top 50 singles in the space of 90 minutes, while interspersing their set with the odd lesser known gem such as 'Supa Shoppa' and the hangover referencing 'Badhead'.

Some of the biggest screams of the night were for Alex James who took centre stage to idle his way through 'Far Out'. The first – and last time – the song was ever performed at a Blur gig, 'Far Out' continued to raise a Roger Moore-sized eyebrow. On the one hand, the bassist's whimsical tour of the universe could well have been the prodigal son of Pink Floyd's similarly themed 'Astronomy Domine'. On the other, it remained a lightweight ditty in search of a proper ending. Whichever side of the fence one sat, 'Far Out' was greeted with something approaching hysteria by the soaked masses at Mile End. After a four song encore that included a punky run-through of 'Girls And Boys' and a strong-jawed 'For Tomorrow' (with The Kick Horns and long-time keyboardist Cara Tivey providing additional uplift), Blur were almost ready to take their leave. To no great surprise, but almost deafening applause, Phil Daniels bounded on stage to help Blur out with 'Parklife'. Five anarchic minutes later, and they still couldn't get rid of him as the actor jokingly clung onto Damon's microphone during a disordered rendition of 'Daisy Bell'. Daniels knew better than to stick around for 'This Is A Low', Blur's finest moment bringing down the curtains at Mile End in a blaze of melancholic style. "Not a dry eye left in the bloody house," James joked.

With its neon-lit 'Zeal Zone', giant floating hamburgers and overarching video screens, Blur's Mile End experience was a natural extension of Alexandra Palace seven odd months before, albeit on a super-sized scale. "There were some people at Mile End who hadn't been to a gig before, or certainly a gig of that size," said Alex after the event. "I suppose we were the first band of our age to play someplace like it, and that made it special. The atmosphere there, it was... par excellence."

James' point regarding the audience that attended Mile End was telling. In 1990, the front rows of a Blur gig had been comprised of scruffy students, a few friends and the odd muso. Now the band had to contend with row upon row of screaming teenage girls, their old fan base lingering at the back of the stadium looking on with a mixture of resentment and shock. "What's 40 yards long, got no pubes and goes 'Aaaaaaaaaaaah!!!'?," Alex quipped. "The front row of a Blur concert." Somewhere in Bournemouth, a comedy cymbal crashed to the floor...

Despite the off-colour nature of the joke, James was essentially correct. *Parklife* had proved a game changer for Blur, their indie roots and atonal beginnings completely irrelevant to the majority of people who bought the CD. As time would quickly show, the music press were still to play an important role for the band, the support of certain journalists key in maintaining their credibility and position with an older, more serious audience. But the days of Blur defining "art school cred" were long gone. In the months leading up to Mile End, British tabloid *The Daily Star* began running a daily cartoon entitled 'The Blur Story' – a witty, occasionally surreal account of the band's rise to power. "Oh, the weirdest thing was the cartoon strip, no contest," said Rowntree. "If you're going to be a pop star, they should let you know in advance so you can prepare for it. But it happened overnight. What an extraordinary time that was." Elsewhere, the quartet regularly appeared in the pages of teen magazines such as *Smash Hits* and *Top Of The Pops*, their opinions on hairstyles and fashion more important to readers than the influence of Brel, Brecht or even Bowie on their work.

Though Damon had fought to stem the tide by occasionally penning articles on British youth culture for the likes of *Modern Review*, or airing his views on Martin Amis to upmarket men's periodical *GQ*, the war to be taken seriously was being compromised elsewhere. In a marvellously wayward piece of journalism, *Sky* magazine dressed up three of their reporters in windcheaters, spectacles and trainers and sent them packing into the London night with the question "Does dressing like Blur impress women?" Sadly for two of the reporters at least, it really didn't. However, the article did underline the fact that certain sections of the media were now treating the band as sex objects as much as serious musicians. Again, Albarn was drawn into the light in an effort to address the issue with the publication concerned. "If you go out to project yourself as a sex symbol, sure, you might become some kind of sex symbol," he told *Sky*. "I don't really write about sex in our songs. I guess it's not really a big issue in my life. I get most of my inspiration watching adverts. Though it is a faintly sexual experience when you throw yourself into a crowd and you're getting, well, fondled by 40 pairs of hands..."

In truth, Blur were on a precarious high wire completely of their own making. Sticking to a game plan devised in 1992 and developed admirably in intervening years, they were now Britain's pre-eminent pop group. Yet, while controlling the strategy within the confines of the music press had proved easy enough (after all, both were beneficiaries), managing their profile across a wider spread of media was becoming more difficult. With *Loaded* and *FHM* pushing the 'new lad' angle, and *Smash Hits*, *Just Seventeen* and *Sky* obsessed with the cut of their jib, Blur were all things to all men and women, their image stretched every which way to suit the ethos of the publication concerned. As Blur's most unwilling participant in matters of fame, Graham Coxon was beginning to find it all rather onerous.

"You become totally aware of your every action," he grumbled. "It's a very weird thing not to be able to walk to the shops without thinking of yourself as the guitarist in Blur walking to the shops."

If the cracks were waiting patiently to appear, Blur's honeymoon period with the press and public was about to reach a crescendo in the summer of 1995 when it was announced that their new single 'Country House' was soon due for release. Previewed to an ecstatic response at Mile End, 'Country House' brought together all that was good, bad and totally absurd about Blur in one huge burst of primary colours. Opening with a cart-wheeling bass and piano line courtesy of Alex and Damon, the song quickly turned into a 'Theme From Minder' for the nineties, as trombone slides, falsetto harmonies and ski-wiff guitar parts all dovetailed in and out of the mix. Sitting on top of this undeniably pleasant din was Albarn, his Mockney drawl telling a tale of an ailing city gent taking refuge from the woes of life in the warm environs of his country pile. "'Country House' is about panic attacks," Damon explained. "I wrote it when Kurt Cobain died because I think he might have suffered from them. But it's not about him, it's about myself (because) I was feeling pretty fucking down at the time. Then, somehow it mutated into this jolly, up-tempo comedy fucking record."

Given Albarn's health concerns in recent months the explanation was wholly plausible, but there were other possible inspirations for the lyrical content of 'Country House'. Shortly after 'Girls And Boys' had hit the Top Five, Food Records boss Dave Balfe had decided to sell the company to EMI, with Andy Ross staying on to manage it as a sub-label within the larger group. "Andy had told me that *Parklife* was going to be massive," Balfe later told *The Guardian*, "but we'd had grunge for a few years and it was really depressing and I thought, 'Fuck this, I want to go and do something else'." However, the now former Food boss – who incidentally owned a substantial mansion in the countryside and had been experiencing his own health issues of late – returned to see Ross just before Blur's latest single was released. "I popped into the office and on Andy's desk there was a cassette labelled 'Country House, Blur'. So I said 'Is this about me?' I could tell from Andy's face that it was. Though the song is obviously not full of praise, it's still incredibly flattering. It's like getting my portrait in the National Portrait Gallery. You're not there because of your own fame, but because of the painter's."

Like the single 'Parklife' before it, Blur were intent on 'Country House' having a big and bold video to accompany its release. On the suggestion of Alex James, Brit-art enfant terrible Damien Hirst was hired to direct it. An acquaintance of the bassist since their time together at Goldsmiths – and now a fellow drinking buddy at James' beloved Groucho Club – Hirst had been making his own headlines since 1992, when he sold a shark contained within a vitrine and pickled in formaldehyde for an impressive £60,000 at London's Saatchi Gallery. By the time of 'Country House', Hirst had also won himself the prestigious Turner Prize, this time delighting critics with an installation of a bisected cow and her calf (again preserved in methanol) with the title *Mother And Child, Divided.* Opinions were (and remain) divided on whether his work is truly art or simply a device to separate the rich from their money but Damien Hirst carried both commercial weight and critical kudos – two factors that would do Blur nicely. "I'd always been preaching that idea... that artists and pop groups, bright young things could come together and produce something of real value," said Albarn. "But in the end, (the video for) 'Country House' ended up being perceived as an exercise in laddism."

New to the world of video making, Hirst kept his original idea for 'Country House' sharp, sweet and simple. "I think it's fairly self-explanatory," Damian said at the time. "Neurotic pop stars buying big houses in the country. I just added a board game." It didn't quite end there. In addition to a giant board game specifically designed for the band to run around, the artist also added several glamour models, a few bath tubs, one or two pigs and actor/Groucho Club stalwart Keith Allen to spice up the story, turning Blur's study of a Prozac-addicted businessman into a lost episode of *The Benny Hill Show.* "I mean, God, we had Page Three models in it," Albarn later groaned. "I didn't even know we'd (hired) Page Three models. I only found out on the second day of shooting when someone brought in a *Club* (magazine) and said 'Eh? Eh? Look that picture, that's Joanne Guest', nudge, nudge.' Call me naive, but I really didn't know. That's the truth."

With new lad culture approaching new heights at the time, the idea of hiring a few topless models to splash around in the bath alongside Blur while a stray pig walked by the camera might have been viewed by some as pure genius. Unfortunately, Damien Hirst's promo for 'Country House' caused significant friction within the group's ranks, with Graham and Damon distancing themselves first from the video, and then Alex's Groucho Club buddies. "I fucking hated it," Graham Coxon later told *Select.* "Videos in general I feel completely awful about... but I regretted 'Country House'. It became Page Three and Benny Hill and I don't think I had the sense to complain about it, which was my fault. I didn't realise what dirty minds Keith Allen and Damien

Hirst had." Coxon's viewpoint was unsurprising given the fact he was in a serious relationship with Huggy Bear's Jo Johnson at the time. A committed feminist and guitar player with one of the original riot grrrl acts (Huggy Bear had actually supported Blur at the Hibernian back in 1992), Johnson had little truck with new lads or Hirst's new vision of Blur. Graham was wont to agree. "It's all *The Guardian*'s fault for saying football was OK. Apparently, you could kick someone's head in as long as you could write an essay about it," Coxon said of all things new lad. "You had to go on about tits, but if you knew why you were doing it that somehow makes you less of a pig. It was all an excuse to just act horrendously." Behind-the-scenes resentments and ideological clashes meant sides being taken and the single hadn't even been released yet.

Then things got get really interesting.

Since signing to Creation/Sony Records in May 1993, Oasis had been playing a rapid game of catch-up with Blur as Britain's biggest band. Formed in Manchester two years before, the quintet were led by guitarist and principal songwriter Noel Gallagher, though his younger brother Liam – who handled vocals – often had something to say about who was actually in charge. "Nobody fucking *leads* Oasis," he once hissed. Matters of governance aside, Oasis officially announced themselves to the public with the release of their first single 'Supersonic' in April 1994. Though it only reached number 31 in the UK charts at the time, the tune was a superb demonstration of what to expect from them in future: raw, coarse and brooding, 'Supersonic' was also immaculately structured, intensely melodic and featured some of the best stream of consciousness lyrics since The Beatles' 'I Am The Walrus'. "Listen, I want to outdo The Beatles," said Noel at the time. "If you don't outdo The Beatles, then it's just a hobby."

Like Damon Albarn, Noel Gallagher was not a man lacking in either confidence or ability. Though their second single 'Shakermaker' failed to crack the Top Ten, Oasis' third release 'Live Forever' did, nicely paving the way for their debut album, *Definitely Maybe* at the end of August 1994. Breaking Suede's old record for "fastest selling debut of all time in the UK", *Definitely Maybe* went straight to number one with a proverbial bullet. Tellingly, it also reached number 58 in the US charts, some 30 positions higher than Blur's best effort *Leisure* had achieved across the pond in 1991.

A band perfectly built for the times, Oasis' post-Stone Roses haircuts, loose shirts and no-nonsense approach to stagecraft immediately struck a chord with the average British pub-going male, making them the new doyens of the new lad movement. Noel Gallagher's optimistic lyricism was also a strong lure to many, his championing of hedonistic youth and living in the moment a stern rebuttal of what had come before. "There's not enough humour in music," he said in 1994. "Look at Suede with all this 'Together in the nuclear sky' bollocks. I'm sorry, Brett, but the cold war's over. Let's talk about beer and fags and lasagne."

Equally, Oasis were a more muscular proposition than many that surrounded them, as happy to draw their inspiration from classic rock as from pop. Again, this gave them an edge and credibility with those seeking a little grit and bite with their melodies. "To me, we're more a cross of The Who and the Stones with a bit of The Beatles," Noel said. "I'd like our records to sound like T-Rex. 'Get It On' and 'Hot Love' sound like there's 500 people there doing the handclaps, having a party. I want that vibe on our records." But Oasis' strongest suit was surely their directness. Within moments of hearing one of Gallagher's songs, one felt an intimacy with it, each verse and chorus drawing the listener directly into the band itself. "The best thing John Lennon ever said was how he always went for the most obvious melody he could get, no matter how naff it sounded, and I agree," Noel told *Loaded*. "The best songs are the most obvious because the listener becomes part of the record and knows the chord changes before they happen."*

Given that they shared a few of the same influences and were both championing a return to British music after the dominance of grunge, one might expect that Oasis and Blur would become friendly. And so it

* While this philosophy of following "the most obvious melody" did well for Oasis, it occasionally ended in charges of plagiarism too. In fact, the band's second single, 'Shakermaker' was so melodically similar to The New Seekers' 1971 hit 'I'd Like To Teach The World To Sing (In Perfect Harmony)', Gallagher and Co. were reportedly forced to pay $500,000 in damages to its writers.

proved, at least at first. In fact, to his enduring credit, Damon Albarn's expressive speech at the Brits was only his latest rubberstamping of the Mancunians' worth. Yet, each successive compliment seemed marked by incident of equal ugliness beforehand. In late September 1994, for instance, both bands were playing gigs in San Francisco a day apart. Grasping an opportunity for some mutual promotion they agreed to appear together as guests of *Live 105*, a radio station local to the Bay area. Within minutes, what began as good-natured ribbing between the two camps had descended into full blown insults and a few choice swear words. A month or so later, they were at it again, with a drunken Liam Gallagher berating an equally soused Graham Coxon at Camden's Good Mixer. Though Gallagher got thrown out for his trouble, the duo picked things up at the nearby Underworld club, where their argument continued on and off into the small hours.

It seemed even the presentation of honours couldn't stop both groups from finding fault with each other. At *NME*'s Brat Awards, where Blur took four gongs and Oasis scooped the exalted Writers' prize for 'Album Of The Year', the night was again marred by their boorish behaviour. After Coxon planted a joke kiss on Liam Gallagher's cheek, the singer flew into a rage before temporarily stomping off to the bar. Not to be outdone, Noel then tried to stick the finger of his Brat award up Damon's nose during a photo session. Reluctant to miss out on all the fun, a returning Liam took objection to Damon's dancing, telling Blur's frontman that he was "Full of shit", before taking a swipe at his band: "I'll tell you to your face, your band's full of shit. I'm not going to do a photo with you." At a cursory glance, such enmity appeared to be little more than drink (or possibly other substances) talking, with two groups already known for their cockiness now getting cocky with each other. But there was also an element of genuine competition brewing between them that was hard to blame on just drink.

Things came to an irretrievable head in early May, 1995, when Liam Gallagher bumped into Damon Albarn and producer Stephen Street at The Mars Bar in London's West End. In an expansive mood because Oasis had just scored their first number one UK single with 'Some Might Say', Gallagher was "giving it large" to all concerned. "Liam came right up to Damon's face, being very arrogant and lairy, with his finger up saying 'Fucking number one'," Street later said. "I remember Damon looking at him saying 'Yeah Liam, whatever'. But I could see him thinking 'Right, we'll see...'" Days later, when Blur were onstage at Camden's Dublin Castle, Gallagher's latest outburst was obviously still very much on the band's mind. "This is the best song!" shouted Albarn from the stage. "What, 'Cigarettes And Alcohol'?" replied Graham, referring to another (quite brilliant) Oasis hit. "No, *this* is the best song!" at which point Blur launched into 'Parklife'. It is perhaps worth noting that when Albarn was once asked what his most unpleasant characteristic was, the reply was immediate: "One-upmanship..."

Pinning down exactly what happened after the events of The Mars Bar and Dublin Castle is no easy task, with Blur, Oasis, various journalists, editors and record company staff all telling slightly different stories at slightly different times. However, the gist of it remains essentially the same. Both bands were due to release singles in the summer of 1995, with each release staggered to allow the other a clear run on the charts. At some point, however, one of the parties (probably Blur) changed the plan and both singles were scheduled for release on the same day: August 14, 1995. Approximating the words of the immortal Joe Strummer, war had just been declared and battle thrown down for the UK number one spot. "It's quite exciting, really," said Damon, "I just wish I wasn't the victim or victor of this." Perhaps, but it was crystal clear that he also wanted to win the big first prize. "I'm going away on holiday that week, and I'm not getting involved," he continued. "(But) I'm going to leave very specific instructions that if I come back on (that) Sunday and we're not number one, someone is going to suffer some sort of grievous bodily harm..."

Realistically, there was no clear frontrunner in the race for number one. As usual, Blur had a strong single on their hands – more a saucy picture postcard of a song than a bonafide classic – but still immensely hummable, with a resolutely catchy chorus. And whether they liked it or not, Damien Hirst's video for 'Country House' would do them no harm at all, its gaudy colours and gaudier cast almost guaranteeing blanket rotation on MTV. "It's just about a business man who walks around a board game," joked Hirst, "There's no characterisation there, darling."

With Oasis, things were slightly less encouraging, but again, nothing to call the doctor about. If truth be told, their candidate for the top spot – 'Roll With It' – was a bit of a duffer in comparison to 'Live Forever', 'Cigarettes & Alcohol' or even their most recent hit, 'Some Might Say'. Coming on like a composite of Slade and Creedence Clearwater Revival, 'Roll With It' jogged along nicely enough but didn't seem to really take off at any point, its melody line content to spin rather than spiral. The accompanying promo was no great shakes, either. A simple in-concert performance that had a white-clad Liam and Noel singing and strumming away as blue light bathed them from all sides, it was hardly the stuff of future legend. But Oasis were still the band in form, their public profile increasing at the same velocity Blur's had in 1994. More, they had just scored their first chart-topper and were eager to repeat the trick. "We're on one," Liam helpfully pointed out at the time.

Oasis' campaign got off to the flying start when the band debuted 'Roll With It' at Glastonbury on June 23, their set later televised by the BBC. Under the canny guidance of Creation's Alan McGee, they were also one of the first groups with a strong on-line presence, their website numbering over 100,000 followers, all primed to buy the single. Yet, touring commitments overseas took them out of the UK's public eye for 10 crucial days in the run up to 'Roll With It''s release, a less than ideal situation for Oasis and their PR team. Blur, on the other hand, had only six concert dates to fulfil during the same period, with one of those to an audience of over 30,000 at Milton Keynes Bowl, where they supported R.E.M. on July 20. Even if only one in ten of those attending purchased 'Country House', that was still roughly 3,000 copies more for the Gallup chart assessors to add to the count. Blur also had a real masterstroke up their sleeves in the form of *Britpop Now*, which was shown by the BBC two days after the release of 'Country House'. As stated, this show was a compendium of Britain's best and brightest of the time, with Damon acting as both linkman and master of ceremonies between acts. Of course, Blur used the opportunity to promote 'Country House' to maximum effect on *Britpop Now* – Coxon and Albarn resplendent in matching deerstalker hats, with the latter donning a bow tie, waistcoat, tweed jacket and jodhpurs to drive home the essential Britishness of it all (to no one's great surprise, Oasis did not participate in the show).

Away from the concerts and TV appearances, both bands also took the odd opportunity or two to rubbish their competition. When invited on DJ Chris Evans' morning BBC breakfast show, Damon sang the melody to 'Rocking All Over The World' over the top of 'Roll With It', adding that the Gallaghers should re-christen their group 'Oasis Quo'. Alex later modified the term to 'Status Quoasis'. Justine Frischmann was also on hand to offer her boyfriend support, reportedly describing Liam Gallagher as "thick as shit" to *NME*, though she later softened her remark considerably. "I'm in the anti-Oasis camp by association, (but) I just think they're very average," Justine told *The Face*. "It's kind of cock rock – the whole... stadium, world domination thing – and I don't think there's anything very interesting going on, musically or lyrically. They're just... OK. The Mantovani of rock, really... an average white-boy rock band."

Never a man to let an insult slide, Noel Gallagher hit back hard, focusing his ire on Blur's occasional lapses into 'Mockney'. "They're not even Chas & Dave because Chas & Dave meant it," he growled. "We're the band of the people and we always will be. Right now, they might be the biggest, but they're not the best."

In the week before 'Country House' and 'Roll With It' were released, the media went into overdrive. Always complicit in Blur's previous sales campaigns (a service they were now also happy to offer Oasis), *NME* Editor Steve Sutherland pushed the face-off onto the paper's front page with the headline 'British Heavyweight Championship: August 14, the big chart showdown.' There was also a distinctly working class vs. middle class/north vs. south angle to the accompanying coverage, turning a simple battle for the number one spot into something distinctly wider in its implications. From the start, matters of class and regionalism were never going to be kept out of the Blur/Oasis showdown. Like The Stone Roses before them, Oasis had traded heavily on their northern roots, promoting themselves as of the people, for the people. That the Gallagher brothers actually came from Burnage – one of Manchester's better suburbs – was by the by. Oasis' image was that of the quintessential Mancunian band, heavy on attitude and arrogance, and proud of their down-to-earth origins. Blur, on the other hand, were the stereotypical southern softies. Well educated, middle class and bohemian-leaning, their creation of Britpop could be viewed as much 'strategic' as of the street. Noel Gallagher certainly thought so. "Blur," he said, "are a bunch of middle-class wankers trying to play hardball with a bunch of working-class heroes."

Gallagher's rhetoric was impassioned, but also clever. By playing the class card, he was not only establishing his own band's identity for the masses, but also questioning the authenticity of Blur's music and image. It was a viewpoint the press was quick to pick up, and which Albarn somewhat uncharacteristically failed to see coming until the damage was done. "The only thing that really annoyed me was the press turned it into a middle class vs. working class thing," he later said. "Because of that, a whole body of people – people who'd enjoyed our songs as good pop songs – were (told) that I'd been looking down on them when I just wasn't. As a result, they didn't want to know anymore. I hate to make it sound so simplistic, but that's how it felt. Mind you, I'm not saying I'm a victim, that's just bollocks."

For the time being, the issue of Blur's credibility was still a somewhat oblique topic, their recent success rendering it a passive rather than active debate. But the peculiarities and newsworthiness of 'The Battle of Britpop' was a different matter altogether, pushing the story out of the music papers and straight into the national press. As a consequence, everyone from *The Daily Star* to *The Guardian* were giving their opinion on who was going to win. And no-one could really blame them. From the Stones and The Beatles in the Sixties to Duran Duran and Spandau Ballet two decades later, groups were known to tread carefully when it came to the charts, politely staying out of each others' way to maximise their own sales. More, rivalries between such bands were often the invention of their managers, record companies or PR teams, with everybody content to raise a drink at the resultant press coverage.

However, Oasis and Blur were not only breaking that tradition by going head to head for the number one spot, they also seemed to genuinely dislike each other. Throw in north vs. south and council estates vs. country estates and one really couldn't find a better tale to tell. "The Blur/Oasis war was a media wet dream," Noel later said. "This lot from Manchester, this lot from Colchester. It couldn't be more contrasting, really. They went to art school, this lot were robbing shit. Perfect."

In the same way that the tabloids and broadsheets had wrested control of the 'Battle of Britpop' from *NME* and *Melody Maker* for their own circulation purposes, Channel 4, ITV and even the normally more reserved BBC could not resist entering the fray. On the day both singles were released, news reports on all three networks took Blur and Oasis into the living rooms of Britain. "I've bought 'Country House' because I like the song more, and to be honest, I quite fancy Damon," an enthusiastic shopper told Channel 4. "But I will buy 'Roll With It' next week because Oasis are pretty good too." As stated, the BBC were also keen to get their tuppence worth in, using class and regionalism to further stoke the debate for their viewers. "It's been described as the British pop music heavyweight championship," said reporter Clive Myrie. "In one corner, four young middle-class men from the south of England collectively known as Blur, and in the other corner, five young working-class men from Manchester called Oasis. They're the two most popular bands in Britain, having sold millions of records, and they're currently engaged in a chart war that's set the music industry alight."

In a week when Saddam Hussein was supposed to have begun gathering a nuclear weapon stockpile and war continued to rage in Bosnia, such coverage was plain ridiculous. But it was also too late to put a stop to it. "With hindsight, it was unnecessary because we both had a certain amount of respect for each other," Noel Gallagher confirmed. "But we were all too drunk or too high to say otherwise."

Having possibly put the whole thing in motion, Damon Albarn had hoped to escape his responsibilities by holidaying with Justine Frischmann in the run-up to D-Day. Unfortunately, Elastica were offered a last minute spot at the Lollapalooza Festival and the idea was scuppered. "With Elastica doing so well in America, it's to be expected really," he said at the time. "You know, I haven't seen (Justine) properly in months. I expect that people in America have seen more of her than I have in the last year. (But) we both realise that because of our careers we're not going to have a 'normal' relationship. It's a risk, but if you invest in one side of your life, you can seldom invest in the other. It's the price you have to pay for a slice of pop immortality."

Still keen to get away from all the furore, Damon took a brief vacation with his parents in Mauritius instead, though he was still back in London the night before Gallup made their crucial announcement. "I'd been getting really agitated (on holiday)," he told *NME*. "So when I got back, I went straight to the cafe on the corner of my street and the lady filled me in on all the press we'd be getting." It wasn't just Albarn who had succumbed to nerves. Sick of the whole affair, Coxon completely withdrew from sight during "finals week" while Rowntree took his wife to France. Even James ran scared, holing up with Damien Hirst and several dozen bottles of wine in a Devon cottage.

By the time the UK singles chart was announced on the evening of Sunday, August 20, Damon Albarn already knew Blur had won out over Oasis, the fact confirmed when Food's Andy Ross arrived drunk for their usual game of football that morning. For his sins, Alex James heard the news like everyone else, the bassist's car stereo tuned into Radio One as he drove back to London from the West Country. "We were number one, they were number two. Job done, I think." By nine o'clock that night, the whole band were in full possession of the facts and celebrating their victory at a party in Soho. For Damon, the news was all good. "Do Blur deserve it?" he said. "Of course we do." Graham's mood, however, was a little different. Having tried to throw himself out a window while the festivities were in full swing, he then left for the seaside to gather his thoughts. "I wanted to enjoy it on my own terms," he later told Q. "I didn't want record company people slapping me on the back. Contrariness has always been one of my biggest sins."

In the end, Blur had scored a comfortable enough win, selling 270,000 copies of 'Country House' to Oasis' 216,000 for 'Roll With It'. Sure enough, marketing had played its part, a point Oasis' management team

'We did a couple of gigs and got signed almost straight away. We were really arrogant, but that's part of this job. You need arrogance and self-confidence..." The band formerly known as Seymour pose for the camera in one of their early publicity shots, (L-R): Dave Rowntree, Damon Albarn, Alex James and Graham Coxon. JAMES JORDAN/RETNA UK

The actor and the artist. Damon and Graham contemplate alternative careers while attending Stanway Comprehensive School in the mid eighties. ANGLIA PRESS/REX FEATURES

Blur backstage at Reading Festival in 1991. GEOFFREY SWAINE/REX FEATURES

"There were times when he was in a world of his own..." Nigel Hildreth. Damon Albarn lost in the moment at Reading Festival.
REX FEATURES

Alex James in semi-classical pose backstage for a charity gig at Colchester Sixth Form College on December 16, 1994.
CAMERA PRESS/PAUL POSTLE

On the way to superstardom. Blur promote the release of *Parklife* at Walthamstow Stadium on April 26, 1994.
ILPO MUSTO/REX FEATURES

Damon Albarn at the helm. JAMIE REID/RETNA UK

Warming up for the big event, Blur play an intimate gig at Camden Town's Dublin Castle on May 18, 1995 in advance of their historic Mile End Stadium show three weeks later. JOHN CHEVES/RETNA UK

The best British guitarist of his generation." Graham Coxon throws a shape or two on his Gibson Les Paul. JAMIE REID/RETNA

Clean sweep. Blur pick up one of a record-breaking four gongs at The Brits in February, 1995. Presenter/comedian Vic Reeves (pictured in background) looks mildly pleased for them... RICHARD YOUNG/REX FEATURES

The last days of Britpop. Damon and Pulp's Jarvis Cocker captured at the Empire Awards in February 1996.
RICHARD YOUNG/REX FEATURES

/leeting a hero. Damon and The Kinks' Ray Davies read from ıe same hymn sheet before performing 'Waterloo Sunset' and 'arklife' on Channel Four's *The White Room* in March 1995. IARTYN GOODACRE/RETNA UK

Avid Chelsea supporter Albarn in charity cup-winning form at Wembley Stadium, March 1996. NEWS GROUP/REX FEATURES

Iey, Mr. Tambourine Man. Damon onstage with Blur at Scotland's T In The Park festival, 1999. DREW FARRELL/RETNA UK

"Killers of baggy, vanquishers of grunge." Blur contemplate the creation of Britpop. (L-R) Graham, Damon, Alex and Dave.
RETNA USA

were keen to draw attention to. In addition to the fact that 'Country House' was sold at £1.99 per single rather than the £3.99 Oasis were asking for 'Roll With It', Blur had also put out two different versions of said single, each with different track listings. Faced with the dilemma of which one to buy, the serious Blur fan would obviously opt for both, thus rendering the band two sales rather than one. Creation further claimed there had been problems with the barcodes on the CD case for 'Roll With It', resulting in the faulty recording of actual copies sold. No-one in Manchester, it seemed, was quite ready to admit that 'Country House''s final success might be down to the fact it was simply the better tune. "Fucking chimney sweep music," said Liam.

Suffice to say, the hostility between Blur and Oasis did not end with 'The Battle Of Britpop', as both sides continued to duke it out in the press. To his enduring shame, soon after 'Roll With It' failed to make the number spot Noel told *The Observer* that he hoped Blur would "catch AIDS and die", a remark he has been apologising for ever since. "As soon as I'd said it, I had (my head in my hands)... My whole world came crashing down around me then. If it wasn't for our kid Liam (saying) 'It's all right, you just said something daft', I don't know what I'd have done." More 'moment of madness' than 'malice aforethought', Alex James was content to let Gallagher's indiscretion slide by on grounds of diminished responsibility: "The trouble with Oasis is they take too many drugs."

However, Albarn was still capable of mixing his compliments with arsenic when the occasion warranted it. "It's important that Oasis are rude about everybody and that they get drunk," he told reporters. "That's what people like you want, and you encourage them. Fair enough. It's nice, isn't it? But it's nothing to do with me. They came to see us in Manchester and they were very pleasant boys. Very nice. I'd like to see that as a quote: 'Oasis are very nice boys'."

Nearly two decades on and it was all a very different story, as Damon and Noel's emotional jets had cooled with age. "That whole thing... well, it's something we were partially responsible for, so there's accountability there I suppose," said Albarn. "But all the (insults)... he said that, you said that, you learn about that at school. It's nothing, really."

Gallagher was equally philosophical of their battle over the skies of Britpop. "The truth is that it was manufactured by *NME* and the people in Blur's camp who moved their single to coincide with ours," he told BBC's Mark Lawson. "What really annoyed me was that everyone blamed it on us because we were seen as the manipulators. In the end, we all sold a lot of singles off the back of it, and we all became wealthy because of it, so I'm really not complaining."

At the time, however, victory would come at a price for Blur. Before the chart skirmish, they had carried the essence of everyman in their kitbag, their songs and image emblematic of better days for British pop. After the event, they were to become known as entitled southerners, their authenticity soon to be tested by anyone with an interest in promoting class war for a quick headline. "The Oasis thing came precisely at the re-emergence of lad culture, and it sold into that perfectly," Damon said in 2010. "Unfortunately, we were soon being sold as the middle-class (option). Perhaps I shouldn't have gone on so much about how much I loved Chelsea."

Whatever the damage, 'The Battle Of Britpop' remains an almost perfect moment in British music, with two fine bands fighting low, hard and occasionally dirty for the number one spot. More, it has seldom been topped for pure entertainment or media spectacle, the likes of *X-Factor* and *Pop Idol* paling in comparison to an episode in which the miracle of pop actually seemed to matter to an entire nation. For that alone, the Blur/Oasis war should really be taught in schools. "You don't get something for nothing," said Dave Rowntree. "That whole thing took us both to the next level, but we also became each other's baggage. Forever linked, like a perpetual joust. Blur versus Oasis for eternity. Really," he concluded, "we should dress up as fucking knights and get on horseback..."

Chapter Eleven

Into The Blue

On its release on September 11, 1995 Blur's fourth album *The Great Escape* was deemed a masterpiece. Hailed by critics as a perfect encapsulation of the band's sound and a bold signifier of the Britpop movement they had arguably created, *The Great Escape* was "kaleidoscopic", "restlessly innovative" and "a triumph" all at once. Then, all of a sudden, it wasn't. In fact, as the years progressed, *The Great Escape* not only began to lose its lustre with reviewers and commentators, it also found its way to the back of many a fan's record collection, occasionally spun for reasons of nostalgia, but little more. Even Blur took to making excuses for it, a wry smile or wave of the hand offered by way of explanation for its fall from grace. "*The Great Escape* was hailed as the most important release of the decade," Damon Albarn later said. "That didn't quite turn out to be the case."

On the way, there have been a few half-hearted attempts to re-appraise the disc's worth, to listen to it with new ears, so to speak. In the main, however, it has remained something of an embarrassment to those who first lauded it "the second coming", and a bit of a head-scratcher among Blur's own back catalogue. From "Painstakingly brilliant" to "The black sheep of Britpop" all within the space of a decade. For the man who wrote it, the problem was simple: "*The Great Escape*'s just messy," said Albarn. He was undoubtedly right. But it wasn't all that bad either...

Blur had begun the recording of *The Great Escape* in January 1995, again using Maison Rouge Studios as their main base of operations. Housed between women's dress shop and Fulham Broadway Methodist Church, Maison Rouge was also about a quarter mile from Stamford Bridge, the home of Damon's beloved Chelsea FC. Returning as producer was Stephen Street, who was delighted to learn that Albarn had brought no fewer than a dozen near-complete songs with him at the start of the project. "We just applied ourselves (and) got into the rhythm of it pretty quickly," Street told *Super Deluxe Edition.* "The actual process of making the record... well, we were like a well-oiled machine at that stage. We just went into it and carried on pretty much in the same mode that we were in when we did *Parklife.*"

Working to a long established schedule, Blur, Street and trusted engineer John Smith arrived at 10a.m. and left between 10 and 12 hours later, only breaking for food in the mid-afternoon. To instill further discipline, no alcohol was taken during these hours, though a fearsome number of cigarettes were smoked. When extra help was required, brass section The Kick Horns were on call, as were The Duke Strings Quartet and backing vocalists Angela Murrell, Teresa Jane Davies and Cathy Gillat. For a change of scenery – and the melding of orchestral/vocal parts to one or two songs – the whole troupe moved to Townhouse Studios in nearby Shepherd's Bush during mid-March, though they were back at Maison Rouge soon enough. By May, it was all finished: "We always saw ourselves as just putting on the white coats and going into the lab," Albarn said at the time.

Seeing their latest effort as a conclusion to "a trilogy of sorts" – and with their last two discs called *Modern Life Is Rubbish* and *Parklife* respectively – Blur felt a degree of pressure to get the word 'Life' somewhere in the title of their album. 'Darklife' and 'Nextlife' were both jokingly considered before 'Sexlife' became something of a real (if quite awful) contender. Thankfully, Alex broke new ground by suggesting 'The Great Escape', a phrase that seemed to capture both the mood and sentiment of Damon's newest collection of songs.

Agreed by all, James' idea also informed the cover of the record, with design firm Stylorouge once again providing a striking image, this time by photographer Tom King. Half-way between holiday snap and catalogue picture, the shot of an unidentified swimmer diving from a speedboat into the waters below was all blue skies and beckoning seas. "We thought it was an ambiguous image and it was blue as well," said the bassist. "We really wanted it to be blue because that's the colour of escape." Yet, when expanded in the accompanying CD booklet, King's photo was doctored to include the stars above, and rather worryingly, a shark swimming beneath the ocean surface. "The album understands that when you're up in the sky, you can either fall to earth...or not," said an arch-sounding Albarn. To further befuddle, the back cover sleeve featured Blur dressed as young, well-heeled businessmen gathered around a computer, their shirts and ties pristine, their hair gelled to oily perfection. Idyllic locations, sharp suits and a Great White shark thrown in to boot. As ever, it was all very mysterious indeed.

Coming on the heels of Blur's extremely well-publicised victory over Oasis in the 'Battle of Britpop', *The Great Escape* was released to something approaching hysteria in mid-September, 1995. Outselling the rest of the UK's Top Ten combined in its first week on the shelves, the album not only went to number one with a proverbial bullet, but was also awarded a platinum disc within weeks. As previously described, the only thing perhaps more feverish than these sales figures were the reviews that greeted the record, with most every music commentator in Britain falling over themselves to praise Blur from the critical rooftops.

"*The Great Escape* puts their talents beyond question," said *The Observer.* "Painstakingly crafted, brilliantly played... it represents an evolutionary leap forward from *Parklife* (and) is also the most truthful mirror modern pop has held up to Nineties Britain." Q quite liked it too. "*The Great Escape*'s rich tapestry is matched by music of kaleidoscopic surprises," they said. "Not since the 1960s has a mainstream UK band shown the capacity to develop this far and this fast over the course of four albums." *The Independent* was also keen to offer their praise. "Rich and three dimensional, *The Great Escape* consolidates Blur's position as the benchmark against which all current British bands must be measured."

Having championed Blur for the best part of five years, *NME* were in no mood to be outdone by these Johnny-come-latelys. "The work of a band approaching the height of its musical powers. (It is) Blur's real triumph... their finest hour." But it was *Melody Maker* who surely said it best: "*The Great Escape*. 12/10."

As time has come to show, *The Great Escape* was neither a band at the height of their powers nor a perfect record by any stretch of the imagination, with many a critic perhaps still caught up in the glorious undertow of the Blur/Oasis war when asked to offer their opinion. That said, there were some substantial truths hidden among all the platitudes. For one, there was little doubt that Blur had once again excelled in illustrating their understanding of the British pop idiom, the group drawing on myriad influences across many a decade to form *The Great Escape*'s musical spine. Further, they had proved themselves ceaseless experimenters in sound, adding new sonic hues and rhythmic brushstrokes to those already displayed on *Parklife*. In fact, there were now Glockenspiels, trombone solos and even Kazoos fighting to be heard. But whichever way you cut it, while *The Great Escape* might have occasionally trumped its predecessor in terms of daring and novelty, it also lacked its sense of clarity and purpose.

When *The Great Escape* was good, it was very good indeed. With 'Stereotypes', Blur had a brand new stadium anthem on their hands, Coxon's cutting riff and Albarn's trebly organ fills pushing the band as close to 'rock' as they had yet come, before a big, fat, pop-friendly chorus pulled them back from the breach. 'Mr. Robinson's Quango' also had an aggressive side, its thumping bass line, elephantine power chords and rumbling brass parts all adding to the song's overall sense of menace. Debuted at The Dublin Castle and Alexandra Palace respectively, 'Stereotypes' and 'Mr. Robinson's Quango' would both take up forceful residence in Blur's set list over the coming months. Less forceful perhaps, but certainly no less proficient was 'Entertain Me', a subtle, uneasy tune that might have lent a little too heavily on David Bowie's 'Modern Love' in the melody department, but which the band made their own nonetheless. The sleepy, yet blissful 'Best Days' was also worthy of mention, Graham's endlessly descending solo able confirmation that he was becoming untouchable as "an alternative guitar hero for the Nineties".

Unfortunately, *The Great Escape* also had its fair share of musical disappointments. 'Top Man''s unusual melding of Adam Ant-like baritone backing vocals and Teardrop Explodes-style chord changes was diverting for a moment or two, but soon began to outstay its welcome. 'Dan Abnormal' made an equally promising start, again pulling on Bowie and Julian Cope for inspiration.* But in spite of Rowntree's spirited tub-thumping and some flavoursome bass fills from James, it was more filler than killer. Supercharged chorus aside, 'Globe Alone' was another let down, the tune rabidly chasing its own tail in search of a suitable home (it would probably have found one on an early Cardiacs album). Worse, in comparison to former punk-pop thrashes such as 'Jubilee' and 'Advert', 'Globe Alone' had a somewhat contrived air to its sense of anarchy, feeling more forced than feral. This manufactured aspect to *The Great Escape* also hung over the glistening pop tones of 'Charmless Man' and 'It Could Be You'. Though beautifully constructed, carefully arranged and deftly played, both songs were also curiously utilitarian, sounding as if Albarn had written them as theoretical exercises rather than lasting statements. In protest, Coxon's guitar work grew so loud and irritated on the latter track, he sounded as if he wanted to do it actual harm. "At times," he later conceded, "*The Great Escape* just sounded too cleaned up and soulless."

One might have said the same for 'Country House'. When functioning as a stand-alone single, it carried itself well, a song obviously written with multiple radio plays in mind. But when sequenced alongside the muscularity of 'Stereotypes' and the more stately 'Best Days', 'Country House' now sounded calculated and hollow, its deliberately brash chorus and clanging chords just too clever for their own good. At the

* A slim tune by anyone's estimation, 'Dan Abnormal' actually took its title from re-arranging the characters of Damon Albarn's name: "It's a name Justine gave me," he said. "Dan's (character) represents a lot of my less savoury habits... (It's) about the fact that I spent a lot of time getting drunk... (and) would find myself in Soho at three in the morning."

time, Graham defended it for those very reasons. "We have a real knack for writing sarcastic chord progressions," he confirmed. "It's a strange thing to say because it all seems so abstract, but we can always come up with a 'Whoops! How's your father?' tune. It's one of our... strengths." Two years on, and it was all change. "I just can't listen to it anymore," he complained. "Everything's a bloody hook." As author of 'Country House', Albarn summed up Coxon's dilemma better than most. "It'd be a brilliant song at the end of a musical," he said. "Actually, *The Great Escape* really was a musical..."

If, as Damon Albarn contended, *The Great Escape* was indeed a theatrical affair, it was also one with some very opaque lyrical undercurrents. Unlike the "mod gangsterism" of *Modern Life Is Rubbish*, or the "Cockney nouveau" of *Parklife*, there were precious few fattened families, Sunday supplements, chirping sparrows or jolly dustmen making an appearance on *The Great Escape*. Instead, Blur – or at least their principle songwriter – seemed obsessed with conveying feelings of loneliness, isolation and detachment, with 10 of the album's 15 tracks either referring to, or revelling in, such emotions. Of course, Albarn being Albarn, said feelings were again hidden in various characterisations and caricatures, sly wordplay and subtle badinage. But there was also little doubt that while everyone else in Britain was suddenly in the mood for a party, it appeared the man providing the soundtrack was trying to find the nearest exit.

"The title *The Great Escape* refers to the fact that in all the songs, the characters are removing themselves from their lives in one subtle way or another," Damon said by way of explanation. "That affects us all in one way or another. Escapism is a very powerful urge." For Stephen Street, Albarn was probably not speaking of the 'universal everyman' on this occasion. "I think Damon was feeling the pressure more than he actually let on at that time," the producer later said. "(In fact), looking back at it, I think inside he was slightly cracking up, to be honest with you."

There were few doubts that Damon Albarn felt the burden of fame in the run up to *The Great Escape*. Troubled by panic attacks, various illnesses and exhaustion, he also had to contend with being 'The Face of Britpop', his opinions constantly sought after, his time seldom his own. There was a very good argument to suggest that Albarn had always wanted it that way, pursuing stardom with considerable vigor and unerring accuracy. But the reality of his position and the demands of having to write an entire album's worth of material as good as *Parklife* must have cut to the quick. Even if he was willing to laugh it all off at the time – "My 'pop personality' has made me feel more normal. I was actually uncomfortable with not being famous" – penning lyrics devoted to escape in all its myriad forms was probably the sanest response he could muster.

Hence, *The Great Escape* was awash with men and women seeking exits on a sexual, materialistic and psychological level, their proclivities, ambitions and foibles specifically designed to provide egress from their everyday existence. In 'Stereotypes', a housewife aches for the moment her husband leaves their guesthouse so she can live out her fantasies with the clientele within: "She's most accommodating when she's in her lingerie..." The titular 'Mr. Robinson' was another choice Albarn creation, his dedication to public service masking a predilection for cross-dressing, sexual harassment and various other indiscretions: "I'm wearing black French knickers under my suit, I've got stockings and suspenders on, and I'm feeling rather loose..." For 'Top Man', it was all about plunging into money and prestige, the keys to a "Little boy racer" jangling nicely in the pocket of his Hugo Boss suit as he orders yet another double in a high street bar. 'Charmless Man' was even more cheerless: "Educated the expensive way," and knowing his "Claret from his Beaujolais," Damon's public school bore harbours secret dreams of life as an East End gangster, though no-one will listen to him long enough to hear them. From 'Best Days''s taxi driver looking for a "Fare to the sun" to 'Globe Alone''s nervy, covetous protagonist ("He wants it, needs it, almost loves it"), most every character in *The Great Escape* was either absconding, fleeing or running headlong towards someone or something else.

With its all-pervading notions of discontent and dislocation, Blur's fourth album had an undeniable sense of gloom and longing to it. But that self-same cheerlessness was a key factor in helping realise its five outstanding tunes. In the case of 'The Universal' (which we will return to), Albarn used images of "Prozac, corruption and quilted utopias" to outline his bleak future world-view. 'Fade Away', on the other hand, was set squarely in the present. Brilliantly described by writer Jon Ewing as a tale of "suburban purgatory", 'Fade Away' matched the sound of 2 Tone to the story of a couple slowly disintegrating behind the walls of a soulless, satellite home. "That song is about places like Coventry and Milton Keynes, and people with no souls leading empty lives," Alex James later observed. "It needed that sort of 'Ghost Town', Specials sort of feel… that sort of scary, sinister feeling." With its mournful trombones (courtesy of The Kick Horns' Neil Sidwell), swaying percussion and tremulous guitars, 'Fade Away' was the best song Terry Hall had never written. 'He Thought Of Cars' was even better. Beginning with a wave of mechanical discordance, '…Cars' soon morphed into a ballad of utter class and real distinction, its subtle, surprising melody line underpinning yet another wet-eyed fable of escape, as lottery winners take to the moon and "everybody wants to go into the blue…"

For some at least, 'Ernold Same' was one step too far into utter despondency, with no back door left open in Albarn's crushing lyrics. But it was also *The Great Escape*'s bravest experiment, as then Labour politician – and soon to be Mayor of London – Ken Livingstone droned inexorably on about a man slowly dying from the boredom of his own existence. "There is something fundamentally awful about getting on a train and doing the same journey every day of the week, so you can go to work and put food on the table," said Damon by way of explanation. "Wearing a suit, conforming. It can break the human spirit. And that's what makes it good subject matter for songwriters. It's human and emotional." Propped up by a delightfully wobbly orchestral arrangement Kurt Weill would have been proud of, and with several vocal interjections from Albarn in his very best "Anthony Newley guise", 'Ernold Same' might have been soul-destroying. Yet, at the same time, it was inordinately entertaining. "Doesn't it make you want to commit suicide, though?" Alex later joked to *NME*.

The Great Escape's final track also carried a sense of weariness to it, though it was more the pang of aching loins than the pain of existential crisis that drove Albarn's subject matter on this occasion. Written from the perspective of young lovers working at the same Japanese car factory, 'Yuko And Hiro''s days are spent toiling away – their only real time together being on Sunday afternoons before the week threatens to begin once again: "I never see you, we're never together, I love you forever..." With Damon having seen his girlfriend Justine Frischmann for only three weeks throughout 1995, it was obvious where the inspiration for 'Yuko And Hiro''s lyric had come from. "With Elastica doing so well in America, it's to be expected, really," he said. "It was the same when Justine had to put up with continually being associated with me when she started getting recognition in England." Featuring a quaint backing vocal from session ace Cathy Gillat and a novel, undulating keyboard line from Damon, 'Yuko...' finished *The Great Escape* in some style, even if there was a faint suspicion the song had been specifically designed to appeal to Blur's ever-growing Far Eastern fan base...

Though there was satire in abundance ('It Could Be You''s sneers at the National Lottery system was especially pleasing) and spells of humour throughout ('...Quango', 'Charmless Man' and 'Stereotypes' all had their moments), *The Great Escape* was still the darkest, most complex work of Blur's career. Pointing a well-aimed torchlight behind all those twitching curtains, the work was still quintessentially British in its concerns and characters, and as such concluded Albarn's ambitious trilogy into the mind (and now bedrooms) of a nation. "It was a weird time (for me)," said Albarn, "so I wanted to punish my characters accordingly." More, his central theme of taking flight – both metaphorically and literally – was also well conceived and ably delivered. Yet, *The Great Escape*'s various emotional twists and turns, its musical leaps and lapses made the album difficult to bond with: its tone uneven, tense and sometimes tiring.

For Graham Coxon, this sense of anxiousness and exhaustion was at the heart of the record. "It's funny," he later said, "*The Great Escape* was made under the pressure of collecting awards for *Parklife* in the evening and making the album in the day. And I do think you really feel the tension in that record."

There was far more tension to come as Blur embarked on a comprehensive touring schedule in support of their latest disc. The game kicked in earnest with a live daytime broadcast from the

BBC Radio Theatre on September 7, 1995 in front of an audience numbering just 200. Somewhat predictably, eight of the 10 songs aired were directly lifted from *The Great Escape*, with only 'Badhead' and 'Popscene' marking Blur's progress from past to present. That said, the band's rendition of the latter track raised several eyebrows among BBC staff, including those of hosts Jo Whiley and Steve Lamacq. Intent on creating a bit of a stir, Albarn and his cohorts tore into 'Popscene' like a starving animal, their take of "Britpop's lost classic" more akin to the atonal anarchy of Seymour than their new, shinier incarnation.

Damon was up to his old tricks again just a week later when Blur played a short set atop the HMV building at the heart of London's West End. The appearance was meant to mark the official release of *The Great Escape* to shops, but when Albarn decided to dangle his microphone into the crowd of hundreds gathered below, then hoof across the building's edge in time to 'Parklife', there were genuine fears he might well fall off: "That didn't happen when The Beatles first did it in 1970..." one critic wryly observed.

Canny marketing techniques were also at the heart of the group's next move, when they performed seven intimate shows during September at various seaside resorts around the UK, including Cleethorpes' Pier 39, Morecambe's Dome Club and Oscars' in Clacton. Roughly taking their tour directions from the enchanted handkerchief Alex gifted Damon in 1993, Blur even ended up in sunny Dunoon, the first British chart-toppers to visit the remote Scottish holiday town since Pink Floyd appeared there some 25 years before. A brilliant opportunity for local fans to see previously faraway heroes up close and personal, 'Blur's Seaside Extravaganza' was going like the clappers until the quartet arrived in James' beloved Bournemouth on September 18. In a scheduling conflict from hell, Blur were lined up to appear at the miniscule Showbar while Oasis were simultaneously plying their trade at the considerably larger International Centre just up the road. Fearing that rival supporters might turn Bournemouth High Street into an impromptu boxing ring, an agreement was hastily sought by both parties to avoid any trouble. Thankfully, a temporary bust up in the Oasis ranks saw them pull out of their show at the last minute, much to the obvious glee of Damon Albarn.

"The other band weren't hard enough to play tonight," he shouted from the stage. The Gallaghers would have their revenge soon enough.

The remaining months of 1995 was totally given over to the promotion of *The Great Escape*. In late September, Blur travelled once again to the States and Canada for 11 select dates – a tasty precursor to a much more wide-ranging campaign scheduled for early 1996. Following their transatlantic excursions, it was then on to Sweden (where the record debuted at number two),* Norway (five), France (14) and Germany (a less respectable 35) before veering left for Japan in early November. Again greeted as returning idols to a man, the band's latest Japanese dates saw them appear at both Fukuoka's cavernous Sun Palace and Osaka's prestigious Festival Hall to an audience of thousands. With *The Great Escape* now riding high at number five in Japan's charts, Blur capped things off nicely with a show at Tokyo's premier venue, The Budokan on November 8. As stated, this gig was recorded, then later released as the double album *Blur: Live At The Budokan*, even if the group's version of 'She's So High' was in fact taken from their performance at Tokyo's smaller NHK Hall the following evening.

With *The Great Escape* now well past the million sales mark at home, it was wholly inevitable that Blur would return to Britain for a more comprehensive tour by the end of the year. Having broken onto the stadium circuit at Mile End only five months before, there was mild surprise when the band confirmed they would be playing only arenas on this occasion (it was winter, after all). Albarn already had his answer ready. "We made the step up at Mile End," he told *NME*, "and that was the best gig we've ever done. These shows will be like that, except they'll be indoors so it won't rain."

In the end, Blur's 16-date trawl of "the biggest aircraft hangers in Blighty" was an unqualified success, the group's stage set taking on a

* After Blur performed in Stockholm's Annexet on October 19, a fire broke out at their hotel. It didn't worry them unduly. "It was odd," Rowntree later said. "There was a loud quaking noise in the room, so I thought 'I'd better get up.' I went into the corridor and there was a cleaning lady doing the room opposite. I said 'Is there a fire?' She said 'No' so I went back to bed..."

surreal, almost carnival quality as chaser lights, huge banks of neon and an omnipresent mirrorball shone out over crowds from Glasgow's SECC to London's Wembley Arena during November/December. To keep it interesting for both themselves and their audience, Blur threw in the odd surprise. 'Mr. Robinson's Quango' for instance now morphed into 'Mack The Knife' towards the song's end, Damon again referencing the genius moods of Kurt Weill and Bertolt Brecht. 'For Tomorrow' also benefitted from a major uplift, with the band extending the track into a mad jam session with their ever-faithful brass section, The Kick Horns. But perhaps the most welcome addition to the set came at encore time when – if they fancied it – Blur would launch into a note-perfect rendition of The Knack's immortal 'My Sharona'. "I always loved that song," laughed Coxon.

Another novel addition to the quartet's stage design at this time was a humongous-sized white tablet that was lowered over the heads of the audience to announce the arrival of Blur's newest single, 'The Universal'. One of *The Great Escape*'s finest moments, the tune had actually been around in one form or another since the *Parklife* sessions of early 1994. Starting life as a Calypso, Albarn had subsequently re-written it several times in intervening months before shyly re-presenting the song to his co-workers at Maison Rouge a year or so later. Even then, he wasn't sure. "I think I was a bit scared of it," Damon later confessed, "but the band said 'we've got to record this.'" Inspired in part by an American TV documentary concerning the ready availability of the anti-depressant Prozac, and Albarn's own, extremely brief experience of the drug when it was reportedly prescribed to him for panic attacks, Blur's singer ran with the ball until he had a lyric that satisfied him. "I saw Prozac as 'a harbinger of the universal bland'," he said, "so I wrote that song as a sort of send-up of my own state of mind." That send up was to become a vision of a future dystopian state where the panacea for all life's woes was a small white capsule ('The Universal' of the title) granting its users a sense of unquestioning, idiotic bliss: "It really, really, really could happen," Damon warned during the tune's swelling chorus, "When the days seem to fall straight through you, you just let them go..."

Married to a gorgeous orchestral arrangement full of lilting strings, sailing brass and gospel-tinged backing vocals, Albarn's cautionary tale of imagined worlds devoid of imagination had hit single written all over it. As with 'Girls And Boys', 'Parklife' and 'Country House' before, 'The Universal' just required a sympathetic video maker to bring out its charms. The man given the job was future *Sexy Beast* director Jonathan Glazer, then best known for his innovative, popular and extremely lucrative commercials for *Guinness*. Filmed in France on "our fucking day off", Glazer's promo for 'The Universal' cast Blur as white-suited futurists or "quasi Droogs" in an obvious homage to Stanley Kubrick's 1971 movie *A Clockwork Orange*. With Damon wearing eyeliner remarkably similar to chief 'Droog' Alex DeLarge – played to perfection in the film by Malcolm McDowell – and being told to make the best of his "Byronesque underlook", promoting Blur's frontman as a heart throb was never in doubt. "Alex looks beautiful in it too, though," he later quipped. But the video for 'The Universal' also carried a sense of genuine unease, with its anesthetised-looking extras, curious 'red men' and blank, endless corridors conveying at least something of Albarn's original, grim vision. "'The Universal' was about another world, and we thought 'Let's make another world'," said James. "It turned out to be quite a chilling one." Released on November 13, 1995 in various CD formats (some featuring the wonderfully rude 'No Monsters' and 'Ultrano'). 'The Universal' didn't quite give Blur the Christmas number one they were surely looking for, with the band having to make do with a number five placing in the UK charts. That said, in spite of its seemingly endless use by British Gas to advertise their products, the tune has grown hugely in stature during intervening years, the poignancy contained within its lyrics and melody even appealing to those with only a cursory knowledge of the group. "The British have always been very good (with) sad pop music," Alex confirmed. "It's something we do very well..."

Unfortunately, as Blur were 'all smiles' for the cameras and their audience at the end of 1995, tempers were beginning to seriously fray backstage. Having been in each other's proverbial pockets for the best part of six years, this might have been expected, but their private feuds were also starting to make their way into the press. Graham, in particular, seemed very angry at Alex 'Champagne Charlie' James. "I hate a lot of things that Alex stands for and I don't want people to think it's what this band is about," he hissed. "All that Groucho Club bollocks and him going on about birds and boozing all the time, I hate that." For his sins, James was only too aware of his 'pop star' ways. In fact, he loved them. "Perhaps I did take to it most enthusiastically," he later told *Select*. "Dave had stopped drinking, just got married... and settled down for a quiet life. Damon was with Justine. And my (long term) girlfriend, Justine Andrew… well, she couldn't bear what I'd become. I was like 'Whoarr! I am gorgeous!' I'd become impossible to live with... arrogant, greedy and selfish. So she moved out and I was suddenly on my own, living in the West End, in the coolest band in the world with loads of money and an expensive champagne habit..."

For Coxon, the buck didn't just stop with Alex James' champagne-assisted behaviour, as Damon Albarn also came in for something of a tongue lashing from his oldest friend. "If Damon goes on about football and page three girls, that means we all get associated with it," he said. "I hate football and I hate page three girls, but people always want to hear Damon's bloody opinion." As usual, Albarn boxed clever when such bear-baiting quotes were brought to his attention. "The passage between irresponsible adolescent to level-headed adult is difficult enough," he told *Q* at the time. "But when you're spending three quarters of a year together on a tour bus drinking, it becomes extremely hard. All in all, I think we're handling it quite well." The man probably handling it best was Dave Rowntree, even if Graham jokingly believed him to be "an alien". Drink-free, then happily married and the proud owner of a brand new single engine aircraft licence, Rowntree was four years older than his peers, and by the sounds of it, possibly four years wiser. "It all comes suddenly and ferociously," he said of the fame game in 1995. "One day you're no one, the next you're on the front of all the newspapers. It's really not something that human beings are designed to deal with." According to the drummer, the very thing that brought him to music in the first place had suddenly become of least importance. "The more famous you become, the less important the actual *playing* becomes, at least in a way. The actual periphery of just being in a band seems to take over. It's one and a half hours on stage. The rest is..." It was a thought he failed to finish.

Booze, bad tempers and pilot's licences. It was all becoming very rock'n'roll. Yet, one was also struck by how tired Blur sounded at the end of 1995, the band more resembling burned out soldiers returning from the front than fresh-faced pop stars. There were reasons. In the space of just one year, they had recorded an album's worth of songs, nine B-sides, performed 68 dates in 13 countries, crossed five oceans, released two singles with accompanying video shoots, filmed countless TV promos and appearances and still made time for the Christmas edition of *Top Of The Pops*. Given their schedule, it was little wonder Blur hadn't murdered one another along the way.

"Strange time, strange pressure, strange euphoria," said Coxon. Of course, what had always brought the group together in times past was a common enemy or goal to fight for or against. Grunge. American influence. Record company ultimatums. All had worked well in creating a united front among them, a call to arms, if you will. The most recent example was the Blur/Oasis war, with Albarn and co. soundly trouncing their opposition in one heady week during the summer of '95. But Oasis hadn't gone away. They had just got stronger.

Some three weeks after Blur had released *The Great Escape*, Oasis issued their second album *(What's The Story) Morning Glory*. Unlike the former, however, the Mancunian quintet's latest disc did not illicit much critical praise, with reaction to it decidedly sniffy from certain sections of the press. "*(What's The Story)...* doesn't sound like much sweat went into it, and its teeth aren't that sharp," said writer Steve Sutherland. "Too much Paul Weller, too little John Lydon, (there) is too little Liam, too much Noel to qualify *...Morning Glory* as the classic the group want it to be. Ultimately," he concluded, "*(What's The Story)...* falls well short of greatness. Measured against an album like *The Great Escape*, Blur are better."

An old friend of the band from their *Leisure* days, it was perhaps unsurprising that Sutherland had placed his flag firmly on the side of Blur. But he wasn't the only one to do so. Several other commentators also dismissed *(What's The Story)...* as a poor follow-up to *Definitely*

Maybe, calling the record "laboured and lazy", "Beatles-lite" or just plain "knackered". Again, it seemed Blur were going to be clear winners in the latest heat of the 'Britpop' stakes. As time quickly came to show, this didn't turn out to be the case.

During its first week in the shops, *(What's The Story)...* shifted a whopping 350,000 copies, its seven day tally making it the biggest seller since Michael Jackson's *BAD* eight years before. Then came the release of 'Wonderwall', a single of such simple, yet stultifying brilliance it made a laughing stock of those who had recently dismissed the Gallagher clan as "one trick ponies" or "Slade copyists". As yet however, there was still no clear victor between Oasis and Blur, with the race still too close to call. Both parties' albums had gone platinum soon after release, and each had sold over 150,000 tickets for their autumn/winter tours. Of further significance, neither side had managed to translate their British and European successes across the Atlantic, where like Blur, Oasis had no discernible profile. "The only thing we've got in common with Oasis," said Damon in December, 1995, "is the fact that we're both doing shit in America."

Albarn's remark did not hold water for long. Unlike *The Great Escape*, which had racked up a total of 122,000 units in the States thus far, (*What's The Story*)... began to pick up speed at a frightening rate, moving from a sales rate of 10,000 discs per week to 100,000 by January 1996. Come spring of that year, Oasis had achieved what Blur could not: a platinum selling, top five album in the USA.

In hindsight, Oasis' Stateside triumph was wholly understandable and completely deserved. While British critics were correct that *(What's The Story)...* broke little in the way of new musical ground, it was never really constructed for that purpose. In fact, Noel Gallagher's ambitions as a songwriter seemed antithetically opposed to any such notion. Instead, he was interested in penning "tunes built to last", great, big, bold anthems that were easily digestible, emotionally reassuring and pleasingly familiar to the ear. Like his heroes John Lennon and Paul McCartney, Gallagher realised that a melody did not have to be particularly novel or complex to make its point. It just had to be understood and sung along to. Like Britain and Europe before them, America had found little difficulty in responding to that directness and simplicity, and rewarded Oasis accordingly.

It was, of course, Blur's strict adherence to another set of principles entirely that made them such a difficult sell in the States. Arch, clever and a tad too knowing, the band's crafty brand of artful pop was not as easily translatable to the stateside market as Oasis' big beats and rock-friendly choruses. At times musically oblique – and chockfull of lyrical references to cross-dressers, wife-swappers, ailing Freemasons and asthmatic city gents – *The Great Escape* could not have been more English in its concerns or more British in its appeal. Like The Kinks, David Bowie, Roxy Music, The Specials and The Smiths before them, Blur's conceits were instinctively understood on home soil. In fact, their ability to reflect the extremity, banality and occasional foolishness of their culture and time was surely cause for celebration.

But America had a poor track record with such deliberate indirection or artistic sleight of hand, preferring music of grander gestures and simpler pleasures. This rule was underlined in crushing terms by Queen's 1984 single 'I Want To Break Free'. A massive hit throughout Europe, the song had been commercially buoyed by a witty promo that had the band dressed in drag and singer Freddie Mercury mincing playfully for the camera. However, when the video was first aired by MTV *in* the States, the reaction was grim. "I actually watched (the presenters') faces turn green," said Queen's Brian May. "They just took it off." Subsequently struck from the music channel's playlist, the clip was also banned in several US states. "It single-handedly ruined our career over there," May concluded. With their roaming pigs, bowler-hatted bankers, strange red men and *Clockwork Orange*-style 'quasi-Droogs', the promos for 'Country House' and 'The Universal' may not have caused as much offence, but were just as poorly assimilated. "I go to America, sit in a diner and just go cross-eyed looking at it all, at how inadequate I am in this environment," said Albarn at the time. "(I understand) how badly I've translated what I think is necessary to translate. I just haven't succeeded at all..."

As events would later confirm, while Blur were not welcomed by Uncle Sam in the same way as Oasis, their 16-date small theatre tour of the States in support of *The Great Escape* during January/February of 1996 did prove of inestimable value to them. But for the time being, there was much work to be done on the other side of the pond. In a mad dash to visit as many countries as possible before spring, the group performed a further 22 shows in Spain, Germany, Italy, France, Holland and Belgium, all neatly tied in to the European release of their latest single, 'Stereotypes'. With its blunt trauma guitars, stop-start rhythms and off-hand vocal delivery, 'Stereotypes' was not the most obvious track to be set free from its parent album. Additionally, the supporting video was a simple 'in-concert' affair, with Blur perhaps missing a trick to make the best of Albarn's risqué lyrics in a more plot-driven, sexually charged film clip. Yet 'Stereotypes' did brisk enough business, going Top 10 in several countries on their recent touring list as well as debuting at number seven in the UK. Somewhat comically, the band's TV appearances in support of the single had seen various members either replaced by road crew or even cardboard cut outs, with Graham attending to the purchase of a house back in London (he bought it for cash), while Dave had his wisdom teeth removed.

In April 1996, Blur were at it again as *The Great Escape* yielded one final single before being put out to pasture. This time, it was 'Charmless Man'. With its title inspired by a piece of graffiti Albarn had seen in the gents' toilet of Grantham railway station when on the way to visit his grandmother, 'Charmless Man' was jaunty enough. But it also skirted perilously close to self-parody, as if Damon were writing a song 'in the style of Blur' rather than seeking to stretch the group's boundaries in any meaningful fashion. It was a view Justine Frischmann in part subscribed to when asked about *The Great Escape* some years later. "I thought it was a truly awful album," she said in 2002. "It was so cheesy in parts, like a parody of *Parklife*, but without the balls or intellect." A tad harsh perhaps, but 'Charmless Man' did sound tired and lacking in invention, its melody line more show-tune than show stopper. Backed by Jamie Thrave's *Groundhog Day*-referencing video that had Blur endlessly stalking a London gangster type, the single again sold well, this time reaching number five in the UK charts. However, in the same way that for Albarn "Adam Ant was the full stop after punk", 'Charmless Man' was to be the end of an era for Blur. "'Charmless Man' really was the end of something, the end of Britpop," said Damon. "For us, anyway..."

Just two days before the release of 'Charmless Man', the unwritten rules of the Oasis/Blur chess game had changed yet again when the Gallaghers' band performed two shows at Maine Road stadium, then home to their beloved Manchester City FC. With 70,000 tickets for both gigs selling out in a matter of hours, Maine Road was final confirmation that while Blur had led well from the front, Oasis had caught them in the long grass. Liam Gallagher in particular was loving every minute of it. "Our last album sold double the Blur album, and that was our first album," he said at the time. "If they still want to fight, I can stand the four of them up. That's what it boils down to at the end of the day. Damon first, then your bass player, then the other two. I'll knock 'em down like dominoes." Gallagher then went for the kill shot. "They've had four albums to our two (but) we took the world by storm. I think Elastica are better than Blur. (Albarn's) bird does it better than him. That's sad. I wouldn't have no bird of mine playing rock 'n' roll better than me. You're not coming home if your bird's doing it better than you..."

Pressing ahead with his advantage, Liam homed in on this potentially sensitive angle in the Oasis vs. Blur stakes by indicating that his admiration for Justine Frischmann went a good deal further than simply liking her band. Such impertinence was part of Liam's rough and ready charm, of course, and might have been construed as tongue-in-cheek were it not for the fact that at a recent Mercury awards ceremony he had actually made a pass at her, albeit in his own unpolished non-PC way. "I was double rude to Justine the other night," he admitted after the event, "going 'Go on and get your tits out'. It's her boyfriend innit, 'cos I love getting at 'im 'cos he's a dick. If anyone said that to my bird, I'd chin 'im. But I fancy her big style. I'm having her, man. In the next six months it will be all over the press... I'll have been with her. Don't say it, though, 'cos I'm mad for her and that'll screw it right up."

This sort of comical entertainment made great copy for the music press whose appetite for juicy gossip was almost as rabid as the tabloids, but after the stupidities of the press war between her former beau, Brett Anderson, and Albarn, Justine was having none of it. "It started off with Liam saying, 'I'd give his bird one' and ended up with 'I know she likes me really, and she's desperate for it'. Liam's frighteningly photogenic, but when you meet him... Well, I had a bizarre experience with him at the Mercury Awards, where his opening gambit was, 'Get your tits out!' Then he ended up grabbing me by the wrists and said, 'Come and talk to me'. I just left because I didn't really want to speak or deal with him... I just find him totally uninteresting, and I knew it would lead to some big media thing that I just didn't want to get dragged into again..."

In fact, having sold almost two million copies of *The Great Escape* since its release in September 1995, it should have been a time of flag-waving and sky-borne rockets, with Blur again ascending to their rightful throne as Britain's best-selling act. "I'd like to be the biggest band in Britain, not the world," Albarn had said just a year before. "That'll do." Yet, just like Blur before them in 1994, Oasis had plugged right in to Britain's cultural zeitgeist, their northern bluster and peerless braggadocio even more emblematic of 'New Lad' than Blur's softer-sounding southern-referencing pop. "Oasis," said once critic in early 1996, "are a band built for our times." Further, by losing the original 'Battle of Britpop', the Mancunians had established themselves as working-class underdogs. And as everyone knows, there's nothing the British like more than an underdog. Again, it was Dave Rowntree that cut to the quick of Blur's latest dilemma. "I think we genuinely believed we could control the situation like puppet masters and you can't," he later confirmed. "It just... gets away from you."

To their credit, Blur had done better than most in attempting to control their engagement with the public via the media. Though Albarn still skirted perilously close to disaster with outrageous pronouncements regarding Blur's manifest destiny on occasion, there had always been a wry smile or glance into the far distance to accompany his boasts. After all, the frontman was more or less following a standard promotional script established in the Fifties by the likes of Little Richard and Jerry Lee Lewis, before being taken up by Bowie, Bolan and myriad others throughout the decades. To wit: "When confronted by doubt or cynicism, keep talking yourself up." Unfortunately, the Brothers Gallagher were also naturals at playing this aspect of the fame game – their assertions even more extreme, their sense of essential entitlement beyond the barbs of certain critics. In their minds, right was now on Oasis' side, and Damon was probably too exhausted or bored to even contemplate a counter attack.

Tired, potentially trapped by a movement they had in large part created, and now "the second best-selling band in Britain", Blur once again returned to the drawing board. Somewhat improbably, they resolved their problems by falling into the arms of America.

Chapter Twelve

Essential Repairs

Despite selling nearly two million copies of *The Great Escape* in less than 12 months, being aboard what Alex James deemed "The good ship Blur" in early 1996 was proving no pleasure cruise even for its senior staff. In fact, if reports of the time are correct – and there is little reason to doubt them – the band were becoming progressively more sick of each other with each passing month. Graham, for instance, had taken to chewing on Alex like a wasp in the press, while Damon fired another pot shot at the bassist during a bad-tempered live interview with DJ Chris Evans on Channel Four music show *TFI Friday*. Though James' occasional descents into "rock stardom" were more often than not the reason for Coxon and Albarn's ire, the two were also beginning to get on each other's nerves, reportedly seeing little or nothing of each other when not on stage.

"Graham was torn between wanting to make art and the demands of the business at that time," Alex later said. "I think he was tormented by the fact that 'Country House' wasn't our best record, but it sold more than anything else. That was what he was famous for, but not what he was proud of."

There were other factors behind Coxon's occasional bouts of ill temper. Battered by the pressures of endless touring and publically having to back an album he privately felt to be sub-standard, the guitarist had again turned to drinking heavily to assuage his feelings of discontent. The results could be nasty. "It's just frustration, really," he told *Q* in the spring of 1996. "I don't like being on the road... there's no emotional stability to it. (But) I'm not a 'punchy' bloke. I just get uptight. It's the pressure."

Alcohol-free for a year, Dave Rowntree was watching it all from the wings, though his newfound position of sobriety among three moderate to heavy imbibers brought about its own set of challenges. "They didn't seem to understand why I gave up," he later said. "I'd have been the same if it had been someone else, because it's quite threatening to drinkers to have one in your midst quit. It makes you ask a lot of questions about yourself."

While Coxon and Albarn's communication problems would be resolved in due course, the damage done by Blur's recent skirmishes with Oasis was going to be harder to remedy. At the beginning of it all, the media coverage surrounding both bands had done them precious little harm, and quite a lot of good. With endless articles about class roots and regional divides, pop vs. rock and "art school vs. no school", journalists had helped turn a simple chart brawl into a nationwide battle, resulting in every teenager, student, and in all probability, pensioner expected to take a side. Sales for 'Country House' and 'Roll With It' went stratospheric as a result. Yet, when the robustly right wing *Daily Mail* chose to toast Blur's success with the headline 'The pop victory that makes it hip to be middle class', one instinctively knew trouble lay ahead. "The most interesting thing that surrounded the press about the single was that it revealed this open sore in our society," said Damon, "our fascination with the divide between working-class and middle-class people."

It seemed such coverage might die away with 'The Battle of Britpop'. But following the initial wave of euphoria which greeted *The Great Escape*, Oasis' subsequent triumphs and the victory rolls that accompanied them had re-activated the argument all over again, this time with a subtle, but potentially even more harmful twist. Instead of just focusing on Blur's family backgrounds and southern roots, the band – and again, Albarn in particular – found themselves being accused of looking down on the very audience that had brought them success in the first place. Far from being rich evocations of the rights and wrongs of British culture, the likes of 'Girls And Boys', 'Parklife', 'Stereotypes' and 'It Could Be You' were now deemed middle-class satires of working-class behaviour. In short, while Oasis appeared authentic and real, Blur had been suddenly cast as villains: their lyrics insincere and condescending, their image as 'new lads' bogus and artificial. "The same fans who'd been going bananas to 'Parklife' six months before were now calling me a wanker in the street," said Damon. In keeping with the standards of the culture Albarn had once been so keen to champion, he and Blur were now experiencing one of its distinctly less pleasant traits. To wit, the backlash.

In truth, questions regarding Blur's image and authenticity had been brewing since the heady days of *Modern Life Is Rubbish*. In 1993, both *NME* and *Melody Maker* had openly challenged the band's then current incarnation as post-modern bovver boys, with Paul Stephen's surly photograph 'British Image No. 1' causing all sorts of fuss. Of course, the problem on that occasion was more to do with accusations that Blur were promoting xenophobia rather than patronising their audience. But the reality behind the group's stance as greyhound-loving, beer-swilling lads had again been called into question during the reviews for *Parklife*, when journalist Simon Price accused them of being "less Essex lager louts" and more "bourgeois indie softies who like a bit of rough..." Price was one of the few to venture down that potentially thorny path at the time, the sheer quality of the album invalidating the need for a debate over the band's legitimacy or lack of street credentials. Nonetheless, his argument had never truly gone away, leaving it to steadily fester until Oasis' "Working-class heroes/middle-class wankers" spiel dragged the whole thing back into the public domain.

In fairness to Damon Albarn – for after all, it was largely his corner to fight – he had always been transparent when it came to his lyrical inspirations and cultural standpoints. For instance, the chance discovery of Allen Klein's sardonic 1962 LP *Well At Least It's British* in a local charity shop proved hugely important to the making of, and philosophy behind, *Modern Life Is Rubbish*. "Klein was a sort of Lionel Bart-type figure in the late fifties and early sixties, and wrote the music and lyrics to *What A Crazy World* (a 1963 film with Joe Brown)," he later told Q. "It was one of the first films to take on the British condition and make something of it in a pop-type way. *Well At Least It's British...* (is) a sort of pop music, but very strange. His lyrics appear very innocent, but at the same time, they have an embryo of cynicism which has been taken on board by everyone since. I can't believe David Bowie didn't know him inside out [or] Ray Davies. It's a fantastic record (and) a very important link for me."

Similarly, Albarn was quick to lavish praise on Martin Amis for his groundbreaking novel *London Fields*. A recommendation from Justine Frischmann, Amis' study of a constantly shifting capital peppered with rogues and pornographers was as important to Damon in the genesis of *Parklife* as Allen Klein's tales of "20th century Englishmen" and "danger ahead" were to its predecessor. "That book," he reiterated, "changed my outlook on life."

That Albarn had been crystal-clear regarding where his inspirations came from was never in doubt. That he, Coxon, Rowntree and James made no attempt to hide their bohemian upbringings, art school backgrounds, voluminous qualifications or liking of fine wines and champagne on the way to success was equally honest. However, when it came to matters of media or public backlash, previous sincerity was utterly irrelevant. Blur had gone from being cheeky chappies winking at the camera to aristocratic dilettantes writing from a position of power and privilege in the space of just seven months. In stark terms, they were now the anti-Oasis, and Albarn was going to pay for it. "By *The Great Escape*, it had all gone wrong," he later said. "I couldn't walk down the street without someone shouting 'Oasis!' I couldn't walk into a shop... or walk down the street (without) people opening their windows and turning up Oasis. It was insane. I mean, try and imagine that. It really was a nightmare, but it made me realise that emotionally, I had a lot of catching up to do."

Albarn chose to do it in Iceland. For so long a remote, strange, almost mystical place that few really knew about, let alone visited, Iceland was probably best known to the average Brit for cold wars and cod wars until the advent of alternative rockers The Sugarcubes in the late eighties. Lively, tuneful and sardonic, the band acted not only as able ambassadors for both Iceland and its independent music scene, but also provided a launch pad for the eventual solo career of their astoundingly talented singer, Björk Guðmundsdóttir. That said, despite accession into the European Economic area in 1994 and the increased political and financial stability it brought, the country remained an improbable tourist destination – its shooting geysers, blue lagoons and splendid glaciers more the stuff of legend than actuality. Suffice to say, this untrammelled destination turned out to be heaven on a stick for Damon Albarn. "I used to have a recurring dream, as a child, of a black sand beach," he later told *The Guardian*. "And one day, I was watching the TV and saw a programme about Iceland, and they had black beaches. So I got on a plane, and booked into the Saga hotel. I didn't know it meant Saga holidays, for older people. I just thought it was 'Saga' as in 'Nordic sagas'. But it was actually an OAP cruise hotel. I was on my own. I didn't know anybody. I went into the street, Laugavegur, where the bars are, and well, that was it..."

What Albarn found was a country full of high art, high adventure, friendly bars, and by all accounts, even friendlier people. "They have a real sense of community there," he later said. "Which, coming from Essex, I'd never had before." More, Iceland's combination of small towns and wide open spaces seemed to tidy up Damon's psyche in double quick time. "The fact that it's so untouched made me feel optimistic," said the singer. "It seem(ed) beyond the reach of such idiocy. I guess I just found something there that I'd been searching for. I just felt incredibly happy and peaceful." Never one to do things by halves, Albarn soon bought both a house and part-share in a bar ('Kaffibarinn') at the heart of Reykjavik, though he remained fearful that his own interest in one of Scandinavia's less explored regions would lead to a potentially fatal upsurge in tourism. "I don't like telling people about it," he said. "It's turning into a 'Clothes Show' special..."*

* Albarn's interest in Iceland was no passing fancy. In addition to buying property in Reykjavik, he was to become an extremely vocal advocate of both the country and its art - working with local bands such as Ghostdigital and involving himself in protests against the construction of hydro-electric plants in Iceland's eastern regions. "It's really a fantastic place," he said in 2007, "...one of the most civilised places on Earth."

"Cleansed" by his experiences in Iceland during the early spring of 1996, Damon was back in England by April, with a sly plan gestating in the back of his ever-clearing head as to Blur's next move. Yet, he did not return to music immediately. Instead, Albarn opted to investigate his other great teenage passion: acting. In the first instance, he took a small but important role in director Antonia Bird's London-set crime drama *Face*. Part of a supporting cast led by British cinema icons Ray Winstone and Robert Carlyle, Damon did not have to carry *Face* in the way he did as lead singer of Blur but when it came to the first day of filming, nerves almost got the better of him. "I did everything to put people off," he later confessed. "I even rang my manager (when) I was first due on set. But he said they could probably sue me for a lot of money, so I turned up. Late. But I turned up. I mean, do you really want a pop star in it?" In his guise as the bright, but ultimately doomed Jason, Albarn was actually quite good, his instinctive cockiness and charm put to strong use by Antonia Bird. Though a short, but sweet performance, it won Damon good notices from critics and the respect of his fellow actors when *Face* was finally released in the summer of 1997. "Damon gave *Face* total respect, total commitment and concentration," said Carlyle at the film's opening night. "I'm confident people are going to be pleasantly surprised."

Albarn was again in Robert Carlyle's company at the Cannes Film Festival where Danny Boyle's none-more-black comedy *Trainspotting* was premiered on May 12, 1996. Based in turn on Irvine Welsh's novel about the ups and downs (but mostly downs) of a group of Edinburgh heroin addicts, *Trainspotting*'s subject matter made for grim, occasionally excruciating viewing. But with its often hysterically funny screenplay and hip young cast – including Ewan McGregor as anti-hero Renton and Carlyle as the psychotic Begbie – the film was destined to become one of Britain's biggest ever box-office successes, eventually grossing over $100 million worldwide. Another key aspect in the movie's fortunes was the quality of its soundtrack, mixing songs by established left-field artists such as Iggy Pop ('Lust For Life') and Lou Reed ('Perfect Day') with the cream of the UK's then current music scene, including Pulp ('Mile End'), Primal Scream (the title track) and Underworld's almost perfect 'Born Slippy'. Unsurprisingly, Blur had also made the cut, with the beauteous 'Sing' and Damon's own composition 'Closet Romantic' both turning up as incidental music within the film. "The book's in a league of its own, and the acting's... well, everyone puts in a real performance, the top of their game," enthused Albarn at the time. "It's just a good British film that doesn't feature Hugh Grant poncing up a hill. *Trainspotting*," he concluded, "is really about blowing a big fart at Hollywood. Proper indigenous film-making."

With the benefit of hindsight, *Trainspotting*'s resolute success was one of the first international manifestations of 'Cool Britannia', a catch-all phrase that would soon replace 'Britpop' in defining the UK as a centre of cultural excellence. While *Parklife* and *Definitely Maybe* might have been the first signifiers that something potentially wondrous was happening, the rest of Britain's artistic and fashion communities had not been slow to catch up. By 1996, the 'Young British Artist' movement (or 'yBa') was making bold splashes abroad, with the work of old Blur cohort Damian Hirst, Tracey Emin, Gillian Wearing and former Goldsmiths graduate Sam Taylor-Wood all exhibiting overseas to strong reviews and the parting of much cash. Coupled with the undoubted gifts of fashion designer Oswald Boateng – who opened his first shop on London's prestigious Savile Row at the tender age of 27 – and promising novelists/playwrights such as Irvine Welsh and Sarah Kane added to the pot, it was no wonder journalists had found a crisp new tag word for their copy.

Even as 'Cool Britannia' was making its entrance on the world stage, Britpop was starting to show signs of death through disinterest. A media-spun phenomenon at the best of times, Britpop had always been frail at its musical centre, with the bands that helped define it very odd bedfellows indeed. In fact, pointing out the differences between the likes of Echobelly, Sleeper, Dodgy and Powder was often much easier than identifying their similarities. Of course, recent events had conspired to dig the hole Britpop would soon fall into. Oasis' resounding victories at home and abroad ensured they no longer needed any restrictive slogans or cloying catchwords to aid their progress. Likewise, Pulp had also achieved escape velocity, their wonderful set at 1995's Glastonbury festival and platinum selling *Different Class* allowing the group to blossom on their own terms. With its flagship bands now sailing out of port for bolder horizons and bigger profits, Britpop's second tier of talent should – in theory at least – have been able to make hay in their absence. In the case of Supergrass, and to a lesser extent, Cast and Shed Seven, this turned out to be briefly true. However, when Britpop's latest poster boys Menswear stumbled after a hit single or two, it was the first real sign the movement was experiencing difficulties in sustaining public interest.

Of equal importance here was the fact that the terms of reference surrounding Britpop were also shifting by mid-1996. Originally the province of guitar-led bands with a distinct indie-facing attitude, the advent of Spice Girls and their monster hit 'Wannabe' again moved the demographic and sound of what actually constituted 'British pop music'. While perhaps not quite pure of heart, Spice Girls were pop in its purest form, an unfathomably marvellous burst of primary colours, mad clothing and wobbly group harmonies. That the best the quintet could summon in the way of a manifesto was shouting 'Girl Power!' at every passing journalist proved no harm to their cause either. Conforming to Noel Gallagher's edict that music didn't have to be politically clever or intellectually driven to sell in the millions, Spice Girls' winning simplicity had stolen the very notion of Britpop away from the hipster contingent and placed it in the hands of children.

But by far the single biggest signifier that Britpop was past its resuscitation point came from the mouth of its inventor. "It is all over now," Damon Albarn told *NME* in May 1996. "We killed Britpop. We chopped it up and put it under the patio long ago. And any band that is still Britpop in a year's time is in serious trouble." Having already taken responsibility for the demise of baggy and grunge, Albarn's latest pronouncement shouldn't have come as any great surprise. After all, some might argue Britpop was his to kill. On this occasion, however, Damon's stony rhetoric was less about establishing critical distance between himself and any flagging movement, and more about saving his own band before it all ended in tears...

While *The Great Escape* might have done brisk business for Blur, the album and its aftermath had taken a considerable toll on their collective psyche. Once the doyens of the music press with an audience to match, the group were now selling a goodly proportion of their records to pre-teens and proto-adolescents hooked in by the Cockney charms of 'Country House'. All great for the bank balance, of course, but death on two legs for their credibility. "When I was a teenager, I deliberately listened to the most obscure music," said Alex. "And I'm sure there are loads of people out there who've come to hate Blur because their little sister now likes them. I mean, you can't listen to music your little sister likes when you're 16. That's partly our fault, because we sold a million bloody records."

There was more to it than kid sisters spoiling the party for surly teenagers. As we have seen, the damage done by Blur's wars with Oasis had also hurt them, with Albarn's need to bring the Gallagher brothers to book re-shaped into a class/regional struggle that cast him as the evil emperor. "After being the 'People's Hero', Damon was the 'People's Prick' for a short period," James continued. "Basically, he's become a loser in a very public way." Albarn could probably tolerate such loss of face. A man seldom quick to turn away from an argument when the occasion warranted it, he might even have secretly enjoyed scuppering his reputation with the new lads and general public. But for Graham Coxon, the nonsense had to stop. "I always wanted us to be really good," he said. "Not just some big... pop group."

As previously described, by early 1996 it was no great secret that Coxon was no longer enjoying his time with Blur. Aside from the Herculean levels of drinking and the metaphorical hanging of Alex James in several cattish press interviews, the guitarist had grown tired of playing "pleasant ditties" to 13-year-olds. Feeling the band had lost much of what had made them genuinely interesting in the first place, and that Damon's increasing control over Blur's recorded output and public image might be doing them more harm than good, Graham's feet began to dig in. "I didn't want (us) to wallow in Britpop filth for the rest of our lives." Given that *The Great Escape* was well on its way to two million sales and Blur had several solid months of touring still ahead of them, Albarn felt any conversations regarding future musical direction could wait. More, he was in no mood to communicate with Coxon when the guitarist was doing his side of the talking from the bottom of a bottle. "It totally ruined our ability to get on with each other," he later said. "When Graham was drunk, he'd be as likely to tell a journalist to fuck off, or I'd hear reports about him being unconscious somewhere in London at four in the morning. It was upsetting because he was my closest male friend."

Ironically, it was another annoying facet of Coxon's nature that ended up being a contributory factor in the repair of that friendship. Desperate to escape the sound of anything remotely British in terms of sound or influence, Graham had taken to monopolising the stereo of Blur's tour bus during their road wars of 1995/1996, playing a plethora of American punk, hardcore, post-rock, indie and newer 'Lo-fi' bands for his own amusement. "I was just a bit bored of Britpop guitar playing," he later told the BBC. "It was all a bit like playing chords and strumming. The Americans though, Sonic Youth, Pavement, Sebadoh and Slint, they seemed to have a freedom of approach that Britpop wasn't offering. So I just started playing that type of stuff on the tour bus, boring the others with it." At first, his colleagues – and Damon in particular – were unsure regarding the worth of Coxon's CD collection. Yet, slowly but surely, the songs started to stick and Albarn began to listen more intently.

The bands Coxon had brought to his friend's attention were not traditionally easy listening. Nor did they offer the pristine production values and perfectly crafted choruses of Green Day or The Offspring, two US pop punk outfits then basking in multi-platinum success throughout the States and Europe. Instead, 'Lo-fi' groups such as Pavement, Sebadoh and Royal Trux were trading in cleanliness and tight arrangements for energy, groove and spirit – these acts were more interested in capturing the immediacy of the moment than working their songs to a perfect death. Inspired by the likes of The Pixies, Pere Ubu, The Butthole Surfers and The Swell Maps, 'Lo-fi' bands basked in an almost arcane fuzziness, often bouncing their sound down onto one track to create a rich soup of scratchy drums and strange harmonic overtones. Not so much a movement per se – "No, but the more I've thought about it, there was something that brought us all together," Sebadoh's Lou Williams later said – this latest wave of independently-minded Americans was soon to influence Blur as much as My Bloody Valentine did seven years before.

One who witnessed that change at close quarters was Diana Gutkind. A classically trained pianist and previously a member of proto-trip hoppers The Sandals, Gutkind had found herself at John Henry Studios in London's Kings Cross auditioning for the role of Blur's touring keyboard player just weeks before 'Country House' was released. "Yes, Damon was holding auditions at John Henry's," she remembered. "He didn't think it was fair to bring the whole band down, so he did it himself." Though the rest of the country was in the throes of Blur fever at the time, Diana only had a small inkling of who they actually were. "I was part of a completely different musical scene at the time, really," she said. "The Sandals were trippy dub with quite a hard edge, and that's what I'd been playing. To be honest, all I really knew about Blur was the song 'Parklife'. I actually had to ask Damon his name. He was quite taken aback at that, I seem to remember..." One imagines he was. Evidently, Albarn did not take Gutkind's enquiry too much to heart. Instead, he gave her the job. "I had two days to learn four albums worth of material before going onstage at the Roskilde festival on July 1, 1995. No pressure then."

From Roskilde onwards, Diana became an integral part of the Blur touring machine, her onstage responsibility to add orchestration and flavour, while also duplicating the keyboard lines Damon had previously recorded. As such, she became extremely familiar with the contents of *The Great Escape*. "*The Great Escape* was an incredibly English record, not so much 'British', but 'English' in its truest sense," she said. "It was very quirky, very culturally specific and therefore not given to breaking America, which is exactly what Blur were trying to do at the time."

As described, Blur's previous Stateside campaigns had not gone without incident, ranging from the promising gigs that accompanied the release of *Leisure* to the extreme tortures of 1992 and beyond. But having dispensed with SBK Records after their tepid efforts to promote *Modern Life...* and *Parklife*, the group's recent signing to Virgin US now provided mild hope that *The Great Escape* might do for Blur yet. "This album is probably more relevant to our American cousins than our previous work, which is more in the 'English' idiom." Albarn improbably offered. "(But) we're English boys. The thing that's always bugged us is that American people can sing about America and that's fine with the rest of the world, which sort of gobbles it all up. Yet, it's a big deal if you come from England and you sing about England. It really shouldn't be such a big deal, though. It's where we come from, and it's what we're best at doing. The whole world wants us except America," he concluded. "So America's a market we're determined to crack..."

As time would show, Oasis took that honour before Blur. But petty feuds, recent losses, future ambitions and a clear commitment to ending the band's adventures in Britpop all coalesced into a magnificent whole when Blur once again toured America in the early months of 1996. Having been steadily bombarded with Pavement, Slint and Sebadoh by Coxon, Albarn was coming to understand and even appreciate what these groups offered. More, he – like the rest of Blur – was enormously taken by the music of The Rentals, who were then providing support for their latest round of Stateside dates. A delightful amalgam of rock undertones and pop overtones, The Rentals' quirky mix of Moog keyboards, fuzzy guitars and 'woo woo-ing' female backing vocals had scored them a mini hit in the US during 1995 with 'Friends Of P'.

According to Diana Gutkind, this odd but endearing sextet might well have helped Damon finally connect the dots from Graham's recent American enthusiasms to his own more melodic-leaning sensibilities. "On that US tour, The Rentals were supporting us," she said. "Everyone just loved them, with these two girl keyboard players on either side of the stage – which was great for me, by the way – because I was usually the only girl among all these men. Now, The Rentals had a very particular sound, which inspired all of us at the time, and I think Damon was really inspired by them too. Anyway, he'd written a couple of songs while on the road in the States. And I remember him playing them to us at sound check (over there). I personally suspect they were very much influenced by the sound of The Rentals. The tracks were 'Chinese Bombs' and 'Song 2'." One of these little explosions in sound would soon be the cornerstone of the new, and some might say, improved Blur.

Progress was quick and sustained. 'Tame', the B-side to 'Stereotypes' and recorded while the band were still in the States, was the first hint that real change might be on the horizon. Full of theremin-sounding synth blasts, sludgy guitars and half-spoken, half-sung vocals from Albarn, 'Tame' took the music of *The Great Escape* and put it through a malfunctioning cement mixer. By April 1996 Blur were back in London and Damon was taking tea with Pavement's sardonic frontman, Steven Malkmus. An acquaintance of Justine Frischmann – who toured alongside Pavement as part of 1995's Lollapalooza festival – Malkmus' reputation among the American indie crowd was impeccable, with his band's 1995 disc *Wowee Zowee* then the very definition of lo-fi. Invited to stay awhile with Albarn and Frischmann at their home in Westbourne Grove, Steven had his own particular take on what Blur were working towards. "They were trying to take back their career and be more personal, I think," he later told *Uncut*. "They were also getting turned on by American Indie music. I guess it was a move. You own yourself and you can do what you want. You're the artist."

Predictably, when news travelled to the music press that Damon was "holding talks" with a doyen of the US alternative scene, journalists were quick to paint Blur's singer as back to his old, bandwagon jumping ways. "Fucking hell, I should be running the government, shouldn't I?" said an aggrieved-sounding Albarn. "I'm so calculating about everything, if my critics are to be believed. (This) whole thing about Steve Malkmus. He's got people telling him, 'You know Damon's only talking to you because he wants to use you for his own evil ends'. It's (just) ludicrous..."

Formally accepting Graham Coxon's challenge to make music that "scares people again", Blur reconvened with producer Stephen Street at Mayfair Studios in London's Primrose Hill during the summer of 1996 to set about making their next album. As usual, working hours were set in stone, with the band seldom straying past their allotted 10-hours a day schedule. However, there were deviations from previously established protocol. Unlike *Parklife* and *The Great Escape*, where songs arrived for recording semi-complete, this time Blur took to playing around with Damon's ideas, giving his new tunes a sense of real urgency and box freshness. "It was the first time we sort of 'jammed'," Coxon later revealed. "We'd never really jammed before. We'd been quite white-coaty, overall about recording, like in a laboratory. (But) we actually felt our way through just playing whatever came into our minds, which was really exciting." To further aid the process, Street's recent purchase of a new piece of recording equipment (the 'Radar' hard disk system) allowed the producer to sample loops and cut-and-paste entire sections of the band's experiments into workable form. "It was great because there was this sort of re-thinking of approach from them," he said. "I also had this great new recorder which enabled me to have the editing capabilities I wanted."

This combination of genuine playfulness and new techniques seemed to put an immediate spring in the step of all concerned, with Blur and their producer once again enjoying the very idea of making music. "They had gone through the whole era of the Blur/Oasis wars, and *Parklife* being in the album charts for over a year and all that and I think they were feeling really burnt out," Street later said. "But (those songs) sort of rekindled their love of making music together by going back to a slightly lo-fi approach."

There was further cause for celebration. After a near decade abusing his liver, Graham Coxon had decided to follow Dave Rowntree's example and completely dispense with the booze. In its place was a new addiction, this time to chocolate-covered peanuts. "Chocolate does the same thing (as drinking) for your happy centres," Graham said. "But you (don't) have ten Mars bars, then end up rolling around on the floor insulting people, shouting and crying for no reason..." Coxon's decision to clean up brought further benefits, not only for his own health, but also his overall relationship with the band. Happily content to avoid each other only months before, Graham and Damon once again found themselves the best of friends, the two often huddling up together in photo sessions at the time. "It's the big love," quipped Albarn. Even Alex James found himself back in Coxon's good books. "Oh, it's nothing bad between me and Alex," the guitarist said. "We're just very similar. If he wants to be The Average White Band, then I'm going to be Gang Of Four. I'm cutting against him all the time because he's a sexy musician and I feel shy and clumsy. So I try and fuck up his funk. It's basically teenage jealousy."

There was little sense of funk to be had on 'Hanging Around', the one and, mercifully, only single by James' new supergroup, Me Me Me. A collaboration between early Duran Duran frontman Stephen Duffy, Elastica drummer Justin Welch, Alex and his friend Charlie Bloor, Me Me Me were originally conceived to write the backing track for Damian Hirst's 1996 short film – the titular 'Hanging Around'. However, along the way, someone had the bright idea to release the song as a single. Remarkably similar to the Sixties novelty hit 'Come Outside', 'Hanging Around' crawled its way to number 19 on the UK charts in August 1996, thanks in large part to James' connection to Blur. But as Alex wheezily chirped his way over a soupy concoction of *Parklife*-referencing brass parts and clanging chords, one was again reminded that while he might have been a thoroughly engaging chap, James was no singer. "I don't do backing vocals," he once said. "I prefer to look cool and smoke a fag." Indeed.

By the autumn of 1996, Blur had almost completed work on their new record. While the majority of tunes were cut in London, Albarn and Stephen Street had ventured north to Iceland for two further weeks, adding more backing vocals and keyboards at a small studio Damon found on his earlier travels. The rest of the band joined them on September 8 for a one-off concert at Reykjavik's Laugardalshöll arena, playing a 23-song set that featured three new three tracks, including Blur's next single, the odd but still beautifully affecting 'Beetlebum'. A genuine shock to the system, 'Beetlebum' had little or nothing in common with what had come before. No overt displays of Cockney jollity. No sly referencing of The Kinks, Madness or The Smiths here. Instead, this was the sound of a group re-constituting itself, in terms of music, image and ambition.

Beginning with a deceptively simple guitar figure from Coxon, its thick tone containing no real treble to speak of, 'Beetlebum' was slow to warm, the song crawling toward the listener on the back of Albarn's sleepy, listless vocal. Of course, Blur had done drowsy before, with 'Miss America' and to a lesser extent, 'Best Days' both coming to mind. But 'Beetlebum''s intro was almost somnambulant in its delivery, the mood solemn and downcast as a result. Then, seemingly out of nowhere, the song's chorus leaped into life, immediately creating a wave of hesitant optimism before things again plunged back into the black. On first hearing, this strong juxtaposition of light and shade was jarring to the ear. Yet, like 'Girls And Boys' before, 'Beetlebum' was that most wondrous of things. It was a grower. "When we first took it around, 'Beetlebum' was perceived as commercial suicide," said James. "Then it went to number one."

Attached to a suitably moody promo from respected video maker Sophie Mueller that somehow made the best of the bags beneath Albarn's tired eyes, 'Beetlebum' was released to utter confusion, then sustained delight on January 23, 1997. As Alex was happy to confirm, it also went to number one in the UK with a bullet. "I think 'Beetlebum''s representative of the fact that as the band's got older, the songs have become more simple," he said at the time. "Now, we can play with them a lot more feeling." An assortment of lo-fi-leaning production, Beatles-like descending harmonies and thudding guitars, 'Beetlebum' was Blur's personal riposte to a post-Britpop, post-Oasis world. Yet, Albarn's lyrics were bereft of any clever social comment or pithy reference to petty rivalries. Nor was he using a character to tell a story. Conversely, 'Beetlebum' was written entirely in the first person, and seemed to be making clear reference to drug use, the term 'Chasing the beetle' common code among users for the smoking of heroin: "I just slip away and I am gone," sang Damon, "Nothing is wrong, she turns me on..."

During 1996, there were persistent rumours that the delays surrounding Elastica's second album had less to do with artistic differences or exiting founder members and were more a case of spiralling drug habits, with heroin often mentioned in connection to the band. For obvious reasons, Frischmann would not care to admit to any such allegations at the time, but by 2002, stringent denials had turned into partial admissions. "There was a fair bit of truth in that, yeah," she told *The Guardian's* Andrew Smith. Given the facts, it is only fair to suggest that Albarn had been a witness to some of the band's difficulties. Yet, while 'Beetlebum' was largely written from the perspective of observer, it also seemed to imply a certain level of participation too, with Damon's understanding of the drug and its effects made crystal clear in the song's narcotic lyricism.

Again, in 1997, no one was asking any probing questions of him on this issue. But that all changed in 2012, when *Guardian* writer John Harris broached the subject directly, enquiring of the songwriter whether his critics and audience simply chose to ignore the fact he might have been experimenting with such drugs. "I thought everyone *did*," Albarn replied. "I thought everyone was just being really nice, and not making too much of a deal of it. Because, you know, although I totally agree with your astute observation, the reality of any experimentation is that it can become habitual, and it can take over your life. I would never, ever disagree with the enlightening abilities of drugs, I also respect their... potency. You have to have very good intentions, otherwise... even the best intentions in the world can go awry." Though his answer was neither concealed nor evasive, it was also not particularly revelatory. In the end, one was left to draw his or her own conclusions.

A song specifically designed to cut stylistic ties with the recent past, 'Beetlebum' proved an able precursor for the band's fifth album – the self-titled *Blur* – which was released internationally on February 10, 1997. As ever before, the CD cover was immediately striking, its smudged image of a patient being rushed through a hospital corridor on a metal gurney the first time Blur had used their hazy name to draw a direct correlation with their commercial image. The work of former Stylorouge designers Chris Thomson and Richard Bull, the out-of-focus photo was meant to convey a sense of "both optimism and scariness", though as critic Mark Bennett ably deduced, it could also be read as a subtle nod to Blur's ailing status of some months before. With the mood now set, it was time for the music to do its job. In keeping with their declaration to abandon Britpop in favour of "something much more personal and involving", *Blur* delivered 14 songs of varying quality: some quite brilliant, others perhaps less so. Yet, one could never accuse the band of resting on their laurels or cynically trading on former glories. In fact, *Blur* promoted change and revision on most all fronts, though its later reputation as their "American album" remains something of a misnomer.

The first thing that struck like a hammer was how loose and intimate *Blur* sounded in comparison to its forbears. In fact, the disc was full of instruments bumping or even tripping over each other, this sense of music unfastening itself from the shackles of song arrangements ably enhanced by Stephen Street's paradoxically tight, but never invasive production. Similarly, Albarn's previously dogged pursuit of 'the big chorus' was largely absent, with tunes allowed to find their own level instead of being sternly instructed to follow a preordained path. Obviously, the band's recent penchant for jamming had helped them well in this area. Also noteworthy was the room given to experimentation in its purest form. In fact, each member of Blur seemed to be having the time of their life trying out new approaches to the business of guitar, bass, drum, keyboards and vocals. Sometimes the results could be cacophonous, even primal in their energy and execution, but they were seldom less than interesting for it. "Blur had decided that commercial pressures and writing hit singles wasn't going to be the main consideration anymore," Street said by way of explanation. "The mood in the studio was very different to when I'd first worked with them. Once we got past those first few days, where I felt everyone was treading on eggshells, there was a great atmosphere." Thankfully, said atmosphere was wholly translatable to the listener.

Blur's musical highlights were many, varied and sometimes barking mad. On 'Country Sad Ballad Man', the quartet had somehow managed to incorporate elements of pastoral psychedelia into a low-fi cowboy song, with James' stand-up bass and Albarn's warbling falsetto offset by Coxon's squealing guitar interjections and a rogue Jews harp. 'Theme From Retro' was even more unusual, its fusion of dub and trip-hop flavours all mingling within a tune that still recalled the very best of 2 Tone. Full of Drumatix beat boxes and rattling sound FX, 'On Your Own' also owed a debt of gratitude to the early eighties, though Damon and Graham's howling, Swell Maps-influenced backing vocals reclaimed the song from that decade and pushed it nicely towards the new millennium. 'Chinese Bombs', however, was pure American hardcore via the mosh pits of the East End, the track still as aggressive, disjointed and atonal as it had been when Albarn first played it to his bandmates in the States a year before. Conversely, 'I'm Just A Killer For Your Love' was aurally comparable to falling in the door after a big night out, its bleary fuzz-tone guitars, walking drums and deadpan vocals as inviting as a comfy sofa following one too many drinks.

Of *Blur*'s other tunes, 'Movin' On' slyly reworked the melody line of 'Country Sad...' into an up-tempo lo-fi treat, albeit one with some distinct Wire and XTC influences on tap. Another set of British institutions were also at the heart of three more tracks. The most backward-facing song on the album, 'Look Inside America' could easily have been an out-take from *Parklife*, its gentle opening strains and clean orchestral sweeps again recalling the work of The Kinks, The Beatles, and most tellingly, Blur's own 'End Of A Century'. In 1994, this would have been no bad thing at all. But in the band's newly re-imagined universe of stereo-defying bumps, grinds and bleeps, 'Look Inside America' now soundly curiously old-fashioned, or "yesterday's sound today" as one critic sourly put it. Thankfully, 'Strange News From Another Star' fared much better. While clearly in thrall to 'Space Oddity'-period David Bowie, this endearing, winsome ballad still had enough about it to trade on its own terms, the tune's free-jazz ending a genuine surprise after nearly three or so minutes of perfectly meshing chord patterns and dreamy keyboards. 'M.O.R.' couldn't outrun its inspirations as easily. A naked update of Bowie's 'Boys Keep Swinging' and Brian Eno's 'Fantastic Voyage', both composers allegedly came forward with their lawyers in tow when Blur released 'M.O.R.' as a single in September 1997. Thankfully, an accommodation over royalties and songwriting credits was soon reached, with 'M.O.R.' peaking at number 15 on the UK charts.

So far, *Blur* had offered much, its mix of Coxon-approved new influences such as Pavement, Sebadoh, Swell Maps and even Beck proving no great challenge to Albarn's abilities to absorb them as a songwriter. "This album's neither particularly American nor British, you know," said Graham at the time. "It's more a... hybrid." That said, two of Blur's strongest tracks were distinctly American and quintessentially European in their sensibilities. With 'You're So Great', Coxon had fashioned one giant love letter to Alex Chilton's Memphis power pop quartet, Big Star. Sung with gusto, if no great voice by Graham himself, 'You're So Great' was still an exquisite little song, its tale of a hung-over man held up by coffee and the affection of his partner no doubt taking its standpoint from his own recent battles with alcohol. "When we recorded 'You're So Great'," he confessed, "I was sitting under a table and had the lights out." Damon's 'Death Of A Party' was just as good, if not better. Conjoining his long-time affection for The Specials to a recent romance with Krautrock in general and Faust in particular, '...Party''s hypnotised feel and 'Ghost Town'-like structure resulted in a "headfuck of a tune" that had one foot in Seventies Bremen and the other in Eighties Coventry. "Damon's obviously gone off his head a bit more with this album," Coxon laughed.

Though it was unlikely Albarn had actually lost his marbles, the singer's wordplay on *Blur* did reveal a new degree of seeming honesty, with characters like 'Tracy Jacks', 'Bill Barrett' and 'Dan Abnormal' forever consigned to the lyrical dustbin in favour of a clear, first-person narrative style. Indeed, if Damon was speaking from his own personal experience, then the last year had been no great picnic for either him or the band. 'Country Sad...', for instance, was awash with notions of failure, its references to planning "a comeback roll" stymied by crushing exhaustion, physical inertia and a desperate need for sleep: "I've had my chances," he sang, "And they had me... I'm a ballad man, I've gone and fucked it." 'Strange News...' wallowed in similar feelings of regret and loss of direction, with Albarn using the title of German romantic author Hermann Hesse's collection of short stories to inform his own plunge into uncertainty. "I wrote that (song) entirely in Iceland, the first time I went there," he later revealed. "It was very dark at (that) time of year... it doesn't get light until half past 12 and then it gets dark again at three o'clock. So it's a very strange place to be and it's very quiet. There was a lot of snow..."

'Death Of A Party' and 'Essex Dogs' were even bleaker in their sentiments. In the former's case, Damon appeared to be wallowing in Morrissey-like notions of guilt and self-recrimination, the song's drudging backbeat a suitable companion to lines such as "Go to another party and hang myself gently on the shelf..." This really was the stuff of emotional torpor. "They're just sad songs," he said at the time. "We're quite good at sad songs. 'Death Of A Party' is (about) melancholy reminiscences. Just being a male... a drunk male." 'Essex Dogs' required an even stronger constitution. A "tonal poem" accompanied by some very atonal blasts of guitar from Coxon, '...Dogs' found Albarn channelling his inner Martin Amis. However, with its talk of dead-end bars and soldiers looking for a fight, it was hard not to tie Albarn's gangster-referencing slang to his own experiences of getting into scraps with crusties and squaddies as a teenager in Colchester.

Thankfully, it wasn't all doom and gloom. On 'M.O.R.', Damon managed to simultaneously honour and satirise David Bowie's famous 'cut-up' lyric technique, with repeated refrains such as "It's automatic (it's automatic)" and "I need to unload (need to unload)" cheekily recalling the Grand Dame's work on *Lodger* and *Scary Monsters*. (Of course, Albarn did end up paying for his cheek in reduced royalties.) 'Look Inside America' was also given to bursts of humour, with Blur's frontman blearily pulling himself together the morning after a late night US show: "Good morning, lethargy, drink Pepsi, it's good for energy..." Further, 'Look Inside...' seemed to finally extend an olive branch in the direction of a country Damon had repeatedly wrestled with in times past: "Look inside America," rang the song's chorus, "she's alright, she's alright." If not quite the stuff of beaming smiles and hearty handshakes, it was at least a start...

An album of surprising intimacy and sometimes great immediacy, *Blur*'s clever jumble of US and European influences placed the band who made it firmly in the middle of the Atlantic Ocean, doffing a cap to their surrounding land masses for inspiration, and no doubt, possible sales. As importantly, the record's more abrasive edges and displays of tonal primitivism also confirmed that in the same way Spice Girls had appropriated the notion of Britpop to serve their own purposes, Blur were now intent on stealing back their music from the teenybopper set and re-directing it towards an adult market. "We've been very courageous, I think," said Coxon. "I don't see any of our contemporaries being courageous with their music at all." Indeed, such was the shock at some of *Blur*'s cacophonous wares that some felt Graham had staged a musical coup within the group's ranks, the once shy guitarist now giving orders to Albarn. It was an opinion both he and his bandmates were keen to refute. "It's not 'Graham's album'," barked Rowntree. "There was four people's influence on the (last) four albums, but on this one, it's more four people pulling in the same direction." Coxon was equally strong on the notion that Blur remained a democracy. "I don't know why people think it's (my album)," he said. "Maybe I just had some strong ideas this time. I had an awful lot of sounds and styles in mind, so I collected them together, put them through my sieve and then applied it to Damon's songs. And it applied very easily, which was very lucky..."

With its music and lyrics given to extremes of emotion and sound, and no easy inroads offered to listeners on first hearing, *Blur* was bound to divide opinion on release. On one hand, some (including *The Guardian*) loved it. Others (mainly *The Independent*) hated the sight of it. Yet, it was left to a previous naysayer to offer the most balanced and insightful review of the disc's wobbling charms. "To fans who've been there since 1990, Blur will sound like progressive regression, a necessary retreat," said *Q*'s Andrew Collins. "Simply, it takes the abiding punk guitar instinct of Graham Coxon and the all-round artfulness that's always driven the band and plays them upfront – leaving the music hall comedians, the commuters, trumpeters and Phil Daniels on the bench. In this Stalinist rewrite of history, it's like 'Country House' never happened. *Blur*," he concluded, "does not have the required four hits on it – unless the world is a cleverer place than it looks – and that's all right. Blur, the band, have no need to split, or more importantly, worry about what 'the other lot' are up to. They are now – on the strength of (this) truly difficult fifth album – officially on different planets." Sound points all.

A successful, if somewhat dissonant re-invention, *Blur* not only saved the band from the embarrassment of going under with Britpop or being bullied off the musical playground by Oasis. It also strongly re-established their commercial profile, debuting at number one in the UK (where it went on to sell over a million copies), while also going Top Ten in Japan and several countries in Europe. "Our heads are a lot more sorted now," said Rowntree. "No more real distractions." Yet, there was one market that had always held out on Blur, keeping its modesty and pocket money at arm's length from both their image and music. If Damon Albarn truly wanted to make good on his promise that Blur would change things at a fundamental level then they had to crack America. "We've never liked chickening out of something," said the singer, "and the States is still a challenge." In the end, it took only two words for the USA to finally succumb to Blur's charms.

Woo and Hoo.

Chapter Thirteen

Political Gains, Personal Losses

America, then. Food boss Dave Balfe had coveted it. Damon had spent nearly five years hauling it over the coals, writing songs about it or telling it to wake up. Graham even suggested it was full of racoon hunters. But one way or another, America had hung over Blur's career like a light-sapping tree since they first visited the country in 1991. "We do really well on the coasts," Alex said. "New York, San Francisco. Sadly, the middle bit tends to ignore us, which is a shame, because that's where most people live. We just haven't entered the farmers' consciousness yet."

As stated, the reasons were manifold. Blur were too British – perhaps too English – to truly make sense in the States, their music arch and artful, their image and references a tad self-contained. Without a grand gesture to understand or embrace, America had got on with the business of largely ignoring Blur. After all, they had their own groups to attend to. "We're pretty used to achieving mediocre record sales in the USA," Damon sighed. "It's something I've learned to live with." Though not necessarily give up on.

Since signing with Virgin US in 1996, Blur had once again redirected some of their efforts to cracking the States, touring there early in that year and plugging their songs on various radio shows and music TV networks. They even tried the direct route, performing 'Charmless Man' in front of an audience of millions on *NBC* talk show *Late Night With Conan O'Brien.* As *The Great Escape*'s brief appearance at number 150 on the *Billboard* charts confirmed, that hadn't worked either. The group's new album *Blur,* however, offered a modicum of new hope. While the contents were often more perplexing than its predecessor and the music's sharp angles occasionally requiring a protractor to calculate, *Blur* also drew direct influence from American sources: the lo-fi grit of Pavement and Sebadoh as present in its grooves as The Specials or Faust. Even if such acts were on the sharp end of the US market, their absorption into the Blur sound machine meant that Coxon's efforts to seek new inspirations from outside their own self-invented walls wasn't in vain. "It was the arse end of Britpop," said Alex, "and we just wanted to run away from it and listen to something new, something... American." It turned out to be a wise decision.

As Blur's touring keyboardist Diana Gutkind confirmed, Damon Albarn had presented the band with two brand new songs at a soundcheck while on tour in the States during early February, 1996.* In the case of 'Chinese Bombs', the title summed things up rather nicely, its stop-start chords and maniacal rhythm packing a hardcore-approved wallop to the senses. 'Song 2' was very different, though perhaps no less American. Again, according to Gutkind, Blur's admiration of their quirky, alt-rock support band The Rentals may have played into what Damon had in mind for the track – with Petra Haden and Cherielynn Westrich's chirping 'Woo a woo' backing vocals on 'Friends Of P' of minor inspiration to him. But 'Song 2' was no idle homage or calculated rip-off. In fact, when Albarn first played it to his colleagues, the tune was a simple, mid-tempo shuffle with its now famous 'Woo Hoo' refrain completely absent. Instead, Blur's frontman simply whistled over the chorus, his mind not fully made up on how to take things forward at the time. More, he wasn't even sure that

* Though no one can remember for sure, Albarn's demonstration probably took place at Atlanta's Cotton Club on February 6, 1996. Both 'Chinese Bombs' and 'Song 2' made their live debut at Sweden's Hultsfred Festival on 15 June 1996.

'Song 2' merited any great attention, feeling that it was more passing fancy than potential hit. "I genuinely didn't know it was a single," he later said. "I mean we ended up cutting it in a couple of hours, one of those songs you almost didn't know you'd recorded. Guess I got that one completely wrong."

Albarn wasn't lying about the almost flippant nature of how Blur recorded 'Song 2'. Actually cut to tape in 30 minutes some four months later at Mayfair Studios, its bopping rhythm was achieved by Graham shadowing Dave on a separate drum kit, the former's imprecise patterns clattering nicely against Rowntree's more methodical approach: "It's expensive to do it that way, but it made it sound really punky." As more astute ears will already know, Coxon's terrifyingly brilliant quiet/loud guitar wasn't even properly tuned during the session, a fact no-one picked up until after the event. "Yeah, my guitar was out of tune for most of the bloody song," he later laughed. James' decision to completely drop out of 'Song 2''s verses was quite deliberate, however. Feeling that his bass packed more punch if he only used it on the track's super-overdriven chorus, this only added to the ad hoc nature of things. But it was Albarn's part-laconic, part-lunatic vocal that placed the proverbial cherry on top of the cake, the singer's explosive entrance at the start of the track then dialled down to the level of casual conversation before once again tearing at the speakers: "Woo Hoo! When I feel heavy metal!"

A tune Damon was so diffident about that he didn't even bother to give it a proper title, 'Song 2' eventually became the second single to be released from Blur's fifth album, making its way into shops on April 7, 1997. Backed by another marvellous video from Sophie Mueller that had the group packed into a tightly confined, carpeted space while being simultaneously buffeted by "demonic kinds of wind", 'Song 2' was probably expected to do quite well, but no more than that. "We knew it was strong," said Rowntree, "but it wasn't a traditional single, either."

What happened next was a genuine surprise to all. Not only did 'Song 2' do well for Blur in the UK, where it went straight to number two in the charts, but it also began picking up real momentum in

Canada and the USA. "Literally overnight," joked Coxon, "we were the 'Woo Hoo!' band." Within weeks, they had shot to number one in the Canadian Alternative Top 30 and also found themselves at number six in *Billboard*'s 'Modern Rock' chart. At long last, Blur had their American hit. "I suppose 'Song 2''s got everything it needs in the first five seconds," Damon later told *VH1*. "The vocals, the enormous guitars. It's perfect as a sound bite, it's immediately recognisable. Looking back, I'm really glad it did well in America, because people were always saying that we wouldn't do it there. It was... gratifying to prove them wrong."

Gratifying and extremely profitable. Though 'Song 2' didn't quite push its parent album to Oasis-like heights in the States (*Blur* actually peaked at number 62 in the charts there), its prolonged shelf-life as backing music for American/Canadian advertisements, soundtracks and sports events proved astoundingly successful for the band, with Labatts beer and Intel Pentium two of the tune's earlier licensees. By 1998, Matt Groening had come on board too, using it for an episode of his rather wonderful *The Simpsons* TV show. Hollywood wasn't far behind either, as director Paul Verhoeven and actress/producer Drew Barrymore picked up the track for their movies *Starship Troopers* and *Charlie's Angels* respectively. Video game makers also came calling, with 'Song 2' providing later incidental music for *Rocksmith*, *Guitar Hero 5*, *Lego Rock Band* and *Madden NFL 11*, among others. But it was US and Canadian athletes that turned Blur's little bundle of punch into something of a sporting phenomenon, with the Vancouver Giants, the Pittsburgh Penguins, the Ottawa Senators and the St. Louis Blues (all hockey teams) as well as the Pittsburgh Steelers and Wilmington Blue Rocks (both baseball) using 'Song 2''s 'Woo Hoo!' chorus to mark a goal or touchdown. By the end of the millennium alone, Blur were better off to the tune of £2 million for just half an hour's work. "'Song 2''s a bit unsophisticated and thuggish," Graham later said, "But that's what some people like..."

A commercial hit and advertising monster that was also nominated for two MTV Video Awards and two more Brits to boot, 'Song 2''s success both at home and abroad realistically meant that Blur would never have to work again. However, while Albarn and Co. were content to licence the tune where they felt appropriate, they did have their standards. This fact was driven home with stern force when the US military reportedly approached the group for its use to unveil their new Stealth bomber in 1998. The grandson of a Quaker/life-long pacifist, and strongly anti-war in his own moral sentiments, Albarn – and indeed, his bandmates – were having none of it. Sports, movies and computers were one thing. Invisible planes and transatlantic bombing capability were quite another. "Everyone has their own way of justifying getting involved in advertising," said Albarn, "but we obviously turned that down..."

Buoyed by the reception given their latest work, and with *Blur* the album well on its way to two million worldwide sales, the band spent most of 1997 on the road, with America now unsurprisingly a continuing target in their sights. After a raft of UK and European appearances at the start of the year, Blur headed to the States in April for 11 high profile gigs, including one notable stop-off at San Francisco's legendary Fillmore theatre. Such was their level of confidence at this point that the group chose to open their set with the lazy charms of 'Beetlebum' before regaling the audience with older standards such as 'Popscene', 'Colin Zeal' and even rarer gems like 'Coping', 'Inertia' and 'Sing'. In New York, they went one further, pulling out the mellow psychedelic charms of 'Beetlebum' B-side 'Woodpigeon Song' for the benefit of several hundred bemused onlookers at Tower Records. That said, this pinballing strategy of mixing the anomalous with more established fare seemed to be doing them no harm at all. "It's funny," said Albarn, "but *Blur* is our biggest selling album to date."

The touring circus continued without respite. After the first leg of their US campaign, Blur returned to Europe for 28 further arena/theatre shows, meandering across Belgium, Germany, Austria, France, Spain and Italy throughout May before once again hopping a plane for Japan. Here, fans were treated to a brand new song called 'Swallows In The Heatwave'. Perhaps the group's most obvious attempt yet to trump Pavement and Sebadoh, 'Swallows...' sounded as if it was literally falling apart at the seams, with Graham's anarchic guitar stabs and Albarn's 'Oo woo oo hoo' vocals on the cusp of lo-fi pastiche. Cleaned up, tightly arranged and given a shiny production treatment, the tune might well have been another single. But that was hardly the point anymore. Blur were back to testing both the perimeters of their sound and audience in a way they had seldom engaged in since the heady days of Seymour. ('Swallows...' was later released as one of the B-sides to 'M.O.R.').

June 1997 brought another Blur-related product, this time in the shape of the single 'On Your Own'. A curious little ditty at the best of times, 'On Your Own' again trumped expectations by getting to number five in the UK charts, despite trading on one of the oddest choruses Albarn had yet written. "Actually, it was one of the first demos I did for *Blur*," he said. "I was far more uncompromising (at that point), using weirder sounds. Also, the song wasn't about anyone in particular. More a personal statement." With its talk of holy men tip-toeing their way across the Ganges, bankrupt Californian game show hosts and happy days spent in clubs and discos 'On Your Own' was as much a tonal travelogue as proper pop single. Yet, unlike some of the more maudlin lyrics presented on *Blur*, Damon sounded content with his lot on this occasion, even if there was some acid floating in the proverbial water supply: "Someone stumbles to the bathroom with the horrors," he sang, "Says 'Lord, give me faith, for I've jumped into space...'" Backed by several tracks originally recorded for a BBC Radio 1 session on the patio of DJ John Peel's home in Suffolk on April 22, 1997 (it became known as the 'Peel Acres' tape), 'On Your Own' would take up semi-permanent residence at encore time throughout the year.

Just a month or so after Blur entered the charts with 'On Your Own', Oasis' Noel Gallagher triumphantly strode through the door of number 10 Downing Street. However, despite all his recent successes – two mammoth gigs at Knebworth Park in front of 250,000 people in August 1996, and two more UK number one singles since 'Roll With It' – Gallagher was not there to take up the position of Prime Minister. He was simply meeting one. Since coming to power on the back of a landslide Labour victory in May 1997, Anthony Charles Lynton Blair, or 'Tony' to his friends (of which there appeared many) was basking in the same levels of popular adulation as Oasis' own songwriter. At only 43 years old, Blair was not only the youngest ever PM since 1812, but also a huge fan of rock music, having briefly fronted the band Ugly Rumours while studying law at Oxford University. Sadly, ugly rumours would become something of a recurring theme for the politician during his later years in office.

Back in 1997, Tony Blair was the public face of 'New Labour', a party which after 17 odd years of unbroken Tory rule supposedly represented major change, a fresh perspective and new sense of optimism for the country, and as such one that aligned itself perfectly with all those starry notions of 'Britpop', 'Brit Art' and 'Cool Britannia'. In fact, in charting his progress to power, Blair had proved himself extremely supportive of such movements and the artists who represented them, including Damon Albarn. "I'd met Tony Blair very early on," said Blur's frontman. "I was invited for gin & tonics with him and (Deputy Leader) John Prescott. An interesting chat with them before they got into power, you might say. They asked me what I thought about 'the youth' and where their heads were at. It was all a bit odd, patronising and very cynical. But that was his style of operation, power at any cost, really. It (wasn't) 'Labour' anymore. I'm not sure what you'd call it, but they need to change the name."

When the call came for a gathering of the "artistic tribes" in Whitehall two odd months after Blair took office, Albarn proved unavailable. "You'd already see politicians at the Brits getting their pictures taken with musicians who are a bit drunk. It all stank to me." But not to Noel Gallagher, at least at the time. "I was on the dole four years earlier, then there I was, arriving at 10 Downing Street in a Rolls Royce. What a trip," he later told the BBC. "The Labour Party were trying to reach out to the artistic community. (Our manager) Alan McGee said they wanted to meet me. Well, why wouldn't they want to meet me? Of course, I knew I'd get a lot of flak over it, but I wasn't going there because I thought I was better than anyone else. I was only there because *I was*, nobody else." When hearing that Gallagher had accepted an invitation to meet with the PM, Damon passed on his thoughts via the media: "Enjoy the schmooze, comrade."

As time came to quickly show, Albarn had been right to decline his own invite to number 10, the singer's ability to spot cynical political posturing for the sake of the youth vote both commendable and astute. But by Damon's own admission, the very fact he was on Tony Blair's party wish list at all was worrying of itself. "Emotionally, there was very little connection (with them). I just felt... troubled," he later said. "All those things that went on at that time troubled me. It just felt normal to be introduced to the leader of the opposition. That shows how fucked up it had all become." For some, and they are probably right, Blair's show business reception behind a big black door in Whitehall on July 30, 1997 marked the true death to Britpop, the idea and what it had become now taken from the hands of musicians like Gallagher and remoulded into a political device. "When Tony Blair came along," Noel later told *The Guardian*, "it was like 'Ah, he's going to outsmart all these public school cunts, but then we all got carried away in 1997, didn't we?" As evidenced, Damon Albarn might beg to differ.*

Mercifully, Blur's increased profile in the States and elsewhere meant that Albarn could take flight from all the celebrations and false dawns at home and concentrate his efforts on pushing the group's latest album further up various charts. Now road warriors to a man, Blur completed another 20 dates in the US across June and early July, including a well-received 40-minute set at the 'Tibetan Freedom Concert'. Appearing alongside the likes of U2, Patti Smith and Alanis Morissette at New York's Downing Stadium on June 8, this charitable event also provided the band with another opportunity to see Sonic Youth and Pavement who were in attendance to offer their own support for Tibetan independence from China. "Oh, it was a lovely, lovely, lovely and very sweaty day," laughed James.

Come August, and Blur were back in Europe and on the festival circuit, with stop-offs at Portugal's Sudoeste, Belgium's Pukkelpop and

* In a 2010 interview, Albarn alleged that when he later criticised Tony Blair's decision not to send his children to a comprehensive school, he received a curt note from Whitehall asking that he keep his own counsel on such matters. "Unpleasant," said the singer.

Sweden's Water before returning to England for V97 in Chelmsford and Leeds respectively. Backed by cosmic cod rockers Kula Shaker and surf metallers Reef, Damon was in particularly fine form, with his introduction to 'Chinese Bombs' – "This one's all about tae kwan do" – raising a laugh from his bandmates and the crowd alike. Renewing their acquaintance with Scandinavia, Blur next travelled to the Faroe Islands and Greenland for "a suitably Nordic vibe". Areas usually avoided on most tour itineraries, the locals nevertheless came out in force, especially in Greenland, where approximately one in 45 of the country's population descended en masse on the capital of Nuuk to see what all the fuss was about. "Greenland was pretty insane," Damon told *Select*. "There was only about 1,200 people, but where you consider there's only 45,000 in the whole country, that's a pretty good turnout."

Another month brought another set of dates, as Blur flew back to America and Canada for 24 more gigs in September. By now Diana Gutkind was losing track of not only which country she was in, but also which continent. "It's an incredible thing living out of a suitcase, you know," said the keyboardist. "I remember phoning my mother one morning and her saying, 'Hello darling, What country are you in?' I was just sitting there going 'Errr...'. She then asked 'Well, what continent are you in?' I was so tired I actually couldn't remember whether I was in Asia or North America. You're crossing time zones constantly, moving all the time. Your brain just goes a bit squiffy. In fact, touring's a bit like being back at school, now that I think about it. Waking up in the morning and hearing things like, 'Have you got your uniform on? Have you got your books ready?' You give (your life) over to the tour manager. He's got to get you on that bloody bus and get you to the airport. And Ivan Thomas, Blur's tour manager, was really good at that... dealing with this bunch of abhorrent, tired teenage types growling at him every morning from under their coats..." While the schedule was punishing for all concerned, the rewards were palpable. A year before, Blur appeared to be a lost cause in the States. But by October 1997, they had sold over 500,000 copies of their self-titled album. "There is justice," Dave Rowntree wryly observed.

Determined to see every corner of the globe before the end of the year, Blur next ventured to Australia and New Zealand, a first for the band. Arriving on the back of a Top Five hit with 'Song 2', Blur were treated like visiting royalty by the Aussies and Kiwis, with sold out shows in Auckland, Brisbane, Sydney, Melbourne and Perth. To show their appreciation, the group re-instated their mad cover of The Knack's 'My Sharona' at several concerts.

Leaving Oz behind, Blur flew on to Thailand and Singapore for two gigs at MBK Hall and the famed Harbour Pavilion, before heading home for a 12-date arena tour, culminating with three shows at the more intimate Brixton Academy. Not quite Oasis numbers, of course, but still highly respectable by anyone's standards. "We're still playing the biggest (places) in the country," Albarn said by way of explanation. "10,000 people in Manchester, for instance, so I don't see any great 'alienation'. I've said it ad infinitum, but just to ram home the point yet again, *Blur* is our biggest selling album to date."

Some 127 concerts, 23 countries and islands, and now over two million sales later, Blur finally came to rest on December 17, 1997. The war wounds were many. Chipped bones, recurring bouts of gastric flu, stubbed toes, gashed cheekbones and sleep just a fond childhood memory. Yet, Coxon was still sober, Alex had found a Jacuzzi in New Mexico he particularly liked and they were all still talking to each other, or thereabouts. Further, the band had at last made their presence felt in the USA, picking up the hipster set not only on both coasts, but also "the big bit in the middle". For James, this was especially pleasing. "All these sideways haircuts and vintage sneakers in the audience, it's quite nice to see, really."

Outside the bubble Blur had created for themselves, things were not quite as rosy. Having already ventured around the world for much of the previous year, Damon Albarn flew to Bali with Justine Frischmann in February 1998 in a last ditch effort to patch up their flagging relationship. There was much work to be done. Like Albarn, Justine had spent the last 18 months either touring or recording with Elastica, her band visiting America half a dozen times during that period alone. At first, the couple made concerted efforts to spend time with each other during breaks in their schedule. But Blur's recent good fortune in the States and the continuing (sometimes self-imposed) demands on Frischmann to break Elastica in the same territory meant those occasions were becoming few and far between.

Then there were the rumours, with unfettered drug use and infidelity at the top of the list. Away from stories about beetle-chasing, a supposed dalliance between Justine and former Kingmaker frontman Loz Hardy was first out of the traps and onto the pages of the music press. There was nothing to it. The pair had known each other for years and Frischmann considered Hardy one of her closest confidants. Primal Scream's Bobby Gillespie was up next. Again, it was a case of smoke and mirrors, though Damon's joke that Gillespie should be running a "Rolling Stones museum in Brighton" only added to the level of intrigue. However, Justine's entirely platonic efforts to reconcile her friendship with Brett Anderson after the Suede/Blur wars of 1992/3 solicited much greatest interest. "We're just really cool friends," Frischmann explained in 1997, "and I just hate the thought of investing all this time in someone and they just disappear, and all that time just slips down the drain."

Of course, Albarn had his own corner to fight when it came to matters of prurience. Once described by Justine as "just not that into sex", she nonetheless understood that he might have suffered the "occasional lapse in concentration" here and there. "If someone comes back to me at the end of the day, they can do what they like in the interim," Frischmann once told *Sky*. "With Damon and me, he's away such a lot, or I am, that I really, really can't expect him to be faithful. It's just not practical. You know, you come off stage and might have had 2,000 people screaming at you, and you've had too much to drink and you want that intensity to go on. You want to have that much attention for the rest of the evening. I totally understand that, but it's like there's a part of me that doesn't want people to think I don't know about it. Because it's like, if I'm letting him do this, then I want the credit for it, almost."

In the end, what brought down Albarn and Frischmann was little or nothing to do with notions of faithlessness or possible heroin use, but was more connected to children, or specifically the lack of them. "Damon said 'You've given me a good run for my money, you've proved you're as good as I am, you've had a hit in America, now settle down and let's have some kids." Possibly angered by the ultimatum – and reportedly suspicious that Albarn was trying to manage or control their relationship rather than address its underlying problems – Justine declined his entreaties and the pair eventually split in August 1998. They had been together for most of the decade. "Eight years," said Damon. "The whole of my twenties. When it finishes, it's a divorce..."

The fall out for both parties was sustained. By her own admission, Frischmann became something of a recluse, seeking out old friends to keep her company behind closed doors, while all but abandoning work on Elastica's second album. Albarn, on the other hand, handled things in the time-honoured fashion of many a newly single male. Instead of moving his belongings from Notting Hill to another property he owned in Devon for a much-needed change of scenery, Blur's frontman set up shop at a rented flat just around the corner in Westbourne Grove. "It was horrible," he later told *The Face*'s Sylvia Patterson. "I felt quite alone. It was just a very painful and protracted separation. But when you're in love with somebody, you're in love with them, aren't you?"

Drafted in to help Damon overcome at least some of his difficulties was new flatmate Jamie Hewlett. Born just days apart, the two were first introduced in 1991 when Hewlett was working as a journalist/artist for *Deadline*, a magazine that mixed comic book strips by British creators with articles on music and culture. Having interviewed Blur for the publication, Jamie deemed Damon an "arsey wanker" in the resulting feature. Despite this initial stumbling block, a friendship slowly ensued.*

* Said friendship was a tad messy to begin with. Hewlett was originally chums with Graham Coxon, who had taken an interest in his *Tank Girl* comic. However, when Jamie began dating Coxon's ex Jane Olliver, the artist and guitarist grew apart, with Damon taking Graham's side. Proving time heals all wounds, the matter was eventually resolved to everyone's satisfaction. Hewlett and Olliver would have two children together before breaking up in 1998.

In fact, by the time *Deadline* shut down in 1995, Jamie was far better known for his art work on *Tank Girl* than his way with a journalistic quip. A lush, occasionally insane comic co-created with writer Alan Martin, *Tank Girl* mixed anarchic, neo-psychedelic visuals with the adventures of a pill-popping teenage outlaw who drove an armoured vehicle and dated a mutant kangaroo. Offering a refreshing alternative from all those American heroes who wore their underpants outside their tights and leaped over buildings with a single bound, *Tank Girl* was in its own way as British as *Parklife* or *The Great Escape*. A rascally soul, who had just come out of a long-term relationship himself, Hewlett would provide a perfect antidote (and future foil) for Damon's emotional and artistic woes. "We absolutely hated each other at first," he said later. "Damon was very competitive and I had the whole *Tank Girl* thing going. Then when I split up with (my partner) around the same time he broke up with Justine, for some reason we decided to get a flat together. We'd spend hours watching *MTV* and wondering why every (band) on it was so terrible." They later solved the dilemma.

Ironically, Albarn and Frischmann's love affair began unravelling at a perfect juncture for Blur, who after nearly a year on the road were taking some much needed time off to concentrate on other projects. "The best thing about being in Blur is giving ourselves the time to not just have to be in Blur," said Rowntree. While Damon attended to personal matters in Notting Hill, Graham was busy with Transcopic Records, a new label he had set up specifically for the release of his first solo album, *The Sky Is Too High*. Alcohol-free for the best part of 18 months, Graham's new routine of drinking two pints of Coke in the local pub followed by coffee and TV at home was not enough to sate him of an evening. Instead, he began plucking tunes on the guitar "as part of a therapeutic routine", his first composition being a folk song about a dead boxer which he subsequently donated to the soundtrack of a neighbour's short film. After a while, however, Coxon realised he had stockpiled a goodly amount of material, some of it quite promising. "I decided to exorcise my demons in the studio," he said. "And then some friends of mine told me that I should make an album out of it. It was 11 songs... almost an album's worth, really."

Released on August 10, 1998, *The Sky Is Too High* caught Graham swimming between quiet melancholia and searing aggression, with songs ranging from the fragile balladry of 'Waiting', 'In A Salty Sea' and 'Me You, We Too' to the two chord punch-ups of 'I Wish' and 'Who The Fuck?'. Numbering the cult flavours of Nick Drake, Yo La Tengo, Sonic Youth and Leonard Cohen among his influences, *The Sky...* was never destined to trouble the upper echelons on the charts (it got to number 31 in the UK). But as a starting flag for Coxon's future explorations outside Camp Blur, it worked just fine. More, despite his undoubted abilities as a guitarist, there was no instrumental braying or hour long solos to be had here. Six strings – whether electric or acoustic – were used purely for the benefit of the track concerned. This approach was evidenced to fine effect on 'A Day Is Far Too Long', where Coxon's simple, yet twirling guitar accompaniment to his own weak, but willing voice provided the record's highlight. "(I was) happy to make it, but a lot of the subject matter wasn't happy." he later said. "That's the way it goes. If you write a diary, then six months later you have to come back and read it, and it's embarrassing. You can't understand your feelings then. But now I have to answer questions about it. That's strange..."

If Graham's debut album was a downbeat, lo-fi affair, then Alex James' latest experiment with the perimeters of sound was more about marching beats, vocal chants, shrieking whistles and a melody line played on a one-stringed bass guitar purchased halfway up a Japanese mountain. Like his previous project Me, Me, Me James wasn't taking himself particularly seriously when he wrote 'Vindaloo' with actor Keith Allen. The name they gave their group – 'Fat Les' – more or less confirmed that. Yet, as novelty hits go, 'Vindaloo' wasn't a bad one, if a little wearing after one or more listens. Intrigued by a "loud and clowny" drum pattern they had heard being played by Fulham's supporters at a spring away game, Alex and Keith developed the idea into a song some days later, presumably over several large drinks. With Allen's rumbling, spoken vocal (itself a tribute to the comedian Max Wall) and a chorus that strongly recalled a half-speed version of 'Get A Bloomin' Move On' ('The Self Preservation Society') from cult British movie *The Italian*

Job, the duo had a tune built for the football terraces. No bad thing really, given the fact that the FIFA World Cup was due to start on June 10, 1998, and Damon Albarn had already been approached to write a song by the FA in support of England's efforts at the tournament. When Albarn turned down the offer (other things to do), The Groucho Club's third musketeer Damian Hirst suggested James and Allen rush-release 'Vindaloo' as a single in time for the first match in France. The race, as they say, was on.

Having sold the master tapes to Telstar for an advance against royalties and the covering of promotional costs, Keith Allen fashioned a suitably anarchic promo for what was later deemed "a true hooligan anthem". Full of curry-eating sumo wrestlers, an extra dressed in bald cap, bow tie and black tights (another homage to the aforementioned Max Wall) and a nest of cameos from comedians such as Rowland Rivron, Matt Lucas and Peter Kay, Allen's video not only managed to spoof The Verve's po-faced clip for 'Bittersweet Symphony', but also turn the street it was filmed on into one very large party. Hitting the shops just two days before the first whistle blew at Stade de France stadium in Paris, 'Vindaloo' did considerably better on the charts than England did at the World Cup, reaching number two in the UK and selling close to half a million copies. Rightly, Fat Les should have left the joke there, but they were back again by the end of the year with 'Naughty Christmas (Goblin In The Office)', a song so puerile and lacking in charm it actually hurt to listen to it. James, however, was in unapologetic mood. "Fat Les was just... funny," he said at the time. "Obviously, the records were shit, but you wouldn't get Radiohead making a Christmas record, would you? Anyway, if I want to make stupid records with a bunch of mates from the Groucho, then fuck off, I will."

In its own sweet and sour way, James' involvement with the likes of Fat Les defined why Coxon was given to occasional losses of temper when it came to the bassist. After Blur had fought hard to re-establish themselves as a band for adults rather than teenagers, Alex had once again plunged himself back into the unfettered laddism that defined the worst of Britpop, all those unbuttoned secretaries and salty nurses used to pep up 'Naughty Christmas...''s video recalling the excesses of

'Country House' three years before. Yet, somehow James always got away with it, his continuing adventures at the Groucho Club casting him more as a champagne-swilling "roister doister" than just some sleazebag pop star. He knew it too. "Ah, roistering," said James. "It's actually in the dictionary: 'Indulging in unrefined merry-making'. I just enjoy going out, meeting people and getting drunk with them. There is a danger... of losing who you are, just becoming this hedonistic horror. But as Robert Louis Stevenson pointed out, 'The traveller must be content'." For Diana Gutkind, Alex's buccaneering ways were all part of the appeal. "Oh, Alex is a genuinely lovely and very smart man... a lot smarter than you might think," she said. "All that Groucho Club thing was just his way of pulling together a modern day Rat Pack. There's no harm in Alex."

Ahead of Blur's brief return to public duties in mid-1998, a few stray strands concerning the band and its members came to light. In collaboration with respected classical composer Michael Nyman, Damon recorded a charming cover of 'London Pride' for *Twentieth-Century Blues: The Songs of Noël Coward.* A tribute album curated by Pet Shop Boy Neil Tennant which challenged contemporary artists to re-imagine Coward's work for a brand new audience, Albarn and Nyman's contribution to *...Blues* joined others by Paul McCartney, Sting, Bryan Ferry and Elton John. Finally released in November 1999, all proceeds raised from CD sales went to the Red Hot AIDS Charitable Trust. Proving he wasn't just a pretty face with a knack for penning best-selling football anthems, James also co-wrote and played on the wonderful Marianne Faithfull's latest single 'Hang On To Your Heart', her gritty, nicotine-soaked vocal sitting atop a chorus made for radio. Unfortunately, this winning combination of bright young thing and wily old stager wasn't quite enough to guarantee a hit.

Now the owner of his very own label, Coxon's Transcopic Records released a brand new LP and single by Chicago art punks Assembly Line People Program and Liverpool prog-folksters Ooberman respectively, with Graham also producing the former band's record. "It's nice to put out people's ideas," he said. "I think everyone deserves a piece of plastic out there in the world." There was even time for Coxon and Albarn to remix Bristol trip hoppers Massive Attack's new single 'Angel', its heartbeat rhythms and spells of dissonance vaguely reminiscent of Blur's own 'Cowboy Song', which had just turned up on the soundtrack of the 1998 Hollywood comedy *Dead Man On Campus*. From Damon tinkering with the tapes of Japanese DJ Cornelius' odd, but endearing 'Star Fruits Surf Rider' to Dave working on a computer animation project for *MTV*, even when Blur were meant to be taking time out, the group's individual parts had stayed very busy indeed.

Away from the spotlight for nearly seven months, Blur finally came out of hiding for a one-off gig at Glastonbury Festival on June 27, 1998. In truth, their previous performances at Worthy Farm had been hit-or-miss affairs. In 1992, Albarn's suit only served to confuse the hippies while his botched trip up a lighting rig resulted in the broken foot. Conversely, 1994 was a year of triumph and turnaround, the lyrics of *Modern Life Is Rubbish* and *Parklife* being sung back to Blur by a crowd of thousands. The year 1998 turned out to be somewhere in between, at least for one of the participants. "It was the mud year. The bloody mud year," remembered Diana Gutkind. "Craig Duffy was our (newish) tour manager at that time, and I was always in a separate dressing room because I was a girl. Anyway, there was a large jeep booked to help get us all through the mud in the backstage area and onto the stage, but Craig forgot me and I was left behind. I was standing there asking 'Where is everyone?' and being told 'Oh, are you with the band? Sorry, they've gone.' Duh. Now, this was a bit unfortunate because my keyboard line for 'Girls And Boys' was starting the bloody gig. Well, Damon – rather chivalrously it has to be said – had lent me his beautiful Parka coat beforehand because I didn't have anything for the appalling weather. So I had to run splattering and screaming through the mud towards the stage in his lovely coat so they could start the show. Hope I didn't ruin it..."

Following Albarn and Coxon's brief appearance alongside sixties electronic pioneers Silver Apples at Scott Walker's Meltdown Festival on July 5, 1998 (they performed 'Essex Dogs'), Blur put aside solo projects and disintegrating romances and reconvened as a group to begin work on album number six. This time around, producer Stephen Street would not be joining them. "It wasn't my choice," he later said. "I just think they wanted to stretch out a bit more and having made five albums with me, the best way to do that was to work with someone different who would approach the project in a different way. I understood that perfectly and certainly wasn't offended." For Damon, dispensing with Street's services after nearly seven extremely creative years and three and a half best-selling albums was never going to be an easy decision. "Of course it was difficult," he said at the time. "Stephen will forever be a part of who we are, and ironically, he gave us the tools we needed to go it alone."

Blur weren't quite going it alone. Instead, they were venturing forth with new producer William Orbit. In several ways, Orbit mirrored Blur rather well, his own back story having several commonalities with the band and its personnel. Born in London's East End in 1956 to two schoolteachers, he abandoned formal education at the age of 16 for a life of squats, strawberry picking and guitar playing. When that proved unsatisfactory, William tried his luck in Europe where a string of odd jobs followed, including stints as a shoe factory worker, motorbike messenger, and rather improbably, a trainee draftsman on a North Sea oil rig. Obviously slow to settle, he then divided his time between promoting mini-music festivals in disused West London workshops while also working as a part-time model for fashion designer Takeo Kikuchi in Tokyo, Japan. It was Orbit's brief tenure as an assistant/tea boy type at Basing Street Studios (later known as Sarm West) that ultimately paid the highest dividends. Inspired by his experiences there, and prodded along by the creative gusto of Laurie Mayer and Grant Gilbert – with whom he had formed the short-lived synthpop trio Torch Song – William cobbled enough money together to set up his own recording facility, Guerrilla Studios, in picturesque Little Venice. Successful from the off, Guerrilla's clients came to include The Cocteau Twins, The Fall, Gary Numan and Sting, among many others. Ever ready to expand, Orbit subsequently turned Guerrilla into a record label, releasing vinyl cuts by electronic dance acts such as Underworld and Leftfield, while also re-mixing tracks for Prince, Peter Gabriel and Depeche Mode.

It was precisely this talent for breathing new life into the songs of other artists that led to the next break in William's already varied career. Following the cult success of another of his new groups, Bassomatic, and an underground hit with 'Water From The Vine Leaf' which he issued under the name Strange Cargo III, Orbit had amassed enough wealth to take a year or so out, eventually settling in Southern California for a time. Yet, a chance encounter with Madonna in 1997 at a New York nightclub led to him being offered a producer's chair on her new album. When the Orbit-driven single 'Ray Of Light' became one of the Queen of Pop's biggest-ever selling singles, the native East Ender could just about write his own ticket to anywhere in the music world. "I'm truly grateful to Madonna for seeing what nobody else saw at the time," he later said. "It gave me a global platform for (my) work."

Blur had first sought out Orbit's skills in the spring of 1998 for *Bustin' + Dronin'*, a stop-gap disc predominantly aimed at the Japanese market that combined the band's recent 'Live At Peel Acres' session with some bold new re-mixes of songs from their last, self-titled album. With superstar DJ type Moby providing a hymn-like interpretation of 'Beetlebum' and Sonic Youth's Thurston Moore deconstructing 'Essex Dogs' within an inch of its life, competition to impress was fierce. Yet, Orbit's complete revision of 'Movin' On' was so off-kilter and unexpected, it stopped Blur in their tracks. "The remix he did for us on *Bustin' + Dronin'* was some of the most insane music I've ever heard," said an impressed Coxon. "He really likes the extreme and the ridiculous in music (and) that kind of appeals to me too. There are almost comic distortions that to me and him are so beautiful. To someone else, they'll sound disgusting and ruin the record, but to me and him, that distortion's like a lead vocal." In short, William Orbit was in.

Recorded at Mayfair, Sarm West and Blur's own recently purchased 13 Studios from July 19 to November 20, 1998 (with the occasional visit to Reykjavik thrown in for good measure), advance news on the group's latest album was promising, as both musicians and their producer traded rose-tinted compliments in the music press. "I think that William is giving the music lots of space," Albarn told *Mojo* at the time. "There was always a lot of detail (in Blur), but sometimes it's been hard to hear it... William has made things more peaceful. Not in terms of sounds, but the spirit." Coxon was even more giving regarding Orbit's abilities. "(He's like) an eight-year-old on Christmas Eve using recording desks like Biros. William spoke to me for an hour about how great out of tune guitars are. I mean, no producer has ever fucking talked to me like that. He didn't even make me tune my guitar." Further, William's ability to "rationalise the results" of Blur's various jams, musical sketches and instrumental doodles met with universal praise from all concerned. "We'd improvise, then (he'd) cut it up," said Rowntree. "Then we'd listen and improvise over what we'd got. Then we might add a loop or another improvisation. In a way, it felt counterintuitive, because you were never quite sure what you were getting. But it worked, and made things fun."

In later years, however, it came to light that the atmosphere during these sessions might not have been as harmonious as first thought, with Coxon's recent return to drinking the possible cause of several behind the scenes arguments. "Things were starting to fall apart between the four of us," Dave confessed. "It was quite a sad process making (the album). People were not turning up to the sessions, or turning up drunk, being abusive and storming off."

There were no denials to be had from Graham on the matter. "I was really out there around (that time)," he said in 2010. "(It) made for some pretty great noise, but I was probably a bit of a crap to be around." For William Orbit, these frequent battles and alcoholically-assisted bumps in the road all became a little draining. "There were certain days when I'd get home and I couldn't even get up the stairs," he told *The Face*. "I'd be suffering from the sheer emotional exhaustion of trying to carve out a musical consensus... of trying to harness all this talent." But even if Coxon's difficulties were causing trouble in the ranks, Orbit couldn't deny the depth of his talent. "That man can really cry, really emote on guitar more than anyone else I've ever worked with," he confirmed to *The Face*. "(But) he's also one of the most complicated people I've encountered."

Made under some duress though, as it turned out, with more than a little genius too, Blur's sixth album *13* was released to stores on March

15, 1999. As ever, eyes were drawn to the packaging before exploring the musical contents inside. For the first time, one of Graham's own oil paintings – *The Apprentice* – was used for the cover sleeve. "That cover was completely Graham's baby," said Dave. All golden hues, subtle reds and tarnished browns with the figure of a man stripped to the torso looking shyly to one side, it certainly made for a striking image.* Further, like *Blur* before it, *13*'s liner notes contained no lyrics, only a set of fractal-inspired illustrations that brought to mind the band's stage set of 1991/2. No immediate clues, then. Just a set of clever puzzles designed to intrigue before the small, spinning disc revealed exactly what the hell had been going on over the last year.

As it turned out, Blur had helped Damon Albarn make a break-up album. Not quite as perfect as Bob Dylan's *Blood On The Tracks* or as commercially accessible as Fleetwood Mac's *Rumours* perhaps, but one surely the equal of Nick Cave's *The Boatman's Call* or even Richard and Linda Thompson's *Shoot Out The Lights*. As with any of those fine records, *13* wasn't wholly devoted to matters of the heart. In fact, there was many a moment of sly humour, wry social comment and, in keeping with William Orbit's previous track record as a producer, an energised dreaminess and contrasting lunacy about the disc. But make no mistake, when *13* really delivered, it was all down to Albarn trying to come to terms with the end of his relationship with Justine Frischmann.

Musically, Blur were in brilliant form throughout *13*, building on the lo-fi influences that peppered their previous album while also adding aggressive new tonalities and waves of dense electronica to again challenge the band's existing fan base. 'Swamp Song' was compelling evidence of this, its grinding charms marrying the best of American alt-rockers Weezer with the stern north English charms of The Fall. 'B.L.U.R.E.M.I.' was also as punky as its Sex Pistols-baiting title suggested, the track a feast of thudding basses and sawing strings, with

* Now taking pride of place in the offices of Blur's management company, Eleven, *The Apprentice* was subtly altered for use as an album cover, with the light shining above the titular figure's head added later for a more pleasing effect. The figure 13 in the upper left hand of the sleeve is also absent from the original painting.

Orbit's deskbound manipulations turning Albarn's voice into that of a manic Donald Duck impersonation in the flick of a studio switch. "William is a very delicate creature with a very scientific mind," said James. "A very smart chap, sensitive and indeed, a bit of a genius." 'Bugman' was even more excessive in its attack, allowing Coxon to wig out like some demonic composite of Led Zeppelin's Jimmy Page and David Bowie's "super secret guitar weapon", the wonderful Adrian Belew.

Though the likes of 'Swamp Song', 'Bugman' and 'B.L.U.R.E.M.I.' conclusively proved Blur had lost nothing in the way of ferociousness when the occasion demanded it, they did not define the overall mood of *13*. With 'Battle', the band again showed an interest in exploring spacey textures and even the work of left-field new romantics Japan. "'Battle' was pretty unknown territory for us, with perhaps a heavier William Orbit influence," said Coxon. "I think it really sounds like Japan, the band. There's a kind of darkness to the music, like the darkness you get between stars." Conversely, the lovely 'Caramel' began with church organs, looped Indian-sounding guitars and falsetto vocals before upping gear into a tune Krautrockers Can would be justly proud of – Dave's gyrating drums and Alex's high octave bass fills a fine tribute to the work of Jaki Liebezeit and Holgar Czukay respectively. "'Caramel' was actually written after a couple of big hangovers in Iceland," said a proud-sounding Albarn.

As its title might suggest, 'Mellow Song' was another comedown tune, this time rolling along on the back of finely-picked acoustics and spherical keyboards. Of course, there was always a nod or two to past glories. Blur again turned to The Specials for inspiration on 'Trailerpark', a track originally written for the lawless cartoon *South Park* and debuted at Glastonbury the previous June. '1992' had an equally interesting genesis. First recorded in the year of its title, Damon lost the demo in a house move, only to see it turn up again at the back of a cupboard six years later. Full of spooky organs and majestic swells of feedback, '1992' came from the same stable as 'Sing' and 'Birthday', resembling a relic of simpler, if not necessarily more optimistic times. The instrumental 'Optigan 1' also had something of the past about it, those fairground organs and sad resolving chords Albarn was so fond of again nodding gently, though insistently, to the music of Kurt Weill.

When all's said and done, however, *13* was never just about how well Blur could carry a tune. Of equal – and if we are being honest here – probably more importance was how much Damon was willing to reveal about his state of mind following the events of recent months. Pretty much everything, as it turned out. "When you end a long-term relationship with someone you loved so much, you've got fantastic material, and I don't say that out of disrespect," he said. "Just listen carefully to the songs, and you'll know I loved her very much." Of that, there was no doubt. A man once content to hide behind character and characterisation, Albarn had spilled his emotional guts on the songs of *13*, with most every lyric conferring personal insight and sometimes horrible levels of honesty into the machinations, downfall and aftermath of his love affair with Frischmann.

Whether seeking feverish abandon or narcotic oblivion in 'Swamp Song', or just wallowing in misery on 'Mellow Song' and 'Bugman', Damon's interior journey was all there for the benefit of listeners, with precious little editing done on the way. In fact, 'Caramel' seemed to capture this rollercoaster of emotions in one wretched lump, as he fought towards clarity and cleanliness before once again lapsing into sadness and gloom: "I gotta get over, I've gotta get better," he sang, "I gotta stop smoking... I love you forever, low, low, low." The wondrous 'Trimm Trabb' – all classical pianos, Flamenco guitars and slowly creeping menace – also conveyed the bleak realities of lost love, with Albarn endlessly repeating the phrases "That's just the way it is" and "I sleep alone" until he and his compatriots fall away in a bank of white noise. Given sentiments like these, it was no wonder *13*'s working title had been 'When You're Walking Backwards To Hell, No One Can See You, Only God'. At least Alex could find a funny side to it. "We actually named the album after the studio in which we recorded it," he said. "Good job we didn't make it in Abbey Road..."

Albarn's feelings came to an emotional crescendo on the two songs that bookended *13*: the gospel-tinged 'Tender' and the moaning blues of 'No Distance Left To Run'. Never one to explore such musical forms before, Damon nonetheless made a fine stab at getting them right now. Building from an almost jug band feel to a full-on church-rattling anthem, 'Tender' utilised handclaps, banging floorboards, call and response vocals from Coxon and the raised voices of the London Gospel Community Choir to see its writer finally out of the dark and back into the light: "Come on, come on, come on, get through it," rang the chorus, "Come on, come on, come on, love's the greatest thing..." An intensely personal examination of crushed hopes and the beginnings of shy redemption, 'Tender' was without doubt the most raw, open and honest lyric Albarn had ever committed to tape. There was no going back now. "You've got to be very careful when you write very personal records, though," he later warned. "I've seen a lot of people... be totally open and I think what they're left with is a real confusion about who they are, because they've got nothing to preserve for themselves. It can really fuck you up."

A much more intimate proposition, though no less affecting in its emotive reach was 'No Distance Left To Run', the song's placement just before *13*'s instrumental closer 'Optigan 1' a quite deliberate statement on both Albarn and the band's behalf. "Yeah, that was a nice touch, I thought," said Alex. Accompanied by the clean, concise brushwork of Rowntree, a sympathetically inclined bass line from James and Coxon's crying guitar, Damon sang his goodbyes to Justine Frischmann in the best way he knew how: "It's over, you don't need to tell me, I hope you're with someone who makes you feel safe in your sleeping tonight..." When all faded to black, there really wasn't a dry eye left in the house. "I felt completely fucked up after I recorded that vocal," the singer later confessed. "But I hope it will strike a chord with people. (That) at last, we might have written something that's fucking helpful."

Graham echoed this sentiment in subsequent interviews, seeing 'No Distance Left To Run' as both a watershed moment in Albarn's development as a lyricist and a universal balm for those experiencing similar troubles of the heart. "I think Damon's changed quite a lot recently," he said. "He's realised some vulnerability in himself, and I've always preferred it when he sang about his own personal experiences,

experiences that everyone really has. When he was singing about people travelling to work on trains to London, I didn't feel a connection, and I think that's true for a lot of people, especially those not living in England. I've known him since I was 12, and he now seems to have more confidence to be open... to not hide behind strange stories about strange people."

A beautifully executed album that drew on a spray of musical influences from Mahalia Jackson, Mississippi John Hurt, Black Flag and Tortoise to Beck, Sebadoh, Can and even pioneering electro-punks Suicide, *13* was arguably Blur's most complete set of songs yet. Further, Albarn's lyricism – whether pouring scorn on the inanities of small town America ('Trailerpark'), making coded references to drug use ('Caramel', 'Mellow Song' and 'Trimm Trabb') – or simply revelling in the exquisite sorrow of failed romance had also reached a new high. Yet, there was always the possibility that the songs' inward-facing subject matter and the squalls of electronic distortion that sometimes surrounded them might render the disc impenetrable to all but the most faithful of Blur fans. It was a point not lost on critics. "All said, there's every chance... that the floating Blur fan will simply be confused by *13*, (thereby) sledge-hammering away large chunks of their current audience," mused Q. "Still, it remains a dense, fascinating and accomplished art-rock album. In a sense, perhaps... Blur have come full circle." *Mojo*'s Pat Gilbert also understood the dilemma Blur faced, though in his mind their very willingness to experiment with both sound and word made it worth the risk. "*13* is further evidence that Blur are deadly serious about reinventing themselves as a challenging, experimental art-rock act, melding US noise with European-noir Electronica," he wrote. "But an instinct for great pop still survives in the murk. So, not just another post-Britpop comedown album. Possibly though, the sound of music in the 21st century."

Perhaps the person best equipped to understand *13* was the subject of most all of its tunes. Of this at least, Albarn remained hopeful. "'Tender' was a real plea from the heart," he said. "The duality of the song is probably why it works, the fact that's it's uplifting but also very sad. (But) I hope Justine likes (all) the songs, because there's no going back on them now, is there? Still, I'm sure she'll get the picture." Thankfully, Frischmann was fully on message, even if it hurt to be so. "I think Damon has turned something that might have been very negative into something very positive," she said at the time. "I think songwriting's sometimes like therapy, so his (writing) about (us) kind of made sense to me. It was quite an odd thing hearing a song like 'Tender' on the radio. I guess it was quite a romantic gesture. To be honest," she concluded, "it made me a bit misty-eyed." Job done, then.

Sad and forlorn, though also elevating and enriching, *13* gave Blur another hit record, going straight to number one in the UK (where it soon provided the band with their latest platinum disc), while hitting the Top Ten in Japan, Sweden, Norway, Germany and New Zealand. 'Tender' too, proved quite the best seller, just missing out on the number one spot – though still shifting over 170,000 copies – when released as a single in February 1999. Given its anthemic, bluesy qualities and rousing, 'we're all in this together' chorus, one might have thought the tune would again gift Blur the keys to the States, even surpassing the bold success of 'Song 2'. It wasn't to be. Despite performing 'Tender' with the Harlem Boys Choir to an audience of millions on *The Late Show With David Letterman,* and backing *13* with a select tour of the States and Canada during March/April, single and album sales remained sluggish rather than spectacular. "No.80 with a bullet," laughed James. Once more it seemed, America had managed to wriggle its way out of Blur's grasp after a quick spin around the dance floor...

As the band again struck out on the road in the early summer of 1999 for another round of festival appearances, one could not help but feel that the record Blur were promoting actually closed the door on an era as well as a decade. Though Britpop was long dead, interest in its golden couple had persisted, with Albarn and Frischmann still somehow defining a time when everything was up for grabs and pop might yet take over the world. But as the events of the last 18 months proved, the effort made to create something "utterly brilliant" had exacted a high price. "For a short time, lots of girls were walking about with short hair and Doc Martens because of Justine and a lot of blokes looked like me," Damon said. "It was unusual for two people in a relationship to have such strong identities, you know. But ultimately, there's been a bit of a fucking cock up somewhere..."

In keeping with his nature, Albarn found a way to move on, his personal and professional life taking an almost immediate upturn after the release of *13*. For Blur, however, the wheels were slowly but surely coming off.

Chapter Fourteen

Slip Sliding Away

Back in the heady days of 1995, Damon Albarn railed forth with one of those statements that made you love and hate him all at once. "We're established now," he said. "We're not going to go away. That's an enormous barrier to overcome." With the huge advances of *Parklife* already behind them and a further two million copies of *The Great Escape* sold, he had more than earned the right to brag on his behalf and that of the band. Yet, Albarn's words could also be construed as arrogant, even careerist, with Blur's recent victories confirming the latest stage in a long term plan to hoist the group above any movement or shift in fashion, and establish them completely on their own terms.

Take away any stray strands of egotism, however, and Damon was perfectly correct. After *The Great Escape*, Blur – the idea, the brand, the image – could operate as a singularity, their overwhelming successes assuring they did not have to align themselves with anyone or anything in order to sustain their profile or output. In short, they were their own men, a fact subsequently confirmed by the artistic volte-face of *Blur* and *13*. From now on, it all went wrong, it was down to them and them alone. Which, sadly, made Dave Rowntree's statement of March 1999 a tad concerning. "We're together for the music," he said. "We wouldn't be great friends if we weren't in a band, and it would be stupid to pretend otherwise. Because you get on each other's nerves. You're bound to after ten years." Though he probably didn't mean it to, the drummer's remark set the tone for the next 18 months.

As Blur made their round of summer shows, the band and its future seemed solid as oak, with crowds enthusiastically gathered in Holland, Finland, Germany and Denmark to see them play a set drawn predominantly from their latest album. Translating easily to the stage, the songs of *13* made for great company, with 'Tender' turning into the lighter-igniting anthem it was always destined to be, while the likes of 'Swamp Song', 'Bug Man' and 'B.L.U.R.E.M.I.' kept the festival mosh pits nice and busy. There was also a brand new single from the album to promote. An Albarn/Coxon co-write, 'Coffee & TV' was one of those tunes that got better with each hearing, its odd chords, lilting feel and section-able guitar solo growing like a delightful infection within the eardrum. Drawing partial inspiration from all those nights Coxon had spent huddled up with caffeine and cathode rays, 'Coffee...''s lyric could also be read as a witty commentary as to the pluses and minuses of his decision to quit alcohol during 1997/8. "The first verse is really what's it's like being famous and living in Camden Town," he said. "The second verse is about what it's like not being famous, going to the countryside and just sitting in the pub..."

At first, Graham had had no intention of singing 'Coffee & TV', feeling as ever that an Albarn vocal would do a much better job of bringing out the song's melodic nuances rather than his own, more reedy voice. But fate and time intervened. "The only reason I ended up singing it was that Damon had to do lyrics for other stuff," he later told *Select*. "He said, 'You write a lyric', so I went home and wrote them that night and did the vocal in two takes." In fact, 'Coffee & TV' actually benefitted from being sung by Coxon, the guitarist's more vulnerable tones adding a real authenticity to its tune and lyrics.

"I suppose being a musician is no different than being a painter, really," he later said by way of explanation. "You constantly have a need to express, to capture the beauty of what you're feeling. And because what you're feeling is constantly changing, you have the need to constantly re-express it. It's part of living, part of the effort of being alive."

To give the single its best chance of success, Blur brought in Hammer & Tong's Garth Jennings and Nick Goldsmith to direct and produce a video of suitable worth. What the duo handed back was its own little work of art, as an animated milk carton ('Milky') set out in search of a runaway Graham, only to find multiple hazards and the odd miracle on the way. Heartbreaking and hilarious in equal measure, the promo eventually won a slew of trophies in 1999/2000, including 'Best Video' at *NME*'s Brats and *MTV Europe's* annual awards show (by 2005, it had also been voted the 17th greatest pop video of all time in a poll by Channel 4). However, there was a mild brouhaha when 'Coffee & TV' failed to make the UK Top Ten on its release in late June of 1999, with Blur's manager Chris Morrison arguing that several thousand sales had failed to be recorded properly at retail stage. In the end, the tune had to make do with number 11. Frankly, it deserved much better.

Leaving Morrison to fight the good fight with Gallup, Blur continued to progress across Europe and the UK throughout the late summer, marking their passage with appearances at the Reading and Leeds Festival in late August. To celebrate 10 years at the top (or thereabouts), the band also played one-off sets at Alex and Graham's former home-from-home, Goldsmith's College, as well as a 'B-sides Night' at Camden Town's Electric Ballroom on September 6. Quite the ticket – though it was also broadcast live on the internet – the latter gig saw Blur perform 19 rarities in all, with the likes of 'Bone Bag', 'Uncle Love', 'Polished Stones' and even golden oldie 'Mace' dusted down and taken out for the evening. On the promotional front, Stuart Maconie's excellent official history of the group, *3862 Days*, also saw release, as did *The 10 Year Limited Edition Anniversary Box Set*, a deluxe package collecting 126 songs on 22 CDs, plus original artwork and lyrics for each of Blur's albums/singles. To cap it all off, the *Blur:X* exhibition at Lux Gallery in London's Hoxton Square offered the chance to see not only rare sleeves and photos of the group, but also video footage dating back to 1990, a nine-foot hamburger from the 1995 Mile End show, and indeed, 'Milky' the milk carton. Running for a week in mid-September, the venue chosen to stage the exhibit had a special place in Damon's heart, the singer having spent several enjoyable weeks working there as a teenager in the summer of 1987 or thereabouts.

Either in the mood for continuing their ten year celebrations – or as likely, sending a message to their audience things were about to change quite soon – Blur pulled another rabbit from the hat in the autumn of 1999, when they announced their 'Singles Night' tour. A clever conceit, the six dates planned for early December would see the band play 23 songs back to back, ranging from 1991's double A-side 'I Know'/'She's So High' right up to their forthcoming 45, 'No Distance Left To Run' (then due for release on 15 November). "I ordinarily get pissed off with singles," said Albarn at the time, "but I've decided to leave all that stuff at the hotel. Leave your angst at the door, so to speak. Life's too short to be angry. To get through it you've just got to think of Christmas and children, really. This is my Christmas cheer for this year. It's like the biggest encore we've ever done, just one big encore." Again, Alex was there to provide comic relief in the face of too much bah humbug. "It'll definitely work differently to a normal set," he said. "It's a bit like drinking too much Coca-Cola, it gets a bit nauseating."

Despite their reservations, 'Singles Night' turned out very well indeed. A greatest hits album writ large on the stage, Blur appeared to have a ball exploring the more commercial aspects of their back catalogue, with the group's show at the cavernous Wembley Arena on December 11 akin to a mad Christmas hoolie. "Oh, playing Wembley Arena's magnificent, mainly because... well, you're playing Wembley Arena!" laughed Diana Gutkind. "I think everyone was proud to be doing that gig." Proud, but not necessarily po-faced. Never in danger of taking themselves too seriously, Blur worked their way through baggy mistakes ('Bang'), glorious failures ('Popscene') and career defining peaks ('Parklife', with Phil Daniels in tow) before slowing it all down at the end for a tear-duct activating 'No Distance Left To Run'. "It's over," sang Damon as the crowd got their lighters out, and indeed for the time being, it was.

Nevertheless, the band still had several odds and ends to attend to – picking up their 'Best Act In The World Today' gong at the Q Awards, for instance ("Thank you, though it doesn't seem very objective, because we don't sell any records in America," said Damon) and a promo appearance or two for 'No Distance...' which reached number 14 in the UK charts. When Blur finally downed tools at the end of 1999, there were no plans to reconvene for the foreseeable future. Albarn, Coxon, Rowntree and James, it seemed, were now on sabbatical until further notice. "I'm no longer interested in touring the world and being a pop tart," said an arch-sounding Damon, "but yes, I still love pop music." But surely not enough to let it take him away from his new family...

When Albarn had left Notting Hill for Westbourne Grove in mid-1998, his days as a proverbial bachelor would prove colourful, if relatively brief. Alongside fellow "recovering romantic" Jamie Hewlett, Damon compressed several wild years into nine mad months, as their flat in Golbourne Road became something of a 24-hour party destination for London's bright and beautiful. Though the two fell short of actually installing a bar in the living room, stories abounded of drunken behaviour, swinging from chandeliers (unlikely, as there weren't any) and guests piled high on the couch and a few other places to boot. "Damon's place?" said Alex. "Wooooh..." As the story goes, visitors to Chez Albarn-Hewlett included Radiohead, supermodel Kate Moss and various members of soul pop up-and-comers All Saints – including singer Shaznay Lewis, whom Damon was rumoured to be seeing at the time. On a more surreal note, one particular evening found Pavement and Spice Girls trading drinks and conversation in the kitchen, the fact of which Damon was justifiably proud. "I managed to get Pavement and Spice Girls hanging out together. Jamie and I thought we'd make that place legendary... then bale out."

Albarn finally pulled the ripcord when he met Suzi Winstanley. "Petite, pretty and with a wild shock of black hair above her head," Winstanley had graduated from Central St. Martin's College of Art in 1987, gaining her qualification in a perhaps unusual, though still thoroughly effective way. While studying in London, she became friendly with fellow student Olly Williams, a former bouncer/amateur boxer who shared Suzi's passion for pencil sketches, bold acrylics and watercolours. Within a month or so, the two began collaborating on projects and never looked back. Describing themselves as "an artist", they subsequently left St. Martin's with a joint degree and flew to Syracuse, New York to continue their formal education. During a road trip across the States in 1989, Suzi and Olly encountered various examples of Native American Indian art and mythology, the experience ultimately leading to a decision to capture "nature at its most primitive and wild". By the late Nineties, this mission had translated itself into countless expeditions to remote desert, jungle, Arctic and ocean locations where the two painted "hand over hand" some of the planet's rarest – and indeed – fiercest creatures. "We actually started letting the animals make their mark (on the canvas) as proof of being there, but each mark is also beautiful for what it is," she later said. Given that some of those adding their particular signature included crocodiles, tigers, Great White sharks and the odd lion, one had to commend Winstanley and Williams' bravery as much as their skills with a brush.

Though successful in her own right (Olly & Suzi's paintings command as much as £10,000 per canvas) and counting the likes of Damian Hirst as a patron – "He bought a shark (picture) from us, which is interesting (because) he kills them and we draw them," she said – Winstanley was still shocked at the level of Albarn's celebrity when the two first became friends. "It was funny," she told *The Times'* Rose Shepherd. "We were in my flat in East London, and we had to go west, and I said, 'Oh, it's really quick from here. Just jump on the Central Line.' He said, 'No, I don't think we should go on the tube.' I had literally just met him, and I said, 'What are you talking about? It's 20 minutes. It's the quickest way.' Anyway, we went down to the tube, and there were all these people shouting, all these girls running around, and I suddenly thought, 'I really don't like this...'" However, despite Suzi's initial concerns, the commonalities between the two far outweighed any differences and they were soon an item. "I was always the one going away (before)," she said, "so it was wonderful with Damon, because he goes away (too). And he's passionate, he's like the biggest workaholic I've ever met. But he loves making music, so we can understand each other's thing." By October 1999, Winstanley had given birth to Albarn's first child, Missy. "She looks just like an Eskimo," said the proud father. "It's a slightly bizarre thing for men, really... all I could do was be the comforter. It's still great though."

Such changes on the domestic front for Damon were no doubt a contributory factor in the cessation of Blur-related activity after their mad charges of 1999. But he was still eager to indulge other opportunities, with film soundtracks at the top of his recently drawn list. Re-uniting with Michael Nyman, Albarn had already set to work on the score of director Antonia Bird's latest feature *Ravenous*, a slim, but occasionally entertaining horror story focussing on an outbreak of cannibalism in 1840s California. According to Nyman, Damon arrived on the first day of recording at Hampstead's AIR studios with "a great idea for an Appalachian four piece band with banjo, accordion and loads of samples. (It was) just like a Morricone score." Later described by the composer as "a joint composition, in the sense that Damon composed 60% of the tracks, and I did the rest," the end result was impressive, with the likes of 'Boyd's Journey' and 'Colqhoun's Story' full of expressive instrumentation, odd time signatures and subtle, yet atmospheric drones. "Michael was the man who taught me (to) never waste a note," Albarn said.

Keen to do it all again, Damon next turned his hand to composing the score of *Ordinary Decent Criminal*, a crime caper directed by Thaddeus O'Sullivan and loosely based on the life of Dublin mob boss Martin Cahill. Though the film itself was no great shakes, Albarn made a decent fist of his own contribution, fusing trip-hop beats and Cuban rhythms (part-inspired by Suzi Winstanley's family background) to *Get Carter*-like strings, electric pianos and Seventies cop show brass stabs. "I really wanted to give the film that 'Catholic Latin' quality," he later said, "I only wish I'd had another month on it."

Away from their responsibilities in Blur, Dave Rowntree and Alex James had taken to living on another planet entirely, or at least, dreaming about such a possibility. Always a man with a keen interest in the sun, moon and stars – *Parklife*'s 'Far Out' being the first recorded proof of it – James had often found himself bemoaning the fact there seemed little attention given to matters of astronomy on home soil. Yet, when he and Rowntree actually researched the subject, they learned that Britain did indeed have a space research programme of sorts, with the Open University's ursine Dr. Colin Pillinger at its helm. In fact, alongside his colleagues at the European Space Agency (ESA), Pillinger was hoping to soon launch a rocket to Mars, which in turn would deploy a landing device/soil sampler called 'Beagle 2' to drill below the Martian surface in the hopes of finding life. "Pop music seems a bit silly when compared with the beginning of time," said Alex. There was only one problem with said plan: sending rockets into space cost money, and lots of it, and funds were still well short of the projected target figure. Now utter devotees to the cause, Blur's bassist and drummer hit the campaign trail on behalf of Beagle 2, glad-handing potential investors at drink parties and industry functions in the hopes of raising additional cash. So taken were the duo with making it all work, they even went on BBC 2's *Newsnight* to discuss the project. Keen to show his appreciation of their efforts, Dr. Pillinger appeared with Fat Les on *Top Of The Pops*.*

Graham Coxon, on the other hand, was pursuing more earthbound pleasures during Blur's hiatus. Having tested the commercial waters with his first solo album *The Sky Is Too High*, and finding himself an unlikely lead vocalist on the hit single 'Coffee & TV', Graham delayed plans to exhibit his artwork in several European galleries in favour of making another record. The result – 2000's *The Golden D* – was a much more raucous effort than his previous work, with tracks such as 'Fags And Failure', 'Satan I Gatan' and 'My Idea Of Hell' capable of stripping paint from fast-moving cars. When Coxon turned it down, as with the lovely Nick Drake-ish 'Keep Hope Alive', the guitarist's gift for melody and invention was indisputable, but the disc's resolutely uncompromising nature marked it out as an acquired taste even among his most devoted fans. That said, it was lovely to hear Graham paying homage to much-missed Eighties Chicago post-punks Mission To Burma by covering two of their finest tracks, 'Fame and Fortune' and that rattling hymn to

* Unfortunately, despite funds being eventually raised and launch taking place in May 2003, Beagle 2 proved unsuccessful as all contact was lost with the device on its separation from the body of the 'Mars Express' rocket. James and Rowntree remain hopeful there will be another British attempt to the stars at some point in the future.

disillusionment, 'That's When I Reach for My Revolver'. "'Fame And Fortune' seems to be a cynical song about emotion," he said. "Then it goes into violence and then into resignation at the end. It's the same with 'That's When I Reach For My Revolver'... a steady build up into realisation. That very last bit (of the song) has the guy telling him something very mean."

Away from such thoughts on cynicism and lost innocence, Coxon's circumstances seemed much more stable. Following the end of his relationship with Huggy Bear's Jo Johnson, Graham had found a new partner in Swedish artist Anna Norlander, the couple eventually purchasing Andy Ross' old North London flat to settle in. Capable of turning her hand to drawing, sculpture, sound collages and even metalwork, Norlander was quite the music fan too, dragging her none too enthusiastic boyfriend to several hard rock gigs. Strangely, Coxon found himself liking what he heard. "Well, I was taken out to see the Hellacopters," he said, "and I really like them. I never liked that (sort of) music when I was younger, so I found it very refreshing. Full-on rock, no irony at all. They have a few different line-ups, so they vary how good they are. (But) when I saw them, I just really loved the rock stances and seriousness of it all. I've had enough of all that 'irony'. Entombed, too, they're good. I really like their album. It's just so heavy and serious. I haven't had much opportunity to see rock before. It was always indie." Presumably, Graham wasn't playing much Swedish metal when his new daughter Pepper Bäk Troy Coxon came home from hospital in early March, 2000. "Gosh, I'll be living in the countryside next," he joked at the time.

With two band members now new parents, and an empathic promise issued to fans that there would be little or no activity on the live front during 2000, it came as a genuine surprise when Blur performed a hastily arranged one-off gig at the Royal Festival Hall's Meltdown Festival on July 2. However, it proved to be a bumpy night, with Albarn sounding distinctly non-plussed to be back on stage after an absence of seven months. "Good evening," he said. "This is it, once this year, and the choice (of songs) has been difficult..." Still, once the group settled into opening track 'Battle', it all went professionally enough, even if a peculiar set list sucked some of the atmosphere from the show. Eschewing almost all of their hits, with only 'Tender' and 'On Your Own' to really lift the spirits, it was left to darker material such as 'Death Of A Party', 'Country Sad Ballad Man', 'Trimm Trabb' and 'No Distance To Run' to do their work. Fine tracks all, of course, but somewhat gloomy in rapid succession. When Ken Livingstone emerged from the wings to murmur his way through the suicide-inducing 'Ernold Same', the urge to seek the nearest exit became palpable. Finishing the evening with a new song, the jazzy, but forgettable 'Black Book' – "This is the one new song we are playing, and if you don't like it we're fucked" – Blur said their goodbyes and headed back to their individual lives. No smiles, no encore. 'Singles Night' this wasn't.

Away from the Royal Festival Hall, things went a little better. Graham left behind nappy-changing duties for a UK tour in support of *The Golden D*, while Damon began work on yet another movie soundtrack, this time partnering Sugarcube Einar Örn Benediktsson for the score of *101 Reykjavik*. Directed with some flair by Baltasar Kormákur, the film's plot might have been a tad fanciful (the central protagonist ends up having an affair with his mother's girlfriend), but the location shots were truly eye-catching, with Damon's famous Kaffibarinn bar (also part-owned by Kormákur) a prominent feature throughout. Obviously a man in demand, Albarn next flew to Mali as a goodwill ambassador for *Oxfam*. There to witness the charity's *On The Line* programme, which actively encouraged African countries to trade ideas with Europe and the West, Damon was initially unsure of participating both as a cultural envoy and roving musician, but Winstanley's continuing encouragement and her own positive experiences of West Africa persuaded him to give it a shot.

In the end, it all worked out wonderfully well, with Albarn jamming alongside local bands, singers and performers such as Kola players/local legends Toumani Diabete and Afel Becoum through the evening and on until morning. "It was just a really inspiring, colourful, bright, gorgeous place, you know," he later told *The Guardian's* John Harris. "Apart from the music, which really is like a river that flows through Bamako (Mali's capital), I think the recycling market was the thing that stayed with me.

You have women and children in temperatures up to 100 degrees, (out) on the rubbish, picking out anything that has some use. That's (then) given to cleaners, renderers and preparers, and then (brought) down to where the road is, where there are ploughs, rockets and computers, all for sale." Returning home with a pocketful of recordings Albarn subsequently began a musical dialogue between London and Bamoko, as songs and arrangements shot back and forth between him, Diabete, Becoum and several other players on the internet until everyone was satisfied with the results. Eventually released in 2002 as *Mali Music* on Damon's new label – *Honest Jon's Records* – all proceeds from the disc went to Oxfam. For the Blur frontman, it was yet another reason not to hurry back to band camp. "You can become very insular in a group when you're playing with the same people," he underlined to *Mojo* upon his return, "That's just not healthy. You have to see how wide the world is..."

As much as Albarn might have been enthused by his Malian adventures, there were still Blur-related responsibilities to attend to on the home front, with the band's new CD/DVD *Best Of...* collection landing in shops on 30 October, 2000. Housing 17 of their 23 singles, plus 'This Is A Low' – "It's on there because it's brilliant" – *Blur: The Best Of...* was certainly a sturdy enough item, and made even more sales worthy due to its wonderfully ironic cover. The work of former Goldsmiths graduate Julian Opie, it presented Blur as four cartoon-like head shots: Graham and Dave spectacle-clad and quizzical looking, Alex and Damon a comely splash of ruffled hair and floppy fringes. A primary-coloured marvel, Opie's image was later purchased by the National Portrait Gallery where it still hangs in 2013. Yet, outside those convenient 10-year celebrations, one had to wonder why the album was being released, even if it was destined to sell over a million copies. Usually the province of groups already past their best, or worse, one last marketing ploy by record companies to extract a final penny before their act broke up or was dropped, 'Best Of's were often the death knell in a band's career. Not according to Albarn. "It's a positive end and a new beginning all at once," he said. "Also, we've been around for a while now, and this captures the songs for younger people who haven't perhaps engaged with them before."

While Blur were happy to deny any such gossip at the time, the album's only new track 'Music Is My Radar' showed signs of lethargy on the group's collective spirit. As an advertisement for Damon's developing interest in Latin and African sounds and rhythms, it worked remarkably well. But as a combined effort of wills to produce something of lasting value for the band itself, it was far less successful. Dave Rowntree begged to differ. "With 'Music Is My Radar', the pressure was off," he said. "That often happens with our B-sides, actually. You know you've got the A-side sorted out, so the pressure's off when you're writing and recording. That way, it just flows more naturally."

Reaching number 10 in the UK charts in late October, '...Radar''s airy, Afrobeat feel might have pleased Rowntree, but it was the first time Blur had issued a product that sounded more like a nascent Damon Albarn solo single than a true group effort. "We really weren't getting on well at that time," Albarn later admitted, "but the song we (ended up) producing was utterly bonkers." Damon was right to be pleased. '... Radar' was a subtle forerunner of an idea that had been growing like a multi-platinum disc in the back of his head since 1998: a new music for a new age, so to speak. Of course, to make it all work in the way he envisaged, he needed a new band.

But not necessarily a real one.

Chapter Fifteen

The Killer Awoke Before Dawn

With Blur's activities during 2000 restricted to one live show, a smidgeon of TV appearances, a so-so single and a greatest hits album, the group's self-described "hiatus" had certainly lived up to its billing. Yet, after a decade of road wars, chart battles, emotional and physical batterings, and indeed, children now a part of the mix, one really couldn't begrudge the band their break. "When people start to have families, you cease to be a four-man gang... you're not The Beatles in *Help!* anymore, are you?" said Alex. "You're not going to be recklessly hurling yourself over a horizon when you've got a family at home. The goal posts have moved... of course they have."

As time came to show, James was actually downplaying how far said goal posts had strayed. In fact, they were in danger of being removed from the pitch altogether. "To all intents and purposes (Blur) had finished, because nobody had said, 'Let's make another record,'" Rowntree later revealed. "And nobody was crying themselves to sleep over that." Least of all Damon Albarn. A ceaseless worker whose creativity and ambition often seemed to work in perfect concert, Albarn had wasted little time contemplating the possible demise of Blur. Instead, he had simply got on with the business of forming another group, even if they were made of paint, ink and pixels.

The concept for Gorillaz had come to Damon and Jamie Hewlett while killing time between parties at Golbourne Road in 1998. As previously described, the two would spend their evenings off ensconced in front of *MTV* – beer in one hand, cigarette (or something quite similar) in another, watching the show unfold with a mixture of fascination and sometimes horror. "We were just sitting there, watching," Hewlett later said. "We felt that you had to wait a long time before anything decent came along. There would be the odd Spike Jonze or Hype Williams video, and then the rest would be pretty bad. So we had the very simple idea: Let's do an animated band." This was not a new idea, but it certainly wasn't a bad one.

Before words such as 'animated', 'digital' or 'virtual' came into common parlance, the music world had a long established and extremely profitable relationship with cartoon pop. While Disney studios had used painstakingly drawn characters such as dwarves, wooden boys and even the odd flying elephant to voice songs during the thirties and forties, it was actually Ross Bagdasarian Sr. who took the idea and put it at the top of the US charts in 1958 with Alvin & The Chipmunks' 'The Chipmunk Song'. An infuriating blend of sped-up vocals and anthropomorphic rodents chirping about hula-hoops and Christmas presents, 'The Chipmunk Song' nonetheless sold over four million copies in just two months, proving conclusively that one didn't have to wear blue suede shoes or look like an alien love god to shift obscene amounts of vinyl.

Between 1965 and 1969 The Beatles were featured in a children's cartoon series shown in the US that ran to 39 episodes, though John, Paul, George and Ringo were reported to be less than delighted with their depiction as happy-go-lucky characters beset by ne'er-do-wells over whom they invariably triumphed in the end. This probably explains why the rights were subsequently bought up by Apple and the shows can no longer be acquired legally. In 1969, when The Monkees balked at recording the bubblegum strains of 'Sugar Sugar', cartoon pop went worldwide, as fictional adolescents The Archies were liberated from the pages of a comic and painted into life by a team of artists. Aligned to the honeyed tones of (human) session singer Ron Dante, the two-dimensional quintet (plus pet dog) danced themselves to an international hit. Whether it was The Beatles, having now graduated to a more sophisticated level, albeit fighting blue meanies from their yellow submarine, The Jackson Five spelling out the alphabet or The Osmonds soundly advising that "one bad apple don't spoil the whole bunch", cartoon bands – or bands transformed into cartoons – did brisk global business for much of the late sixties and early seventies.

Though the format had all but disappeared by the eighties, "the world's first digital supergroup" were doing their thing on various music channels at precisely the time Albarn and Hewlett were tuning in to watch. Based on an idea by entrepreneur Jimmie Gray and North London composer/producer David Kelly, 'LCD' or 'Large Cool Dudes' were a computerised band of heavily moustached, heavily overweight men bouncing their way through a Europop version of Mikis Theodorakis' justly famous 'Zorba's Dance'. Cheeky, irreverent, but above all very catchy, 'Zorba's Dance' went Top 20 twice in the UK during 1998/9 and was awarded a platinum disc in Australia, where the country's huge Greek population ensured it stayed in the charts for five months.

"Jimmie asked me to create a techno version of 'Zorba's Dance', which to be honest, I was very reluctant to do as it seemed such a silly idea," said Kelly. "But he managed to persuade me by promising that I only had to spend two days working on it. If it wasn't happening by then, he'd drop the whole thing. In fact, it really did work. But we then had the problem of who – or what – was going to front the project. Boybands were very popular at the time, so I had the idea of inventing a 'cartoon boyband'. My friend Marisa Scott came up with a video storyboard featuring these little round men and Jimmie hired Dave Spencer to do the digital animation. Jimmie then took it to Virgin records who loved it, and the rest, of course, is history."

In fact, LCD'S digitally rendered video showed just how far technology had come since Alvin and his chirping chipmunks some 30 years before. To create the images used for the promo, Dave Spencer spent 24 hours slaving away at his PC to create seven seconds of usable footage. Worse, if the results were undistinguished, the entire sequence would have to be redone. Evidently, while computer graphics was the way forward in the realisation of virtual acts, it still remained an onerous task to make them wholly believable.

Perhaps unsurprisingly, Albarn and Hewlett's vision for their own animated band bore no relation to the techno sound or visual style of LCD. But they were thinking – albeit separately – on similar lines. However, neither artist nor songwriter seemed in any particular hurry to realise their idea, at least at first. "No, there was no great formula or grand plan," Jamie later confirmed. "We just started messing around for about six months. I was doing designs, Damon was doing demos (and) it sort of grew from that." Inspired by the work of legendary animation director Chuck 'Wile. E Coyote' Jones, his own anarchic creation *Tank Girl,* a small, but still important slice of Japanese Manga and somewhat oddly, The Osmonds cartoons of the early seventies ("Genius stuff, you have to watch it..."), Hewlett started pulling together the visual characteristics of the group. "I wanted them to look cool, but not in wacky, animation terms," he said. "I wanted them to each have an individual character that was interesting. As a group together, they needed to project an image that appealed to us – which for us has always been slightly demented, a little bit dark, a bit broken. That was the vibe. We didn't want them to be cutesy characters on skateboards doing street surfing or whatever they call it..."

The result was fresh, clever and genuinely involving. A virtual quartet, Gorillaz were comprised of sweet-faced, but "blank as paper" lead singer 2D, "Asian axe princess" and Haiku queen Noodle, "hip-hop lug of stone & rhythms man" Russel and a black-eyed, bass-playing "prince of darkness" called Murdoc. Ethnically diverse, dressed for a Friday night out in Tokyo's Harajuku district and surprisingly cool for cartoons, Gorillaz were the visual equivalent of a tin of Quality Street. Everyone had their favourite. However, Jamie was keen to point out the end result of his creative endeavours was less down to test surveys and demographic ranges, and more about how the characters looked in his head. "People said I drew a black character, an Asian character and a white character so that it would appeal to everyone," he said. "I didn't. It just came out like that."

While Hewlett laboured away at 'Kong' Studios with a team of six animators to create the perfect-looking pop group, Albarn was already completing work on the music they would 'play' and 'sing'. "The music," Jamie underlined, "always came first." Working in isolation from his art partner, Damon chose to employ the services of esteemed West Coast hip-hop producer Daniel M. Nakamura AKA 'Dan The Automator' to help frame the project. Fresh off his own experiments with the futuristic sounds of Deltron 3030, Dan brought along friend/ fellow Californian MC 'Del tha Funky Homosapien' to provide a rap or two. Eager to sprinkle the sound of Gorillaz with some Afro-Cuban musical textures, Damon also invited veteran singer and Buena Vista Social Club legend Ibrahim Ferrer to take part in the sessions. With recording taking place in Jamaica, America and West London, and Miho Hatori, Cass Browne and former Bob Marley right-hand man Junior Dan on guitar/vocals, drums and bass respectively, Hewlett and Albarn's "idle idea" was now taking final shape.

In hindsight, the manner in which Gorillaz was foisted upon the world proved a stroke of marketing genius. Instead of trumpet cries and torchlight processions being organised for "Damon Albarn's latest band", Gorillaz' first EP – the prophetically titled *Tomorrow Comes Today* – snuck into shops with precious little fanfare just three weeks after the release of *Blur: The Best Of*. Downplaying his involvement to an almost ludicrous level at the time, Damon seemed content to be seen more as a jobbing collaborator than a multi-platinum selling artist indulging himself in some short-lived vanity project. "Dan (The Automator) is a mate of mine and (we've) made this record, this Gorillaz record, in Jamaica. I've just helped out a bit. It's going to come out and everyone can make their own minds up about it."

By pursuing such a strategy, Gorillaz arrived on the music scene unencumbered by high expectations or previous glories, allowing listeners to come to them with their own terms of reference. *Tomorrow...*'s grainy video only enhanced the effect, as Hewlett's animated foursome flitted in and out of shot against a real backdrop of tower blocks, scrawled graffiti (including Banksy's famous ape painting) and West End bars. Even the music was low-key, with Damon's new instrument of choice, the Melodica, piping out a melody that eased itself between splashes of rumbling bass, hip-hop beats and the singer's own forlorn-sounding vocal. Sitting nicely within the overall game plan, *Tomorrow...* debuted at number 33 on the UK charts before slipping back into the night a week later.

It wasn't going to stay that way for long. When Gorillaz's second single hit stores on March 5, 2001, it became clear Albarn and Hewlett had a potential monster on their hands. Gliding in on a Ennio Morricone-referencing 'Spaghetti Western' scream, 'Clint Eastwood''s jumble of Brixton dub, electronic wave forms and a career-defining rap from Mr. Homosapien all combined to produce a record of immediate appeal, and it has to be said, enduring distinction. Jamie wasn't letting down the side either. Handing over an animated promo that featured a scowling Murdoc replete with upside down cross, 2D waking through a lightning-bolt illuminated graveyard and an army of gorilla zombies trying to scare Noodle and Russel out of their designer pants, this was no stray episode of *Josie And The Pussycats*. "You can turn the whole notion of a pop group on its head," Jamie said. "Because when the members of the group aren't 'real', you can make up (situations) for them that are as ridiculous and outrageous as you like, and then suddenly it becomes really interesting."

Further enhanced by a laconic, almost amused vocal from Albarn – "I got sunshine in a bag, I'm useless, but not for long... the future is coming on" – 'Clint Eastwood' went to number one in Norway, Spain and Italy, Top Five in half a dozen other territories while also bagging the number four spot at home. Even America bit this time, simultaneously bestowing Gorillaz with a number three in their 'modern rock' chart and a number six in the 'Hot Dance Club Top Ten'. This was a level of crossover success Damon had never enjoyed before. "Well, I'm really glad people are getting something out of it," he said with no little understatement.

Albarn and Hewlett's next move was as well judged as the slow release campaign that preceded it. Testing the possibility of taking Gorillaz into a live environment, Damon pulled together a band of musicians/rappers for a gig at the Scala cinema in London's Kings

Cross on March 22, 2001. Yet, instead of facing their audience directly, singer and group performed behind a screen upon which were projected images of 2D and his cohorts shooting into the heavens and back again. "We were trying to create something that had no references in rock music," Albarn later said. "It was more like a film score revisited, with some references to film around it." Critically lauded, this combination of behind the scenes action and front of house animation worked a treat, creating in one critic's mind "a hyper-realistic shadow puppet show for the 21st century". This future-facing aspect to Gorillaz's nature was confirmed by the various extras that accompanied the release of their first, self-titled album at the end of March. In addition to 14 original songs, the disc also contained enhanced materials such as screen savers, wallpapers, and an autoplay function which opened the user's intranet browser directly onto the band's new, fully interactive website. Alex James' proverbial goalposts had just been moved to another dimension.

Of course, all this technology needed some real tunes behind it to make the concept of Gorillaz a credible one. Again, Albarn had risen to the challenge at hand, providing a confection of reggae, world music, trip hop, electronic and even punk stylings for Noodle, Russel, 2D and Murdoc to call their own. From the Cuban-tinged, Ibrahim Ferrer-sung 'Latin Simone (Que Pasa Contigo)' to the jazz-friendly, brass-stabbing rap party of 'Rock The House', *Gorillaz* was a record that had appropriated a smidgeon or two from every then fashionable musical form to inform its content and present its style. For some journalists this caused a problem or two, with Albarn's genre-busting antics redolent of a man trying a little too hard to stay down with the kids – or even worse, turning the East Ender/Essex escapee into one of those "sad West London middle-class white boys (who) talk in an embarrassing dubwise patois". Still, despite such occasional sniping, the critical response to *Gorillaz* was mainly positive. "(Gorillaz are the) perfect West London group," said *NME*. "A multi-cultural funky figment of white, indie, suburbanite imagination – an interactive cartoon band who use dub and hip-hop techniques to create sickly-sweet bubblegum pop. It (can) all plod somewhat, (and) it's so in love with the limitless potential of musical gadgetry... that it becomes twee (and) wearisome. Still, well done, Damon. (You) can be the Tom Tom Club as well as Pavement as well as the Kinks. (You) can be west London as well as Essex."

Given *Gorillaz*'s subsequent chart success, Albarn could actually claim to be more world citizen than West London wannabe, as the album became a global best seller. Making its debut at number three in the UK, *Gorillaz* also went Top Ten throughout Europe, Japan and the Antipodes, with gold discs turning platinum as the months went by. The record even allowed Damon to shed his previous shackles as "The woo hoo! Man" in the USA, hitting number 14 on the *Billboard* charts in June 2001 and eventually shifting over a million units. "I suppose the kids who like Gorillaz don't care who's behind it," he pondered at the time. "They just like the music and the characters. It isn't a cartoon jokey band. (It's) something that two years ago we thought was totally revolutionary and it's working so well because it's part of the zeitgeist." Jamie Hewlett was of a similar mind. "For the kids who are really invested in Gorillaz, who went on the website, played the video games, and collected all the interviews, it's become a whole world for them."

A chance idea that eventually yielded over seven million sales, Gorillaz was potentially much more than just an impressive royalty stream for Damon Albarn. If handled correctly, by its very nature the virtual band allowed him an opportunity seldom granted to pop or rock performers: a chance to never grow old. Through the miracle of Hewlett's brushstrokes, Gorillaz could remain forever 21, a perfect group withstanding the ravages of time – and in Murdoc's case – a fearsome smoking habit. No wrinkles, no embarrassing hip replacements or hearing loss. Just perpetual, uninterrupted, dewy-eyed youth. Taking the conceit to its natural conclusion, Damon need never even tour again, with Gorillaz's website, promotional videos and inevitable advances in technology allowing him to stay seated in a West London studio while his animated creations did the work for him. All he and Hewlett had to do was keep the ideas imaginative, the characters grounded in their own alternative reality and the concept truthful to its original intention. The rest, as they say, would take care of itself.

A clever man with a sound head for business, Albarn was already attendant to the possibilities Gorillaz offered and their potential future within the pop idiom. "(Gorillaz) demands that people use their imagination more than pop music generally allows for these days," he told *Metro* in the late spring of 2001. "If you can believe in figures such as Eminem and Marilyn Manson, why not get your head around something which takes that to its logical conclusion? The whole pop aesthetic is more and more about personalities and you can get carried away with that and end up being let down. Humans are such fragile creatures and the whole nature of celebrity screws you up. Look at all the manufactured bands in the world. Even those that claim not to be are, in some way. Bands such as Coldplay are a little bit too clean to be real. Then there's Westlife, A1... (all the rest). Gorillaz is about trying to destroy that and take it further, to manufacture something with real integrity. It just requires a leap of faith."

With a four-colour fountain of youth burbling nicely in the background, one might have expected Damon to turn his back on any former endeavours, and enjoy a life on the animated lam. Yet, true to form, it seemed the 33-year-old songwriter couldn't quite wrest himself away from the real joys of a real group. Given the end result, he might just have taken a holiday instead.

At more or less the same time Gorillaz's second single '19–2000' was climbing its way to number six in the UK charts on the back of another inspired Jamie Hewlett video, news escaped that Blur were to record a new album. Like Albarn, the band's members had been far from idle in intervening months. Having caught the flying bug from Dave Rowntree, Alex James had successfully passed his pilot's licence and taken to the skies in various small aircraft. He had also become quite the fitness fanatic, even eschewing his beloved champagne in an effort to get back into shape. A man for whom Rowntree once said, "If Alex doesn't end up looking like Keith Richards, then he really does have a picture in the attic", James' love of the good life first began catching up with him during Blur's tour excursions of 1999, when the bassist's usually svelte figure showed signs of considerable expansion. Determined to do something about it – "Vanity's always been my saving grace," he once quipped – Alex had run, boxed and swum his way back to good health and an enviable waistline. Perhaps those old rumours that he had his publicity shots vetted by his mother before their release weren't quite as unfounded as they seemed...

Away from the gym, James had been busy contributing bass parts to Sophie Ellis-Bextor's platinum bound debut album *Read My Lips*, as well as co-writing her dub-influenced, Top Twenty single 'Move This Mountain'. In a parallel move, Alex took up the position of occasional presenter on the late night TV show *24 Hours In Soho*, a job that not only gave him the exquisite pleasure of introducing viewers to his favourite part of London, but also paid him for the privilege. James was not quite done with Fat Les either, having recently provided England's football team with another cod-anthem for *Euro 2000*, this time a surprisingly sincere version of the hymn 'Jerusalem'. Keen to steal the old English standard back from far right-leaning political groups, Alex, Keith Allen and Damian Hirst arranged for the track to be sung by both the London Community Gospel Choir (who had previously featured on 'Tender') and the London Gay Men's Chorus. Though not a great commercial hit, 'Jerusalem' was nonetheless a considerable improvement on the risible 'Naughty Christmas (Goblin In The Office)' of two years before.

Also contributing to 'Jerusalem' was Dave Rowntree, whose experiences with marching drums as a child served him well in Fat Les' promo for the song. Unfortunately, it was one of few examples of levity during an otherwise strange time for the Blur man. By his own admission, Rowntree had arrived at the new millennium feeling unsettled and unsure, with even the clothes on his back a source of some distraction. "There were a lot of things I hadn't actually thought about before," he later told *The Guardian*. "Clothes were a big example. I'd been wearing Doc Martens for 20 years or something stupid, but I'd never actually made that decision. I used to hate clothes shopping, because I'd been stuck in this huge room, full of clothes, going, 'Is that a nice shirt or not? How do you know?'"

While not quite a mid-life crisis, Rowntree's quest to understand previous choices while also planning for the road ahead must have been a contributory factor to several major changes to his circumstances at the time. In addition to ongoing work with his animation company Nanomation, Dave also began an Open University degree in Law, with the aim of becoming a qualified solicitor. His always strong interest in left-wing politics began to resurface too, as the drummer attended several Labour party meetings during 2001. Unfortunately, though there was progress made in many an area, Rowntree's marriage did not do as well, with he and his wife Paula divorcing after five or so years together.

Graham Coxon was also experiencing a turbulent period in his emotional life, as his relationship with artist Anna Norlander had floundered some months after the birth of their daughter Pepper, leading to a full separation in 2001. An extraordinarily sad time for the guitarist, his overall mindset can be clearly heard on the songs of his third solo album of the time, *Crow Sit On Blood Tree*. Described by *Q* as a record of "wide-open vulnerability", *Crow...* was a schizophrenic blend of the mournful and angered, with pensive ballads such as 'A Place For Grief' and 'All Has Gone' sitting uncomfortably next to the furious blasts of 'Burn It Down' and 'Empty Word': "This tree is dead and it won't grow anymore," he railed on 'Burn...'s train wreck of a verse, "The park's on fire, the sun don't shine anymore..." When Graham did come up for musical air, as on the folk-tinged 'I'm Goin' Away', his lyrics were often still bleak and sapped of optimism, with things reaching a natural conclusion on the *Taxi Driver*-referencing single 'Thank God For The Rain': "Such a messed up world we're living in today, thank God for the rain, maybe it'll wash that scum away..." A grim tale about the dangers of inner-city life, the fact that Coxon was apparently drawing inspiration from the gun-toting, mohawked avenger Travis Bickle was of some concern itself.

With much on their minds, and varying degrees of success in learning how to deal with it, Blur tested the waters of their potential reunion with a recording session in August 2001 for Marianne Faithfull's latest album, *Kissin' Time*. Contributing the record's title track, the band were among a number of other acts/artists providing songs for Faithfull, including Beck, Pulp and The Smashing Pumpkins'

Billy Corgan. Initially optimistic to be working with one of the true survivors of the first wave of sixties British pop, the atmosphere in the studio soon darkened, as old arguments over musical direction and a few other things besides broke out between Albarn and Coxon. "For the band, it wasn't one of the best experiences," Damon later confirmed. "Partly for obvious reasons and partly for reasons that are private. It just wasn't a good time for the band. We really didn't want to be with each other."

Thankfully, essential repairs appeared to have been made in time for the group's appearance at the 'British Music Roll Of Honour', an annual event held every September by the Music Managers Forum (MMF) at London's Hilton Hotel. On this occasion, Blur's manager Chris Morrison was the subject of the MMF's attentions, winning the Peter Grant Award for his outstanding contribution to the music business over the last three decades. Given the fact Morrison was receiving a decoration named in memory of Led Zeppelin's larger-than-life and none-more-legendary boss, this constituted praise at its very highest. "(It's) a brutal business we're in and anyone who has lasted deserves credit," said Albarn from the podium. "(And) Chris has definitely got us through a lot of weird things..." Performing two songs – 'Beetlebum' and 'Song 2' especially for the occasion, it was Blur's first time on stage together since the 'Singles Night' tour of 1999. "Oh, I enjoyed that," said Diana Gutkind, who was there to offer keyboard support on the night. "Sadly, it was also my last gig with the band..."

However, the real test of whether Blur could recapture the spirit and camaraderie that produced their best work in the nineties still lay ahead as tentative plans for a new album became bold reality in the autumn of 2001. By all accounts, the start date was driven by Dave Rowntree. "I suppose I was trying to force the issue one way or another," he later said. "Obviously, I wanted to carry on (the band) but not if somebody felt they *had* to do it. So, in the end it was about finding some kind of common ground." That said, he remained realistic as to what might happen if it all turned to dust. "There's this unwritten assumption that when Damon's off doing something, I'm (left) drumming my fingers on the table going, 'Come on!'. I have several other lives that I lead. I just don't lead them in the public eye, that's all."

At first, it appeared that Blur were going down a rather unconventional route with their choice of potential producer, as rumour had the band linked with jazz/rock/ambient/new age journeyman Bill Laswell. An industry veteran whose previous clients included the likes of Mick Jagger, Iggy Pop, Sly and Robbie, Yoko Ono and even Motorhead, Laswell's take on Blur would certainly have made for interesting listening, but for various reasons the pairing didn't work out. Instead, the job of overseeing the group's seventh disc went to Ben Hillier. A sensible choice, Hillier had cut his studio teeth as an engineer on U2's odd but endearing *Pop* before being promoted to the production seat for Britpop beneficiaries Echobelly (*People Are Expensive)* and Britpop avoiders Suede (*Head Music*) in 1998/9. Yet, it was his recent efforts on 'Music Is My Radar', Fat Les' 'Jerusalem', Sophie Ellis Bextor's 'Move This Mountain' and Marianne Faithfull's *Kissing Time* that strongly endeared him to the Blur camp. Enthusiastic and methodical, Hillier was also known for his saint-like patience, a quality he would need in spades during the coming months.

Recording for the band's new record was scheduled to begin at 13 studios in early November 2001, and indeed, for at least three members of Blur this proved to be the case. However, at the end of the first day, Graham Coxon was still absent. With the clock already ticking, Albarn, James, Rowntree and Hillier decided to soldier on without him. "When we started the record, the choice was to either sit around and wait for everyone to turn up, which wasn't really going to happen, or to get on with doing the record in the time we had," the producer later told *Sound On Sound*. "So we said 'Here's the two weeks we've set aside to work on it. We start at 10 and finish at six. If you're there you get to play on it, if you're not, you miss out'. So everyone was really hungry to play. If Damon wasn't there and we wanted to record a vocal then Alex would sing. Or if Alex wasn't there, then Damon would be desperate to get on the bass. It was quite competitive but really exciting. Everyone had this real drive to play." Despite Graham not being present, these sessions yielded at least nine usable ideas, though activities were temporarily suspended for the Christmas break, after which Blur's guitarist was expected to return.

And so he did. In late January 2002, Coxon finally joined his colleagues in West London, providing thoughts and even a contribution or two to the material already recorded with Hillier. By March, and with Graham still making the occasional appearance, Blur's song tally had risen to a serviceable 17 as Damon continued to pool ideas from his previous four-track demos with the help of 13 house engineers Jason Cox, Tom Girling and James Dring. "I don't usually work with an engineer, I usually do it all myself, so it's nice... especially nice to have Jason," he said at the time. "He's an awful lot more than an engineer, he's worked with the band for years, and he knows 13 and the band's equipment inside out."

However, Albarn's decision to pursue a live agenda with Gorillaz meant that sessions were again delayed so he could travel to America for several shows. With the animated group's debut album having now sailed past the one million mark in the States, and talk of Grammy nominations already rife, the idea of Gorillaz remaining a virtual proposition was simply untenable. As the Scala cinema performance – and several more UK gigs during the autumn of 2001 – confirmed, there was an extremely lucrative market for 2D, Noodle, Russel and Murdoc's adventures outside the confines of a website or video clip. Given the facts, Damon would be a fool not to take advantage of it and head for the stage. "I think everyone (saw) that I wasn't leaving the band in any way, though," he later said. "I was just filling my mind and my heart with things that gave me a real reason to go and do justice to a group that (Jamie and I) worked so hard on building up." Come early May, and with Gorillaz's US tour obligations now behind him, Albarn returned to 13 in the hope of finally completing work on Blur's album. Then things took an unexpected turn. Graham Coxon was out of the band.

At first, details were sparse. According to some reports, Coxon had bailed due to Damon's continuing obsession with Gorillaz. Others placed the reason for his exit on Graham's own plans for a solo career, a view apparently confirmed by producer Ben Hillier. "Graham's an awesome guitarist and an amazing musician, but he wasn't really that interested in making a Blur album," the producer said. "His solo stuff is what he's into doing and Blur was becoming a bit of a chore for him, so it didn't seem right to have him involved – we're not at school!" The waters became further muddied when Dave Rowntree seemed to imply during an interview of the time that Coxon's departure might well be temporary rather than permanent. "None of us precludes the possibility of getting back with Graham at some point in the future," he said. "Who knows whether that will happen..." With media enquiries increasing by the day, it was left to Albarn to try and clarify Blur's position on their errant guitarist. "Graham just wants to pursue a far more low-key life in every aspect," he told *NME*. "He's been through a very tough time, and hopefully, he's coming out the other end now."

How tough that time was became apparent when Coxon finally spoke to the press in the autumn of 2002. By his own admission, things had been on a downward slide long before Blur began work on album number seven. "Well, 2001 was a funny year for me," he told *Q*, with a level of honesty usually reserved for confession boxes. "I was in two different psychiatric hospitals in March and then November. There were problems with booze and depression."

Profoundly shaken by the end of his relationship with Anna Norlander, while also keen to ensure the well-being of his daughter Pepper, Coxon's troubles were obvious and completely understandable: "I was sad, overwhelmed and just a bit knackered." Yet, it was his decision to quit drinking for good on November 15, 2001, after a month in The Priory that paradoxically caused problems elsewhere. A clinic renowned for its treatment of celebrities with alcohol and drug addictions, The Priory was the perfect place for Graham to stage his recovery, but the timing of his admission clashed badly with the guitarist's responsibilities in Blur. "It was something that I just needed to do," he later said. "It was unfortunate. It was like being on a motorway wanting to pull over but no one's letting you... and knowing that you were going to crash. I just needed to take my hands off the steering wheel. In the end, it was good for me. It meant I could take some time, (and then)... look after my daughter and be at home."

There is absolutely no suggestion that Blur did not support Coxon's choice to seek treatment. In fact, they were probably relieved by the news when they heard it. Unfortunately, according to Damon, Graham hadn't thought to actually tell them of his plans until they arrived at 13 studios to commence work. "What threw us was the fact that we started and the first day Alex, Dave and I turned up but Graham didn't," Albarn later said. "We were given no warning of that, and later that day we were informed that Graham wouldn't be around for a couple of months." When Coxon did eventually join his colleagues, things had changed on both sides, though not for the better. "I'd had a couple of awkward afternoons recording, and I got a few things down," he said. "(But) I was probably a little crackers, still. And very energetic." In fact, Graham's new sobriety and the psychological re-adjustments it brought may well have been key to what happened next. "Quite often, dipsos are easier to deal with when they're pissed, not when they've sobered up," Coxon later told writer John Harris. "When they're sober, they tend to tell the truth a little more. I don't know if I was behaving a little out of turn, but it did feel awkward for everybody. And in the end, Chris Morrison said 'Look, the boys don't really want you to go into the studio today.' And I said, 'Well, when then?' "He said, 'Well, not really at all.' It did make my blood go a bit cold. I went into the loo, and I thought, 'Shit, man, this is like one of those *Behind The Music* things'. I looked at myself in the mirror, and (thought), 'I'm sort of being sacked...'"

Chris Morrison, Blur, and indeed, Graham have all confirmed at various times that he was not technically sacked from the band. In fact, any such suggestion continued to anger Albarn, even a year after the event. "No one was sacked. There was nothing like that," he growled to *The Daily Post* in 2003. "We just started recording and it sounded great. When Graham actually returned, it just didn't work as a four-piece anymore and it was as simple as that. And the spirit of Blur was more important than the individuals. It could have happened to any one of us." Perhaps so, but Rowntree went a little further into the possible reasons behind why it was Graham rather than anyone else that found himself at the sharp end of the stick. "(He) kind of absented himself from the last two or three records," the drummer told *OTWS*, "so it was business as usual (when he didn't turn up). We didn't make too much of a play of it... because we were still hoping that we could patch things up. (But) my best guess is there are now only three of us, so that's one less name for people to have to remember..."

Rowntree's candid assessment of Blur's immediate future turned out to be entirely correct. After the events of May 2002, Coxon did not return to the band, with all communication between both camps strictly confined to the trading of business documentation and legal papers. "Damon... thinks I'm in a mood with him, but I'm not," Graham said. "The truth is I'm suffering from deep embarrassment. I'm like that with a lot of people. Out of shyness, I don't phone them and that turns into an epic of not calling them because I'm embarrassed that I haven't called them." Albarn sounded just as uncomfortable with the situation. "I've known Graham since I was 12, so I sincerely hope that at some point we'll be talking again," he told *NME*. "Otherwise, that's a lifetime's friendship wasted..."

With Coxon now out of the picture – though no-one was yet brave enough to confirm whether the arrangement was temporary or permanent – Blur pressed on with the recording of their new album. Having now amassed some 28 songs (it would soon grow to 37), the trio decided to further extend their perimeters by calling in several additional producers/re-mixers during June 2002. It turned out to be quite the roll call, as Grammy Award-winning duo The Dust Brothers (Beastie Boys/Beck) and Norman Cook AKA Fatboy Slim (an early contender to produce the record) both experimented with Blur's latest material. Though extremely busy at the time, William Orbit also returned to the fold, albeit in his own unique way. "We sent a couple of tunes to William to work on in his studio, working round the clock in a computer environment the way he does," said Hillier. "He's a nutter and works all night. That was quite an interesting juxtaposition, us doing office hours then going to see William after work, just as he was getting up!" Yet, the introduction of all these outside ears only served to confirm that the band was still some way off the finish line, with Albarn in particular doubting the quality of several songs. His solution to this issue was novel: Decamp the whole operation to a barn in North Africa.

Since his experiences in Mali, Damon seemed completely enamoured with both Africa the continent and its people, taking every opportunity he could to travel there either with Suzi Winstanley or close friends. It was on one such trip that he discovered the joys of Marrakesh's vibrant artistic community, spending a weekend in Morocco's capital city at a spiritual music festival. There, Blur's frontman watched as bands literally formed in front of his eyes, with players setting up their instruments, dusting off an old tune, then quickly packing up again to move on to another session elsewhere. "Live music is just everywhere. It's a very important part of the culture, in a much more direct way than it is (in Britain)." Feeling that Blur might benefit from a change of scene, and as importantly, the injection of energy offered by such a vital area, he suggested upping sticks from West London to what locals called "The Western Kingdom". The idea proved so popular, James, Rowntree and Hillier were literally on the plane before him.

Though only there for a month or so, Marrakesh seemed to agree with the band musically, as three new songs were written within a week of their arrival in the city. More, Albarn was determined to get the best out of their location, penning his lyrics under a bank of olive trees but a short distance away from the barn where Blur and Hillier's equipment was housed. Free from the confines of a stuffy studio, he also sang his contributions for the record in much the same way. "All of the vocals were sung outside," he later said. "It was nice. When it's nice weather, it's nice to be outside. I think the big studios are really a con."

There were downsides. Because of Marrakesh's sweltering summer heat, working hours were considerably shortened. These extreme temperatures also brought problems with instruments and technology, resulting in out of tune basses and malfunctioning laptops. Worse, a bad bout of food poisoning caused havoc among band and crew, with a lone bicycle serving to convey various musicians, engineers and producers to a toilet located some 200 yards away from their temporary home. Yet, these ad hoc arrangements were equally responsible for some inspired moments of improvisation, as the band were free to tape background noise, stray percussive effects and even Damon's squeaky leaps on and off a derelict truck, and mix it into the sound of their album. "(This) record is really going to reflect all the environments it was recorded in," Albarn said at the time.

As Blur were making arrangements to leave Morocco in late September 2002, Graham Coxon was busy stealing a march on the trio back at home with the imminent release of his fourth solo album, *The Kiss Of Morning*. Pulled together from songs written after he gave up alcohol a year before, the disc turned out to be Coxon's most focused and coherent effort yet. Whether making a winning stab at sixties psych pop on 'Just Be Mine' or fusing the sound of Syd Barrett with country pedal steels and classical pianos on 'Good Times', *The Kiss Of Morning* proved a neat encapsulation of Graham's past influences and future manifesto – the guitarist obviously willing to try out any musical style that emotionally moved him. Two tunes really stuck out, however. The acoustic-rattling 'Song For The Sick' was a two-minute tirade against someone called 'Taylor', with whom Coxon appeared to be very angry indeed: "You stabbed me in the back, you're lower than a snake, your brains are in your sac, you two-faced fucking fake..." Of course, it was all too easy to read this as a barbed attack on Damon, but Graham was having none of it. "I think the record's more focused on obvious problems rather than me being a screaming brat," he said. But it was 'Mountain Of Regret' that plucked at the heartstrings the most. A sad, resigned but somehow still uplifting account of a love affair lost to the bottle, 'Mountain...' was the most autobiographical song Coxon had yet written: "I turn my back on her true love, all my friends and the lord above, and my drinking dragged me down to the bars in Cabbage town..."

When meeting the press to promote his new record in October 2002, Coxon was equally self-effacing about the problems that had dogged his time with Blur. Never once seeking to duck the issue of his drinking, Graham just shot straight from the hip. "I realise that I've been an arsehole for a long, long time," he told *The Scotsman's* John Mulvey.

"For maybe a quarter of an hour each day I was probably quite nice, probably after three or four drinks. And after that, I was a snarly, nasty, bitter piece of work. Or hung over, snappy and irritable." He was also crystal clear as to the reasons behind his previous behaviour. "Well, I'd drink because of social inadequacy, or nerves, shyness. (I thought) 'If I drink this I can actually talk to people. I can make people laugh... shit, people like me'. Then it turns into a coping mechanism, especially gigging. You're all hyped up after a gig and there's nowhere to put the energy, so you drink and you party and then before you know it, you're up and down and all over the bloody place for 10 years. Then somehow you've got to get off it and it's really difficult, because it's become part of who you are. It's a big change." Away from enquiries as to his newfound sobriety, there was one question that hung like the Sword of Damocles over Coxon's head. To wit: whether he was still a member of Blur. On this matter, Graham was somewhat more evasive. "I am on the Blur record. I was in the studio with Blur. I'm just not in there now," he said. "I can't really say. I'm not taking part in anything Blur are doing right now (and) there's nothing official yet. (But) I haven't really been involved in anything with Blur since May." For the time being at least, no-one was any the wiser.

Following their recent Moroccan escapades, Blur traded in the African sun for the torrential downpours of autumnal southwest England, with the band setting up shop at Damon's old farmhouse in Devon during mid-October to put the finishing touches to their record. Here, songs were tweaked, arrangements completed and any glitches suitably repaired. Again, William Orbit was temporarily on hand to offer his opinion and provide production suggestions, while Norman Cook (who actually visited Morocco for five days) also added his tuppence worth. By November, Blur finally had something they wanted to release. In an effort to test the waters – and perhaps duck any uncomfortable queries as to Graham Coxon's status within the group – they issued 1,000 copies of a semi-anonymous, vinyl-only single entitled 'Don't Bomb When You're The Bomb', its title quizzically written in Arabic on the 45's bright red-label. As a lyrical precursor to Albarn's anti-war sentiments for the band's next disc, it was next to perfect, even if the title was the only line in the song. Unfortunately, as a piece of music, 'Don't Bomb...' was profoundly disappointing. Somewhere in between the sound of seventies synth-punk duo Suicide and a half-speed electro-take on Krautrockers Faust, the tune meandered amiably, but aimlessly for four odd minutes before throwing itself on the listener's mercy. So shocked were fans at Blur's apparent new direction that Damon was actually forced to placate their concerns. "It's definitely going to be a rocking record," he said of Blur's forthcoming album, "(In fact), two tracks are among the most rock-orientated tracks we've ever done." In just two sentences, Albarn had steadied the horses.

But before Blur could truly step back into the light, there was one critical matter to attend to. They managed it with the consummate skill of seasoned politicians. "Graham Coxon always was, and always will be, *the* Blur guitarist and one of my best friends," said Dave Rowntree as he and his fellow bandmates introduced Blur's new "touring" guitarist Simon Tong at a record company showcase on February 7, 2003. Of course, as events came to show, Rowntree was being neither duplicitous nor furtive in his comments. He was just doing the best with the cards he had been dealt, covering both Blur and Coxon's relative (and possibly legal) positions at the time and for the future.

A fine musician and steady fixture in the alternative rock community for nigh on a decade, Simon Tong first came to prominence in 1996, when in a similarly fraught situation he had the unenviable task of replacing guitarist Nick McCabe in The Verve. Proving himself more than up to the task, Simon was even asked to stay when McCabe returned a year later, playing on some of the group's biggest hits, including 'Bittersweet Symphony', 'The Drugs Don't Work' and 'Sonnet'. Following The Verve's dissolution in 1999, Tong moved on to a promising, but short-lived alt-rock outfit called The Shining before taking up his latest post with Blur. However, no-one – least of all the group he was now attached to – were labelling Simon Tong as Graham Coxon's replacement. Nor would he play on the group's new album. Instead, Tong was to fill in for Blur's former lynchpin on an upcoming world tour, of which more details were to follow. "He's done the impossible, really," said Dave. "He's come into what could have been a really awkward situation... and he's fitted in perfectly." As ever, no official doors were being closed on Graham Coxon. Blur were just getting someone in to attend to a few cracks around the framework. "Oh, it's 25% different (without Graham)," said Alex, before quickly reassessing his percentages, "Or perhaps 33% different, actually..."

In keeping with industry practice, Blur released the first 'official' single from their forthcoming record on April 15, 2003. Entitled 'Out Of Time', its brooding melody and Afro-centric rhythms soon put to bed any notion that the group could not handle life without Graham. A shockingly good tune imbued with the same sense of serenity and sadness that made 'Beetlebum' such wonderful listening in 1997, 'Out Of Time' also featured a bravura performance from James and Rowntree: Fully supportive, but never intrusive, Alex's spare bass figure and Dave's tempered brushwork carried Albarn's vocal just as well as the violins, cellos and auods provided by the 'Groupe Regional du Marrakesh', who also guested on the single. And a fine vocal it was, too. Sounding more fragile and honest than he ever had before, Damon sang out his lyric of a planet spinning in the wrong direction, where people were either too busy or preoccupied to notice that everything was "turning the wrong way round".

Part intimate love song, part socio-political statement, 'Out Of Time' benefitted from an excellent video by director John Hardwick that emphasised the band's point of view without having them actually appear in it. Using footage culled from a BBC documentary (*Warship*) that depicted life on board the American aircraft carrier USS Abraham Lincoln, 'Out Of Time''s promo conveyed the inner dialogue of a female crew member as she stared out to sea, her own thoughts on a crumbling relationship appearing as subtitles at the bottom of the screen: "Two days after I get home, he leaves. It's just too hard. I used to love him. But you can't love someone you don't know anymore..." Without recourse to showy graphics or multi-angle perspectives, Hardwick's clip still packed a mighty punch. "It's the antithesis of the *Top Gun* image of the American military machine," explained Albarn. "It focuses on the loneliness of somebody working on an aircraft carrier and the fact that a six-month tour of duty means that relationships break down and children go without their parents. That's the reality of it." A fine and emotive comeback, 'Out Of Time' reached number five in the UK charts, nicely setting things up for the album to follow.

Arriving on May 5, 2003, *Think Tank* was as good a record as Blur could have made under the circumstances, with Graham's unfortunate exit from the group partially compensated by a strong set of tunes and much more rounded world-view. As ever, the sleeve was notable. With Coxon having provided such an expressive cover image for *13*, one might have thought Blur would return to design firm Stylorouge to fill the gap. Instead, they had approached cult graffiti artist Banksy for help at their time of need. Despite his previous distaste for engaging in commercial work, the notoriously reclusive stenciller agreed to provide a suitably 'Banksian' illustration of a couple locked in an embrace, albeit with divers' helmets on their heads. "I've done a few things to pay the bills, and I did the Blur album," he later explained. "It was a good record, and (the commission was) quite a lot of money. I think that's a really important distinction to make. If it's something you actually believe in, doing something commercial doesn't turn it to shit just because it's commercial." Another in a long line of impressive sleeves from the band, *Think Tank*'s cover art was eventually sold at auction for £75,000 in 2007.

Previously, there had been much talk that Blur's recent trip abroad, Damon's previous escapades in Mali and 'Out Of Time''s Moroccan-assisted orchestration would result in the band making "an African-themed album", or at least one that would skirt close to the West London sound of Gorillaz. This turned out to be not quite the case. While there were surely elements of Afro-beat and trip-hop throughout *Think Tank* – and a strong reliance on rhythm to convey mood and pace – the record was as much influenced by punk and electronica as it was by the work of Fela Kuti, Toumani Diabaté or Vieux Farka Touré. "I love The Clash," Albarn said, "and they're a real inspiration on this album." Too true, as the Norman Cook-produced 'Crazy Beat' and growling thrash of 'We've Got A File On You' both recalled the trim spirit and fighting talk of Joe Strummer's men. "'Crazy Beat' actually started off in such a different way, though," Albarn confirmed. "The nearest thing I could compare it to is a really bad version of Daft Punk. So, we got sick of it, and then put in that descending guitar line over it to rough things up a bit." In Graham's continuing absence, Damon had actually covered the vast majority of guitar parts on *Think Tank* himself, with Alex and Dave only stepping in to assist on one or two cuts. In the main, he had done a fine job of it too, though on one occasion even Albarn had to accede his place to an old master...

When Blur weren't paying homage to lost punk heroes or Damon establishing his credentials as a fledgling axe hero, they were busy getting into the groove or visiting the chill out room. In fact, *Think Tank*'s opener 'Ambulance' – with its squidgy keyboard line, stop-start percussion and sailing vocals almost begged for a dance re-mix – though in Alex James' mind, the track actually represented the first signs of group recovery after the woes of May 2002. "That was the first song that I thought, 'Right, this is Blur again'," he said. "Like 'I'm (back) in the right place again...'" If one were looking for any such nods to the past, then 'On The Way To The Club' delivered admirably. A dreamy little thing that bubbled along on a stream of light loops and treated piano, 'On The Way...' was the latest example of "The Blur Hangover Remedy", taking up where 'Mellow Song' had left off several years before: "Yeah, [it's] a 'hangover song' which we sort of write from time to time," said Damon. The William Orbit-produced 'Sweet Song' was another sleepy gem, its title confirming Albarn's interest in naming his ideas for the mood he wished to convey. "That's another African thing I've picked up," he said. "They call (songs) things like 'Tree Song'. You know what I mean, they give it (a title) that's something quite simple. It doesn't have an agenda so much, it's just offered out as a nice bit of music to everyone."

This was undoubtedly true of the melodic aspects of 'Good Song'. Tranquil as a summer's day, it was easy to imagine Damon stretched out under a Cypress tree when he wrote the track, though given its similarity to U2's 'Stuck In A Moment You Can't Get Out Of', a transistor radio might well have been playing in the background at the time. From the lush Malian blues of 'Caravan' ("It makes me think about the sun going down... with an immense sense of calm," said James) to the Fatboy Slim-assisted 'Guns Of Brixton' – referencing 'Gene By Gene' – *Think Tank* was an album that "either soothed the senses or shook the socks", as one critic delightfully put it. Sadly, there was also the odd dull moment or stretch too far. Despite some growling sound FX and spitting atmospherics, 'Brothers And Sisters' was a little too close in tempo and running order to 'On The Way...' to make much of an impact for itself. Similarly, while cleverly arranged and structured, 'Jets' resembled a cannibalization of pre-existing material – its only saving grace provided by Mike Smith, whose uncanny sax solo arrived mid-song as if from another planet.

Unfortunately, 'Moroccan People's Revolutionary Bowls Club' seemed lazier in its ambitions. A pleasant enough ditty displaying a huge North African influence at its sonic centre, the track confirmed Blur's ability to absorb the spirit of Marrakesh into their musical bones. Yet, '...Bowls Club' could also be read as simple pastiche, with the band more interested in emulating the sounds they heard around them than taking ownership of them. Still, when the going got tough, there was always 'Battery In Your Leg' to fall back on. Ending *Think Tank* in gorgeous fashion, 'Battery...' was a serene and majestic reminder as to how bloody marvellous Blur could really be. Redolent of *Gentlemen Take Polaroids*-era Japan, but with a sly hint of gospel thrown in to help ramp up the emotional value, Albarn's "poignant elegy to good times and old friends" was also the only track on *Think Tank* to feature the spidery guitars of Graham Coxon: "This is a ballad for the good times," Damon sang tellingly, "and all the dignity we had..."

With the possible exception of 'Battery...', anyone looking among the lyrics of *Think Tank* for further clues or coded explanations as to what exactly happened between Blur and Coxon during the early months of 2002 was wasting their time. This was not an album given to either personal ruminations or professional recriminations concerning the band's recent past. Albarn would have probably found any such notion obvious, perhaps even vulgar. Instead, *Think Tank*'s twin engines of lyrical thrust were concerned with "love and politics", though not necessarily in that order. "What are you supposed to do as an artist other than express what's going on around you?" asked the singer.

Since the formation of Blur in 1990, Damon had always walked a judicious line when it came to matters of government and policy. On the one hand, he made no bones about his distaste of American influence and its spread to the land of his birth. Indeed, for a time he and Blur seemed to be fighting a one-sided war against such things, championing home-grown music and values in the hope that once again, British pop culture might resume its previous importance on the world stage. And it had worked, though not exactly in the way that Albarn might have hoped or wished for. Yet, despite his artistic family background and occasional support of left-leaning causes, Damon had remained suspicious of hoisting his or Blur's colours to any political party or agenda. This approach was exemplified when he refused to get sucked in to the cartwheels and fireworks of 1997, marking himself out as one of the few artists not to turn up for a free lollipop at 10 Downing St. when Labour's Tony Blair came to power. But recent circumstances had at last forced him out of the dugout and onto the political pitch.

After the events of 9/11, the international 'war on terror' had begun to escalate, with a series of planned military operations slowly but surely building towards fruition. By November 2001, Afghanistan had been invaded and American and British troops were at the heart of the fighting. With fears of a prolonged campaign and the slim but palpable threat of the use of nuclear weapons hanging over everyone's head, Albarn had in turn used Gorillaz's acceptance speech for 'Best Dance Act' at the 2001 MTV Europe Music Awards to convey his point of view. Striding onto the stage with Jamie Hewlett, and wearing a T-shirt emblazoned with the Campaign for Nuclear Disarmament logo, Damon's speech was brief, but intense. "So, fuck the music and listen," he said. "See this symbol here? This is the symbol for the Campaign for Nuclear Disarmament. Bombing one of the poorest countries in the world is wrong. You've got a voice and you have got to do what you can about it, all right?"

As the war on terror escalated throughout 2002, so did Albarn's political involvement. Following intelligence that Iraqi leader Saddam Hussein was supposedly sitting on a stockpile of 'weapons of mass destruction', United Nations investigators entered the country in search of them. When it became clear that America and Britain were planning to invade the country despite no definitive proof of WMD, or indeed, a legal resolution from the UN to proceed with such action, one million people took to the streets of London on March 26, 2003, in protest against the imminent war. This time, Damon was among them. Though his planned speech at Hyde Park never transpired,* Blur's frontman had already clarified his position concerning possible fallacies and misunderstandings around Arabic nation states with the release of 'Don't Bomb When You're The Bomb' four months before. "I feel there's so much misconception surrounding Arabic culture in general," he said. "I decided to translate the lyrics on that song (into Arabic on the label) because I thought it was an appropriate message. And I sort of proved my point because all of the reviews of it in Britain called it an 'anonymous 7-inch accompanied by mysterious Arabic writing'. Well, it's not mysterious. All you need to do is get somebody who speaks Arabic, and they'll translate it for you. It forces people to consider that issue, which for me is one of the most pressing issues of our time: cross-cultural understanding."

With 'Don't Bomb When You're The Bomb' acting as a primer, and the group's video for 'Out Of Time' another little push in the same general direction, Damon Albarn and Blur's recent politicisation was fully extended into the lyrical veins of *Think Tank*. Picking up on punk

* Reportedly, Albarn was too emotional to address the crowds at Hyde Park, the possible cause being the recent death of his grandfather Edward while on hunger strike as part of an anti-war protest. However, he did speak to the BBC while there: "I feel this is something I was brought up with, that war is never the answer. I don't think we've been consulted as a democracy. It is the wrong war. If we're going to depose (Saddam Hussein), we need to look at the elements in the West that created him..."

band Discharge's old trick of endlessly repeating one line to ram home an intellectual point, 'We've Got A File On You' made Orwellian play of shadow dossiers and shady governments while 'Jet''s circular refrain found Damon likening speeding bombers to star-like objects: "Jets are like comets at sunset..." Despite its sunny disposition, 'Good Song' also caught Albarn in a political frame of mind, his references to "lying on an atomic bomb" and turning off the TV to get the war out of his head both clear pointers to Iraq and Afghanistan. The swaying 'Brothers And Sisters' – with its sardonic name-checking of most every drug known to man – prescribed MDMA "for the war machine" before coming to the conclusion that "We're all drug takers" of some sort or another. Even the humorously titled 'Moroccan People's Revolutionary Bowls Club' wasn't immune from comments on the greenhouse effect, conservation and the looming threat of destruction through war. "(Uncertainty) forces people to value what they've got," said Damon at the time. "And that, hopefully, will pay dividends and help change the world to a better place. Hopefully. Touch wood..."

As if to provide an antidote to his concerns about world peace and world policemen – or as likely, underline the better parts of human nature – *Think Tank* was also given to lyrical bursts of affection, camaraderie, and above all, love. 'Ambulance' was one such strong example, with Albarn taking succour from the strength of his relationship ("I ain't got nothing to be scared of") while promising faithfully to "stay to the end". 'Caravan' too, extolled the virtues of partnership and family as Damon surrendered himself to the greater whole: "I believed I was strong, but you are the one..." Even the pseudo-dub of 'Gene By Gene' provided Blur's frontman with a chance to sing out his fondness for new friends and new places: "Fatboy and the barn is jumping, it's all right, it's just tight... deep down happiness." Evidently, if the world was going down in a ball of flames, Albarn was determined to see out its last moments with a smile on his face and his comrades around him.

Realistically, however, *Think Tank* was not Blur's finest moment. On occasion, it lacked clarity and songs often had a habit of bleeding into each other, their distinctive qualities lost in a miasma of like-minded tempos and electronic trickery. Also, the playfulness, surprises, venom and spite that Graham Coxon always brought to the band were for obvious reasons missing in action, and therefore sorely missed. But the album still had the power to please immensely, with the likes of 'Out Of Time', 'Ambulance', 'Caravan' and the superb 'Battery In Your Leg' providing a hazy soundtrack for Blur fans to revel in. The critics were wont to agree. "Thankfully *Think Tank* does still sound like a Blur album, but it is, in the main, a record oddly devoid of guitars," said BBC's Dana Tallis. "In their place are keyboards and dance beats (of the chilled out, dub variety). Album highlights are 'Caravan' and 'Sweet Song', two mellifluous songs that overflow with moving beauty, reminding me of 'This Is A Low'. (But) don't buy this if you're expecting the Blur of old. The past has been blurred, welcome to the future." *The Guardian*'s Kitty Empire followed a broadly similar tract in her own review of the record. "It's hard to fault (their) spontaneity, but *Think Tank* is not Blur's *Pet Sounds*, a work of skewed genius that will redefine them in years to come," she said. "It's the sound of a band at play in a 21st century tinker's caravan. Sometimes, the sense of freedom is infectious, the burbles and squelches welcome, but often, it's just a passing rattle and hum, like watching someone else's round-the-world holiday video. You're glad they had fun, but it won't change your life."

Not one to buck a trend, *Think Tank* gifted Blur their latest number one album in the UK, though this time, it fought hard to repeat the trick in other territories, often taking a mid-table position rather than heading straight to the top of the charts. Still, Albarn's high profile in the States with Gorillaz might have been a causal factor when selling *Think Tank* across the Atlantic, as the record debuted at number 56 on the *Billboard* Hot 100, the highest position Blur had yet achieved with a 'long-player'. "As an album, it came together extremely quickly, which was quite exhilarating, the sheer immediacy of it," said Alex with typical enthusiasm. "In fact, I think it's the best thing anyone's ever done." Rowntree was also pleased, even going as far as to compare *Think Tank*'s wares and general attitude to times long past. "If I had to pick a record that *Think Tank* sounds like, it'd have to be *Parklife*," he said. "(It's) the sound of starting again. That time, it was to piss our record company off. This time was because we'd lost our guitarist." Of course, there was one opinion of *Think Tank* that everyone wanted to hear. It came like the sound of wasps. "(I wish they) chucked the computer out and actually worked on making music instead of playing with Lego electronics, I suppose," Graham Coxon told *Q*'s Ben Mitchell. "That's about it... oh, and written songs. Sorry, I try not to be bitchy because bitchiness is just stupid..."

Ignoring the thoughts of their wandering guitarist, Blur seemed determined to take their new record to as many places as possible throughout 2003, with the band striking out on a world tour that soon rivalled their never-ending travels of 1999. Kicking things off with a spray of secret gigs to select audiences in America and Europe during early spring, the show truly got on the road at Mexico City's Auditorio Nacional on April 22, where Blur played a 20-song set chock full of *Think Tank* tunes, including 'On The Way...', 'Out Of Time', 'Good Song', 'Brothers And Sisters' and a corrosive rendition of 'Crazy Beat'.

By May, the group was in back in London for a five-night stand at the Astoria Theatre, where English fans could get their first good look at Simon Tong. Not one given to displays of overt showiness, Tong nonetheless held down his side of the stage admirably well, handling Coxon's guitar parts with some aplomb while also lighting a fire under new material such as 'We've Got A File On You' and 'Gene By Gene'. For some old school attendees, the former Verve man was simply human kindling, his very presence an affront to Blur's missing link. Yet, this was a somewhat sour view with too much focus given to the rear view mirror. Things were as they were and unlikely to change for the foreseeable future, even if Damon still held out a smidgeon of hope that Graham might one day make it back to base camp. "I genuinely cannot believe that we won't play together in the future," he said. "And that's because we had such a great time." He would have to wait a while yet.

The release of two further singles punctuated Blur's travels around the globe. On 7 July, 2003 while the band was shooting between the USA and Europe's festival circuit, 'Crazy Beat' escaped from *Think*

Tank to try life on its own. Sadly, despite its Clash-friendly energy and aggressive spikes in sound, the track was compromised by some particularly irritating quack-like "Yeah Yeah Yeah"'s courtesy of producer Norman Cook. Never destined for true greatness, 'Crazy Beat' fell out of the UK charts after one week at number 18. 'Good Song' fared even worse when released in October, the tune's sunny disposition proving no real antidote to the onset of autumn. Proffering Blur their worst chart position since 'Sunday Sunday' 10 years before, the single limped to number 22 at home before disappearing altogether. Still, for those seeking one last dance with the guitar of Graham Coxon, 'Good Song''s B-side 'Morricone' was of ineffable help. Recorded at 13 studios before his exit from the group, this Mamba-like shuffle featured Graham's distinctive noodlings throughout, those subtle splash chords and probing melody lines a gentle reminder of what he had once brought to the party.

If Blur's singles were not quite hitting their marks, then at least the band's live shows were picking up positive reviews, with their two-hour performance at Reading Festival on August 23 akin to the second coming in one critic's mind. "Tonight will probably be remembered as one of the greatest Blur shows of all time," said *NME*'s Krissi Murison. "From Damon falling off the stage during 'Beetlebum' and putting a dent into the ground beneath him, to Phil Daniels joining them for a tin-pot, acoustic version of 'Parklife', Blur make every spare moment a memorable one." Murison also drew attention to one aspect of Blur's performance that might have been initially sticky to negotiate, but had now been turned into a highpoint of their set. "Putting bad blood behind them – '(But) without wishing to be too sentimental (said Damon)' – Blur drew attention to the gaping vocal hole in 'Tender' by asking the crowd to sing along to Graham's part."

As the Blur war machine rattled vigorously forward toward the winter of 2003, Damon Albarn issued *Democrazy*, a vinyl-only collection of "lower than lo-fi" song ideas he had committed to a four-track tape machine in various hotel rooms while the band was touring the States earlier in the year. "There's some potentially very good stuff on there if I developed it, but you have to have an understanding of musical process to be able to hear that," he warned. "I don't want people to buy something they're not going to appreciate. I just don't want people to waste their money on it." Albarn's caution made horrible sense when actually confronted with the EP. Unfortunately, though these little snippets of sound might have provided a rare, behind-the-scenes insight into his "music-making process", they were of limited use to those not inside Damon's head, with listeners straining to join the melodic dots from the sketchiest of materials. Receiving a critical mauling upon its release on Honest Jon's Records, many a reviewer took aim at what they thought to be nothing more than a "self-important vanity project" from the Blur/Gorillaz frontman: "On the evidence of *Democrazy*," said *Dot Music*, "the wrong self-indulgent flake got fired from Blur..." Perhaps so. But when Albarn later returned to one of the EP's song skeletons – the creaky 'I Need A Gun' – he ended up turning it into the Gorillaz 2005 single 'Dirty Harry'. The tune subsequently went to number six in the USA and was nominated for a Grammy. Perhaps the singer should have called it 'Having The Last Laugh'...

Following an 18-date tour of the UK and Ireland that included four nights' work at Brixton Academy and three sold out shows at Dublin's Olympia, Blur came to the end of the road at Bournemouth International Centre on December 12, 2003. A superb gig (with Alex's parents both in attendance), the band ended their set with no fewer than five encores, running the punk swank of 'We've Got A File On You' into their final number of the evening, 'The Universal'. The tally was rich enough. Eighty odd gigs across the year, one million plus sales for *Think Tank* and the now usual slew of superlatives for their efforts, including 26 placements in various Album of The Year polls. "I think the whole notion of the 'pop star' is about to explode, though," said Alex. "(With) the internet, and all that's followed. It's like the last days of Rome."

Blur could no longer be called 'pop stars' in the traditional sense, however. Now men in their mid-to-late 30s, the band's glory days as "The architects of Britpop" were almost a decade behind them, with even their youngest fans of the time long out of school and ably assimilated into a nine-to-five existence. In fact, trying to contextualise exactly what Blur 'were' in the Noughties remained something of a puzzle. Unlike Elastica, who finally fell on their sword in 2001 after years of inactivity before one last, very patchy album, Albarn and Co. had persisted, moving beyond the confines of the movement that established them towards new life and artistic reinvention. More, they had largely avoided the traps Oasis had recently succumbed to, with no bloated, average-sounding records to blight their back catalogue or celebrity/political photo specials to embarrass their children in future days. Despite the odd similarity, one could not lump Blur in with the likes of U2 or Coldplay either, the group's intrinsic appeal too selective and knowing to sit well alongside the old/new stadium anthems and world-saving antics of Bono and Chris Martin. As ever and always, Blur were simply of themselves, for themselves. "There comes a point when you realise that being in a band's a bit silly, though," Albarn once said. "But you stay with it because you love music too much to leave."

Things were about to change on that front too. Though not undone by the loss of Graham Coxon, Blur were still gravely wounded at the departure of their guitar talisman, with *Think Tank* the first proof of it. Soothing, groove-orientated and extremely listenable, the album also lacked for bite, edge and the "sense of inherent danger" one associated with the very best of their work. There were worries elsewhere. Privately, both Damon and Alex had admitted that the band's recent live performances were just not the same as when Coxon strode the boards beside them, with Damon even going as far as to call some shows "rubbish" in comparison to Blur's world tour of 1999. While he was being a tad too harsh on both himself and the group, Albarn was more than qualified to make such an assessment. That said, Blur were still holding the party line at the beginning of 2004, when they confirmed to the press that an EP was on the cards by year end. As if to prove it, recording studios were booked to accommodate the possibility. "Why make an EP?" Damon said at the time. "So I don't get too much hassle from Alex, really. I know roughly what I want... but that's one nice thing about having something that's been consistent throughout my life... that it's going to sound a certain way. Sometimes that's quite a relief." Yet, 2004 came and went without Blur. As did 2005, 2006 and 2007. Radio silence. Dead signal. Just the sound of an audience twiddling their thumbs waiting for a sign of life.

It would come.

Chapter Sixteen

What Blur Did On Their Holidays

For the best part of five years, Blur would become a ghost, their shadow existence of 2004-2008 confined to occasional, though often unreliable sightings by the press and strange tales of séance-like meetings where various members reputedly, albeit unsuccessfully, tried to raise the band from the dead. The first attempt at reconstitution came in early 2004, when Albarn, James, Rowntree and Coxon convened behind closed doors to iron out the odd legality while also testing the temperature for any future collaboration. It came to nothing. "Actually, it was like meeting up with three ex-wives," Graham later laughed. With their guitarist now seemingly out of the picture, Blur 'the trio' again stepped forward, with recording sessions taking place during May at 13 studios in West London for a proposed EP. At first spirits appeared high, with Dave even hinting at a new album by 2005. Yet, the year came and went without a sound, though Damon did make encouraging noises about a "punk rock record" at some point in the future. More studio time was booked and more songs were cut, but nothing – save an old *Think Tank* demo ('Some Glad Morning') – escaped into the public domain.

The 'Woo Hoo' men. Blur at the steps of Sydney Opera House, Australia in 1997. ROGER SARGENT/REX FEATURES

The big love. Graham and Oasis' Liam Gallagher share a smile and a scowl at the Weenie Roast Charity Concert in America, 1997.
ROGER SARGENT/REX FEATURES

Damon meets his adoring public at London's Astoria Theatre. ROBERTA PARKIN/REDFERNS

On the set of 'Country House'. Blur caught in the headlights among a cast of extras, including Page Three model Jo Guest (wearing a nurse's hat). In the foreground of shot (L-R) are comedian Matt Lucas, actor Keith Allen and artist/video director Damien Hirst.
PAUL POSTLE/CAMERA PRESS

The solo artist. Graham strikes out on his own after the events of 2002. NICKY J. SIMS/REDFERNS

Not just a drummer. Dave Rowntree addresses the Labour party faithful at Westminster Academy School on 25 April, 2010. PETER MACDIARMID/GETTY IMAGES

From city slicker to country gent. Alex James and friend pictured among the hay at the bassist's farm in Oxfordshire. REX FEATURES

A life beyond Blur. Damon performs onstage with one of his various post-Blur projects, The Good, The Bad And The Queen. (L-R) drummer/Afrobeat legend Tony Allen, Albarn and former Clash bassist Paul Simonon. MICK HUTSON/REDFERNS

Making Mali Music. Albarn and singer/guitarist Afel Bocoum together at the Barbican. OLIVIA HEMINGWAY/REDFERNS

Rapper Snoop Dogg joins in the fun alongside Damon and Gorillaz at Michael Eavis' Somerset farm on June 25, 2010. JAMES MCCAULEY/REX FEATURES

Their finest hour? A reunited Blur make Glastonbury's Pyramid Stage their own on June 28, 2009. TABATHA FIREMAN/REDFERNS

The host with the most. Following Blur's cessation of activities in the early 2000s, Alex re-established himself as a successful writer and media personality, appearing on several TV shows including BBC2's *Never Mind The Buzzcocks*.
BRIAN J. RITCHIE/REX FEATURES

War is over. After nearly two decades of personal rivalry and petty insults, Damon and former Oasis man Noel Gallagher finally reconciled in late 2011: "I bumped into Damon in a (club)," said Noel, "and we both had a bit of a laugh about it all..."
DAVE M. BENETT/GETTY IMAGES

Back at The Brits. Blur receive an 'Outstanding Contribution to Music' award for their services to British pop on February 21, 2012. DAVID FISHER/REX FEATURES

"Whatever happened to that grand old British institution, the tea lady?" Comedian Harry Enfield glams it up with Blur and actor Phil Daniels (back to camera) onstage at the Closing Ceremony Celebration Concert for the London Olympic Games at Hyde Park on August 12. BRIAN RASIC/REX FEATURES

Back to the future. Blur collect their 'Best Live Act' trophy at the annual *Q* awards on October 22, 2012. The band will continue to tour throughout 2013. RICHARD YOUNG/REX FEATURES

Come mid-2006, and the game began all over again. "The Foo Fighters are going to wet their pants when they hear this stuff," said Alex of the band's recent efforts at Premises Studios in fashionable Shoreditch. But Coxon still wasn't on board and confidence in their new material was subsequently lost. "There's a horrible hole without Graham," conceded Albarn. On this, they all agreed, though James was still hopeful the band's time would yet come. "I think we'd all like to make another record," he said. "We'd all like to do it with Graham. We may have to beg him a bit though."

By 2007, it seemed the bassist's wish might just be granted when news broke that Coxon had finally re-joined his colleagues after three years of pursuing a separate agenda. Unfortunately, it turned out to be a case of smoke and mirrors. A great story. The finest of ideas. But ultimately no reason to unfurl the red carpet. "I think it's something that might happen when everybody feels ready," said the guitarist in early 2008. "(But) that might be years. And we're all really busy..." On that issue, Graham was wholly correct. For while Blur the band had remained an idea rather than an actuality for the best part of five years, its constituent parts were far from idle.

In Alex James' case, change had occurred at an almost fundamental level, with Blur's very own 'Roister Doister' transforming into a devoted family man living the life of a country squire light years away from the avenues and alleyways of London's West End that once defined his existence. Having by his own admission blown a not inconsiderable fortune either up his nose or at the bottom of a champagne Balthazar, James underwent a 'Road to Damascus'-like conversion on meeting video producer Claire Neate in the spring of 2002. "I bumped into Claire in a club in Soho and we were sitting in a taxi before we knew each other's names," he later said. "She wasn't impressed by fame and didn't even really like Blur. But to me, she instantly felt like home and I never wanted to leave." One whirlwind romance later and the couple married in April 2003, with Alex confirming his status as a bridegroom in one well-rounded sentence: "I'm well chuffed."

The next stage of James' unlikely re-invention came with a move out of the smoke and into the heart of England's green and pleasant land.

While dating, he and Claire had often borrowed her boss' cottage in the Cotswolds and soon fell in love with the area as well as each other, leading to a permanent move after signing the marital register. "We got married at exactly the same time as Blur disintegrated," he later told *The Sun*. "It was like 'Rock Family Robinson'. I had no job, a woman I didn't really know and here I was on a farm in the middle of nowhere. But it really worked. [Anyway]," he concluded, "I think it's inevitable for a certain type of rock gentleman... that trout farm phase." The farm in question was actually a 200-acre property near Chipping Norton in Oxfordshire, though by all accounts, one in need of some work. "The farm wasn't all Ferraris and oak panelling," he said. "It was tractors and mess. I actually sold my plane for a digger."

However, the new locale allowed Alex a chance to finally gain some perspective on his time as "A Blur" while also pondering his recent brush with serendipity. "I was a thrill-seeking nocturnal hedonist living in London who met a girl, fell in love, married within a year and bought a farm on our honeymoon," he said. "We then spent our time in the countryside getting to know each other. So many things that are seismically important depend on tiny coincidences. The whole world that we built together depended on a chance meeting on the first day of spring, 2002."

By early 2004, James was also a father with his wife giving birth to the couple's first child, Geronimo. Proving themselves a dab hand at parenthood, the James family would multiply almost by the year, with twins Artemis and Galileo, and daughters Sable and Beatrix all following in rapid succession. Though Alex didn't realistically want for money, Blur's on-again, off-again status during the mid-Noughties did give him time to pursue other opportunities, at which in most cases, he showed himself to be a natural. After a thoughtful, if ill-conceived collaboration in 2005 with nineties pop singer/songwriter Betty Boo called Wigwam failed to ignite, James' subsequent forays into TV, radio, journalism and autobiography took off like a proverbial rocket. A winning appearance on a celebrity edition of the boffin-testing *University Challenge* acted as a trigger for other broadcasting work, with Alex taking on judge duties on *Channel Four*'s *Mobile Acts Unsigned* and a role as panelist on the BBC's satirical programme *Have I Got News For You*. It didn't end there, as the bassist threw in his lot with the reality show *Maestro* where he trained on camera as a would-be classical conductor, while simultaneously fronting the documentary *Cocaine Diaries: Alex James in Colombia* – a subject which he reportedly knew much about from a previous life. When not on the telly, James was storming the airways as a presenter on BBC Radio 4's music digest *On Your Farm* which in 2007 became the precursor to his own regular show, *The A–Z of Classic Music* on Classic FM.

But it was arguably Alex's talent as a writer and his passion for "all things cheesy" that bore the sweetest fruit and the most pungent profits. A born raconteur who could spin a yarn out of wool, James' contributions to a wide range of broadsheets – *The Independent, The Observer, The Times* and its sister publication, *The Sunday Times* – as well as other music/culture periodicals such as *Q, The Spectator* and *The Idler* all confirmed him as a journalist of some note. Yet, it was his own autobiography *Bit Of A Blur* that made James a best-selling author. A candid, often self-flagellating account of his adventures and indiscretions in Britpop, and eventual escape to the safety of his very own country house, the book was required reading for those with only the smallest interest in the lives of pop stars and what made them tick. "I got married (and) that was the end of 'rock 'n' roll' and the start of something else," he said of his preliminary journey towards the writing of *Bit Of A Blur*. "I did look at my diaries, but they all seem to have been written by a drunken idiot." Remedying such lapses of memory by following the chronology of the band – single by single, album by album – Alex ended up with a tome that sold by the bucketload and covered him in critical rose petals.

James' quest to become a monarch in the world of cheese was perhaps a riskier venture for both his credibility and pocket. On the one hand, it might all go swimmingly well, with Who singer Roger Daltrey's successes as a trout farm owner and Bono/The Edge's recent acquisition of Dublin's Clarence Hotel strong proof that rock stars could make enormous financial gains outside the confines of album sales and live shows. On the other, Mick Fleetwood's regrettable forays into real estate management and MC Hammer's disastrous brush with thoroughbred racehorses were bold verification they often couldn't, as both performers were declared bankrupt after efforts to diversify their business interests.

Thankfully, Alex James belonged to the former rather than latter category. Benignly obsessed with curds, rinds and conserves since childhood, James had been in training for nigh-on three decades before branching out as a cheese-maker, and the end results spoke for themselves. Creating three signature brands – 'Blue Monday' (named for his favourite New Order song), 'Little Wallop' and 'Fairleigh Wallop' – the latter actually won Alex 'Best Goat's Cheese' at the 2008 British Cheese Awards. A range of more populist flavours titled 'Alex James Presents...' would even find their way onto the supermarket shelves, the Blur man's conjoining of Cheddar with salad cream, tomato ketchup and even tikka masala proving extremely popular with kids, adults and the post-pub brigade.

There was, of course, another area of endeavour that James still fondly doted upon. Always as given to matters of astronomy as he was with the merits of Stinky Bishops and Wensleydales, the bassist continued to find wonder in the stars. A keen and continual proponent of Beagle 2 (He and Blur wrote a song/call-sign of the same name that was sent up with the ill-fated probe into space), Alex was finally honoured with the title Artist In Residence by Oxford University's Astrophysics department in early 2007. "The scientists are a great bunch," he said, "(and) I think science is pretty rock 'n' roll." Already a member of the British Astronomical Association (and later to receive an honorary doctorate from Bournemouth University), this pat on the back for his previous fundraising work and still ongoing efforts to promote one of Britain's more neglected sciences was but the latest confirmation that his days as a reveller were long, long gone. "Getting a record deal was like boarding a transatlantic flight," he once said. "There's somebody coming with a drinks trolley all the time." Alcohol and drug free for the best part of five years, James had obviously learned to study the heavens instead of the in-flight wine list.

If Alex's incursions into broadcasting, cheese-making, space probes and the inner circle of the 'Chipping Norton Set' were significant, then Dave Rowntree's chameleon-like shift from pop star to would-be Labour politician was perhaps even more surprising. Still, there were precedents and previous behaviours that hinted that Rowntree wasn't just a bog-standard pop drummer defined by a love of fast cars, fine women and a framed death certificate by the age of 32. The first member of Blur to knock drinking on the head and settle down in a traditional sense, he had already set up his own successful animation company (Nanomation) while also directing two series of Channel 4's *Empire Square*. First aired in February 2005, *Empire Square* was a pixel graphic-led show in the same anarchic vein of *South Park* – its three streetwise, animated leads forever chasing a quick buck as they avoid the attentions of crack dealers, prostitutes and other ne'er-do-wells living around them. Something of a cult hit both in the UK and USA, it not only confirmed Rowntree's standing in the area of computer graphics, but also led to his opinion being sought for academic-themed research papers on the heady subject of non-photorealistic rendering, whatever that might be...

Beyond Dave's interests in animation, there was his musical involvement with The Ailerons to consider. Formed in 2005 and consisting of Rowntree, Blur/Gorillaz's occasional touring keyboardist Mike Smith, guitarist Dan Beattie and the wonderfully named Grog and Charity Hair on bass and vocals respectively, one might be forgiven for not expecting much from a drummer's side project. Yet, The Ailerons turned out to be very good indeed, their four-track EP *Left Right* being a delightful assortment of sci-fi keyboards, weird film samples and screeching guitars. Had luck been on their side, the band could even have scored a potential hit with the endearing 'Dig A Hole', the song's chorus as catchy as anything that had escaped Blur's clutches in recent years. But despite the odd good review, The Ailerons came and went quickly.

This was not something that could be said of Dave Rowntree's political interests. As previously described, Rowntree was always a man who kept up with the machinations of Whitehall, even while travelling the world with Blur. Once a teenage Marxist "squat punk", much had changed for Dave in intervening years, with twin-engine Cessna airplanes long having replaced the dodgy vans that blighted his days in France as a touring busker. Still, the drummer's commitment to leftist principles had never really left him. Instead, it just percolated on the back burner until the time was right: "Instead of getting a red sports car and a 19-year-old girlfriend, I (trained) to be a solicitor and went out knocking on doors for the Labour party," he said.

Becoming a fully-fledged member of the Party in 2002, Rowntree's recent Open University studies in law were also enormously beneficial in opening a potential door into politics, providing him with a solid foundation on which to approach complex legal issues and parliamentary processes. By the time he passed his final exams and began training as a solicitor at the offices of an East London criminal defence firm, the move towards representing a local constituency on behalf of Labour was almost inevitable. "The two (were) linked," he later told *The Guardian*'s Gareth Grundy. "It was seeing who the clients were... the same people over and over. One-man or one-woman crime waves, who (were) largely drug addicts, or who had mental health problems or who come from generations of crime. 99% of these people have never had a chance." In terms of career moves, Dave's emergence from behind the drum kit with Blur to prospective Member of Parliament was little short of astounding.

A resident of the area for several years and Chair of the 'West End' branch, Rowntree's decision to stand as the Labour candidate for the Marylebone High Street seat of Westminster City Council in April, 2007, was wholly logical, even if he knew the odds of winning such a strong Tory ward were stacked against him. In the end Rowntree lost, though it didn't deter him from trying his luck again in 2008 when he fought the Labour sweat of Church Street. "Labour's a people party," Dave later said. "What Westminster needs, and Labour can bring, is putting people... ahead of big business and property speculators. I think a lot of people are quite angry at the way the Tories are running (this area), and somebody needs to make a stand and become a rallying point for these disaffected people and put over their point of view." This time he lost again by a 14.1 swing to the Conservatives, but Dave kept coming back for more*. "People assume I want a free ride and I don't," he said. "So I have to work very hard to show that I'm interested in what I can give, not what I can get."

Of course, there was one aspect of Rowntree's work on behalf of the Labour Party that might have led to the odd impassioned debate with another member of Blur: his clear support of the invasion of Iraq. In a strange, if pleasant twist of fate, Dave had begun dating Michelle de Vries, the daughter of nurse Daphne Parish, who in turn, was arrested with journalist Farzad Bazoft just before the outbreak of the first gulf war. Though Bazoft was hanged in Baghdad, Parish was later released after the campaigning efforts of de Vries and others. Privy to much behind the scenes information about Saddam Hussein and how he conducted his country's affairs, Dave came to a markedly different conclusion than Damon Albarn on the need to depose Iraq's then leader. "I was getting an inside perspective on what was going on there, which is why I think Saddam was an evil bastard," he later said. "While I don't think he should have been killed – I'm extremely opposed to the death penalty** – getting rid of him was the right thing to do."

In comparison to Alex James' gallivanting between jobs and Dave Rowntree's dual career as legal aid lawyer/Labour Party Candidate, Graham Coxon's voyages outside Blur's established domain seemed wonderfully traditional and reassuringly quaint. Fortunately, they were also quite exciting. With his "services no longer required" after the events of May 2003, Coxon had resisted the urge to become depressed or maudlin about his lot and simply got on with the job of establishing himself as a successful solo artist. "My hobby was (now) a job," he said. "Actually, it was a 'Jobby...'" Being a clever sort, the guitarist enlisted the help of Stephen Street in making his next post-Blur record, 2004's

* In February 2008, Rowntree was selected by London and Westminster Constituency Labour Party to run for Parliament at the 2010 general election. He came second, with 8,188 votes. In 2011, Dave contested the Labour candidacy for Norwich South at the next election. He again lost, this time to a former soldier. As of 2013, he remains a solid Labour Party supporter.

** Rowntree has long been a patron of Amicus, an organisation that provides legal representation to those on Death Row in the USA.

Happiness In Magazines. Previously given to recording his work with gusto, but no great production values, Street's valuable input helped Coxon transform those crackly lo-fi musings into something far more commercially enticing. "My input into Blur (was) always an abstract thing, a capturing of sound," he said. "(But) my own stuff ranges from tantrums to other, freeing (of) emotions..."

If *The Kiss Of Morning* confirmed that Graham possessed the necessary frontier spirit to move past his days with Blur, then *Happiness In Magazines* proved he also had the songs. Flying in on the back of a top twenty single – the neat and tidy 'Bittersweet Bundle Of Misery' – *Happiness...* gave Coxon his first solo hit, with the album reaching number 19 on the UK charts. Moving from bluesy, even danceable tunes such as 'Bottom Bunk' and 'Hopeless Friend' to the squawky punk of 'Spectacular' and chunky new wave of 'Freakin' Out' (a limited edition 45 that got to number 37), the record was one in the proverbial eye to those who thought his days as a pop star were over when he was shown the door at 13 Studios. "Nearly every tune (on *Happiness...*) is milkman-friendly hummable," said BBC Music's Ian Wade. "A bit of a pop genius on the sly, Coxon claims that the songs pleaded with him to be recorded properly this time and he's done them proud. Producer Stephen Street, the man who had a hand in the first five Blur albums, has done wonders here, reflecting a more upbeat and happier Coxon, making this a joy to listen to. Whatever his real reasons for leaving Blur, on *Happiness In Magazines*, Coxon has shown he most certainly doesn't ever need to go back."

While Graham was far too much a gentleman to confirm such a view, he still wasn't averse to clarifying the downsides of his time with the band. "Life in Blur could be pretty confusing," he told *Music-Room.com*. "There wasn't much time to get your head together. It was tour, record, write songs, tour, record, write songs. I guess the record company's idea was 'Strike when the iron's hot', but it was hard." Equally, regardless of previous friendships, the possibility of reconciliation and the continuing expectations of Blur's fan base, Coxon didn't seem to be in any rush back into the arms of his former bandmates. "I think I made some decisions that were right," he said. "You do start out as mates and have a shared goal. But the whole nature of the music industry moulds you into a business partnership rather than mates. You have to do that to survive."

The proud recipient of *NME*'s 'Best Solo Artist' of 2005, Graham gamely soldiered on throughout the year, playing his first solo US tour in March before releasing an in-concert DVD/EP capturing his performance at Oxford's Zodiac club on June 3, 2004. A warts and all document that made the best of Coxon's onstage charm and high energy set, *Live At The Zodiac* also featured a marvellous cover image by photographer Penny Smith. Shot in grainy black & white as Graham leapt into the air with Telecaster in hand, Smith's work was an obvious homage to her own career-defining photo for the sleeve of The Clash's seminal 1979 LP *London Calling*.

By March 2006, Coxon was back again with his sixth solo disc, *Love Travels At Illegal Speeds*. With his own Transcopic Records now defunct, he had returned to EMI/Parlophone for distribution and marketing purposes. However, the album bore no real signs of corporate influence, its contents still retaining the resolutely indie-pop/rock edge of both *The Kiss Of Morning* and *Happiness In Magazines*. Again helmed by producer Stephen Street, *Love Travels...* wasn't quite as commercially successful as its predecessor, though it did have the odd corker or two to commend its purchase. The single 'Standing On My Own Again' (number 20 in the UK charts in March 2006) was one such moment, the track's snappy chorus and insolent vocal delivery demonstrating how far Graham's singing voice had come since the days of 'You're So Great' in 1997. 'I Don't Wanna Go Out' was also a grimy little bugger and perfect reminder of why Coxon was still a guitar player to watch, his Hendrix meets John McGeoch-like riffing at the song's end as ferocious and inventive as Blur's own 'Bugman' or 'Trimm Trabb'. "That was a riff I had for ages," he said of 'I Don't Wanna Go Out'. "I just really liked that 'Rarr, rarr, rarr' thing. It's about getting TV fever, not wanting to leave (the living room), just... 'Despondo rock'. That phrase is one of mine, by the way. At least, I've never heard it before..."

Obviously not one to rest on his laurels, Graham spent the rest of 2006 either in the studio or on the road. A minor involvement with

England's 2006 FIFA World Cup anthem came first, as Coxon teamed up alongside old punk stagers Sham 69, DJ Christian O'Connell and actor Brian Blessed for a bumpy remake of 'Hurry Up Harry', now re-titled 'Hurry Up England' especially for the occasion. Though nigh on impossible to work out Graham's exact contribution (he was absent from the song's video and Sham's own Dave Parsons seemed to take care of guitar duties rather nicely), 'Hurry Up England' nonetheless went to number 10 on the UK charts in June 2006. Four months later, Coxon was at it again, with the release of *Burnt To Bitz: At The Astoria*, a 27-track double disc recorded live at the West End venue on October 25. Thanks to the wonders of modern technology, the CD was actually on sale at the Astoria immediately after the gig. But it was Graham's cover of The Jam's short but sweet 'All Mod Cons' on *Burnt To Bitz...* that provided a subtle clue as to his next collaboration.

A "humongous" fan of Paul Weller since he was old enough to dream about Rickenbackers and skinny black ties, Coxon's teenage reveries were duly answered in the spring of 2007, when it was announced he and the former Jam frontman were to collaborate on a new single called 'This Old Town'. "As a long time admirer of Paul, I never dared imagine getting a chance to work with him so I was bricking it when we first met," gushed Graham, "but he's an absolute gent and a shockingly great singer and musician." By the sounds of it, Weller was quite pleased to be part of their team-up too. "I've always been a big fan of Graham's and love his work, so it was exciting for me to work on something new with him." Propelled along by the drums of Zak Starkey (The Who's first choice drummer and also the son of The Beatles' Ringo Starr), 'This Old Town' sounded exactly as one might expect, its chiming guitars and earthy, shared lead vocals redolent of not only The Jam, but also of The Kinks and The Pretty Things. Released as a download and limited edition 45 on July 2, 2007, 'This Old Town' reached number 39 on the UK charts, while Paul and Graham reunited a year later (March 2008) for a gig in aid of the homeless charity Consequences at the Camden Roundhouse.

Another huge obsession of Coxon's as a teenager was art, and just as with his love for The Jam, that passion had never really gone away. A keen painter whose work first came to public view in 1999 with the bronzed-hued cover of Blur's *13*, each of Graham's subsequent solo albums featured one of his own designs/canvasses on the front sleeve. From the almost childlike elephants and cartoon faces of *The Sky Is Too High* to the primary-coloured splendour of *Love Travels At Illegal Speeds,* Coxon's way with a brush or pencil was as striking as his delivery on a Telecaster or Gibson Les Paul. Yet, many of his own more personal paintings had remained hidden from view until a two-day exhibition at the ICA's Nash & Brandon rooms in late October 2004 allowed punters to study them at close quarters. A small, but well-reviewed enterprise, it opened a door that Graham couldn't have shut if he wanted to. In January 2006, there was a show of the artist's prints at the Vice Gallery in East London where the work was on sale. So successful was the response that Coxon later updated his own website to accommodate interest from art buffs and music fans alike.

An extremely fertile, and indeed, hellishly busy period for Graham, his creative endeavours were however matched by Damon Albarn, whose own work rate from 2004–2008 could only be described as ceaseless. At a certain point in his career, one might have reasonably expected the songwriter to fill his downtime outside Blur with the odd acting role. After all, the short, sharp performance he gave as the doomed Jason in Antonia Bird's 1997 movie *Face* had picked up good notices and subsequent offers of employment from several other British film directors. But the decision he made following his negative experiences at East 15 back in 1987 held firm well into the new century. "With acting I'm a bit of a coward really and I'd only really do it with mates," Damon said. "If it's on a professional level then I can't... I'm not really committed enough to do it properly." Instead, Albarn ploughed on with music, his work rate putting others of his ilk and stature to permanent shame.*

* For the record, it should be noted that Damon lent his voice to Gunnar Karlsson's 2007's computer animated film *Anna and the Moods,* his work on the project taking place just before he was awarded an honorary Master of Arts degree from the University of East London.

Seldom one to turn away from a good collaboration when it presented itself, Damon's name was attached to many projects during Blur's wilderness years, though he first picked up the habit long before when providing uncredited keyboard parts for Elastica's 1995 debut album. Since then, Albarn had popped up on other songwriters' material like a musical jack in the box: a few odd tunes with former Special Terry Hall (to be found on 1997's *Laugh* and 2002's *The Hour of Two Lights*), and a lightning stopover for old friends The Rentals' 2000 album *Seven More Minutes* (he appears on 'Big Daddy C') were two such examples. Damon's blink or you'll miss it appearance on Dan The Automator's 2001 downtempo electronica project *Lovage* ('Love That Lovage, Baby') and Massive Attack's 2003 disc *100th Window* ('Small Time Shot Away') were two more. Yet, as Blur ceased to exist in any meaningful sense between 2004 and 2008, Albarn's love of working with other artists reached a new high, as he mixed, produced, wrote for or simply guested on a plethora of tracks, EPs, records and other sundry cuts. From the lovely 'Last Song' on Marianne Faithfull's 2005 album *Before The Poison* and British rapper Roots Manuva's 'Awfully Deep (Lambeth Blues)' of the same year, to Fatboy Slim's *Palookaville* and Kano's *London Town*, Damon sang, spoke or composed for his friends: Ghostdigital, U-Cef and The Black Ghosts; Eslam Jawaad, Abdel Hadi Halo and Amadou & Mariam. The list, as they say, was endless. "Music is infinite," he said of such creative partnerships, "And that's why, for me, it's a life long journey."

But it was outside Albarn's admirable championing of Malian, Lebanese-Syrian, and indeed, British artists that his more commercially-themed work was being done. Having altered the perimeters of what might be achieved with a virtual band alongside co-creator Jamie Hewlett, Damon returned to Gorillaz for 2005's outrageously successful *Demon Days*. Buoyed by the contributions of Zen rappers De La Soul, Happy Mondays' Shaun Ryder, Neneh 'Buffalo Stance' Cherry and actor Dennis Hopper to name but a few, the record went Top Five in seven countries, while also claiming the UK and US number one and number six spots respectively. With four more hit singles – 'Feel Good Inc.', 'Dare', 'Dirty Harry' and 'Kids with Guns/El Mañana' – to add to the overall tally, and 21 platinum discs gleaned from various points around the world, Damon and Jamie's "little idea" had taken on an overwhelming life of its own. "(Gorillaz) helped sidestep the inevitable problem of being an aging art-school rocker," he chuckled to the *New York Times* in 2005.

Based around the loose concept of 'a long and unsure journey into the night' that was in part inspired by Albarn's own train trip from Beijing to Mongolia in 2004, each of *Demon Days*' 15 songs represented some form of confrontation with personal (and possibly professional) demons. However, working out whether these evil spirits were related to Damon and Jamie's own fears or those of their imagined virtual characters was never difficult. Perhaps the first genuine clue laid in the track 'Fire Coming Out Of The Monkey's Head', which tackled the notion of diminishing global oil resources. "That (song) came from a very naive idea, which is 'what is going to happen when they've taken all of the oil out of the earth?'" said Albarn. "Aren't there going to be these vast holes? Surely those holes shouldn't be empty. Surely there is a reason why they had all of this in. It's like bad plastic surgery, eventually it (all) collapses." This theme of treating the Earth as one giant fast food restaurant also surfaced on 'Last Living Souls', 'O Green World', and most especially, the album's title track where the London Gospel Community Choir sang out Damon's concerns for all to hear: "It's so hard for your soul to survive, (when) you can't even trust the air you breathe..."

Despite its pessimistic nature and "minor key, trip-hop melancholies", *Demon Days* acted as a launch pad for another wave of Gorillaz-related activity, with the band's website boldly re-launched and a set of toy figures soon arriving in shops. Live dates and various promotional appearances also followed, with Gorillaz performing the single 'Dirty Harry' at the 2006 Brit Awards, where they were nominated for both Best British Group and Best British Album. Things then took a turn towards the incredible the following year, when holographic renditions of 2D, Russel and a Y-front wearing Murdoc duetted with a very real Madonna on 'Feel Good Inc./Hung Up' at the 2006 Grammy Awards. "I think playing with holograms at the Grammys was partially successful,"

Damon said. "It looked great on TV. It had a great atmosphere about it. You know, just being able to be as eclectic as we continue to be visually and musically (was) our primary motivation for doing this." The first stage of a new plan to tour the world with holograms created using Musion Eyeliner technology during 2007/8, Albarn and Hewlett's globe-trotting ambitions were later stymied due to spiralling costs for the project. "It was extremely expensive, extremely difficult, (and) a million and one things (could) go wrong every second that the thing's playing," said Jamie. Still, with the combined sales of *Gorillaz* and *Demon Days* soon hitting 15 million, their disappointment was probably cushioned a little...

As Hewlett laboured on with a proposed Gorillaz movie throughout 2006 that would take his virtual quartet from their website home and onto the cinema screen (sadly, the film never materialised), Albarn returned to matters of making music, this time with a new band: The Good, The Bad And The Queen.* Originally reported to be the title of Damon's first solo album, the songwriter soon changed his mind and formed a group instead. And quite the group it was. In addition to Blur's touring guitarist Simon Tong, Albarn also managed to rope in fellow West London resident/former Clash bassist Paul Simonon and Afrobeat genius Tony Allen to complete the line-up. A long time legend of punk, and a fine artist on his days off, Simonon's pedigree was beyond dispute. In fact, his old band had inspired at least three of *Think Tank*'s better tunes. However, Tony Allen was perhaps less well known outside musician's circles, his previous tenures with the likes of Fela Kuti, King Sunny Ade and jazzer Archie Shepp more cult in their appeal than mainstream in their sales figures. Dig a little deeper though, and Allen's reputation as one of the world's finest drummers was a matter of record. "Tony Allen," the godlike Brian Eno once said, "Is perhaps the greatest drummer who ever lived." Damon Albarn wasn't one to disagree. Picking up on Allen's gifts during his initial explorations of

* Albarn has repeatedly stressed that 'The Good, The Bad And The Queen' is the name of the album and that the band itself has "no real name." However, to keep matters simple here, the group will be referred to by the record's name.

African music, Damon had actually ended the lyrics to Blur's 2000 hit 'Music Is My Radar' with the spinning refrain "Tony Allen gets what a boy can do, really got me dancin'..." Journeying to the drummer's home in Nigeria to work with his hero at various points between 2002–2005, Damon subsequently released Allen's *Lagos No Shaking* on his own Honest Jon's Records a year later. That said, Albarn's appreciation of Tony's 'eager hands and restless feet' was no one way street. "The lyrics, the melodies, the way (Damon) creates sounds. I would call him a genius," said Allen in 2007. "It's five years I've been working with him now, is that not enough for me to know?"

With revered producer and occasional Gorillaz contributor Danger Mouse at the controls, Albarn and his latest group worked through the summer of 2006 before releasing their first single 'Herculean' on October 30. It was a bit of a shock. Neither super-charged street punk nor particularly danceable, 'Herculean' was more like a movie soundtrack than anything else, with deep choir-like voices floating over a background of fluffy pianos and eighties-sounding synths. Yet, when one's ears finally adjusted to accommodate the surprise, there was definitely something quite special there. Preceded by the group's debut appearance at BBC's *Electric Proms* and dutifully followed by a four-song show at Abbey Road on December 13, 'Herculean' held the line until The Good, The Bad And The Queen's debut disc arrived on January 22, 2007.

As with *Demon Days* before it, *The Good...* proved to be another loose concept album, though this time, Damon had turned his attention to life in England's capital rather than stray imps and devils. "(It's) really a postcard from London," he advised at the time. With his lyrics devoted to looming tower blocks, "falling off the palace walls", ravens circling overhead and "a stroppy little island of mixed-up people", Albarn certainly delivered on his promise, presenting London as a part-mythic, part modern city built on horror, dreams and more than a little magic. But it was the music of *The Good...* that really drew one in. Full of space and invention, tracks like the dubby 'Behind The Sun', the slippery 'Northern Whale' and the spiralling 'The Bunting Song' had a certain filmic quality to them, conjuring odd, sometimes disturbing images in the mind's eye. Paul Simonon concurred. "The good thing is, we all appreciate cinematic music," he told *Pitchfork*'s Bret Gladstone. "I know that Damon does, and also the stuff that Simon plays... the nature of it is very atmospheric. It's about that idea of creating a picture, so the combination of all the flavours and this vision was whirling around everyone's minds. That's why it came out the way it did."

For some, *The Good, The Bad And The Queen* was "an oblique but worthy successor to *Parklife*," its camera-like capture of London's streets and beats acting as proof that while Albarn's head and body was now often to be found in Africa or America, his heart had stayed firmly at home. For others, that sense of devotion sometimes made for a rainy Sunday in old London town: "*TG, TB&TQ* feels under the weather, downcast and dejected... (and) the biggest surprise is how rarely this scratch supergroup really swings at its full potential," said *Uncut*'s Stephen Troussé. Yet, he also conceded that Damon hadn't lost his ability to pen a fine tune when required. "What ultimately saves this album is Albarn's unwavering pop compass, (and) his knack for hook and melody. Like Bowie – with whom he has a thing or two in common – his heart remains in Tin Pan Alley (and) it's this pop sensibility that's made his greatest hits."

Given an understated marketing roll-out by Virgin Records (with whom the band had signed), *The Good, The Bad And The Queen* nonetheless managed to enter the UK charts at an extremely respectable number two, with the album soon achieving gold status on positive word of mouth. More, in spite of its London-centric aspects, *The Good...* also managed to crack the US Top 50, sneaking a quick appearance at number 49 in the *Billboard* Hot 100. "You know, we just sort of played," said guitarist Simon Tong. "We tried the songs in lots of different ways, and we weren't afraid to just scrap a whole recording session, or scrap a song and try something completely new. It was just a matter of keeping that sort of magic... (to) try to keep the album as unpolished and natural as possible, I suppose."

Supported by a small tour of the UK and America, *The Good, The Bad And The Queen* again verified how easy Albarn made the business of creating music appear, though he was keen to share the honours equally. "We were there informing each other and playing together," he said, "and that's the reason *The Good, The Bad And The Queen* really works."

It wasn't the songwriter's most ambitious project of 2007, however. Stretching his talent to its logical extreme, Damon next set his sights on realising an opera, though he would also take Jamie Hewlett along for the ride. The back story to this monumental undertaking actually started three years before, when Chinese director Chen Shi-Zheng approached the head of Paris' Théâtre du Châtelet Jean-Luc Choplin to discuss staging an opera based on Wu Cheng'en's classic 16th century novel *Journey To The West*. After broad terms were agreed, and Chen began work with writer David Greenspan on how to bring the story to the stage, Choplin set about finding a composer for the music. Following a conversation with Manchester International Festival director Alex Poots, the Frenchman was pointed in the direction of Damon Albarn.

At the time, Damon was actually planning a residency for Gorillaz at Manchester Opera House, but still jumped at the chance of meeting with Poots and Choplin to discuss the proposal. Within weeks, he was travelling to China alongside Hewlett to talk ideas with Chen Shi-Zheng. Brought to the countryside to hear and record native Chinese musicians while Jamie took photographs of the people he saw and the clothes they wore, the duo later returned to London with a fistful of concepts on how to take forward the compositional and visual aspects of the production. Three long years later, and with the financial backing of the Manchester International Festival, the Théâtre du Châtelet and the Staatsoper Berlin, it was finally ready for the stage.

For those of a certain age, the story of Monkey cannot easily be divorced from the Japanese TV series of the same name that ran like clockwork after school hours throughout the late seventies and early eighties. Depicting the titular character's birth "from an egg on a mountain top" to his becoming "the funkiest monkey that ever popped", the show was one of the most bizarre and brilliant examples of bonkers telly ever to be transmitted on British screens. In fact, if one shouted 'Pigsy!', 'Sandy!' and 'Horse!' in rapid succession on an average high street even now, several heads might well nod with approval before the inevitable arrival of a police van. In its own way, Shi-Zheng, Albarn and Hewlett's realisation of *Monkey: Journey To The West* was just as memorable as its televisual predecessor when it made its debut at Manchester International Festival on June 28, 2007. Closely following Wu Cheng'en's original tale of an arrogant primate that incurs the displeasure of Buddha before being finally granted paradise for his good deeds, the opera was a feast for both the eyes and ears. Featuring bold set designs, wild costumes and several animated sequences courtesy of Jamie, *Monkey...* was also awash with flying acrobats, martial artists, plate spinners and a very frisky pig. Audacious to the point of insolence, the production even flashed LED-assisted English subtitles of its Mandarin lyrics to the audience as they were sung by performers on the stage.

Clearly cautious of not straying too far beyond his limits as a composer, Albarn made no great attempt at trying to capture the subtle nuances and technical exactitudes of Chinese music. "You don't want to be pastiching (that)," he ruffled to *The Sunday Times*. However, his score did capture much of their spirit, with Damon (and musical advisor David Coulter) assembling a 25-member orchestra that utilised both Western and Chinese traditional instruments alongside more exotic sounds such as a klaxophone, musical saw and the Theremin-like 'ondes Martenot'. For a visiting Nigel Hildreth, Albarn had clearly excelled himself this time around. "I was at the first performance of *Monkey...*," said Damon's former teacher. "It was an amazing combination of drama, music and art, but all in very different expressions within the (overall) form of 'Opera'."

Beset by several technical glitches on opening night (Damon spent much of the time charging towards the mixing desk to solve recurrent sound problems), *Monkey...* still drew mostly strong reviews for the critics. "It's a high-octane, 90-minute rock 'n' roll circus," said *The Guardian's* Alfred Hickling, "performed in Mandarin and featuring over 50 Chinese acrobats, martial arts experts and a team of tiny contortionists so pliable they could have flown over as cabin luggage." Yet, when it came to Albarn's score, Hickling was slightly less positive.

"Though the stunts can be breathtaking, the musical and dramatic development is fairly inert," he said. "Albarn has certainly extended himself, encompassing a vast, brashly amplified mélange of Chinese percussion (and) esoteric electronica. Yet, surprisingly for someone with (his) melodic gift, there are no arias, thematic development or even much in the way of a memorable tune." Others begged to differ. "I don't know much about Chinese opera, but I do know what I like," reasoned *The Independent*'s Andy Gill, "(and this) is 90 minutes of fascinating music by Damon Albarn in which Oriental and Occidental forms are skillfully combined."

Following a near two-week run at Manchester's Palace Theatre, *Monkey...* journeyed on to Paris, Berlin and even South Carolina, where the production was staged at the Charleston's Spoleto Festival in July 2008. Within months, it had returned to England, with the show first running at London's Royal Opera House before moving to the much larger O2 arena. A popular hit, *Monkey...*'s soundtrack album also did brisk business when released on August 18, 2008, reaching number five in the UK charts. "This (was) composition, not songwriting, of course, (and) I was apprehensive at first," Albarn said of *Monkey...*'s original difficulties and resultant success. "But people who come from my normal discipline don't tend to go far enough. We wanted to bring more flavour to people's lives... and demystify opera to a degree, destroy its elitist angle. Then for people who do like opera, open them up to new forms of music, too."

The latest, and possibly most taxing, challenge he had set himself since Blur closed its door for business in 2003, *Monkey: Journey To The West* seemed a natural break point for Damon, both as a composer and artist. Having sold CDs in their millions with Gorillaz, crafted a modern day love letter to London with *The Good, The Bad And The Queen* and even impressed his old Head of Music with a well-rendered opera, perhaps it was time for him to revisit the band that had started it all. But like the rest of Blur, putting aside individual projects for the greater good still seemed an insurmountable task. In fact, when the four were spotted having lunch together at the start of 2008, they even issued a joint media statement scotching any notions of reformation. "In light of recent press speculation, blur.co.uk would like to confirm that Alex, Damon, Dave and Graham met for an enjoyable lunch on Monday, but there are currently no other music plans for Blur."

As the saying goes, don't believe everything you read.

Chapter Seventeen

Never Say Never

Away from the hopeful rumours that popped up and down like moles on a golf course a few years into the new century, the reality of Blur actually reuniting their classic line-up seemed very slim indeed. While Albarn, Rowntree and James had regularly met up and even threatened to release new material, Coxon remained at a critical distance, his assisted exit during the recording of *Think Tank* still a point of sadness, irritation and bruised honour for the guitarist. "The idea of bumping into any of them was terrifying," he once said. Behind the scenes, attempts had been made to heal the wounds. Back in 2004, Rowntree brought in a professional mediator to re-establish meaningful dialogue between all parties, but the attempt failed. Reportedly, Graham was still annoyed with Dave, though Alex was back in his good books. Coxon's thoughts on Damon at the time went unrecorded. There was also talk of money and various other legal issues as the real reason for such stilted progress. Yet, none of them really needed another huge pay day on the back of a tour or album that might again go terribly wrong, or further sully the memory of days past. Much more plausible was the fact that until the former Stanway boys put down the bow and arrows and settled their differences as gentlemen, Blur were basically scuppered. "Look," said Albarn, "It can never be defused, and never be resolved, until Graham and I, face to face, sort our differences out. And that would be really nice, obviously. But whether it will actually happen or not, I just don't know..."

In the end, it was all settled over an Eccles cake.

On October 22, 2008, Damon was rehearsing for another performance of *Africa Express* at Camden Town's ballroom-like Koko club, the evening's planned entertainment but the latest example of his unceasing commitment to promoting music and culture from that continent. Irked at a "glaring absence" of African musical acts at Hyde Park's *Live 8* concert in 2005, Albarn subsequently met with a coterie of managers, promoters and bands in an effort to bring about closer links between western pop/rock artists and their African counterparts. At first, progress was marginal, with only Fatboy Slim, Martha Wainwright, Martina Topley-Bird and Jamie T making the trip to Mali to work with renowned musicians such as Amadou and Miriam, Salif Keita and Bassekou Kouyate. But things blossomed quickly when Damon took over Glastonbury's Park Stage in 2007, putting on a five-hour show that included the likes of Senegalese singer Baaba Maal, Terry Hall, Somalian rapper K'Naan, Billy Bragg, The Magic Numbers and Saharan trance-blues combo Tinariwen. An unqualified success, Albarn's Somerset extravaganza was followed by another event at Liverpool's Olympia Theatre in March 2008 (this time lasting nine hours and featuring 134 performers) before he pushed the idea Europe-wide with gigs in Paris and northern Spain. At the latter concert, an unlikely supergroup of Led Zeppelin bassist John Paul Jones, Algerian vocalist/political activist Rachid Taha and Clash guitarist Mick Jones ploughed through a lively cover of 'Rock The Casbah' for an audience of 50,000. *Africa Express* had well and truly arrived. "African music is the future of music," said Damon, "that's what you're hearing here, the future..."

When Graham Coxon wandered into Koko unannounced to watch rehearsals for the latest instalment of *Africa Express* in October, there was no one more surprised than Damon Albarn. But he recovered quickly. "Graham showed up, (then) we went round the corner and had an Eccles cake," said Damon. "What was said that needed to be said was said. It took about 30 seconds for it all to be fine again." Coxon also downplayed this meeting of minds, likening the closure of five years of uncertainty to the end of a playground spat. "We had a little chat and a cup of tea, and it felt all right," he confirmed. "There was no 'I don't hate you' or 'You don't hate me'. We never did anyway."

Sticking around for a "bit of a musical muckabout" before heading home, Coxon was back a week or so later to see *Monkey: Journey To The West* at the O2 arena. By now, Alex James had been tipped off something wondrous might be happening. "I was on my way to Northumberland and my manager called," he recalled. "But the bloody signal kept cutting. It was like 'Alex, you've got... speak... Dam... Graham... they're getti... Blur back tog... Turn around!' Anyway, I went to see *Monkey* the next week (November 9) and there was Damon and Graham with their arms on each other's shoulders. It was all back." There was, however, one key component missing. "Yeah," laughed James, "We had to bust Dave out of law school..."

A month later (and with Rowntree temporarily on the run from his East End legal practice), Blur stepped before the press to confirm that they were reforming for a summer show at London's Hyde Park on July 3, 2009. Though still diplomatic in their pronouncements, the odd joke hinted that things were thawing out quite nicely between them. "The hiatus was extremely good for our physical and emotional health," said Coxon. "Blur didn't really stop, though. Like explorers in the twenties and thirties, we just went on expeditions."

Alex was in an equally relaxed mood, his relief that "the world's coolest band" were finally back together coming off him in waves of fluffy delight. "A bit of a long time between band practices, I think," he said, "I wondered whether it would ever really happen again, and now it has. That's made me genuinely excited." Ever the pragmatist, Dave was perhaps more vigilant regarding Blur's volte-face, though he too seemed genuinely happy that a rapprochement of sorts was underway. "What we had before was a real energy about our live performances," he offered, "and I think that's what we have to recapture."

It was left to Albarn to dodge enquiries as to where it all might lead. "I missed that dynamic, that energy that Graham and I had," he said. "I just wouldn't have done Blur again unless he was part of it. (But)," the singer concluded, "this shouldn't be seen as the beginning of a 'brave new statement'. It's more that we want to play these songs again."

As news travelled fast of Blur's summer reunion at Hyde Park demand rose exponentially, with 55,000 tickets sold out in a matter of minutes. Damon appeared in shock. "It was genuinely incredible after doing nothing for years that everyone still wanted to come along and see us," he said. When it became clear that just one show wasn't going to cut it in terms of audience demand, further dates were added, with a headline appearance at Glastonbury on June 28, 2009 one of the last to be confirmed. "You know, we needed to do it for us," said Alex at the time. "We almost forgot other people might be interested." To ensure they were up to the task, rehearsals for Blur's return to the stage commenced in January 2009. For Graham, rejoining his former colleagues in a small space after a lapse of nearly six years was a fearsome thing. "I remember walking in and seeing Dave's drums, my amps and Alex's bass and thinking 'Wow'," he told *Channel Four.* "When I started, I was playing really quietly. Then it just got louder and louder. Funny. It used to be the other way around."

Approaching the challenge a week at a time, the band revisited their entire back catalogue, with over 60 tunes thrown up for possible use before they slowly began whittling them back into a usable set. "We played every single song we'd ever recorded, then knocked it down to about 40 that we could bear playing," said Damon at the time. "Now, we (have to) knock it down to 20 songs so we don't end playing on stage for four hours." There was the odd disagreement or issue to contend with. Coxon was fond of the group's B-side material, with 'Inertia' being his own particular favourite. No-one else was quite as keen. Elsewhere, Albarn struggled to remember lyrics he hadn't sung for nigh on two decades, the effort required to pluck stray words and phrases from the back of his brain both frustrating and tiring. And then there were other non-Blur commitments to consider. Rowntree now had a full-time job, his life in law as important to him as his life with the band. Alex also had several irons in the fire, his journalism, conducting duties *on* BBC's Maestro and recording commitments with New Order-offshoot act Bad Lieutenant all taking up considerable time and effort. But there was no doubt the old fires still burned bright. "It's great fun (and) we all missed it," said James. "When we first came in, sat down, started working together, that kind of spark that was there the first day was obviously still there. You know, that spark that we all felt when the four of us first started playing together. You do wonder whether it is going to be, (but it was)."

Putting a first, cautious foot in the water, Albarn and Coxon emerged from their den in February 2009 for a surprise appearance at the annual *NME* Brat Awards. For the music paper that had so avidly championed their cause at the start, middle, and until recently at least, the end of their career, it was the least they could do. Originally wanting to perform an acoustic rendition of 'Strange News From Another Star' – "The Editor thought it was too esoteric," said Damon – the duo instead dusted the mothballs off one of their finest songs, the beautiful and timeless 'This Is A Low'. Keen to play some part in the evening, Rowntree and James were on presentation duties, the duo handing over the gong for 'Best Solo Artist' to ex-Libertine Pete Doherty. "Graham's always been one of my heroes," said Doherty after the show, "and more so now, actually. He's a fucking geezer is Graham. Watching him and Damon doing 'This Is A Low', well, I got a lump in my throat. I remember listening to that when I was riding my bike to school. Just really, really special."*

With just one month to go before Blur made their live return, the object of Pete Doherty's enduring affections released his new album, *The Spinning Top*. Coxon's seventh solo disc was a grand departure from the indie-pop/punk influences that had defined much of *Happiness…* and *Love…*, as he now doffed a cap to the work of renowned folk guitarists such as Davey Graham and John Renbourn. "I was always seen as a bit

* At the time, Coxon was lending a hand to Doherty on his forthcoming solo album *Grace/Wastelands* (it was subsequently released on March 24, 2009). A diverse record from a special, if troubled performer, *Grace…* ranged from reggae and folk flavours to full-on post-punk, with Graham playing on all but one track.

of an indie beast in (Blur), really. A bit of a contrary, erratic kind of a person," he said. "But hopefully on *Spinning Top*, I've proved myself to be a little more considered and consistent." He had, indeed. Blooming with wistful tunes such as 'Look Into The Light', 'Brave The Storm' and the upbeat 'Feel Alright', not only was *The Spinning Top* a "loose concept album about one man's journey from cradle to grave", but also a continuing testament to Graham's skills with a guitar. Featuring guest turns from singer/songwriter Robyn Hitchcock ("He plays counter-attack guitar"), Jas Sigh on dilruba/jori and folk/rock legend Danny Thompson on bass, the record also benefitted from the watchful eyes and ears of producer Stephen Street.

"Stephen asked me to come in," Coxon later said. "We recorded with two acoustic guitars, then put the other stuff on top. He was in great form, and got taller by the day." Bypassing the compliments, Street seemed just as excited as everyone else by the news that Blur were back on the scene. "I'd been quietly chipping away at Damon and Graham for the past two to three years to get off their high horses and talk to each other," he told *The Guardian*. "Every now and then, I'd be with Damon and say 'Have you spoken to Graham recently?' and the same with Graham. I would put a little thought in their mind. 'Wouldn't it be nice if you spoke?' Initially, neither of them was interested, but I knew that once they got the chance to be in a room together and talk, they would find it impossible not to work together again."

Street was finally rewarded for his persistent efforts on June 13, 2009, as he ventured north to a small hall just outside Colchester to see Blur once again take to the boards. Having not performed as a unit since 2000, Albarn, Coxon, Rowntree and James confirmed the terms of their present reunion by returning to the very site of their first gig as Seymour in 1989. "Well, if you're going to go down memory lane, you may as well start at the top of memory lane," quipped Alex. Strolling onstage in the goods shed of the East Anglian Railway Museum in front of an audience of just 150 (mostly family and friends), the band's opening number was as perfect an emblem of their musical beginnings as their choice of venue: the first song they wrote together, the first single they recorded together and the first

Top 50 hit they had together, 'She's So High' was still pure pop gold. "It's a bit different to last time we played here," shouted an obviously delighted Albarn.

Performing 28 songs from all points of their recorded career, Blur covered the hits ('Girls And Boys', 'Parklife' and 'Beetlebum'), the album classics ('Tracy Jacks', 'Colin Zeal') and even the one that got away ('Popscene'). But there were surprises. Though Coxon was long gone by the time of its release, the quartet struck forth with a poignant version of *Think Tank*'s 'Out Of Time', as well as taking the atonal sound poem 'Essex Dogs' out for a leisurely walk to please the partisan crowd. Yet, it was the last two tracks aired that served to remind where Blur's skills often lay. With 'For Tomorrow', all that was good about the band's initial incarnation was there to hear, the tune's Bowie meets The Kinks strut and strident, London-centred lyricism as valuable and uplifting in 2009 as it had been in the heady days of Britpop. The same could also be said of 'The Universal'. Seen by some as too fey and whimsical on its initial release in 1995, 'The Universal' had grown much in intervening years, its message of a society descending into idiotic bliss now eerily prescient when faced with the likes of *X-Factor* and *Pop Idol*. Given such evidence, perhaps Blur's reappearance wasn't just an opportunity to wallow in nostalgia, but actually a strict requirement of the age.

With their first gig in nine years now out of the way, the band continued to ease themselves back into the saddle with a series of semi-private concerts throughout mid-June. A secret set at London's Rough Trade East coincided nicely with the release of a new – and it has to be said, immaculately chosen - compilation CD, *Midlife*. Another show for close friends at Brixton Academy saw the introduction of backing vocalists, keyboards and a brass section in preparation for the bigger gigs to come. The 'fan club only' set at Goldsmiths College found Graham and Alex revisiting the school they so loved (and that had awarded them Honorary Fellowships in 2005 and 2008 respectively), while Blur's stop-off at Southend's Cliffs Pavilion even gave the group a chance to dip their toes in the sea. Yet, with each passing day, Glastonbury loomed ever closer. Following three more warm-up dates at Newcastle,

Wolverhampton and Manchester, the big day finally arrived. "God," said Coxon, "we were absolutely kakking it beforehand..."

When Blur opened their account at Michael Eavis' big, old farm 17 years before, the Premier League was four months old and the 'World Wide Web' was about to celebrate its second birthday as a public service. On their return in 1994, South Africa had recently conducted its first multi-racial elections and the European Union was just up and running. By the band's third visit in 1998, Dolly the sheep had been cloned, Tony Blair was in government, Princess Diana had passed away and Bill Clinton hadn't had sex with Monica Lewinsky. The Millennium bug, 9/11 and the War on Terror all happened before Graham had left the group. The death of a Pope, Avian Flu and the fall of the banks all happened soon enough after. Britpop wars and the rise of Muse. The birth of grime and the slow implosion of Oasis. One way or another, Blur had been around long enough to see their generation through the best and worst of times. No wonder they were a tad nervous to be meeting 100,000 of them again in a large field in Somerset.

It went well, though. "When we walked on... that noise," said Graham. "It was like the sound of a million cows." Though not the most prosaic description of their expectant audience's combined voice, Coxon wasn't far off the mark. Greeted like returning heroes coming home from some unidentified campaign, the roar that went up over Glastonbury when Blur took the stage was genuinely frightening, its prolonged intensity temporarily stopping the band in their tracks as they realised exactly what they had got themselves into. "I'd actually forgotten the noise an audience can make when you come on stage," the guitarist continued. "It's really quite scary." There are those who contend that the following two hours constituted Blur's finest ever concert, with Damon Albarn possibly among them. "(It was) a highly emotional experience and probably something (I'll) never experience again." Certain polls would also point in that direction, with BBC 6 Music listeners conferring the band's set at Worthy Farm as "the best Glastonbury performance" on record. It just might have been.

Using the taped, fairground preamble of 'The Debt Collector' to help find their bearings before rolling into 'She's So High', Blur threw everything they had into Glastonbury and reaped their just rewards. Of the 24 tracks aired (16 of which were UK Top 30 singles), it was genuinely hard to pick a highpoint. 'Trimm Trabb' was certainly up there, the song's slow build and sense of impending menace providing both sustained tension and delicious release. 'Song 2' also had the power to transport, the assembled throngs moshing themselves into a frenzy before collapsing in an exhausted heap as Albarn sang out his last "Oh yeah!" Even 'Parklife' threatened to steal the honours as Blur's strongest moment on the night, its Phil Daniels-assisted, sing-songing qualities completely removing the veil between band and audience. But as some critics observed, it was the group's long established gift for melancholy that made the deepest connection: "For all (Blur's) energy, it's the sad songs that work best," said *The Guardian*'s Tim Jonze. "'To The End', 'The Universal', 'This Is A Low'. Weirder still is the reaction to 'Tender', a song never really rated (at least by me) as a classic, transformed into a joyous hug-a-long that reverberates around the crowd after the first encore *and* the second encore. It's at this point – when previously dismissed tracks acquire a new life of their own – that you realise something truly magical is going on..."

A triumph for the group, wonderful entertainment for the crowd and an occasion that saw an already visibly shaken Damon Albarn break down in tears during 'To The End', Blur's Glastonbury concert usurped any and all expectations for their reunion. "It was beautiful," said Damon. "We managed to come back intact and do the best gig that we'd ever done. That for me, was a testament to our original friendship." If the band's appearance in Somerset carried heady connotations of both popular re-embrace and emotional closure, then Blur's two-day stopover at London's Hyde Park on 2/3 July was more akin to one giant party. "I'm so proud that I'm going be able to sing 'Parklife' with Graham and Dave and Alex – which is one of the most familiar songs of the last 20 years – in the park it was written about," said Albarn in advance of the celebrations. "You don't get a chance to do that very often in life." In accordance with his nature, Graham was ducking all such hyperbole, his own thoughts more given to getting the songs right than any potential history-making. "I have my own lovely vision of sunny skies and happy faces, you know," he confirmed. "We've just been getting really into rehearsal rather than (thinking about) anything else. I don't get as nervous these days as I used to, anyway."

Given the reception that greeted Blur at Hyde Park, Albarn could have read out the contents of a telephone book for two hours and the band might still have won an encore. In a script quite possibly written by God, London's notoriously fickle weather not only held firm for the duration of both concerts, but also provided the best visual effect any group might conceivably wish for during a show. As Blur prepared to break into 'Beetlebum' on the first night, the sun flared golden yellow in the distance on its way to meet the horizon, turning the clouds overhead into a big ball of orange fluff. "Ah, just turn around now," Damon instructed his faithful from the stage, "Look at the sun... look at how beautiful it is. This song, it's for the sun." Cheesy as one of Alex's Shropshire Blues perhaps, but devastatingly clever stagecraft nonetheless. Another resounding success, James was as taken by Blur's Hyde Park adventures as the fans themselves. "It's the best thing you could do in some ways, split up for ten years," he said. "When we put Hyde Park on sale, it was a punt, really. 'D'you think we can fill it? Ah, fuck it, why not?' Then it (all) sold out in two minutes and we were like, 'Fucking hell! Really?' Actually, that was the most wonderful thing... that (everyone) was still interested." Dave Rowntree concurred. "The sun was shining and I was out with my mates. What's not to like?"

With both shows ably captured for later release on the album *All The People...*, Blur headed to France for a semi-intimate concert (just 4,500 attendees this time) at Lyon's Les Nuits de Fourvière festival, before performing similar honours at Ireland's Oxegen and Scotland's T In The Park on July 12, 2009. However, all was nearly lost hours before the band's appearance at the latter when Coxon succumbed to a nasty bout of food poisoning. "It was dreadful," he said. "I ate some oysters in Edinburgh (for lunch) and then at five p.m, we all met outside the hotel to go over to the site. I thought 'Hang on, I don't feel too well'. I fainted on the stairs trying to get up to my room. I just felt really ill." Things took a turn for the worse when James started playing naughty schoolboy behind closed doors. "It was weird because Alex had been having a crafty smoke in his room and set the fire alarm off," laughed Coxon. "So when the ambulance came, everyone staying in the hotel was out front due to the fire drill. (They all) saw me looking pale and funny being wheeled into the ambulance." By all accounts, after "A cup of tea, a couple of digestive biscuits and a few bags of saline pumped into my arm," Coxon was back on more or less level terms with his digestive system, though doing the show was still a huge concern. "I just thought, I've got to have a go, even if I faint during the set. It would have been awful not to and a big disappointment. I really wanted to do it so I wasn't going to let it stop me." If the guitarist was still feeling queasy, it really didn't show.

T In The Park marked the last date of the 'Summer Of Blur' tour, but anticipation surrounding the band's next move remained high, with fans wanting something more permanent than a fine live album to look forward to. Sadly, they were in for a disappointment. "Bit by bit we got back to the level where we had been in our prime... where it was stadiums and everybody singing and very euphoric." Damon told writer Paul Morley. "And then, after the last gig in Scotland I got on the train and left it all behind. That's it, I haven't thought about it since. For me, it was so nice to do that again and to know that I had left on a good note with Graham, Alex and Dave, but I didn't come off stage thinking, 'I'm a rock star!' at all. I really didn't. I loved every second of it and I felt the songs had lasted. But then when it had finished it was like, 'We've all got to get on with our lives now'. It was like a really nice holiday, a really nice treat and a great honour to experience. (And) you can't underestimate the feeling of 100,000 people at Glastonbury just singing every word back to you... (that's) incredible."

Such sentiments from Albarn might have inferred it was his decision – and his alone – that did for any notion of Blur recording a new record or carrying on in some other meaningful sense. With Gorillaz still an ongoing concern, and talk of more The Good, The Bad And The Queen-related activity on the horizon, stepping away from the group would be relatively easy for him. Yet, the choice to down tools after a summer of fireworks was not just down to Damon. In fact, it was a judgement thoroughly backed by his bandmates who, like their lead singer, all had lives outside the belly of the beast. "We're still in touch and we say 'Wotcha' and all that, but nothing has been mentioned about any more shows or anything else," Coxon said. "Everyone's slipped back into what they do when the Blur creature isn't heaving around. Law and cheese and music, I suppose. But," he sagely concluded, "The 'Summer Of Blur' was lovely..."

Acting as a fine reminder for old school types as to Blur's original value, while also allowing those who missed out first time around to see what the fuss was about, the events of 2009 drew a pleasant, if ultimately bittersweet end to the briefest of reunions. But there was partial compensation offered when *No Distance Left To Run* enjoyed a short theatrical run at selected UK cinemas in early 2010. A 104-minute documentary made by the twin creative team of Dylan Southern and Will Lovelace, *No Distance...* followed Blur from rehearsals for their 2009 tour onto the stage at Glastonbury and beyond, using vintage footage and exclusive interviews with each member of the group to tell their collective tale.

Billed as "The story of an English band, and a portrait of enduring friendship and resolution," the film was both painfully funny and at times painfully frank, as Albarn, Coxon, Rowntree and James faced the camera with candour, bluntness, and ultimately, more than a little love. "We knew from the start that we wanted *No Distance...* to kind of focus on friendship, as much as it did the career of Blur and all of the things that you expect from a music documentary," Southern said. "But, obviously going into it, we didn't know how successful it was going to be, or whether they'd still get on and things like that. So, it could have gone either way."

Receiving its world premiere at London's Odeon West End on January 14, 2010, *No Distance...* was later released to DVD, with Blur's full Hyde Park show attached to the extras to illicit further interest and maximise sales. Several months later, the film also received a much-deserved nomination as 'Best Long Form Music Video' at the 53rd *Grammy Awards*, the first time any Blur-associated product had been in contention for such a prize. "I was skeptical about it at first," said

Damon of *No Distance*... "I felt it was intruding on something (personal) we were trying to do. But sometimes you have to relax and let it go. Now, I feel really glad to have been part of it."

Ever quick out of the traps, Albarn wasted little time in mourning Blur's recent live glories, as he now turned his attention to publicising the imminent release of Gorillaz's third album *Plastic Beach* alongside long-time creative partner Jamie Hewlett. "I'm making this one the most 'pop' record I've ever made in many ways," he said at the time, "But also (using) all my experience to try and at least present something that has got real depth."

Strangely, after the resounding success of 2005's *Demon Days*, Damon and Jamie had contemplated dropping their virtual band origins altogether in favour of a more collective film/music project called Carousel. "Gorillaz now to us is not like four animated characters anymore," said Hewlett in 2008. "It's more like an organisation of people doing new projects. That's (our) ideal model, Gorillaz is a group of people who gave you this, and now want to give you new stuff."

But like their now aborted animated movie, the duo's idea proved hard to implement, causing a quick return to the Gorillaz namesake. While Hewlett worked on a refreshed look for the band's website/promos featuring an "older and wiser" Murdoc and Co., Albarn travelled between Syria, Beirut – and rather improbably, Derby – to record orchestral contributions for the songs he had written. As before, a huge group of guest stars were also roped in for contributions and general fun, with rapper/semi-professional smoker Snoop Dogg, soul legend Bobby Womack, 'Mr. New York' Lou Reed, The Clash's Paul Simonon and Mick Jones, The Fall's irascible Mark E. Smith and a returning De La Soul all turning up to add spice, snarl and humour to the disc.

Released on March 3, 2010, *Plastic Beach* did well enough in re-establishing the Gorillaz brand, making its debut at number two on both sides of the Atlantic, where it sold 74,000 and 112,000 copies respectively in the first week. Yet, the record was neither as tuneful nor compelling as its illustrious predecessor, with none of the four singles eventually gleaned from *Plastic Beach* making much of an impression on the charts. Still, the critics remained more or less on side: "Despite Albarn's protestations that *Plastic Beach* is Gorillaz's most pop album to date, an effortless, irrefutable hit along the lines of 'Feel Good Inc' or 'Dare' is noticeable by its absence," said *The Guardian*'s Alexis Petridis. "That said, what is here does enough to underline the fact that Albarn is the only artist from the whole Britpop imbroglio to whom you could attach the word 'Genius' without causing widespread mocking laughter." *Q*'s Dave Everley was also ringing Damon's bell. "*Plastic Beach* (features) some of the most forward-thinking pop you'll hear this or any year," he said.

There were some out there who were considerably less impressed with Gorillaz's newest platter. "Too many of these 16 hazy, half-crazy tracks," reasoned the *Los Angeles Times*' Mikael Wood, "sound like undercooked studio goofs." Even if one felt Wood was being a little harsh, there was also some uncomfortable truths to be had in his review. While the luxuriant 'Empire Ants' negotiated the tricky move from salsa-themed ballad to full-on Eurodisco with considerable aplomb, and 'White Flag' made one feel they were spending Christmas on a tropical island, there were disappointments. 'Some Kind Of Nature''s insipid backbeat and skeletal orchestrations reduced Lou Reed's usually commanding voice to the level of gravelly cameo. Worse, 'Stylo''s Kraftwerk-referencing intro went all out in search of a chorus that was sadly never found, the track finally grinding to an atmospheric, yet insubstantial halt three minutes later. Perhaps that was the point. But such meandering bravery did little for its chances as a standalone single, the tune limping into the mid-reaches of the US charts rather than dominating them in early 2010.

Given the fact that Damon was gearing up for a near-year's activity with Gorillaz, the appearance of Blur's 'Fool's Day' on April 17 came as something of a bolt from the blue. Released as part of 'Record Store Day' – an annual event conceived by indie shop employee Chris Brown to celebrate "The art of music in its all various forms" – the single was initially limited to only 1,000 copies in 7″ format before being made available as a free download on the band's official website. An arch little tune, though truthfully one that might not have made it as a B-side during Blur's golden years, 'Fool's Day' ambled along pleasantly enough on the strength of a walking drum and Graham's thick, descending guitar lines. But it was Albarn's diary-like lyric that pecked at the ear. Drolly recounting a spring bicycle ride to the studio where he was meeting friends whose "Sweet music we just can't let go", the singer's wordplay seemed to infer there was life left in the Blur machine yet. This fact was semi-confirmed when he later hinted to the press that in lieu of a proper album, 'Fool's Day' might well be the first of many such 45s, giving the group an outlet for their wares without risk of impact on their continuing solo activities. A fine idea sure enough, but as time would come to show, one that was more fanciful than realistic in terms of actual delivery.

After the spring surprise of 'Fool's Day', the rest of 2010 was a Blur-free zone. Graham began recording material for his next solo album with *Think Tank* producer Ben Hillier, while Dave made a spirited, if again unsuccessful stand at the Cities of London and Westminster ballot box against Tory MP Mark Field. When not expanding his commercial interests as a cheese maker of note, Alex threw in his lot with the new ITV1 reality show, *Popstar To Operastar*. "I love opera," he said to camera. "It's like the pop music equivalent of the pyramids. I'm not a singer, though. I'm a bass player. And there's two types of musician. Punchers and strokers, and I'm a puncher. Play loud, sing loud." Sing loud he certainly did, completely murdering one of Rossini's better known arias to the collective delight of the studio audience. Scoring "900%" for pure entertainment value, and commended for a vocal style not unlike "an operatic version of Dennis The Menace", James was nonetheless booted off the programme at the end of the first week.

For Albarn, it was Gorillaz, Gorillaz and more Gorillaz as the virtual band struck out on their first world tour, *Escape To Plastic Beach*. A combination of new videos, big screen projections and Damon's handpicked "village of people" actually playing front of house instead of behind the scenes, he was joined on the 36-date jaunt by a backing band that included old friends Simon Tong, Paul Simonon and Mick Jones. Performing their biggest concert to date at the 2010 Glastonbury festival after original headliners U2 pulled out at the last minute due to Bono's bad back, Albarn's return to Worthy Farm granted him the honour of being the first musician to ever headline on a Friday, Saturday and Sunday night. Handing in an assured set propped up by the presence of singer Bobby Womack and rapper Mos Def, Damon also gave a moving onstage tribute to actor/former Gorillaz collaborator Dennis Hopper, who had sadly passed away some three weeks before. Yet, despite the airing of some fine songs, with 'Kids With Guns' and the teary 'Cloud Of Unknowing' particularly worthy of mention, there were complaints that Damon and Jamie's animated quartet were not sufficiently iconic to close the show. "Many punters didn't know the songs well enough for a headline act," said *The Sun*, "(And) it would have been a different story if U2's 'With Or Without You', 'Where The Streets Have No Name' or 'Sunday Bloody Sunday' had been blaring out. Still," the paper conceded, "it was a top gig and a privilege to have been a part of the crowd in Pilton. I'd give it a three out of five." Albarn was probably overcome with joy.

As with the preceding year, 2011 brought no real Blur-related activity, though there were a few tantalising bleeps on the radar. In January, the band were spotted jamming in a London studio, immediately leading to speculation that a new single or even – dare one say it – an album might be on its way. But Coxon soon put the kibosh on all such talk when he told the press their recent experiments might turn up on "an LP in six years' time, or something". Graham's pessimism was well founded as his old friend remained ever occupied. Following *Plastic Beach*, Damon had managed to get yet another Gorillaz album out within the space of 12 months, as *The Fall* was uploaded on the group's website exclusively for those belonging to their 'Sub-Division' fan club before arriving in shops on December 25, 2010. Recorded entirely on Albarn's iPad during the American leg of the *Escape...* tour three months before, its 15 tracks might have been more experimental in nature than *...Beach*, but featured far fewer guest spots, with only Mick Jones, Paul Simonon and Bobby Womack on hand to offer real help. Best described as patchy, if well meaning, when *The Fall* was good – as with the grime-laden 'Phoner To Arizona' and the free-flowing 'Revolving Doors' – it was very good indeed. However, its close proximity to the release of ...*Beach* and the demo-quality of some of the material made it an inessential listen. Debuting on the US and UK charts at numbers 12 and 24 respectively before quickly disappearing again, the album raised Prince-like concerns that Gorillaz were now in danger of saturating the market with too much product. Either that, or Damon was simply making hay while the sun shone.

Artistic compulsion. Market opportunity. Whatever the case, Albarn couldn't be stopped. In the spring of 2011, he again shed his pop star skin and announced details of a brand new opera, *Dr. Dee.* Given its subject, this was to be no easy task. A Sixteenth century Welsh polymath, whose genius in the fields of mathematics, astronomy, navigation, alchemy, divination and occult philosophy placed him at the centre of Queen Elizabeth I's royal court, John Dee's life was an explosion of science and magic, his ideas still rattling the senses some four hundred years after his death. "He connected to mathematics, religion and superstition, and even suggested that some of the early Britons had got as far as America," said Damon. "So some of these ideas, these... mad ideas were fed into a (bigger) idea that became the British Empire. In that sense, he's an integral part of our national identity, but one that's (now) been completely sidelined."

The concept of *Dr. Dee* had its origins in a completely separate project, as Albarn and Jamie Hewlett sought to collaborate with renowned graphic novelist/comic book creator Alan Moore on an opera about superheroes. The fertile mind behind *Watchmen*, *Swamp Thing*, *The Killing Joke* and *From Hell*, Moore was justly famous for inverting the idea of strangely-powered men in tights into something far more fantastical, yet still somehow grounded in reality. However, the bearded writer was not particularly interested in returning to his old stomping ground of red-caped Kryptonians or lantern-jawed vigilantes, and suggested concentrating on the life and times of John Dee instead. But when Albarn and Hewlett allegedly failed to provide copy/art for Moore's new comic (*Dodgem Logic*), he quickly removed himself from the fray. With Hewlett following him out the door soon after, Damon was left to soldier on with theatre director Rufus Norris.

Opening at the Palace Theatre on July 1, 2011 as part of the Manchester International Festival*, *Dr. Dee* drew reasonably strong notices, with its Elizabethan masque structure, innovative set and costume designs (bowler hats and punk rockers abounded), and animated projections all to be admired. "The opera is fresh, original and heartfelt," said an impressed Rupert Christiansen at *The Daily Telegraph*. Further, Albarn's mixing of 16th Century instrumentation such as the shawm, dulcian and crumhorn with African Koras and the inventive percussion of a visiting Tony Allen were further cause for celebration. But at times, parts of the production felt rushed and even unfinished, a fact Damon would later concede. "Well," he said, "it was all made in an eight week work-shopping period."

That said, where *Dr. Dee* really succeeded was the boldness and imagination of its music, the title character's sad fall from grace due to his doomed 'Hermetic partnership' with the spirit-medium Edward Kelley playing itself out over 18 bucolic and extremely expressive tunes, more often than not sung by Albarn himself. "Whenever I get excited about something, the best way forward is for me to express that excitement as clearly as I can," he later said. "And *Dr. Dee* made some weird connections for me in that I've rediscovered my own folk traditions." It was a point well made. On the likes of the bird-song filled 'The Golden Dawn', acoustically-propelled and flute-laden 'Apple Carts' and the choir-like strains of 'Oh Spirit, Animate Us', Damon hadn't just channelled the esoteric thoughts and scientific deeds of the good Doctor. He had also crafted an opera that in its own way was as 'British' in its preoccupations and sense of history as *Parklife* or *The Great Escape* – even if the tools used on this occasion were viola da gambas, recorders and lutes rather than electric guitars,

* *Dr. Dee* was but the latest collaboration between Damon and the Manchester International Festival (MIF). Aside from Gorillaz's appearance at the MIF in 2005 and *Monkey: Journey To The West* in 2007, Albarn also composed several tunes for 2009's *It Felt Like A Kiss*, a theatre production focusing on power and politics, which archive footage of Fifties/Sixties Baghdad, New York, Moscow and Kinshasa to make its intellectual point.

drums and synths. A pastoral treat that was later released on CD and even performed at the English National Opera House, *Dr. Dee* was yet another string to Damon's ever-expanding bow of genre-striding successes.

After a trip to the Congo to record music with local musicians under the pseudonym 'DRC Music' (the results can be heard on October 2011's *Kinchasa One Two*), Albarn was back in the UK by the late summer to again record with Blur, though it was nothing to get too excited about. Irritated by the possible cancellation of the Notting Hill Carnival after the English summer riots of August 6–11, 2011, Damon got his old band back together to provide musical backing for poet/activist Michael Horowitz's spoken word protest on the matter. But when the relevant authorities changed their minds and gave the West London festivities a cautious go ahead, said collaboration was filed away, never to be heard of again. During the same period, Graham Coxon was honoured by Fender Guitars with the release of his own 'Signature Model' Telecaster. A sturdy bit of kit based on the same specifications as Graham's long-serving axe, the blonde Tele's honking pick-ups finally gave those who had long sought to bash out 'Song 2' in the privacy of their bedrooms the chance to do so.

While Coxon was giving video demonstrations of his new guitar, James was getting himself in a bit of a pickle. Emboldened by dreams of combining food and music in a celebratory atmosphere, the bass player had put his name to 'Alex James presents Harvest', a festival that took place from September 9–12 in the grounds of his own farm. Unfortunately, despite the presence of artists/acts such as KT Tunstall and The Feeling, master classes by super chefs like Hugh Fearnley-Whittingstall and enough grub to feed a medium-sized army, ...Harvest fell prey to financial problems. "The fact that people didn't get paid really, really upset me," Alex later said. "It wasn't about the money I lost. It's just a mess. It was easily the worst business deal I've ever done. I'm just gutted that some people didn't get paid." To his credit, James tried his best to make amends by pledging to match all funds raised at a benefit concert staged in nearby Chipping Norton to settle the outstanding debt: "I was so happy to do that," he later said.

As Alex struggled on with lawyers, Damon was building another supergroup. First mooted in 2008, but soon deferred because of Albarn's countless other musical commitments, Rocket Juice And The Moon made their first live appearance at the Cork Jazz Festival on October 28, 2011 under the name Another Honest Jon's Chop Up!. Featuring the talents of Damon, Tony Allen and bass guitar royalty/Red Hot Chilli Pepper Michael Balzary (AKA Flea), Rocket Juice... combined musicianly chops with jazz, funk and Afrobeat influences, their overall sound sitting somewhere between Fela Kuti and KC & The Sunshine Band. "As wonderful as it is to stand at the front of the stage with Blur and hear everyone singing every single word of your songs back at you, it's not everything," Damon said of his fourth group since 2005. "I'm just as happy sat at the back of the stage at the piano when there's real magic in the room. Playing with master musicians, you learn so much, about being a musician, about yourself." Flea was equally given to Albarn's quest to create "an unadulterated rhythmic masterclass", with his view of Rocket Juice… taking on almost religious connotations. "We (wanted) to capture a really beautiful moment between three musicians," he told *Mojo*. "It was clear from the moment we met (that) we were all going to click in the studio… just the way we approached music and what we wanted from it. We've got a spiritual connection."

Recorded on the hop between Allen's home in Paris, Albarn's 13 studios and any time Flea could find a spare moment in the Chilli Peppers' touring schedule, Rocket Juice…'s self-titled album turned out to be a surprisingly coherent, if loose-limbed affair. Enhanced by the seismic horn blasts of The Hypnotic Brass Ensemble – and with further contributions from neo-soul singer Erykah Badu and Ghanaian rapper M.anifest – the snapping funk of tracks like 'Hey Shooter' and slip-sliding rhythms of 'The Unfadable' were yet more evidence of Damon's contention that all musical roads led back to Africa. "Everything goes back to Africa," he said. "Music itself, the Western model, those '60s beat groups that set the template for rock classicism, they were into R&B and soul, which came from gospel, which came from the plantations, which came from Africa. The nature of what we are doing here with Rocket Juice & The Moon is built on the spirit I've carried from that first experience in (Mali) to this day… that sense of community and togetherness that the musicians have when they are playing music."

Perhaps not everyone's cup of tea (the record's quick jumps between playful wooziness and rhythmic abandon could easily jar), *Rocket Juice…* still received a cautious pat on the back, if not huge sales, when later released in March 2012. "First, you should be aware that this is a funk album," said BBC Music's John Doran, "A very odd funk album, but a funk album nonetheless. If you do not like funk, there is every chance you will not enjoy it. Second, this is a jam album, and if you're averse to looseness then this just isn't going to cut it. But for those wanting a herbalised oddity that tips its scruffy, psychedelic cap to Fela Kuti, William Onyeabor, the Ohio Players, Fred Wesley, Augustus Pablo, the BBC 'Radiophonic Workshop' and Bootsy Collins, this album is a genuinely enjoyable find." Something for everyone, then.

Conclusively proving that a month seldom went by without some form of Albarn-related activity, the end of 2011 found the songwriter again fronting The Good, The Bad And The Queen for a sold-out show in support of Greenpeace's 40th anniversary. Staged at the Coronet Theatre in London's Elephant & Castle district on November 10, the gig marked the first time the band had played together in three years, though it might not be the last. "You just never know..." said Paul Simonon. Regrettably, the same could not be said of Gorillaz. Just two weeks after The Good...'s appearance on the New Kent Road, the cartoon quartet's latest – and quite possibly last – album popped up in the shops. Stretching from 'Tomorrow Comes Today' to 'Doncamatic', *The Singles Collection: 2001–2011* was a sprightly 15-track compilation focused on a decade of international hits. However, the record (which was also released as a 7″ and 12″ box set) was less about establishing an artistic holding pattern and more about presenting a 'full stop' to Damon and Jamie's long-running virtual soap opera.

Since 2008, there had been reports that all was not wine and roses between the duo, with Hewlett's graphics on *Plastic Beach* allegedly not gelling with Albarn's music, and vice versa. A supposed quote from the artist saying he was "fucking sick" of drawing the same characters didn't help the story go away either. More, Damon's persistent flitting from project to project outside the perimeters of their working relationship was another source of ongoing tension. Yet, Gorillaz had persisted, with 2010's world tour, a new song ('DoYaThing') and even a range of Converse trainers tying into the overall brand all signifying things were still reasonably healthy behind closed doors. All was well, then, until suddenly it wasn't. In an interview with *The Guardian* in early 2012, Albarn confirmed that any further Gorillaz music or visuals was "unlikely", while Hewlett spoke concurrently to the media of wanting to "do some of my own stuff". Though both creators later readjusted their comments so as not to preclude the possibility of future endeavours, the message was still reasonably clear: Murdoc, 2D, Russel and Noodle were sunning themselves on *Plastic Beach* until further notice.

They say nature abhors a vacuum, and so it proved with Blur. At almost the very moment Gorillaz pulled down the shutters, Damon, Graham, Dave and Alex were back for their "21st anniversary" with an appearance at the Brits. Scheduled to receive an 'Outstanding Contribution to Music' award for their services to British pop at the ceremony on February 21, 2012, this latest decoration brought back a plethora of emotions for Coxon. "I've been to the Brits only two or three times," he said. "I remember the one where (we) won a lot of Brits and we were, unfortunately, next to the Oasis table. I was getting a lot of gyp from Liam Gallagher. It was all very worrying, but it was an amazing night. I felt slightly guilty about winning them all. That's just how I am. I should just have enjoyed it. But I was worried that people would think we were spoilt brats. This time, sod it, I'm just going to lap it up I think." Alex was of a like mind, at least on the last point. "We're going to play, which is brilliant," he said. "It's like putting the Blues Brothers back together..."

Joining a distinguished list of performers that included the likes of The Beatles, Queen, David Bowie and U2, Albarn's acceptance speech on receiving "The big gong" offered not only genuine gratitude to the assembled crowd, but also a quick trip down memory lane. "The last time we were here was 17 years ago," he said, "and what happened that night seemed to have a really profound effect on our lives, so it's nice to come back and say 'Thank you' for this honour." Singling out Dave

Balfe, Andy Ross, EMI Chairman Tony Wadsworth, Stephen Street and a vast number of other producers/contributors, Damon ended his discourse by dedicating Blur's newest trophy to their long-serving and extraordinarily proficient manager, Chris Morrison. "You're a very dear friend and a very special person," he smiled. "Thank you for putting up with us."*

Following Morrison's rightful acknowledgement from the podium, the group then proceeded to head backstage in preparation for a live medley of their biggest hits, while Britain's latest multi-million seller Adele picked up the evening's last trophy 'Album Of The Year'. Yet, after only about 30 seconds of thanking the world, her dialogue was abruptly cut short by the show's producers as they battled to put Blur in front of the cameras before the advertisements beckoned. Rightly irked at the slight, Adele pulled out her middle finger at those to blame as the opening bars of 'Girls And Boys' signalled the end of another classic Brits cock-up. "We were standing behind a curtain just waiting for it to lift so we could get on with it," said Damon. "Personally, I'd have been happy to wait for another 10 minutes. Blame the adverts."

Blur's five-song set at the Brits was only the opening salvo of six months' work, as the band once again re-entered the limelight after an absence of three years. Still, there was some confusion as to exactly what their 21st anniversary reunion might yield. "It's pretty nice... getting the Brit award," said an enthusiastic Graham at the time. "We haven't planned the rehearsals yet, but there will definitely be another Blur album." Two days later, he withdrew the remark, having been cautioned (by parties unknown) for announcing something that might – or might not – transpire. Wary of repeating a similar mistake, James stuck to the newly abridged script. "Who knows what will happen," he said, "but there is a lot to look forward to..."

Before all became totally clear, the recently chastened Coxon went on the promotional/touring trail for his eighth solo disc, *A&E*. Released

* With Morrison stepping aside for Blur's latest reunion, their ongoing managerial affairs have become the responsibility of Eleven's Niamh Byrne and Regine Moylett, two long-time associates of both Chris and the band.

on April 2, 2012, the album marked a winning return to more familiar territory after the lovely, but "hard to perform live" acoustic folk of *The Spinning Top*. Offering 10 tracks (though 21 songs were actually recorded in all), *A&E* was justly described by *Uncut* as "A series of heavy squalls rather than a settled spell of fair weather", its use of piercing, vintage synths and on-their-last-legs drum machines giving Graham's latest batch of tunes an abrasive, almost tetchy edge.

With influences running from Kraftwerk and Krautrock to late-Sixties rock and new wave/post punk touchstones like Magazine, Subway Sect and even The Cure, *A&E* also had a schizoid quality that sometimes didn't make for the easiest of listening. That said, there were rewards. 'Seven Naked Valleys' was Creedence Clearwater Revival's 'Run Through The Jungle' for the post-Jesus And Mary Chain generation, Coxon's caustic guitars and low-slung saxes prowling along like an angry panther with a thorn in its paw. 'Running For Your Life' took things even further, managing to marry Graham's distorted vocals to a riff both Jimi Hendrix and Neu!'s Michael Rother would have been proud of. Lyrically given to subjects such as England's North/South divide, lonely men "working undercover" in their bedrooms and the perils of replacing someone else's record at a party, *A&E* was Coxon at his most ornery, individual and as subsequent reviews confirmed, "willfully awkward". The guitarist appeared quite happy with all such descriptions. "I removed any temptation to be flowery, pretty or sentimental," he said. "*A&E* has a more sinister edge, but I was in a good place when we were recording. It was fun despite some of the bleakness, and I hope it's not depressing." A huge musical argument on a small sliver disc, *A&E* reached number 39 in the UK charts.

By the time that Graham had finished his final round of interviews in service of *A&E*, Blur's plans for 2012 had become much clearer. In addition to the release of new material, the band would also be taking on the responsibility of headlining the Closing Ceremony Celebration Concert for the London Olympic Games at Hyde Park on August 12. A huge honour and equally huge undertaking, Blur were nonetheless looking forward to their latest date with destiny. "Three of us still live in London," said Albarn, "and we really wanted to participate in a city that's so galvanised by the event." The only member of the group having to take a train to the gig, James was no less enthralled with the prospect of Blur's return to Hyde Park. "Well obviously," he laughed. "Doing the Olympic show was something we really couldn't say no to." Yet, though the crowd at Hyde Park was expected to top 80,000, Blur were only to receive a paltry £300 for their participation. With London having been in the throes of recession since the collapse of the banks in 2008, and no end to it anytime soon, Damon wasn't wont to grumble. "When you divide that between four and add publishing, management and tax, it's down to about a quid," he said. "But that's not why you agree to do it... I love this city." And no doubt, the city would love him back equally with the purchase of downloads, CDs and DVDs long after the event.

As Blur's management negotiated the logistics of Hyde Park with various Olympics organisations, civil servants and groundkeepers, the quartet busied themselves with the imminent release of two new songs, though their path to sunlight was not without incident. As far back as January 2012, producer/old friend William Orbit had confirmed that he was to work with Blur on their latest studio sessions, his Twitter feeds on the subject full of enthusiasm and wry anticipation. "I'm in the studio with (Damon) from Wednesday!" he said, before later adding "Loving the guitars you laid down, (Graham)! Vocal session March 3!" But soon enough, the love-in was all over. "Blur could have been good," William tweeted to a fan, "but Damon, brilliant and talented though he is, is kind of a shit to the rest of Blur." Obviously angered by his experience, Orbit was still on the warpath when he spoke to *NME* in mid-March. "The new stuff sounded amazing," he confirmed. "Then it all stopped suddenly. It was all over with Damon and the rest of the band were like, 'Is this it?'". With the facts unclear as to exactly what happened and why – Albarn chose not to respond to Orbit's missives – Coxon finally decided to step forward on his friend's behalf. "We had a go (with William), and we just didn't like the way it turned out," the guitarist told *Vulture*. "We were just like, 'Shit, this is not what we're after'. And we decided to go it alone."

With Orbit no longer at the helm, Blur undertook the task of realising the songs themselves, as 'Under The Westway' and 'The Puritan' were eventually released first by Twitter stream (via a live performance above 13 studios) and then 7″, CD and download on July 2, 2012. Originally performed by Damon and Graham at a pre-Brits charity show in aid of War Child during early February, 'Under The Westway' was by far the better tune, its keening nature, sad/happy undertones and piano-based chords musically recalling something of both 'This Is A Low' and 'End Of A Century'. More, the song's lyrics were classic Albarn, his descriptive powers this time pointed at a life played out beneath the dual carriageway that had hung magnificently above his head since moving to West London in the mid-Nineties. "I always loved living underneath (the Westway)," he said, "Having to go past it every day, and I love getting on it... flying over, and minutes later, you're in a totally different part of London. It's just a metaphor for London and something that's constant."

Unfortunately, 'The Puritan' gave one less to shout about. Admittedly a much jollier proposition than 'Under The Westway' – though also much more wearing – the track again recalled Blur's heyday, with its "La, la, la, la" vocal refrain picking up precisely where 'For Tomorrow' left off. But when compared to the bouncing 'Jubilee', free-wheeling 'Advert' or even the sly giggles of 'Magic America', 'The Puritan' was more impoverished second cousin than proudly returning prodigal son. Alex, however, was having no such criticisms. "'Under The Westway''s a cry-your-eyes-out type tune, whereas 'The Puritan' is much more a jump up and down and sing along song." At first, there was some confusion that Blur's new double A-sided single had been written specifically for the forthcoming Olympics. But though Albarn was inspired by the games and what they might bring to London, it was never his specific intention to wax lyrical about the event in either 'Under The Westway' or 'The Puritan'. "No," he said. "I wrote something that would have a life outside the event. I don't think Muse will be playing (their Olympic) song in a few years' time, will they?"

Reaching a disappointing number 34 on the UK charts on release, 'Under The Westway/The Puritan''s release was somewhat overshadowed by another Blur package dropped on the public at the end of July. Often rumoured, but never realised until now, *Blur 21* was in the words one pithy critic "a never-ending nocturnal emission for Blur fans the world over". Chronicling the vast majority of the band's recorded career, the 21-disc box set offered not only expanded formats of their seven studio albums, but also four more CDs worth of rarities, demos and unreleased material. With three further DVDs containing never-before-seen group footage, two stage shows and more atypical video gems, *Blur 21* was the gift that kept on giving, as the whole kit and caboodle was topped off with a 7″ single of the Seymour-era live track 'Superman' and a hardcover book recounting the quartet's story with exclusive/previously unpublished photographs.

Both a perfect way to mark Blur's 21st anniversary on the earth, and astounding stylistic proof of their musical evolution from baggy usurpers to something completely of themselves, the band were rightfully proud of it. "It's a whopper, isn't it?" laughed James at the time. "*21* was a year in the making (and) took enormous amounts of time. We've all been through our attics, combed our archives (and) found all kinds of crazy stuff that's triggered avalanches of memories." But while Alex and Co. were perfectly willing to share previously hidden treasures such as the first ever recording of 'She's So High' and the surprisingly peaceful ballad 'Sir Elton John's Cock', the Blur hunters' Holy Grail remained tantalisingly beyond reach. "Blimey, no." said the bassist. "Our version of The Buggles' 'Video Killed The Radio Star' will forever remain a secret."

With only 12 odd days to go before the Olympics Closing Ceremony Celebration Concert, Blur reactivated their old habit of playing a spray of warm-up gigs in advance of the big night. Two live sessions for BBC Radio 6 started the ball rolling on July 31, while sweaty sets at Margate's Winter Gardens and London's tiny 100 Club soon followed. By August 5, Blur were ramping up the size and scale of the venues in which they appeared, with Wolverhampton's Civic Hall playing host to back-to-back shows before the group headed to Scandinavia for further concerts at Denmark's Smukfest and Sweden's Way Out West festival.

For Coxon, Blur's latest manifestation offered him the chance to walk between two worlds at once. "I'm lucky," he said. "I can do the big, posh shows (with Blur). Big guitars, big amps, big audience. Then I can go back and do my grubby, more raucous, smaller solo gigs. I'm really quite happy with having the best of both worlds." Just as well, because they didn't come much bigger than the one he was about to play. After a quite magnificent – and in keeping with the essence of the nation – quite unexpected performance by Great Britain at the Summer Olympic Games, London was in the mood for quite a party on August 12 at Hyde Park. Having seen the likes of Jessica Ennis, Mo Farar, Chris Hoy, Bradley Wiggins and a host of other sportsmen and women take a whopping number of medals in the best possible atmosphere, national pride seemed for once to be at an all-time high. "The Games were a tonic for the whole country," said Albarn. Now, he and Blur had to follow it.

Bounding onstage just as the official Closing Ceremony was nearing its conclusion at Stratford's newly created Olympic Stadium 10 miles away, Blur were out for their own set of honours at Hyde Park. Greeted by a sea of Union Jacks, visiting royalty – Prince Harry had been roped in especially for the occasion – and 80,000 people in search of even more to celebrate, the band opened the show with 'Girls And Boys' and never really looked back. Performing beneath a huge replica of Damon's much-loved Westway, Blur were as much an embodiment of British national pride on the night as any athlete, rower or dressage team. Yet, for all the pomp and circumstance, it was also a surprisingly intimate gig, as each song played into a time or place that defined the group's personal history.

Whether it was Albarn pecking Coxon on the cheek as the guitarist sang "Oh my baby" during 'Tender' or the apocalyptic, white-noise ending to 'Beetlebum' that recalled their mad days as Seymour, Blur's performance was as much for themselves as the crowd. This fact was underlined by their choice of tunes. For every 'Sunday Sunday', 'Country House' or 'End Of A Century', there was a 'Caramel', 'Sing' or even 'Young And Lovely' – the long lost and luscious B-side to 1993's 'Chemical World'. From the band's very own 'Stairway To Heaven' ('Trimm Trabb') to a raucous take on 'Colin Zeal', every blast of feedback, megaphone-assisted vocal or rhythmic whack brought back its own minute, moment or memory for those on stage.

Of course, Blur were not oblivious to the huge crowd gathered in front of them, and when the grand gesture was required, it was despatched with all guns a blazing. Never one to miss a big event, Phil Daniels was on hand to lead the audience through a bawled rendition of 'Parklife', though this time he brought a guest along with him. Emerging from the wings dressed as tea lady replete with stacked trolley to refresh those on stage, comedian Harry Enfield looked both bewildered and delighted to find himself serving hot drinks to the band as they belted out their best-known Mockney anthem. "To that great British institution, the tea lady!" shouted Albarn as the mischievous Enfield kissed him sweetly. A rare break in proceedings before 'Song 2' brought yet another surprise, as Damon successfully got an entire field of revellers to do the 'Mobot' in honour of track star and double-gold winning medallist Mo Farah. "You know," said the singer, "What an extraordinary two weeks we've had in this country, and there are so many people to celebrate. But because he's been a real breath of fresh air... and such an inspiring human being, let's all do the Mo!"

An emotional evening which again saw Albarn visibly overcome during set closer 'The Universal', Blur's Hyde Park revelries drew an appropriate, and some might even suggest, glorious line at the end of the 2012 Summer Olympics*. However, it again raised a question that now followed the band around like a stray dog from gig to gig and town to town, forever snapping at their heels until it got a definitive answer. "As Albarn's bandmates deliver the rousing instrumental finale to 'The Universal', the frontman gazes into the crowd, blinking back tears, struggling to take it all in," said *The Guardian*'s Chris Salmon.

* A download of Blur's performance, the cunningly titled *Parklive*, was released just a day after the gig. Subsequent deluxe CD/DVD editions also included songs from the band's warm-up concert at the 100 Club and elsewhere, as well as a full concert film shot on August 12 at Hyde Park.

"Tonight, London has bid farewell to one of its finest fortnights. (But) whether it's also said goodbye to one of its best bands seems to be something Albarn himself is wrestling with as he bangs his fist to his heart and exits the stage."

In short, the answer was "No."

Epilogue

I Have Seen Glimpses

October 22, 2012

A little over two months after Blur had finished the Olympics their way, the band arrived at Grosvenor House in London's Mayfair to pick their latest gong at the Q Awards for 'Best Live Act'. The last time anyone from Blur was a recipient of such honours was 2007, when Damon accepted the Q Inspiration Award for his outstanding services to music. Cast the net back a few years and there were even more trophies from the magazine in the group's already stuffed cabinet: 1999's Best Act In The World, 2003's Best Album, the list went on. So many cups, and not just from Q either. The South Bank Awards, the Brits, the Brats, the *Mojos*, *Smash Hits*, MTV Europe, though curiously not the Mercury Prize. One way or another, Blur had been collecting crowns, medals, plaques and plates for almost two decades.

However, on October 22, 2012, things were a little different. Dave arrived at the ceremony on an afternoon off from work, the 48-year-old now as successful a criminal lawyer (with a neat sideline in computer/internet crime) as he was a drummer. Graham too, was also on a timer, his long-time partner – artist/photographer Essy Syed – having given birth to the couple's new daughter Dorelia just a day before. In fact, in stark contrast to the bleary days of 1995, it was only Damon and Alex that actually made it to the pub afterwards for a quick drink. That said, the bassist sounded his usual, ebullient self. "Happy days," he told *Q*'s Paul Stokes. "It's always a good do this one, and we were really, really thrilled to win Best Live Act." Further, the group's recent show at Hyde Park brought back only the sweetest of memories. "It was like looking out at a CGI scene from *Lord Of The Rings: Return Of The King*," said James. "A million faces twisted with joy." But when the questions came as to Blur's probable future, the answers became a little more guarded, though on this occasion there was real news to be had. "Well, this is the first time we've actually been in a room together since Hyde Park, though we are getting a bit better at communicating individually," he confirmed. "But there are some dates in Europe next year, so..."

A small sentence, but quite an important one, nonetheless. Obviously, Blur's reunion for the 2012 Olympics went so well that the band had decided to push on into the next 12 months. And while Alex remained extremely cautious about the possibility of any new recorded material – "No plans, no..." – there was at least small hope that something of a more permanent nature might eventually surface. Still, the very thought of a new Blur album continued to befuddle Graham. "Oh, I can't remember the answers I've already given," he laughed. "It's not a 'No', but it's not a 'Yes' either. We're in a good place right now and getting along really well, but we have to consider our legacy. There is a bit of pressure to do more, but we have to make sure that if we do, it's got to be right..."

March 25, 2013

The spring of 2013 and Blur are well and truly back in the public eye, even if they continue to manage the terms of their return with an attention to detail seldom seen outside the offices of MI6. Having confirmed a number of select European festival appearances the previous year, that list has steadily expanded to include not only Spain, Portugal and Belgium, but half the known world too. Mexico, the USA, Hong Kong, Taiwan and Indonesia have all been added to Blur's touring itinerary, as well as Finland, Turkey, Russia and Ireland. Some of these destinations will be first time visits for the band, others already familiar terrain. But whatever the case, it's all a long way from the 'weekend warrior' talk of recent years. "Blur is our sort of 'Sunday' band," Coxon said in late 2012. "We get to hang out with each other and muck about, so now it's sort of nice."

Equally, Blur's choice to play anywhere else but the UK after the victory of Hyde Park may be less about besmirching a wonderful memory and more to do with avoiding the 'Reformation circuit' currently journeying up and down the motorways of Britain. With The Stone Roses, Happy Mondays, Pulp and Suede all back on the reunion trail, Blur's decision to duck out of another British tour seems judicious, selective and well-timed. Crucially, it is also in keeping with Albarn's original pronouncements on how the group might proceed with dignity more or less intact. "We're no longer at a point where our whole world was reliant on the four of us," he said. "It came to a point when that was too much. Now we can re-group and approach Blur with appropriate respect."

Still, one recent event at the Royal Albert Hall in support of the Teenage Cancer Trust saw the thawing of one mighty iceberg. On March 23, Damon and Graham beckoned Noel Gallagher to join them and Paul Weller onstage for a jaunty, if somewhat disjointed version of 'Tender'. A moment that might have caused the collision of ships back in 1995, it somehow all seemed entirely reasonable now. "I think it's great for music fans," said Gallagher after the event. "It's like when you hear about John Lennon playing with Eric Clapton or... well I don't know what the equivalent is. It won't change anybody's life but people could say they were there."

In truth, Albarn, Coxon and Gallagher had matters worked out long before their historic appearance on the boards of the RAH. In the same way that Blur's collective wheels hit a greasy patch during 2003, Oasis suffered a similar accident six years later, when decades of sibling rivalry coalesced into one hot moment that finally did for the band. Just before a gig at Paris' Rock en Seine festival in late August 2009, Liam Gallagher allegedly smashed one of his brother's beloved guitars during yet another heated debate. This time, it was a step too far. "It's with some sadness and great relief to tell you that I quit Oasis tonight," said

Noel at the time. "People will write and say what they like, but I simply could not go on working with Liam a day longer."

By late 2011, the writer of 'Wonderwall' was back not only with a fine new act – Noel Gallagher's High Flying Birds – but also a brand new friend. "Well, I bumped into Damon in a (club)," said Noel, "and we both had a bit of a laugh about (the Britpop war). In fact, we were bemoaning the state of music and the fact that type of rivalry just doesn't happen anymore." Fast forward nine odd months, and Coxon was even touring in support of Gallagher's band, plugging his solo disc *A&E* to a now friendly crowd of formerly rabid Oasis fans at London's Wembley Arena. With worm turned and hatchet buried, Noel, Damon and Graham's rapprochement seems final proof that even the bitterest of wars can have the happiest of endings. At least, until the next argument kicks off...

In lieu of all these changes, and indeed, many more to probably come, it would take a brave man to predict Blur's next steps. Of course, that Albarn, Coxon, Rowntree and James will continue to have a rich life outside the band remains a given. Graham's solo career, for instance, has blossomed from lo-fi musings recorded on a sofa in Camden Town to a highly respectable and diverse body of work, his ability to change musical styles as often as his shoes as commendable as it is intriguing. "I suppose I am pretty happy," he recently said of such things. "I suppose if I'm an artist or whatever, a musician, and the message I'm getting is that what I'm doing is relevant, then yes, I'm happy." Alex too, shows no sign of slowing down any time soon, his ongoing forays into TV/ radio broadcasting and the recent publication of another book – *All Cheeses Great And Small...* – but two examples of the bassist's activities. "Actually, all I think about these days is cheese and children," he joked, "though I'd seriously consider a job as a celebrity astronaut. That'd be a good one, if the job was going..." As for Dave Rowntree, the world would appear to be his oyster. Currently a lawyer. Perhaps one day an MP. "Vote Dave!" sang the crowd in Hyde Park back in 2009. One really wouldn't bet against it.

Invariably, Damon will always have a project or five to attend to, his production duties on the wonderful Bobby Womack's 2012 album,

Bravest Man In The Universe the latest, but surely not the last of such creative endeavours. "I get up at 6.30 in the morning, eat some porridge, do a bit of exercise then go to the studio," he once said. "Then it's all work until I go home about five and put my feet up. I'm a nine-to-five musician." But behind Albarn's surprisingly modest assessment of his own work patterns, there was an iron will to succeed. "I have discipline," the songwriter said. "When I say I'm going to do something I'll do it, for good or for bad. If you don't have that inner strength about stuff you're fucked. But I just generally believe I can get better, and I need to believe... that I can keep going forward so I push myself and those around me to get the best we possibly can. That's what motivates me, this belief in going forward."

Where that will lead for Blur remains deliciously out of reach. Now in their 22nd year of trading, the band has seen off baggy, grunge and Britpop, failed romances, internal squabbles and sad-eyed breakups, only to come back just as strong and always when most required. There have also been occasions, however, when fans and critics' patience has been stretched to breaking point by the band. The constant drum-banging and bear-baiting, penchant for petty wars and unpleasant one-upmanship have all acted at one time or another as barriers to Blur's cause, turning attention away from their music and back to the sound of one's own grinding teeth. Yet, those very irritations are also an essential part of the group's appeal, their contrariness in the face of logic more often than not producing another classic album or unforgettable song. "I think we're kind of perverse, really," Rowntree recently said. "We've never done what's expected of us, we've never done the same thing twice. I think people might have found that very annoying about us for many years, but," he sagely concluded, "now I think they find it all quite endearing..."

Of course, the heart of Blur is still defined by the curious, complex, but still ultimately touching relationship between Graham and Damon. Friends for over 30 years – until for a time, they really weren't – the two's early experiments in sound at the back of a small Portakabin in Colchester have led to a slew of multi-platinum albums, hit singles and for a short, albeit golden period, a very exciting movement in British pop. When they fell out, Blur fell over. But for Coxon, the risk of another such spate won't destroy the work already done or the terms of any future engagements. "Oh, it seems that Damon and I are going to be in each other's lives musically forever, in some way or other," he said. "Whether it's with Blur or without Blur, or even sort of like 'The Old Gits', probably. Which is quite an amusing thought. We just get on very, very well..."

And so to the man who set Blur in motion. Now in danger of receiving a knighthood for his contributions to the British music industry, Damon Albarn can probably look back with both satisfaction and pride on the band he started in a small studio near Kings Cross in 1989. Principal songwriter, frontman, architect of Britpop, and moving target for Oasis fans as a result, Albarn's devotion to the idea of Blur has remained a constant in his life for over 20 years, the group outlasting every side-project, opera, production deal or virtual character he has ever become involved with.

"Blur has got a lot of shared history, you know?" he said in 2012. "We still get on very well, and when we play, it's still a magical experience for us all." But for now at least, there are no clues beyond the 20 dates announced for 2013. A new single. An eighth album. Who knows, *Blur: The Bloody Opera.* If Albarn knows, he's just not telling. "I really don't know what's around the corner," he said. "My mum taught me that, you know. She said 'Damon, you never know what's around the corner, you never know what's round the corner...'"

Acknowledgements

There are many to thank.

During the course of researching this book, I consulted the following newspapers, magazines, television/radio networks, websites and weeklies (some of which have ceased publication). In some cases, I extracted previously published or broadcast material. For this, I remain extremely grateful to: *Absolute Radio, Addicted To Noise*, *Amelia's Magazine, Arena*, *Bang*, *Bass Player*, *Channel Four*, *Daily Mail*, *The Daily Post*, *Daily Record*, *Deadline*, *Detour*, *Entertainment Weekly*, *Esquire*, *The Face*, *FHM*, *The Guardian*, *The Guitar Magazine*, *The Independent*, *ITV*, *Jyrki*, *Launch*, *The List*, *London Calling*, *Melody Maker*, *The Mirror*, *Mojo*, *MTV*, *Music-Room.com*, *NME*, *NY Rock*, *The Observer*, *palestra.net*, *PSL*, *Q*, *Record Collector*, *Repeatfanzine.co.uk*, *Rock Express*, *Rolling Stone*, *Select*, *Sky*, *Sony UK*, *Sounds*, *Sound on Sound*, *Spaceshower*, *The Sun*, *Sunday Times*, *Super Deluxe Edition*, *The Times*, *Time Out*, *Toazted*, *Total Film*, *Total Guitar*, *Triple J radio*, *Uncut*, *VH1*, *Vox*, *The Weekend Australian*, *www.blur.co.uk* and *YouTube* (all thanks due to the thousands of people who have posted rare Blur clips online).

For providing additional source material, I'd like to offer my genuine appreciation to the following individuals/journalists: Toby Amies, Ivor Baddiel, Steve Bateman, David Bennum, Michael Bonner, Nick

Bradshaw, Ally Carnwath, Imogen Carter, Dave Cavanagh, Andrew Collins, Lawrence Conway, Simon Crook, Stephen Dalton, Johnny Dee, Adrian Deevoy, John Dingwall, Danny Eccleston, Valerie Elliott, Matt Everitt, Jon Ewing, Emma Forrest, Pat Gilbert, Simon Goddard, Marsh Gooch, Rose Granson, John Harris, Sharon Hendry, Ria Higgins, Will Hodgkinson, Laura Houghton, El Hunt, Jim Irvin, Mark Kermode, Paul King, Lucy Jones, Phil Jones, Alex Kadis, Karen Krizanovich, Steve Lamacq, Eddy Lawrence, Michael Leonard, Paul Lester, Ceri Levy, Caspar Llewellyn Smith, Emma Love, Steve Lowe, Zane Lowe, Nick McGrath, Stuart Maconie, Sean Michaels, Ben Mitchell, Paul Moody, Paul Morley, Tim Muffett, David Nolan, Paul Du Noyer, Sylvia Patterson, Kat Phan, Andrew Purcell, Amy Raphael, Jay Rayner, Martin Roach, David Roberts, Chris Salmon, Miranda Sawyer, Iain Shedden, Sue Sillitoe, Andrew Smith, Paul Sinclair, Danielle Soave, Marc Spitz, Paul Stokes, Christopher Stocks, Fiona Sturges, Phil Sutcliffe, Steve Sutherland, Jamie Theakston, Graeme Thomson, Stephen Troussé, Alex Turner, Lisa Verrico and Stephanie West.

I must also sing the praises of several Blur-related/dedicated websites which alerted me to a number of facts of which I had no prior knowledge. Kind regards and much appreciation then, to: *blurballs.com*, *blurtalk.com*, *blur.tournant.tv*, *caramel.org.uk*, *damonalbarnunoffical.blogspot.co.uk* and last, but certainly not least, *vblurpage.com,* whose 'Gigography' section was invaluable.

A huge thank you for all those people who kindly gave up their time and thoughts for this project: Marijke Bergkamp, Dave Brolan (better luck next time, I guess), the good people at Eleven, Darren Filkins, Diana Gutkind, Nigel Hildreth, Graeme Holdaway, David Kelly, Steve Power and Jayne Stynes. For all those who provided off record contributions, I also remain truly grateful.

A small, but important number of honourable mentions: As ever, a king big thanks to Chris Charlesworth for his continued guidance, saint-like patience and sage advice. For additional help, humour and the ownership of a very cool coat, hats off to David Barraclough. For publicising my efforts so diligently, I must thank Charlie Harris. And for continuing to find the right photo to fit every page, I am indebted to Jacqui Black.

Some quick personal doffing of the cap: To John Constantine: 300 and out. You can quit smoking now. As always, many thanks to Anthony Cutler, Ben Davis, Stephen Joseph, Mr. Kelly, Andrew Robinson and Colin Stewart for their help with this, and indeed, several dozen other projects. To Kathy Macready: I greatly appreciate your kindness and owe you several stamps. And last but not least, Trish, who really deserves better but won't be told.

One final debt of gratitude: To Damon Albarn, Graham Coxon, Alex James and David Rowntree. Gentlemen, thank you kindly.

Discography

What follows is a selective discography of Blur's recorded output from 1990-2012, focusing on the band's classic releases and various other compilations. Solo albums, side projects & bootlegs are not considered, and all catalogue numbers refer to UK releases unless stated otherwise. Downloads will be readily available for most all of the titles listed below.

Singles
She's So High (Edit)/I Know
FOOD 26 7″ October 1990

She's So High/Sing/I Know (Extended)
12FOOD 26 12″ October 1990

She's So High (Edit)/I Know (Extended)/Down
CDFOOD 26 CD October 1990

There's No Other Way/Inertia
FOOD 29 7″ April 1991

There's No Other Way (Extended)/Inertia/Mr. Briggs/I'm All Over
12FOOD 29 12″ April 1991

There's No Other Way (Edit)/Inertia/Mr. Briggs/I'm All Over
CDFOOD 29 CD April 1991

Bang/Luminous
FOOD 31 7″ July 1991

Bang (Extended)/Explain/Luminous/Uncle Love
12FOOD 31 12″ July 1991

Bang/Explain/Luminous/Berserk
CDFOOD 31 CD August 1991

Popscene/Mace
FOOD 37 7″ March 1992

Popscene/I'm Fine/Mace/Garden Central
12FOOD 37 12″ March 1992

Popscene/Mace/Badgeman Brown
CDFOOD 37 CD March 1992

For Tomorrow (Primrose Hill Extended)/Into Another/Hanging Over
12FOOD 40 12″ April 1993

For Tomorrow (Primrose Hill Extended)/Peach/Bone Bag
CDFOODS 40 CD1 April 1993

For Tomorrow (Single Version)/When The Cows Come Home/Beachcoma/For Tomorrow (Acoustic Version)
CDFOOD 40 CD2 April 1993

Chemical World (Edit)/Maggie May
FOODS 45 7″ June 1993

Chemical World (Edit)/Es Schmecht/Young & Lovely/My Ark
12FOOD 45 12″ July 1993

Chemical World (Rework)/Never Clever (Live at Glastonbury 1992)/Pressure On Julian (Live at Glastonbury 1992)/Come Together (Live at Glastonbury 1992)
CDFOODS 45 CD1 July 1993

Chemical World (Edit)/Young & Lovely/Es Schmecht/My Ark
CDFOOD 45 CD2 July 1993

Sunday Sunday/Tell Me, Tell Me
FOODS 46 7″ October 1993

Sunday Sunday/Long Legged/Mixed Up
12FOODS 46 12″ October 1993

Sunday Sunday/Dizzy/Fried/Shimmer
CDFOOD 46 CD1 October 1993

Sunday Sunday Popular Community Song: Sunday Sunday/Daisy Bell/Let's All Go Down The Strand
CDFOODX 46 CD2 October 1993

Girls And Boys (Edit)/Magpie/People In Europe
FOOD 47 7″ March 1994

Girls And Boys (Edit)/Magpie/Anniversary Waltz
CDFOODS 47 CD1 March 1994

Girls And Boys (Edit)/People In Europe/Peter Panic
CDFOOD 47 CD1 March 1994

To The End (Edit)/Girls And Boys (Pet Shop Boys 7″ Remix)/Girls And Boys (Pet Shop Boys 12″ Remix)
12FOOD 50 12″ May 1994

To The End (Edit)/Threadneedle Street/Got Yer!
CDFOODS 50 CD1 May 1994

To The End (Edit)/Girls And Boys (Pet Shop Boys 7″ Mix)/Girls And Boys (Pet Shop Boys 12″ Mix)
CDFOOD 50 CD2 June 1994

Parklife/Supa Shoppa/To The End (French Version)/Beard
12FOOD 53 12″ August 1994

Parklife/Supa Shoppa/Theme From An Imaginary Film
CDFOODS 53 CD1 August 1994

Parklife/Beard/To The End (French Version)
CDFOOD 53 CD2 August 1994

End Of A Century/Red Necks
FOODS 56 7″ November 1994

End Of A Century/Red Necks/Alex's Song
CDFOOD 56 CD November 1994

Country House/One Born Every Minute
FOOD 63 7″ August 1995

Country House/One Born Every Minute/To The End (Featuring Francoise Hardy)
CDFOOD 63 CD1 August 1995

Country House (Live From Mile End Stadium)/Girls And Boys (Live From Mile End Stadium)/Parklife (Live From Mile End Stadium)/For Tomorrow (Live From Mile End Stadium)
CDFOODS 63 CD2 August 1995

The Universal/Ultranol/No Monsters In Me/Entertain Me (Live It Remix)
CDFOODS 69 CD1 November 1995

The Universal (Live At The BBC)/Mr. Robinson's Quango (Live At The BBC)/It Could Be You (Live At The BBC)/Stereotypes (Live At The BBC)
TCFOOD 69 CD2 November 1995

Stereotypes/The Man Who Left Himself/Tame
FOOD 73 7" February 1996

Stereotypes/The Man Who Left Himself/Tame/Ludwig
CDFOOD 73 CD February 1996

Charmless Man/The Horrors
FOOD 77 7" April 1996

Charmless Man/The Horrors/A Song/St. Louis
CDFOOD 77 CD April 1996

Beetlebum/Woodpigeon Song
FOOD 89 7" January 1997

Beetlebum/All Your Life/A Spell (For Money)
CDFOOD 89 CD1 January 1997

Beetlebum/Beetlebum (Mario Caldato Jr. Remix)/Woodpigeon Song/Dancehall
CDFOODS 89 CD2 January 1997

Song 2/Get Out Of Cities
FOOD 93 7″ April 1997

Song 2/Get Out Of Cities/Polished Stone
CDFOOD 93 CD1 April 1997

Song 2/Bustin' + Dronin'/Country Sad Ballad Man (Acoustic)
CDFOODS 93 CD2 April 1997

On Your Own/Popscene (Live at Peel Acres)/Song 2 (Live at Peel Acres)
FOOD 98 7″ June 1997

On Your Own/Popscene (Live at Peel Acres)/Song 2 (Live at Peel Acres)/On Your Own (Live at Peel Acres)
CDFOOD 98 CD1 June 1997

On Your Own/Chinese Bombs (Live at Peel Acres)/Movin' On (Live at Peel Acres)/M.O.R. (Live at Peel Acres)
CDFOODS 98 CD2 June 1997

M.O.R. (Road Version)/Swallows In The Heatwave
FOOD 107 7″ September 1997

M.O.R. (Road Version)/Swallows In The Heatwave/Movin' On (William Orbit Remix)/Beetlebum (Moby House Remix)
CDFOOD 107 CD September 1997

Tender/All We Want
FOOD 117 7″ March 1999

Tender/All We Want/Mellow Jam
CDFOODS 117 CD1 February 1999

Tender/French Song/Song 2/Song 2 (Video)
CDFOOD 117 CD2 February 1999

Coffee & TV (Edit)/Trade Stylee (Alex's Bugman Remix)/Metal Hip Slop (Graham's Bugman Remix)/X-Offender (Damon/Control Freak's Bugman Remix)/Coyote (Dave's Bugman Remix)
12FOOD 122 12" July 1999

Coffee & TV (Edit)/Trade Stylee (Alex's Bugman Remix)/Metal Hip Slop (Graham's Bugman Remix)
CDFOOD 122 CD1 June 1999

Coffee & TV (Edit)/X-Offender (Damon/Control Freak's Bugman Remix)/Coyote (Dave's Bugman Remix)
CDFOODS 122 CD2 June 1999

No Distance Left To Run/Tender (Cornelius Remix)/Battle (UNKLE Remix)
12FOOD 123 12" November 1999

No Distance Left To Run/Tender (Cornelius Remix)/So You
CDFOODS 123 CD1 November 1999

No Distance Left To Run/Battle (UNKLE Remix)/Beagle 2/No Distance Left To Run (Video)
CDFOOD 123 CD2 November 1999

Music Is My Radar (Edit)/Black Book
12FOOD 135 12" October 2000

Music Is My Radar (Edit)/Seven Days (Live)/She's So High (Live)
CDFOOD 135 CD1 October 2000

Music Is My Radar (Edit)/Black Book/Headist/Into Another (Live)
CDFOODS 135 CD2 October 2000

Out Of Time/Money Makes Me Crazy (Marrakech Remix)
EMI R6606 7" April 2003

Out Of Time/Money Makes Me Crazy (Marrakech Remix)/Out Of Time (Enhanced)
EMI CDR 6606 CD April 2003

Crazy Beat/The Outsider
EMI R6610 7″ July 2003

Crazy Beat/Don't Be/Crazy Beat (Alternate Video)
EMI CDRS 6610 CD July 2003

Good Song/Morricone
EMI 6619 7″ October 2003

Good Song/Me White Noise (Alternate Version)
EMI CDR 6619 CD October 2003

Fool's Day
5099964104874/R 6811 7″ April 2010
Live From The Brits: Girls And Boys/Song 2/Parklife
Available as download – February 2012

Under The Westway/The Puritan
EMI R 6873 7″ August 2012

Under The Westway/Under The Westway (Acoustic)/Under The Westway (Instrumental)/The Puritan/The Puritan (Instrumental)
R 6873 CD August 2012

Albums

Leisure
She's So High/Bang/Slow Down/Repetition/Bad Day/Sing/There's No Other Way/Fool/Come Together/High Cool/Birthday/Wear Me Down
UK CFOOD LP 6 LP August 1991
UK FOODCD 6/ CDP 7975062 CD August 1991

Leisure (Special Edition 2012 Re-issue)
Disc One: She's So High/Bang/Slow Down/Repetition/Bad Day/Sing/There's No Other Way/Fool/Come Together/High Cool/Birthday/Wear Me Down
Disc Two: I Know (Extended Mix)/Down/There's No Other Way (Extended Version)/Inertia/Mr Briggs/I'm All Over/Won't Do It/Day Upon Day (Live)/There's No Other Way (Blur Remix)/Bang (Extended Version)/Explain/Luminous/Berserk/Uncle Love/I Love Her (Demo Version) (Fan Club Single)/Close (Fan Club Single)
EMI CD & Digital Download July 2012 (Vinyl Edition also available)

Modern Life Is Rubbish
For Tomorrow/Advert/Colin Zeal/Pressure On Julian/Starshaped/Blue Jeans/Chemical World/Intermission/Sunday Sunday/Oily Water/Miss America/Villa Rosie/Coping/Turn It Up/Resigned/Commercial Break
CFOOD LP9 LP May 1993
FOODCD9/CDP 7894422 CD May 1993

Modern Life Is Rubbish (Special Edition 2012 Re-issue)
Disc One: For Tomorrow/Advert/Colin Zeal/Pressure On Julian/Starshaped/Blue Jeans/Chemical World/Intermission/Sunday Sunday/Oily Water/Miss America/Villa Rosie/Coping/Turn It Up/Resigned/Commercial Break
Disc Two: Popscene/Mace/Badgeman Brown/I'm Fine/Garden Central/For Tomorrow (Visit to Primrose Hill Extended Version)/Into Another/Peach/Bone Bag/Hanging Over/When the Cows Come Home/Beachcoma/Chemical World (Reworked)/Es Schmecht/Young and Lovely/Maggie May/My Ark/Daisy Bell (A Bicycle Made for Two)/Let's All Go Down the Strand
EMI CD & Digital Download July 2012 (Vinyl Edition also available)

Parklife
Girls And Boys/Tracy Jacks/End Of A Century/Parklife/Bank Holiday/Badhead/The Debt Collector/Far Out/To The End/London Loves/

Trouble In The Message Centre/Clover Over Dover/Magic America/Jubilee/This Is A Low/Lot 105
FOOD LP10 LP April 1994
FOOD CD10/7243 829119421 CD April 1994

Parklife (Special Edition 2012 Re-issue)
Disc One: Girls And Boys/Tracy Jacks/End Of A Century/Parklife/Bank Holiday/Badhead/The Debt Collector/Far Out/To The End/London Loves/Trouble In The Message Centre/Clover Over Dover/Magic America/Jubilee/This Is A Low/Lot 105
Disc Two: Magpie/Anniversary Waltz/People in Europe/Peter Panic/Girls And Boys (Pet Shop Boys 12″ Remix)/Threadneedle Street/Got Yer!/Beard/To The End (French Version)/Supa Shoppa/Theme From An Imaginary Film/Red Necks/Alex's Song/Jubilee (Acoustic) (BBC Radio 1 Session 1994)/Parklife (Acoustic) (BBC Radio 1 Session 1994)/End Of A Century (Cadena 40 Principales Acoustic Version)
EMI CD & Digital Download July 2012 (Vinyl Edition also available)

The Great Escape
Stereotypes/Country House/Best Days/Charmless Man/Fade Away/Top Man/The Universal/Mr. Robinson's Quango/He Thought Of Cars/It Could Be You/Ernold Same/Globe Alone/Dan Abnormal/Entertain Me/Yuko & Hiro
CFOOD LP14 LP September 1995
FOODCD 14/7243 83523528 CD September 1995

The Great Escape (Special Edition 2012 Re-issue)
Disc One: Stereotypes/Country House/Best Days/Charmless Man/Fade Away/Top Man/The Universal/Mr. Robinson's Quango/He Thought Of Cars/It Could Be You/Ernold Same/Globe Alone/Dan Abnormal/Entertain Me/Yuko & Hiro
Disc Two: One Born Every Minute/To the End (La Comedie) (Feat. Francoise Hardy)/Ultranol/No Monsters in Me/Entertain Me (Live It! Remix)/The Man Who Left Himself/Tame/Ludwig/The Horrors/A Song/St Louis/Country House (Live at Mile End)/Girls And Boys (Live

at Mile End)/Parklife (Live at Mile End) /For Tomorrow (Live at Mile End)/Charmless Man (Live At The Budokan)/Chemical World (Live At The Budokan)/Eine Kleine Lift Musik
EMI CD & Digital Download July 2012 (Vinyl Edition also available)

Blur
Beetlebum/Song 2/Country Sad Ballad Man/M.O.R./On Your Own/ Theme From Retro/You're So Great/Death Of A Party/Chinese Bombs/I'm Just A Killer For Your Love/Look Inside America/Strange News From Another Star/Movin' On/Essex Dogs
CFOOD LP19 LP February 1997
FOOD CD19/7243 85556227 CD February 1997

Blur (Special Edition 2012 Re-issue)
Disc One: Beetlebum/Song 2/Country Sad Ballad Man/M.O.R./On Your Own/Theme From Retro/You're So Great/Death Of A Party/ Chinese Bombs/I'm Just A Killer For Your Love/Look Inside America/ Strange News From Another Star/Movin' On/Essex Dogs
Disc Two: All Your Life/A Spell (For Money)/Woodpigeon Song/ Dancehall/Get Out Of Cities/Polished Stone/Bustin' + Dronin'/ M.O.R. (Road Version)/Swallows in the Heatwave/Death Of A Party (7" Remix)/Cowboy Song/Beetlebum (Live Acoustic Version)/On Your Own (Live Acoustic Version)/Country Sad Ballad Man (Live Acoustic Version)/This Is A Low (Live Acoustic Version)/ M.O.R. (Live In Utrecht)
EMI CD & Digital Download July 2012 (Vinyl Edition also available)

13
Tender/Bugman/Coffee & TV/Swamp Song/1992/B.L.U.R.E.M.I./ Battle/Mellow Song/Trailerpark/Caramel/Trimm Trabb/No Distance Left To Run/Optigan 1
FOOD LP29 LP March 1999
FOOD CD29/4991292 March 1999

13 (Special Edition 2012 Re-issue)
Disc One: Tender/Bugman/Coffee & TV/Swamp Song/1992/B.L.U.R.E.M.I./Battle/Mellow Song/Trailerpark/Caramel/Trimm Trabb/No Distance Left To Run/Optigan 1
Disc Two: French Song/All We Want/Mellow Jam/X-Offender (Damon/Control Freak's Bugman Remix)/Coyote (Dave's Bugman Remix)/Trade Stylee (Alex's Bugman Remix)/Metal Hip Slop (Graham's Bugman Remix)/So You/Beagle 2/Tender (Cornelius Remix)/Far Out (Beagle 2 Remix)/I Got Law (Demo)/Music Is My Radar/Black Book
EMI CD & Digital Download July 2012 (Vinyl Edition also available)

Think Tank
Ambulance/Out Of Time/Crazy Beat/Good Song/On The Way To The Club/Brothers And Sisters/Caravan/We've Got A File On You/Moroccan Peoples' Revolutionary Bowls Club/Sweet Song/Jets/Gene By Gene/Battery In Your Leg
EMI 582 9971 LP May 2003
EMI 2485 8424201 CD May 2003

Think Tank (Special Edition 2012 Re-issue)
Disc One: Ambulance/Out Of Time/Crazy Beat/Good Song/On The Way To The Club/Brothers And Sisters/Caravan/We've Got A File On You/Moroccan Peoples' Revolutionary Bowls Club/Sweet Song/Jets/Gene By Gene/Battery In Your Leg
Disc Two: Money Makes Me Crazy (Marrakech Mix)/Tune 2/The Outsider/Don't Be/Morricone/Me, White Noise (Alternate Version)/Some Glad Morning (Fan Club Single)/Don't Be (Acoustic Mix)/Sweet Song (Demo)/Caravan (XFM Session, October 2003)/End Of A Century (XFM Session, October 2003)/Good Song (XFM Session, October 2003)/Out Of Time (XFM Session, October 2003)/Tender (XFM Session, October 2003))
EMI CD & Digital Download July 2012 (Vinyl Edition also available)

Collections, Compilations, Special Editions, Remixes, Live Albums and 21

Blur – The 10 Year Limited Edition Anniversary Box Set
CD1: She's So High/I Know/Down/Sing/I Know (Extended Version)
CD2: There's No Other Way/Inertia/Mr. Briggs/I'm All Over/There's No Other Way (Blur Remix)/Won't Do It/Day Upon Day (Live)/There's No Other Way (Extended Version)
CD3: Bang/Explain/Luminous/Berserk/Bang (Extended Version)/Uncle Love
CD4: Popscene/Mace/Badgeman Brown/I'm Fine/Garden Central
CD5: For Tomorrow (Edit)/Into Another/Hanging Over/Peach/Bone Bag/When The Cows Come Home/Beachcoma/For Tomorrow (Acoustic)/For Tomorrow (Primrose Hill Extended)
CD6: Chemical World (Edit)/Young & Lovely/Es Schmecht/My Ark/Maggie May/Chemical World (Rework)/Never Clever (Live)/Pressure On Julian (Live)/Come Together (Live)
CD7: Sunday Sunday/Dizzy/Fried/Shimmer/Long Legged/Mixed Up/Tell Me Tell Me/Daisy Bell (A Bicycle Made For Two)/Let's All Go Down The Strand
CD8: Girls And Boys/Magpie/Anniversary Waltz/People In Europe/Peter Panic
CD9: To The End (Edit)/Girls & Boys (Pet Shop Boys Single Mix)/Girls And Boys (Pet Shop Boys 12″ Mix)/Threadneedle Street/Got Yer!
CD10: Parklife/Beard/To The End (French Version)/Supa Shoppa/Theme From An Imaginary Film
CD11: End Of A Century/Rednecks/Alex's Song
CD12: Country House/One Born Every Minute/To The End/Country House (Live)/Girls And Boys (Live)/Parklife (Live)/For Tomorrow (Live)
CD13: The Universal/Ultranol/No Monsters In Me/Entertain Me ('Live It!' Remix)/The Universal (Live at the BBC)/Mr. Robinson's Quango (Live at the BBC)/It Could Be You (Live at the BBC)/Stereotypes (Live at the BBC)
CD14: Stereotypes/The Man Who Left Himself/Tame/Ludwig
CD15: Charmless Man/The Horrors/A Song/St. Louis

CD16: Beetlebum/All Your Life/A Spell For Money/Beetlebum (Mario Caldato Jr. Mix)/Woodpigeon Song/Dancehall
CD17: Song 2/Bustin' + Dronin'/Country Sad Ballad Man (Live Acoustic Version)/Get Out Of Cities/Polished Stone
CD18: On Your Own/Chinese Bombs (Live at Peel Acres)/Movin' On (Live at Peel Acres)/M.O.R. (Live at Peel Acres)/Popscene (Live at Peel Acres)/Song 2 (Live at Peel Acres)/On Your Own (Live at Peel Acres)
CD19: M.O.R (Road version)/Swallows in the Heatwave/Movin' On (William Orbit Remix)/Beetlebum (Moby's Minimal House Mix)
CD20: Tender/All We Want/Mellow Jam/French Song/Song 2
CD21: Coffee & TV (Edit)/Trade Stylee (Alex's Bugman Remix)/Metal Hip Slop (Graham's Bugman Remix)/X-Offender (Damon/Control Freak's Bugman Remix)/Coyote (Dave's Bugman Remix)
CD22: No Distance Left to Run/Tender (Cornelius Remix)
FOOD CD BLURBOX10 August 1999

Blur: The Best Of
Beetlebum/Song 2/There's No Other Way/The Universal/Coffee & TV/Parklife/End Of A Century/No Distance Left To Run/Tender/Girls And Boys/Charmless Man/She's So High/Country House/To The End/On Your Own/This Is A Low/For Tomorrow/Music Is My Radar
FOOD LP 33 LP October 2000
FOOD CD 33 CD October 2000
A 'Limited Edition' double CD of *Blur: The Best Of* provided an additional 10 tracks recorded on 11 December, 1999 at Wembley Arena as part of the 'Singles Night' tour: She's So High/Girls And Boys/To The End/End Of A Century/Stereotypes/Charmless Man/Beetlebum/M.O.R./Tender/No Distance Left To Run
FOOD CDS33/7243 52985821 CD October 2000

Midlife: A Beginner's Guide To Blur
Beetlebum/Girls And Boys/For Tomorrow/Coffee & TV/Out Of Time/Blue Jeans/Song 2/Bugman/He Thought Of Cars/Death Of A Party/The Universal/Sing/This Is A Low/Tender/She's So High/Chemical

World/Good Song/Parklife/Advert/Popscene/Stereotypes/Trimm Trabb/Badhead/Strange News From Another Star/Battery In Your Leg
EMI 099996 630723 CD June 2009

Blur Present 'The Special Collectors' Edition'
Day Upon Day (Live)/Inertia/Luminous/Mace/Badgeman Brown/Hanging Over/Peach/When The Cows Come Home/Maggie May/Es Schmecht/Fried/Anniversary Waltz/Threadneedle Street/Got Yer!/Supa Shoppa/Beard/Theme From An Imaginary Film/Bank Holiday
EMI Japan TOPC 8395 CD October 1994

Live At The Budokan
The Great Escape/Jubilee/Popscene/End Of A Century/Tracy Jacks/Mr. Robinson's Quango/To The End/Fade Away/It Could Be You/Stereotypes/She's So High/Girls And Boys/Advert/Intermission/Bank Holiday/For Tomorrow/Country House/This Is A Low/Supa Shoppa/Yuko And Hiro/He Thought Of Cars/Coping/Globe Alone/Parklife/The Universal
EMI Japan TOCP 89067 CD May 1996 (Original Japanese Release)

Bustin' + Dronin'
Movin' On (William Orbit Mix)/Death Of A Party (Well Blurred Remix)/On Your Own (Crouch End Broadway Mix)/Beetlebum (Moby's Mix)/Essex Dogs (Thurston Moore's Mix)/Death Of A Party (Billy Whiskers Mix)/Theme From Retro (John McEntire's Mix)/Death Of A Party (12" Death)/On Your Own (Walter Wall Mix)/Popscene (Live at Peel Acres)/Song 2 (Live at Peel Acres)/On Your Own (Live at Peel Acres)/Chinese Bombs (Live at Peel Acres)/Movin' On (Live at Peel Acres)/M.O.R. (Live at Peel Acres)
EMI Japan TOCP 50444 5 CD February 1998 (Original Japanese Release)

All The People: Blur Live At Hyde Park
She's So High/Girls And Boys/Tracy Jacks/There's No Other Way/Jubilee/Badhead/Beetlebum/Out Of Time/Trimm Trabb/Coffee & TV/

Tender/Country House/Oily Water/Chemical World/Sunday Sunday/ Parklife/End Of A Century/To The End/This Is A Low/Popscene/ Advert/Song 2/Death Of A Party/For Tomorrow/The Universal
EMI CDLHN57 & CDLHN58 CD August 2009

Parklive
Girls And Boys/London Loves/Tracy Jacks/Jubilee/Beetlebum/Coffee & TV/Out Of Time/Young & Lovely/Trimm Trabb/Caramel/Sunday Sunday/Country House/Parklife/Colin Zeal/Popscene/Advert/Song 2/No Distance Left To Run/Tender/This Is A Low/Sing/Under The Westway/Intermission/End Of A Century/For Tomorrow/The Universal
Released as a download (August 2012) and two CD pack: CD LHN 100R December 2012
(A bonus edition 'Triple CD' of *Parklive* collects various other live shows on an additional disc, including: Under The Westway (Live From Studio 13)/The Puritan (Live from Studio 13)/Mr. Briggs (BBC Maida Vale)/ Colin Zeal (Civic Hall)/Young & Lovely (Wolverhampton Civic Hall)).

Parklive: CD/DVD Deluxe Edition
This deluxe edition extends *Parklive*'s 2-CD format (listed above) by two further discs, plus a DVD. Bonus materials include live performances from BBC Maida Vale, Wolverhampton's Civic Hall and 13 songs recorded at Blur's 100 Club appearance on 2 August, 2012. A film of the band's Hyde Park concert concludes the package.
Disc Three: Under The Westway (Live from 13)/The Puritan (Live from 13)/Mr. Briggs (BBC Maida Vale session)/London Loves (Live from Wolverhampton Civic Hall)/Young And Lovely (Live from Wolverhampton Civic Hall)/Colin Zeal (Live from Wolverhampton Civic Hall)/The Puritan (Live from Wolverhampton Civic Hall)/No Distance Left To Run (Live from Wolverhampton Civic Hall)/This Is A Low (Live from Wolverhampton Civic Hall)
Disc Four: Girls And Boys/Jubilee/Beetlebum/Young and Lovely/Colin Zeal/Oily Water/Advert/Bugman/The Puritan/Trimm Trabb/For Tomorrow/Under The Westway (All tracks live at the 100 Club)

Disc Five (Live DVD): Girls And Boys/London Loves/Tracy Jacks/Jubilee/Beetlebum/Coffee & TV/Out Of Time/Young & Lovely/Trimm Trabb/Caramel/Sunday Sunday/Country House/Parklife/Colin Zeal/Popscene/Advert/Song 2/No Distance Left To Run/Tender/This Is A Low/Sing/Under The Westway/Intermission/End Of A Century/For Tomorrow/The Universal/Under The Westway (Alternative take)/The Puritan (Alternative take)/Under The Westway (Lyric Video)/ The Puritan (Lyric Video)/Under The Westway (Alternative take)
Released in December 2012 (catalogue number unavailable at time of printing)

21
For Blur fans, this lavish release must seem like manna from heaven. A deluxe 21 disc set chronicling the band's entire career, it not only offers expanded formats of all their seven studio albums, but also adds four more discs worth of rarities and over three and a half hours of previously unreleased material. In addition to the music, there are three DVDs, including over 120 minutes of unseen footage, two concert shows and an exclusive disc of video rarities. Completing the set is a collectable 7″ single of the Seymour-era live track 'Superman' and a hardcover book telling Blur's story with new interviews and previously unseen photographs.
The first 14 discs of *21* – comprised of the band's seven original studio albums, each with a corresponding disc of outtakes, alternative versions, etc. – were also released as stand-alone 'Special Edition Re-issues' in July 2012. As such, their contents are already listed in the 'Albums' section of this Discography. To avoid further duplication, what now follows are the details of *21*'s remaining seven discs, plus the 'Superman' single:
CD15 – Seymour and *Leisure* rarities: Dizzy (Seymour Rehearsal & Demo)/Mixed Up (Seymour Rehearsal & Demo)/Birthday (Seymour Demo)/Sing (To Me) (Sing Demo) (Fan Club Single)/Fool (Seymour 4-Track Demo)/She's So High (Seymour Rehearsal)/Won't Do It (Demo) (Fan Club Single)/I Know (Falconer Studio Demo)/Repetition (Falconer Studio Demo)/High Cool (7″ Master)/Always (I'm Fine Early Version)/Come Together (Demo) (Fan Club Single)/I'm All Over (Demo)/Wear Me Down (Demo)

CD16 – *Modern Life Is Rubbish* rarities: I Love Her (Alt Version)/Popscene (1991 Demo)/Beached Whale (4-Track Demo)/Death Of A Party (Demo – Fan Club Single)/Pap Pop (4-Track Demo)/Pressure On Julian (Demo)/Colin Zeal (Demo)/Sunday Sunday (Demo)/Never Clever/Advert (Demo)/Star Shaped (Demo)/She Don't Mind (Blue Jeans demo)/Coping (Andy Partridge Version)/Sunday Sleep (Sunday Sunday Andy Partridge Version)/7 Days (Andy Partridge Version)/Kazoo (Turn It Up Early Version)/The Wassailing Song (The 7″ Giveaway at Fulham's Hibernian Club)/When The Cows Come Home (Demo)/For Tomorrow (Mix 1 – Early Demo)/Magpie (Early Demo)
CD17 – *Parklife* and *The Great Escape* rarities: Parklife (Demo)/Clover Over Dover (Demo)/Jubilee (Demo)/One A Minute (One Born Every Minute Demo)/Badhead (Demo)/Far Out (Electric Version)/The Debt Collector (Demo)/Trouble In The Message Centre (Demo)/Rednecks (Take 1)/Rednecks (Take 2)/Alex's Song (Demo)/Cross Channel Love (Home Demo)/Ernold Same (Demo)/Saturday Morning (Demo)/Hope You Find Your Suburb (A.K.A. Eine Kleine Lift Musik Vocal Demo)/Rico (Fade Away Demo)/Bored House Wives/Entertain Me (Early Version)
CD18 – *Blur*, *13*, *Best Of* and *Think Tank* rarities: Beetlebum (Demo)/On Your Own (Mario Caldato Jr. Mix)/Woodpigeon Song (Original Full Length)/Battle (Jam, Mayfair Studios 11 August 1998)/Caramel (Ambient Version)/So You (Alternative Version)/Squeezebox (Music Is My Radar Alternative Version)/Jawbone (Black Book Alternative Version)/"1" (Bill Laswell Session, 2000)/ "3" (Bill Laswell Session, 2000)/Sir Elton John's Cock/Avoid The Traffic/Money Makes Me Crazy (Deepest Darkest Devon Mix)/Don't Bomb When You're The Bomb/Nutter/Piano/Kissin' Time/Fool's Day/Under The Westway
DVD1 – 'Showtime: Live At Alexandra Palace, 7 October 1994': Lot 105/Sunday Sunday/Jubilee/Tracy Jacks/Magic America/End Of A Century/Popscene/Trouble In The Message Centre/She's So High/Chemical World/Badhead/There's No Other Way/To The End/Advert/Supa Shoppa/Mr. Robinson's Quango/Parklife/Girls And Boys/Bank Holiday/This Is A Low

DVD2 – 'Singles Night, Live at Wembley 11 December1999': I Know/She's So High/There's No Other Way/Popscene/For Tomorrow/Chemical World/Girls And Boys/To The End/Parklife (With Phil Daniels)/End Of A Century/Country House/The Universal/Charmless Man/Beetlebum/Song 2/On Your Own/M.O.R./Tender/Coffee & TV/No Distance Left To Run
DVD3 – Rarities: B.L.U.R.E.M.I. (Live 13 at London Depot, 10 March 1999)/No Distance Left To Run (Live 13 at London Depot, 10 March 1999)/Tender (Live 13 at London Depot, 10 March 1999)/Battle (Live 13 at London Depot, 10 March 1999)/Beetlebum (Live 13 at London Depot, 10 March 1999)/Bugman (Live 13 at London Depot, 10 March 1999)/Trimm Trabb (Live 13 at London Depot, 10 March 1999)/Mellow Song (Live 13 at London Depot, 10 March 1999)/Song 2 (Live 13 at London Depot, 10 March 1999)/Seymour: Dizzy/There's No Other Way (BBC Eggs & Baker) (Blur's 1st TV Performance)/To The End (La Comedie) Feat. Francoise Hardy (French Promo Video)/It Could Be You (Japanese Promo Video)/Music Is My Radar (Promo Video)/Out Of Time (Promo Video)/Crazy Beat (Promo Video)/Good Song (Promo Video)
7″ SINGLE: 'Superman' (Recorded December 1989 at The Square in Harlow, Essex)
N.B. Blur's seven studio albums were also released as 'Blur 21: The Vinyl Box' in July 2012. Housed in a sturdy case, replete with original replica sleeves and weighing in at 180g per item, this box set surely represents the definitive collection for vinyl junkies everywhere.

Videos & DVDs

Starshaped
Intermission/Can't Explain/There's No Other Way/Inertia/She's So High/Colin Zeal/Popscene/When Will We Be Married/Sunday Sunday/Wassailing Song/Coping/Day Upon Day/For Tomorrow/Chemical World/Advert/Commercial Break
MVP VHS 4911453 September Video 1993 (Reissued 1995)

Showtime
Lot 105/Sunday Sunday/Jubilee/Tracy Jacks/Magic America/End Of A Century/Popscene/Trouble In The Message Centre/She's So High/ Chemical World/Badhead/There's No Other Way/To The End/Advert/ Supa Shoppa/Mr. Robinson's Quango/Parklife/Girls And Boys/Bank Holiday/This Is A Low
MVP VHS 4914023 Video February 1995

Blur: The Best Of
She's So High/There's No Other Way/Bang/Popscene/For Tomorrow/ Chemical World/Sunday Sunday/Girls And Boys/To The End/Parklife/ End Of A Century/Country House/The Universal/Stereotypes/ Charmless Man/Beetlebum/Song 2/On Your Own/M.O.R./Tender/ Coffee & TV/No Distance Left To Run
FOODVHS 001 Video November 2000
FOODDVD 001 7243 492433 92 DVD November 2000

Starshaped (DVD re-release)
Intermission/Can't Explain/There's No Other Way/Inertia/She's So High/Colin Zeal/Popscene/When Will We Be Married/Sunday Sunday/Wassailing Song/Coping/Day Upon Day/For Tomorrow/ Chemical World/Advert/Commercial Break
DVD Extras - Live In Kilburn: Popscene/Fool/High Cool/Bad Day/ Oily Water/Slow Down/There's No Other Way/Turn It Up/She's So High/Wear Me Down/Come Together/Day Upon Day/Sing/Explain/ Commercial Break
DVD Extras – Live At The Princess Charlotte: Won't Do It/There's No Other Way/High Cool/Wear Me Down
EMI 24349 08999 DVD October 2004

No Distance Left To Run (The Making Of)
No Distance Left To Run (Live)/The Making of No Distance Left To Run/Interview with Dave Rowntree, Graham Coxon, Damon Albarn and Alex James/Tender (Live)/Battle (Live)/Beagle 2 Footage
FOODDVD OO2 DVD November 1999

Blur – No Distance Left To Run
Disc One: Feature length film.
Disc Two: Blur Live In Hyde Park 2009 – Intro/She's So High/Girls And Boys/Tracy Jacks/There's No Other Way/Jubilee/Badhead/Beetlebum/Out Of Time/Trimm Trabb/Coffee & TV/Tender/Country House/Oily Water/Chemical World/Sunday Sunday/Parklife/End Of A Century/To The End/This Is A Low/Popscene/Advert/Song 2/Death Of A Party/For Tomorrow/The Universal
EMI/Pulse 5099960 974594 DVD February 2010

Parklive
Girls And Boys/London Loves/Tracy Jacks/Jubilee/Beetlebum/Coffee & TV/Out Of Time/Young & Lovely/Trimm Trabb/Caramel/Sunday Sunday/Country House/Parklife/Colin Zeal/Popscene/Advert/Song 2/No Distance Left To Run/Tender/This Is A Low/Sing/Under The Westway/Intermission/End Of A Century/For Tomorrow/The Universal
DVD December 2012 (Catalogue unavailable at time of printing)

Index

Index

Index